Down The Hatch

A Magical Misfits Mystery

Lina Hansen

Literary Wanderlust | Denver, Colorado

Published in the United States by Literary Wanderlust LLC, Denver, Colorado. www.LiteraryWanderlust.com

ISBN print: 978-1-956615-18-0
ISBN digital: 978-1-956615-19-7

Cover design: Pozu Mitsuma

Printed in the United States of America

1

IN AT THE DEEP END

A bang rolled through the village car park, sending the rooks skyward in a rattle of wings. When a series of rapid pops followed, I stopped in my tracks, and so did quite a few of the tourists milling around in the cobblestoned Main Street. Sweat trickled down the gap between my breasts, and my lungs strained to breathe air turned to syrup in the sultry heat. My friend Jenna's five-year-old twin boys, however, hopped up and down with unconcerned glee.

"Uncle Marty, it's Uncle Marty."

"Oh dear, and here's me hoping the garage would have fixed Bro's blasted van," Jenna said. "You two are not haring off, do you hear me?" She tossed me a concerned look. "Are you okay, Myr?"

"Eh, yes, sure." I relaxed my grip on the gym bag with my swimming gear. Neither a gunshot nor magical misfire, after all. Only my imagination—and memories of last spring—run amok.

The tourists resumed their parade past the pastel-colored cottages lining the street, the roofs bristling with thatch and the front gardens so packed with flowers they crowded the gnomes. More visitors clustered around the Purple Emporium, our New Age shop run by Mel, a coven member as feisty as she was stout. The rest of the visitors flooded in and out of the village grocery store. Where others of its kind had shut down long ago, their windows barred and empty shelves unlikely to see wares again, this one thrived. It sold wilted greenery to the guests, together with overpriced ChapSticks, spaghetti rings, and garishly colored drinks the twins had better not remember. Otherwise, we would never make it to Knick-Knack's and my appointment with Dottie Wytchett, Jenna's grandmother.

On second thought, perhaps that wasn't such a bad idea. The woman made my toes curl.

"We'd better move on." Jenna pushed aside a lock of maroon hair too heavy for her elfin face. "Gran's a stickler for punctuality."

I shoved down the sigh that threatened to rise in my throat and forced my unwilling legs into motion. To my left loomed the chunky tower of the church, where starlings noisily warred for viewing space on the four pointy spires. A few steps ahead of us, Jenna's boys were weaving past the visitors, chittering like the birds.

"Let me guess, weeks and weeks of hospitals and rehab didn't improve Dottie's mood, right?" I asked.

Jenna winced. "Don't call her that. She hates it. It's Dot, okay? People keep getting it wrong. Otherwise, spot on. It didn't help that in early May she bounced back, only to get worse than ever, poor Gran. Anyway, she should be better now. Listen to her proposal. It'll help. You don't have to do anything yet." Jenna shot me a sideways glance from under thick, dark lashes. With mine that would never have worked, since they matched the strawberry blonde of my hair and were almost invisible.

Nowhere to hide.

A procession of people robed in white, chanting solemnly and radiating waves of patchouli and incense, ambled out of the narrow lane that led to Knick-Knack's and the car park. All pedestrian traffic, the boys included, ground to a halt, and the smartphones came out.

The group of Druids headed for the stone circle, no doubt in search of wisdom. Perhaps joining them might be a good idea.

I stopped and swung around. "Listen, I'm not sure I can carry on where my aunt left off. It's clear that Dot's heart troubles make it hard for her to run the coven. It doesn't help that our lot are . . . a bunch of odd ducks, though that's not my biggest issue. To be honest, I'm still not comfortable with the m-thing."

I was talking about magic, of course. To say my wayward skylles frightened the socks off me was the understatement of the year. Magic had killed my Aunt Eve.

Making gunshot noises, the twins galloped into the lane, a green tunnel shaded by acacia trees. Misgivings on my mind, I followed.

"Given how you got ambushed in spring, it's not surprising," Jenna said. "Unfortunately, before we even consider general training to strengthen the skylles, we must understand how they work. For that we need people to share the documents they have inherited, and the database is the best solution."

"The database isn't the issue."

"No, but you're the best person to coordinate both the project and the people. Gran's not fit enough, and with Jeff thankfully out of the picture, the boys need me more than ever."

She raised her hands and let them drop at her sides, the gesture possible only because she was carrying a rucksack. Like her hair, it seemed too weighty for her slender frame. But Jenna's strength ran deep.

"I'll chip in whenever I can," she said.

"Oh, I know that. But once that lot is trained, they'll be even more keen to try things out. What if we get discovered?"

"With a bit of caution, we should be fine. After all, we're supposed to be supernatural wusses."

"What's a supper national wuss?" Johnnie—or Robbie—asked. Children always had ears too big for their shoe size.

"Shh," I said. "Not so loud."

"Come on, the number of Druids and Wiccans in this place boggles the mind. We'll fit right in." When she laughed, Jenna reminded me of Tinkerbell.

The small car park next to the café came into view, and as usual every slot was taken, which was most likely the reason a scratched white van, its doors open, blocked the entrance. Inside slouched a man in his thirties reading a newspaper.

"Uncle Marty, Uncle Marty." This time there was no holding back, and the twins raced ahead.

The man looked up, grinned, and folded his paper. "Hey, little guys. Hello, ladies. How was the swimming pool?"

"We're not little," Robbie—or perhaps it was Johnnie?—protested.

"Afternoon, Marty," I said. "I'm so hot again, I could do with another dip."

Jenna's laugh jingled into the translucent teal of the midday skies. She gave my shoulder a gentle squeeze. "Come on, you can't stay away from the action forever."

She had a point, and we both knew it. I was a witch—and unlike my aunt, I had so far survived to tell the tale.

I hugged my friends goodbye and headed for the gift shop. Behind my back, Marty fired up the van with an oily bang that reverberated through the car park. This time, I remained unfazed. Despite sweating in the heat and sheltering a posse of magical misfits, idyllic Avebury was entirely the wrong place for murder.

2

A QUIET UNEASE

I entered Knick-Knack's attended by the clanking of cowbells. Cool, fresh air fanned my cheeks. Saturated with the scent of lavender, the draft carried a faint moldy whiff from the old brickwork. Modern spotlights cast a glare from the ceiling, leaving not a single nook or cranny unlit. The gift shop's narrow aisles were lined with wooden racks, all of them crammed with cheerful paper napkins, tablecloths, postcards, guidebooks, and scented candles on one side and homemade wines, dips, and marmalades on the other.

The bells stilled. Silence pressed on my ears as I brushed past the vases, crystal figurines, and other fragile trinkets that made me feel like the proverbial heifer in the china shop.

"Can I help you?"

With a yelp, I backed into the nearest shelf. Luck was with me, and instead of hitting something breakable, a reassuring wooliness tickled my bare legs.

A figure blocked my path. It stepped closer, and I recognized the curvy shape of my cousin, decked out in a sleeveless coral tunic with rhinestone flowers that framed a bust even more substantial than mine. It was half-covered by her auburn braid, the rest of which snuggled along her neck like a cuddly toy.

Rats. Among all that stressing about Dottie—Dot's—plans, Daisy and her many troubles slipped my mind.

"Hullo, cuz. Saw you on candid camera." She grinned and pointed at a small box with a gleaming red light mounted under the wooden ceiling.

"Hello yourself." I knelt to pick up the mohair blankets my hasty retreat had pushed off the shelf.

"Let me sort that for you." The heels of Daisy's golden strap sandals clacked on the stone floor, her perfume heavy like armor. She shook out the hairy fabrics, folded them with reverent fingers, and bedded them in their resting place. Then she swung around and tilted her head, the grin fading from lips painted a shade of orange that would make me look like a trollop.

There's nothing wrong with my body. I cherish every single one of my freckles, eyes the color of stonewashed jeans, my flyaway strawberry hair. However, my cousin clearly outclasses me when it comes to looks. So unfair.

"Where have you been?" Daisy pointed at my grass-stained white tee.

Fashion wasn't my forte, though with the help of my friend Sergeant Sarah things were improving on the clothing front. I might still be a bit of a mess, but at least I now was a color-coordinated mess.

"Since it's Saturday and it's hot, I went to the Swindon Sports Pool with Jenna and the kids. I needed a break before the next load of guests pops up. How about if we go together one day?"

Daisy shrugged. She sashayed past me, heading toward the cash counter. "I might have the time actually, since Dot's back." She whirled around, the sudden movement slicing her braid through the air. I spotted a telltale furrow between her eyebrows.

Uh oh. Yet another problem that hadn't blipped on my trouble radar. Dot had set up the shop, which Daisy had been running in her absence, and no doubt Dot would want to take over.

Steeling myself for a rant, I stopped beside a bright blue door half-hidden between two shelves. The next moment, the cowbells over the entrance clamored away and Daisy's nascent scowl morphed into a welcoming smile.

With a shuffle of flip-flopped feet, a group of Wicca practitioners pushed through the central aisle and then fanned out. One woman, probably of Caribbean origin to judge by her skin color, slanted eyes, and grizzled afro, made a beeline for the shelf filled with cotton sachets and glass vials arranged next to the cash counter. She passed me in a flutter of dark robes that clashed with the leather pilot case she was carrying. Once arrived at the shelf, she trailed her fingers over the neat rows of bags before choosing a brown vial that she deposited on the counter.

"If I was at home, I would prepare my own calendula extract," the Wiccan said, her voice a warm gong. "But I've made so much suntan lotion, I've run out of it. I must have missed your herb and plant section the last time we shopped. When I tried the Purple Emporium, the owner sent me straight back here."

Daisy smiled as she wrapped the bottle in silky paper. "Oh, sorry for that. We prefer to split things up between the two shops."

The Wiccan tapped her generous lips. "No worries. Actually, you gave me an idea. Would you be able to order something for me?"

"I'd love to, but it depends on what you need."

The woman pushed her sleeves up a set of well-toned arms, the scent of sandalwood filling the air. She exuded an aura of quiet competence and authority, as if at home with her beliefs and happy being who she was.

"I shouldn't be thinking about work right now, but I've run

out of foxglove. In my practice, not here. Whenever possible, I buy my herbs in a proper shop instead of ordering stuff on the Internet." She handed her credit card to Daisy. "I'm a physician, you see?"

Daisy gave the woman an apologetic smile. "Frightfully sorry, but I won't be able to get that for you. Peppermint, ginger, coneflower—that kind of thing I can order any time and quickly as well. However, we're not licensed to sell proper herbal medicine."

"Never mind," the woman said. "It was worth a try. At least I know where to get the oil. We're camping next to the river, and there's not a lot of shade."

The irony of the situation wasn't lost on me. Here was a modern witch, perhaps lacking in the magic department but missing neither purpose nor competence. Our coven was what Greg, our pubkeeper from the States, would call a dumpster fire. Embarrassing, really.

Chatting among themselves, the rest of the group placed bottles of country wines, dips, and jams on the counter. Daisy did a super job. She rang up the purchases, laughing and joking with the Wiccans, before pointing out how the silk scarves would go nicely with the swirly skirts and do double duty as sunscreens. Unsurprisingly, she sold the lot.

"You're a natural," I said, when the women had left the shop.

Daisy noted something in a ledger and gave me a grateful smile. "You reckon? I love dealing with people. Barkeeping was fine, but here the customers don't chat me up all the time."

Daisy put the ledger away. The furrow reappeared between her elegant brows.

"I can't imagine Dot will ever be able to work full-time. You'll still be needed," I said somewhat hastily.

The furrow smoothened. "She told me the same thing. It's not just the shop, mind you. Before she fell ill, Dot asked me for help. Mum's job was to trace the families while Dot checked the magical lore the newcomers brought with them. Like, spells and stuff? That's where I came in. Wasn't that easy. You know how they hate sharing."

"Oh, yes." After centuries of keeping secrets, mistrust had become the witches' second nature, even among their own kind.

"Mum never involved me. She thought I was a dummy or something." Daisy raised her chin in defiance.

Guilty as charged, Aunt Eve. But so was I.

"If Dot relied on you for coven matters, I'm sure she will do so again," I said in as soothing a tone as I could muster.

Only a creak and the faintest of drafts heralded the arrival of a third person. When I whirled around, Dot had closed the door to my right and stepped into the spotlight.

Dot shared her granddaughter's slight build and doe eyes set in a heart-shaped face. In Jenna, they were authentic. In Dot, they were deceptive. Neither her eyes nor the embroidered blouse hid the steely character underneath, even when she smiled, as she did now.

My heartbeat gathered speed. Ridiculous, when I had done nothing wrong and the woman meant no harm.

Instead, she appeared to be under pressure herself. Perspiration beaded a forehead flecked with pale liver spots. Her wiry white hair had been cut short enough to make a drill sergeant proud. Not my idea of a cuddly grandmother.

Like a trapped moth, something fluttered at the base of my throat. I swallowed it down. "Oh, hello, Dottie . . . Dot. Glad to know you're feeling stronger. It's good to have you back. We need you."

Instead of responding, Jenna's grandmother gave me a regal nod and headed for the swivel chair beside the counter. Hurriedly, Daisy turned it around.

"Thanks, both of you." Dot sank into the upholstery and placed her handbag on her knees.

"After my medical odyssey, I'd love to slip back into my old life, but I'm not as fit as I would like to be." Dot grimaced. "Not fit enough to run the shop or lead the coven, or even hex, for that matter. I'm to avoid all stress, but tell me how I'm supposed to do that when these wretched tourists are crawling all over our sacred site, eh? Never mind, I'll cope." She toyed with the chain of her reading glasses. "Thank you for chipping in, Myrtle. That'll make a real difference. The Coldrons and Wytchetts must stand together."

I hadn't agreed to anything yet, but I would hear her out.

"The coven is a shambles. Most of our members have nothing left but a few scraps of ratty parchment or some garbled oral lore."

"Trying to safeguard traditions across the centuries is a real beast," I said. "Otherwise, I fear it's a case of wanting to be among fellow witches and flex their magical muscles while brooding over their family heirlooms like jealous hens."

A smile pulled at Dot's tired face. "You have a wonderful way with words."

Daisy played with her braid. "That's what gave Mum the idea for the database. By donating their scraps, they gain access to the rest of the knowledge."

Dot heaved a sigh. "I might not always have seen eye to eye with Eve, but she had a good head on her shoulders. It's imperative that we share our heritage, no matter what these people think. Once done, we can try to train them."

Bugger. Decision time.

By bringing the last witches together at the Avebury henge, Dot and Aunt Eve had augmented our feeble skylles. So far, only a few of us had hexed anything. But it was only a matter of time until the rest followed, especially with the solstice on the horizon. I would have to crank my bum into gear a lot faster than Jenna had promised, but then I had known that already. It was that or abandon the coven.

In the end, the choice was as clear as the summer skies. Yes, magic could kill, but it was so special. The world had almost lost it once, and I couldn't let that happen again. At least we now had Dot to lead the way.

"Sorry I've been missing in action," I said.

Dot's face softened. "You came late to your skylles. Makes it even more of a shock. That, and the way Eve died."

Silence settled on the store, growing and swelling like an invisible cloud. I was searching for something to break the spell when a muffled ping sounded from Dot's handbag.

Daisy shook herself like a soggy dog. "Why don't I close the shop for a while and drive you home?"

Dot heaved herself upward. "No, you've done more than enough, girl. I'll call a taxi. I'm not decrepit yet. Okay for a coven meeting tomorrow?"

"Go ahead. I'll be there," I said. "Daisy?"

"I guess so."

Dot's impish wink reminded me of Jenna. "I appreciate that, I really do." Her face went serious again. "Especially since you're the only one who . . . well, you know."

"Has survived serious hexing?"

Daisy exhaled in a soft rush. Dot looked grim.

My worries, those dark, little thoughts that besieged me at night, bubbled up, and I couldn't stop them from spilling. "Look, I know people think me standoffish, but as you said, I have my reasons. All we know is that magic comes at a cost. Until now, the fallout was on the practitioners. What if I trigger something inadvertently? What if I mumble my way through what I believe to be a recipe for biscuits and a demon pops up in my pantry?"

I snapped my mouth shut, but the words seemed to have taken on a life of their own, their echo haunting us.

Daisy's eyes had grown huge. "Eek," she said.

"Hush." Dot stepped closer and patted my arm. "No need to fret. That's not how it works. Firstly, there are no demons. Even if there were any, we're too weak to call them. I'm sorry I wasn't around to explain, but I would have expected Jenna to step in."

"She tried, but I didn't give her a chance. Yeah, I know, so not clever of me."

Dot donned her glasses and regarded me calmly. "The skylles

won't go away, so it's better to know what you're up against. Let me explain the basics. Strong emotions are the key to our magic. They power your magical skylles. You must be deeply in love. Or you're scared or shocked. Whatever. Yes, there can be side effects to hexing—what you called 'fallout.' Yes, they usually affect the practitioner or their property, especially when they're inexperienced, and especially when they're under stress. One thing is paramount. There's got to be a purpose underlying it all, meaning you want or need something to happen. You can't just read out a spell, or think or dream about things, and the world goes bang. No way." Dot muttered something under her breath that sounded suspiciously like, "Doesn't take witches for that."

"Side effects?" I asked.

"Think flickering candles. Or a headache. Nothing to write home about. There's also backfire, which definitely hits the practitioner, but that only happens if they bend the rules."

"What about Myrtle's magical primula?" Daisy asked.

"Born of grief and loss. Myrtle wanted Eve to live. The flower must have recently withered away when Myrtle touched it, and she brought it back." Dot fiddled with her glasses. "That gun you shifted into a cactus? Myrtle, you were stressed, you were afraid, you were furious all at once, plus you wanted to save my grandson, my great-grandson, and your young man. So, you did."

I couldn't help myself. "Chris isn't my young man."

Not because he was descended from witch hunters. He'd made it clear what he thought of his ancestors. But in the eight weeks and three days since he had left for an IT project somewhere in the wild Welsh mountains, he'd messaged me a total of six times. For him that might well be the epitome of chattiness. For me, it wasn't enough.

A smile deepened the crinkles around Dot's eyes. "That's a shame, since I took your agreement for granted and hired him to continue with the database. Eve trusted him, and I think she was right, no matter what the others might say. Unless I'm mistaken, that ping we heard earlier was him. He said he would contact me once he was back." She retrieved her phone and checked the message. "Just as I thought. I like punctuality in a man. I rented the holiday flat over the café for him. Why don't you go across and say hello?"

—

After the blessed coolness of the shop, the heat in the carpark pounced like a wild beast. Thoughts buzzed through my brain, and my insides hosted a beehive. It would take time to digest Dot's words. Right now, I needed to cope with her actions.

My inner voice sang, "Chris is back." Its grumpy twin responded with a daunting, "Oh no." With that cerebral racket going on, I didn't watch where I was going, which is why I slammed straight into a hard obstacle. I snapped my gaze from the dusty gravel and took a step backward.

"Ouch," said Chris. "We must stop meeting like this."

Night-black eyes twinkled at me. They were framed by a mop of curly dark hair and an impish grin on his stubbled face, a grin that would have made the horned fiend proud, a grin that never failed to rile me.

It did so now.

"Ice cream?" He waggled a cone of Cadbury's Flake in front of my face.

The long fingers of his other hand clasped a second cone, already unwrapped. "I saw you entering the shop. Since your last message sounded less than cheerful, I reckoned I needed a peace offering."

Food in any shape or form has always been my downfall, so I wasn't surprised when my treacherous hand reached out and snatched the cone. For a split second my fingertips touched his, and the *zing* in my belly had nothing to do with witchcraft.

Chris grinned. He would.

"Shall we sit on that bench, so I can try to redeem myself?" He pointed at a rickety wooden contraption close to the historical dovecote. We were wearing shorts, his more expensive than mine. Haute couture notwithstanding, we would both end up with splinters in our respective backsides. Still, it might be worth the risk to listen to him grovel.

I lowered myself onto the bench and unwrapped my ice cream. "I'll take about five minutes to eat this."

Chris sauntered across and sat on the other end of the rough plank where he stretched out his long legs and nibbled at his sweet.

I bit into the vanilla goodness and some ice cream attached itself to my nose. A surreptitious swipe with the heel of my hand took care of that minor problem.

Chris's grin widened. "Glad to see you haven't changed."

Above us a breeze stirred the summer air, and the glossy green leaves rustled in response. A ray of sunlight tickled my nose, and my mood soared. This was the normal world—the one without witches in it. The one featuring Chris.

I slammed a lid on the thought and raised my brow. "Four minutes," I said around a mouthful of ice cream.

He laughed and finished the rest of his cone. Then his face turned serious. "Sorry. I could say I've been super busy in recent months, which I was, but that's not the only reason I made myself scarce."

"Mh?"

"Eh, quite a few of your newfound friends aren't keen on my presence. Can't blame them."

"Rubbish. Nobody in their right mind would hold you responsible for the deeds of your ancestors."

"Some do. In fact, I'm one of them."

In his need to make up for the crimes of his witch-hunting predecessors, Chris approached my aunt, and she had entrusted him with her last words. Well, either that or the simple fact he'd been the only person around at the time.

"And having a moving and shaking super-rich slimeball for an uncle doesn't help either," Chris added. "Especially if he keeps interfering with you guys."

This time I couldn't stop the snigger. "Haven't heard from him since April. If Uncle Bob isn't your role model, I'm fine."

Chris snorted. "You should know me better than that."

"How?"

His face softened. "You're right. I didn't make things any easier for you."

My ice cream was a sticky memory of vanilla and chocolate on my tongue, and the air clung to me like a wet, warm sheet. Yet I experienced no urge to move.

Chris leaned forward, his eyes like black holes sucking me in. "Myrtle, I—"

My shorts vibrated. The theme music from *Miss Marple* warbled from the pocket. Chris raised an inquiring brow.

I rubbed my sticky hand against my bare thighs, tossed him an apologetic smile, and fished out my phone. "Hello?"

An unintelligible echo tortured my ear. It sounded as if the speaker was sitting at the bottom of a metal bucket.

"Can't understand a word, whoever you are."

"Myrtle? That you?"

Even if the melodic strains of North Carolina were distorted by a poor signal, I recognized the voice as belonging to Greg, the temp keeper of the Whacky Bramble Pub and Daisy's lover.

"Yes?"

"Would'ya have some time? I mean, like now?"

"Sure, is there a problem? I'm around the corner, actually. With Chris."

"That's swell. Please, I'm gonna need your help."

"Okay, but what's up?"

"Uh, could y'all come over here? I've got a body in the basement."

3

TERMINALLY PICKLED

The babble of thirsty tourists in the Whacky Bramble's beer garden quieted once Chris and I had slalomed our way past the last of the wooden tables and benches. A wind was blowing across the plains, but the heat remained fierce. Sweat steamed from my pores, and the pool was a distant memory. Our sprint, as short as it might have been, made things worse, despite me dumping my bag in the trunk of Chris's car.

"Hold on a second. I need to catch my breath." I leaned against the rough plasterwork of the pub and Chris followed my example. His presence did nothing for my inner cool.

"I hope you know where we're going."

"Sort of. Greg says the cellar is at the back. I've only ever been in the kitchen."

We moved on at a slower pace and soon found ourselves in a small courtyard framed by ramshackle garages. A cool breeze fanned my face, teasing my hair. Strangely enough, the air current, reeking of mildew and hops, rose from the ground.

"Greg doesn't expect us to jump down his beer drop, does he?" Chris pointed at a shed-like extension bulging from the pub like a carbuncle. In front of it gaped a square opening, two metal doors lying flat to the left and the right of the hole in the ground. A rough wooden skid led into the musky darkness of underground spaces. My stomach lurched, but since we came to help, I risked a peek into the depths.

Fortunately, I detected no bodies. Only a dented aluminum keg sat at the foot of the skid.

"There's got to be another entrance." Chris hadn't finished the last word when a hollow voice drifted from the basement.

"Go around the storeroom. Turn left when you see the kitchen. Back door's open."

"Greg, is that you?" Chris asked.

"Yeah. The other guy ain't talking."

My stomach lurched again.

Once we circumnavigated the storeroom, we hit upon a row of black commercial wheelie bins. Thankfully, their lids were shut tight. However, the small window in the wall of glass blocks stood open, and my nostrils were assaulted by an aroma of frying fat. My stomach, now seriously pissed off, sent an acid note of protest up my throat.

"Let me guess. We found the kitchen," Chris said.

He hesitated. So did I. On our left, as promised, yawned an open door. I licked my lips, as dry as the tarmac in the court-yard.

"This isn't quite how I envisaged our joyous reunion," Chris said.

"Nope. Actually, I envisaged nothing, since I wasn't aware you'd show up. I'd sort of written you off. For the record, I'm pleased to have you here."

Lips twitching, Chris sketched a bow. "Just like in spring. Chris Lentulus, IT Solutions, at your service. Though I don't think my coding skills will be of any use here." His face became serious. "Sorry, don't mean to be flippant."

"No worries. My sentiments entirely. Ready for this?"

"No, but who cares."

We entered the shed and found ourselves in a storeroom jam-packed with assorted foodstuff. A battered metal door was set into the right wall, presumably leading to the kitchen. The other side of the room featured a staircase, no doubt the access to the basement of doom. My heartbeat shifted gears.

Chris stepped past the racks and headed for the opening. Then he stopped. "That's odd."

His words prodded my heartbeat into a sprint. My friend Sarah, a copper at Swindon CID, teased me about my superior reasoning skills, but I sucked as a detective, just as I sucked as a witch. At no time during my stint as an amateur sleuth earlier this year did I face a corpse.

"What do you mean by 'odd'?"

Instead of responding, Chris entered the row between the nearest racks.

I followed, though I could have moved faster. When I caught up with him, he was bent over some sort of sack in NATO khaki. Next to it, on a neatly folded white plastic carrier bag, stood two unopened cans of spaghetti rings and baked beans, a glass jar with peas, and a half-empty bottle of mineral water. A faint whiff of sweat and old grease hung in the air, increasing as I approached.

I stopped. The folds of the drab sack were unlikely to hide a complete body. However, they might contain parts of one.

Chris nudged the stained fabric with his foot. "A sleeping bag, I would say. Has seen better days."

At least it was empty. "Looks like an overnight guest."

"Mh, yes. Definitely more pleasant in here than it is outside."

Chris was right. With my heart banging away and adrenaline coursing through my system, the coolness of this place hadn't registered before now.

"Where are you?" Greg's voice boomed from down below.

"Coming," Chris hollered back and then translated his words into action.

There was no spit left to swallow, so I breathed in twice, regretted it, and followed Chris into the basement. With every step I took, the temperature dropped. At the bottom of the rough staircase, my breath billowed out in a whitish haze. As if to pay respect to the departed, the fine hairs on my naked arms and legs rose in unison.

Greg, a giant of African American descent and the kindest person in the world, waited for us at the entrance of a good-sized room illuminated by strip lighting. Kegs, cables, and gauges lined up along one wall. The floor was modern, the same epoxy resin paint we used in the utility rooms of the Witch's Retreat. A faint hissing and humming filled the place, slipping away whenever I tried to focus on it. Otherwise, the cellar was as silent as, well, a grave. It smelled of chemicals, not soil, and the yeasty tang of beer, together with something more unpleasant. Something that recalled the many times I played around hedges as a child—hedges other people had used as a makeshift toilet.

Greg's face was a dark mask of misery. "Thanks, guys, for coming. I sure appreciate it."

"It's fine," I said. "You couldn't exactly call Daisy."

"Oh, no way. She's too fragile." He shook Chris's hand. "Great to have you back. Sorry about the chill down here, but it's better for the beer."

Chris waved him off. "No worries, mate. Where is he? Or she?"

"He." Greg pointed at a bundle of brownish rags squeezed between two of the kegs. Underneath, half-hidden by the fabric, was a splash of white. I squinted and immediately wished I hadn't. The white bit was a hand, with funny pinkish splotches on it. A dead man's hand.

Nausea flooded my innards, and my head swam. *Breathe, Myrtle.*

I sucked in air, released it on the count of four, and did a repeat performance. Despite the funky smell, the cold draft flowing in and out of my nose kept the sick down where it belonged. After a couple of breaths, the toilet stench, if that was what it was, bothered me no more. Surely the glacial temperatures in the cellar would have refrigerated the body?

My teeth chattered like a set of wind-up dentals. The movement must have shimmied my brain into action, because I remembered a lesson I had learned earlier this year.

"Eh, could this be a crime scene? Should we even be in here?"

"Probably not." Chris withdrew toward the doorway. "Did you alert the cops, Greg?"

"Yeah, I called emergency. Not hailing from around here, I figured I wanted some friendly faces with me when the sheriffs arrived. And Myrtle has that tough cookie in the CID for a friend. Thought she might be able to help."

Sarah and I had planned to meet tonight. With her crazy hours, girls' nights out were always a hit-and-miss affair. She wouldn't be amused if I messed with her much-deserved free weekend without a good reason. The poor man might have died of nothing more sinister than heat stroke.

"Did you touch anything?"

Greg swung around. "Uh, I thought he would be a goner, but I had to be sure, right? So, yes. I figure he suffered from digestive problems."

I turned away and focused once more on my breathing, trying to block out the cold and ignore my protesting stomach. The exercise sort of worked, but I took longer than before to calm things down.

"He's got a rash on his skin," Greg added. "Would be better if a pro had a look. To be sure it isn't anything serious."

"Thanks," I said. "Too much information. Okay, I can take a hint." I fumbled for my smartphone. When I found it, my fingers slipped on the screen. Somewhere in this blasted device had to be a list of contacts. Twice I fingered the wrong icons. Finally, I got a connection. The phone rang. And rang.

"Hello? Swindon CID, Sergeant Widdlethorpe speaking?"

"Sarah, I'm glad you're there. It's Myrtle."

"I gathered as much," an amused voice said. "Your number is on the display, and your dulcet tones are unmistakable, even if you sound a bit hollow. What's up? Don't tell me you won't make it tonight?"

"Uh, actually you might be the one with the problem. A corpse problem, to be precise."

Static buzzed into my ears. "You're joking, right?"

Talking to an official quelled my nausea. "I'm afraid not. I'm in the basement of the Whacky Bramble. With Chris . . . Mr. Lentulus, and Mr. Winters, the landlord. And a body. Mr. Winters found him. He doesn't look good."

"Who? Mr. Winters?"

"No, the stiff. The deceased, sorry."

A deep sigh fluttered into my ear. "They never do. Can you confirm the person is deceased? Have you called this in? Is it a man or a woman?"

"Greg did. And it's a man. As to the rest, hang on."

I moved the phone away from my ear. "Greg, are you sure that bloke's dead?"

"He's as stiff as a board, isn't breathing, and his eyes are open. He hasn't blinked once since I found him. No pulse either. I betcha he's gone," Greg said.

"Okay, I heard that." Sarah's voice had turned brisk and business-like. "Let me ping Constable Cameron. He's in the village already. With the solstice crowd, things are getting lively on your end. I don't need a dead body in the mix, even if it's natural causes, but we need to go through the motions."

I couldn't stop myself. "Don't bodies tend to be dead?"

"Myrtle, English lessons are the last thing I need. You can do me a favor, though. Get out of that basement and hold the fort until Cameron turns up. If it happens to be a crime scene, I don't want it contaminated."

On that hopeful note, she disconnected.

"And now?" Greg asked.

"Now, we wait for the cavalry and make sure nobody gets down here." I gave them the condensed version of my conversation with Sarah.

"Sounds like a plan. I'll put a garbage container in front of the shed, which should block unwelcome visitors. Don't know about you, but I need a drink." Greg was already headed for the steps.

I risked a quick glance at the dead man behind us. A sad heap was all that remained of a life, discarded like a bunch of old clothes, smelly and soiled. What a rotten way to go.

—

When we emerged from the dungeon, a thin layer of clouds blanketed the sky, and the sun floated in the haze, mimicking a glowing egg yolk. Cold to the core as I was, even the oppressive warmth was welcome.

"Come into the pub," Greg said, once we returned to the beer garden. "AC's at full blast. No idea why these people insist on sitting outside during a scorcher."

"Us islanders, not graced with the benevolent climes of our colonies, must make the most of whatever heat wave we get," Chris said.

Greg guffawed. "I'll give you colony."

Once inside the Whacky Bramble, I headed for the nearest seat. Inset into a bay window, the high-backed bench was smothered in colorful taffeta cushions, their fabric smooth under my bare legs. The diamond shapes of the windowpanes gave us a distorted view of the touristic hordes outside, which had doubled since we went down to the basement. The waiters rushing in and out of the pub had their hands full.

Greg returned with a tray on which sat a pitcher with lemonade, two glasses, and a bottle of lager for Chris.

"I'll be right back," he said. "The sous chef is freaking. Looks like we've run out of arugula. In the meantime, help yourselves."

He tramped off.

How I envied Greg. He had mundane disasters on his hands, which would keep his mind off things—like the bundle that had once been a man.

Chris swigged half of the bottle of lager before I even filled my glass with lemonade. I downed my drink in one go, cool fluid heading for my stomach with a sweet and sour bliss I would no doubt regret later.

"Ahh," said Chris. "Just what the doctor ordered." He stopped swigging and stared into space, undoubtedly harboring thoughts similar to mine. No doctor in the world could help the man in the cellar.

For a short while, there was nothing but a supercharged stillness between us, broken only by the din from outside that drifted through the half-open window. Not eco-friendly with the air-conditioning running, but I couldn't conjure up the energy to do something about it. Instead, I grabbed the pitcher and was refilling my glass when a police car rolled into view and stopped at the entrance to the beer garden.

Outside, heads turned. Hands lifting glasses froze. The door of the police vehicle opened, and a swarthy man in plainclothes climbed out and headed toward the entrance of the pub. Constable Cameron, Sarah's sidekick, and I had first met in spring after the attack on my cousin. Back then, he'd still been in uniform.

Cameron entered the pub and his gaze found mine. A grin split his face. "Afternoon, Ms. Coldron. The sarge tells me you're causing trouble again," he said, his strong Scottish accent at odds with features that hailed from the Indian subcontinent.

That was unfair of Sarah. I had done nothing of the sort. "The landlord, Mr. Winters, discovered the body and called us in. Mr. Lentulus and I supplied moral support."

Chris raised his bottle in a salute and swigged his beer.

Cameron moved closer, as silent and graceful as a lynx. Seemingly guileless, he radiated goodwill. It didn't wash with me for a second. Whoever worked for Sarah would be competent. Unfortunately, she couldn't pick her boss.

"Don't fash yourself. I was trying to lighten the mood. Any idea where I would find the landlord?"

"I'm here." Greg headed for his bar. He pulled down the pump handle, and beer frothed into a glass. "Be right with you. Would you like anything, officer?"

"Thanks, but nae." Cameron's gaze skittered here and there, taking everything in.

Greg placed three full glasses on a tray, which he handed to a pimply youth wearing a burgundy apron over his jeans. Then he dried his hands on a towel and leaned on the bar, his frown creating a six-pack on his perspiring forehead. "About that body . . ."

Constable Cameron pulled a tablet from the inside of the light sports jacket he wore over a crisp white shirt. "The sarge's called the doctor. While we're waiting for him, you might as well tell me what happened and why you saw the need to call for re-inforcements." He winked at me.

Greg's jaw muscles clenched. "Despite popular opinion, even in the U.S. we don't stumble over corpses every five minutes. I couldn't face things on my own."

Cameron nodded. "Understandable. Run me through your movements, will you?"

"About an hour ago, I was preparing for a delivery. I un-locked the beer drop before making my way to the back. See, the cellar can only be accessed through the storage shed."

"How does one get in there?" Cameron asked.

"Either from the courtyard or through the kitchen, but that door is warped and a bastard to open. Unless you know the trick, you won't get far. I noticed the open door to the storeroom straight away. Next, you'll ask about security. There are motion sensors and a camera at the back. Neither of them reliable."

Cameron looked up from his tablet, his eyes sharp.

Greg raised his ham-like hands. "Before telling me off, be aware this isn't my pub. My friend Jack is on a world tour, and

I'm standing in for him. I always wanted to run a British pub. He keeps telling me he's coming back, and then he extends his trip. I reckon I'll be around for a while yet, so I've ordered replacements for both doors and somebody will fix the alarm. Have you tried to find a competent maintenance worker recently? It's a nightmare. Got people lined up for next week, but of course now it's too late."

"It always is, unfortunately." Cameron's face gave nothing away.

"The storeroom door is a joke," Greg added. "All it takes is a credit card and it'll pop open."

"The guy down there doesn't strike me as somebody who would own credit cards," Chris said.

"If he did, they're probably maxed out," I said. "Oh, sorry, didn't mean it that way."

"Has anything been stolen?" Constable Cameron spoke with exaggerated patience.

Greg shook his head. "I checked, and it doesn't look like it. Anyway, my next thought was vandals, which is why I dashed down into the room holding the equipment. That's where I found him."

"Funny vandal who arrives complete with sleeping bag," I said.

"Sleeping bag?" Cameron tapped away on his tablet.

"Yeah," Greg said. "Between the racks. To the left of the cellar entrance. He must have brought some cans and a bottle of mineral water with him. They're not mine, for sure. Apart from those peas, perhaps."

Cameron faced first Chris and then me. "Can you corroborate this story?"

"Yes," Chris said. "There's an old sleeping bag and the ingredients of a rather spartan meal. If you ask me, that bloke was looking for a place to eat and doss. He had dinner, or breakfast or whatever, and something was off and caused food poisoning."

"Doesn't work, since the cans and the glass jar weren't open,"

I said. "Only the water."

Cameron sighed and stowed away his tablet. "Let's not jump to conclusions. Okay, I'd like you to show me the body, Mr. Winters. As to your friends, unless they wish to share further observations, they're free to go. If necessary, we know where to find you." He bared his teeth at me, a pearly crescent in his face.

Since neither Chris nor I had further observations to share, we were soon alone in the restaurant.

Blast, my guests. I checked my watch as surreptitiously as possible.

Chris caught me in the act and rose. "Right. We better make ourselves scarce. I still need to move some stuff into my apartment, and you must be busy with your tourists."

"Eek, yes. The first lot is due to arrive in fifty minutes, and I still have to change. Maybe I can borrow my cousin's wheels."

"Let's return to the shop, and I'll drive you. It's the least I can do."

My heart did a happy skip and hop. "Much appreciated."

He pulled a face. "Yes, because I need to desert you again, even if it's only for a short while. I've got to finish a job tomorrow."

Rats. "On a Sunday?"

"I'm freelance, which means no free time. I'll be back for the coven meeting. If it takes place, that is. Mrs. Wytchett was a bit vague on that front."

My stomach knotted and bubbled up a sour greeting from the lemonade. As unpleasant as the experience had been, the corpse wouldn't be my problem. The coven, however, was, and Chris's involvement would aggravate matters something chronic.

Those were my thoughts at the time, but then premonition didn't feature in my scanty bag of magical tricks.

4

MEET AND GREET

Auntie's beloved bed and breakfast, now my home, rose before me in full Georgian splendor. The symmetrical cream facade glowed in the evening sunlight, which the latticed windowpanes reflected into the front yard we used as a car park. Oddly enough, the place was empty. My spanking new cherry-red minivan stood in the shade at the back, but I would have expected the Simpkins sisters to have arrived by now. If I hadn't known better, I would have said Chris took a wrong turn somewhere. The drive from Dot's shop took much longer than the usual ten minutes.

Still, the trip was much too short.

A quick glimpse at my smartwatch told me I was cutting things close. I shifted the heavy gym bag to my other hand, ran up the steps, and stopped between hanging baskets bursting in a riot of geraniums. The plant's fragrance teased me with sweetness while I rummaged in the bag for my keys. As usual, the blasted things had dropped right to the bottom and were entangled in my soggy swimming costume. Key retrieved, I unlocked the front door and entered an L-shaped corridor filled with the homey smells of fried bacon, Clorox, and rose potpourri.

"Ladies, I'm back," I shouted.

There was no response. Then the door at the end of the hallway creaked open. The mottled furry shape of my cat, Tiddles, slunk through and padded alongside the coconut runner, her claws clicking on the wooden floor. From the now-open private parlor behind her came swishing and whooshing, followed by a chink as something hit the windowpane.

"Petty, stay where you are," I hollered. "We've got people coming. You'll get your water later."

The cat I could explain to the guests since she featured in our brochure. My other companion was something else entirely. The last thing I needed was Petty on the prowl when the visitors arrived. Not that she had been out and about much recently. After almost getting composted when she saved my life, my magical primula had been taking things easy.

Tiddles slipped under the saloon-style swing doors into the kitchen and an imperative yowl emerged soon after.

"Come on, it's not six o'clock yet."

I panted up the stairs, carpeted in midnight blue. Once arrived on the second floor, I dashed past the linen cabinet and room number seven, which had been my home until two days ago. With the season in full swing and bookings coming in hard and fast, removing myself from number seven had been the obvious thing to do. Still, I had dithered. I might have inherited Auntie's business, but usurping her private space seemed downright wrong. It took Greg's polite inquiry whether I could accommodate a friend from the States to kick me into action.

Since it was impossible to hire reliable decorators this side of doomsday, I ordered only a new bed—Auntie's was perfectly serviceable, but I had to draw the line somewhere—hung a pair of floor-length blackout curtains in a chartreuse chintz, and took possession of her room. Of course, the last two nights had been somewhat restless because the unfamiliar surroundings interfered with my sleep patterns, and I kept banging my shins on the way to the bathroom.

Once inside my new abode, I headed for the shower, my stained T-shirt halfway over my head. For reasons best known to himself, Chris had never cared about my appearance. He even seemed to find my lack of chic amusing.

A short but refreshing interlude later, I emerged from a cloud of vanilla-scented steam and padded into the bedroom. I had left the door ajar, but the stubborn quiet in the house remained unbroken. Where were the Simpkins sisters? Since the day I met them, the two housekeepers always arrived at least ten minutes ahead of every appointment, their stiffly sprayed poodle perms bristling with anticipation and their work-worn hands reaching for the nearest mop as soon as the ladies crossed the threshold.

Unfortunately, there was no time to fret over their whereabouts since the guests were overdue as well. I wriggled into a linen shift dress that Sarah had discovered during our latest visit to the Swindon outlet centers. The pale gold fabric would never have been my first choice, plus the dress fitted rather snugly over my hips, but it made me look cheerful and had been reduced in price twice, so I couldn't say no. I was fiddling with eyeliner when the doorbell gonged.

My hand jerked, creating a black wriggle where it didn't belong.

"Cripes." I reached for a tissue but decided against it. Fixing the eyeliner would take too long, so I raced back downstairs. When the coconut runner scratched the soles of my feet like an oversized Brillo pad, I stared at my feet. In my haste, I forgot the shoes.

The doorbell gonged again.

"I'm coming," I yelled. Drawing in a deep breath, I turned the brass knob and opened the door.

—

Two men in their late thirties squeezed into the scanty shade thrown by the covered porch. The darker and shorter of them stuck his nose in a hanging basket and was inhaling the scent of the geraniums. He wore a burgundy polo shirt, its sleeves displaying arms almost simian in their length and hairiness. To compensate, the legs poking out of his tan Bermudas were too short for his torso, as if somebody had glued together different halves of two bodies.

You've got bodies on your mind, girl.

I slapped a friendly smile on my face. "Welcome to the Witch's Retreat B&B. I'm Myrtle. Sorry to keep you waiting."

My gaze fell on his companion, and I couldn't help but stare. Translucent dragonfly wings rose from the back of a shirt as milky pale as the man's arms. His gossamer mop of blond hair fringed eyes sunken in their sockets as if they shied away from the fright called life.

Don't gape.

Both men grinned at me instead of replying. My botched mascara must have spread.

"Oh, did I rush you?" asked the human locust, a twinkle in his hooded eyes. "So sorry, but I like the sound of your doorbell."

A closer inspection revealed the shimmering wings emerged from some sort of rucksack he was carrying and not his back, which I found reassuring.

"I'm Pan. This is Gerry." He pointed at his partner and tossed me a coy glance from under his bangs. "We've booked for a week."

A shy smile at the other man drew a rapt expression, and my synapses clicked. They had to be our honeymooners.

I checked the couple in and showed them to number three. My aunt, in a fit of warped humor, not only named her establishment the Witch's Retreat but also gave each room an occult label. Where my old digs featured a teal numeral seven and a broomstick, for number three she had picked a cauldron and a bright red three. Pan and Gerry's temporary home was the best and largest in the house. Like the other two rooms at the front, it overlooked the car park, but it was busy for only a few hours in the mornings or evenings and otherwise quiet. As a bonus, robust beeches grew on the boundary to the house next door and threw their shade over the windowpanes of number three. I, however, hadn't relied on nature alone but kept the air-conditioning running. As a result, the room was cool.

"Oh, isn't this wonderful? And look at that." Pan dropped his pack with the wings and launched himself onto the covers of the antique four-poster bed that dominated the room. He flapped his arms twice before closing his eyes with a contented sigh.

Gerry grimaced. "Pan's a statistician. His job is all about number crunching, so in his free time he likes to explore different lifestyles."

"Then you've come to the right place. Avebury during the solstice is not of this world. Would you like me to show you how the Jacuzzi works?"

He opened his mouth, but the doorbell cut into his response.

"We can figure it out. Please don't worry about us," Gerry said.

"You're a star. Enjoy your stay." I closed the door on them as an unearthly yowl rose from below. The cat of the Baskervilles, reminding me of my substandard catering.

Where had Cecily and Alma disappeared to?

I dashed past number two, which was occupied by my friends and fellow coven members Damian and Rosie Ragwort until they moved into their new home. Number one awaited Randy Johnston, who was part of the long string of sales reps bunking down at the Witch's Retreat. We always kept the room for them, come hell or midsummer. They usually visited during the week, but Randy loved the village so much he had booked for an extended weekend. I could have rented out his room for thrice the usual price. Instead, I gave him a special deal.

The doorbell rang again and again, as if somebody's finger was glued to the button.

"Coming," I hollered. Patience was a virtue that some people apparently did without.

I threw open the door to a couple, middle-aged, rake thin, and clad in beiges and browns, which fit the blandness of their features. Despite that, the man looked vaguely familiar. Or rather his handlebar mustache did. I had seen it before, but I wasn't sure where. The chap stepped forward, executed a stiff bow from the hip, and thrust his hand at me for a shake. It was hard not to drop his clammy, spongy appendage.

"Enderby's the name, James Enderby. This is my wife, Anne." His voice sounded familiar also, but before I could rifle through my memories, another hand thrust out at me. Fortunately, Anne's grip was firm and dry.

"Sorry about the doorbell," she said with a grim glance at her husband, who slipped a stopwatch into his trouser pocket. He picked up two battered brown leather suitcases in a style and design that had gone out of fashion with poodle skirts.

"My apologies for making you wait. I was busy with guests who arrived before you. My housekeepers seem to be missing in action." I ushered the Enderbys toward reception while racking my brain for where I might have met the man. The woman I had never seen before.

"Oh, no, have they left? Your housekeepers, I mean?" Mr. Enderby asked, anxiety tugging at his voice. "It's so difficult to find the right place for a holiday. In a job like mine, one sees too many nasty things. But I thought here we would be safe."

I had no idea what the guy might be on about, so I gave him the friendlier of my landlady smiles, the one with concern in it. "They should be around soon. I'll take you to your room, and then you can fill out the registration form at your leisure."

"Eh, see—I'm allergic to mites and bees. Especially the latter. I should have asked when I booked. You haven't got any here, have you?" Bulging eyes beamed anxiety at me. "One sting and I might be done for. I always carry an EpiPen with me." He fumbled with a fawn wrist bag and retrieved something that reminded me of a Magic Marker.

"Please don't worry. There are no beehives anywhere near this place. As to mites, I dare say my cleaners are on top of it."

He gnawed at his lower lip and pulled at his mustache. "Yes, that was my impression."

Like an itch I couldn't scratch, his mannerisms niggled. I had met the man before. Blast, my memory for people wasn't usually this bad.

Plop.

I snapped my gaze away from the tourist brochures I had been about to hand over.

Next to the stairs sat a white plastic bucket with a metal handle. As buckets go, it was solid but unspectacular. Not so the bucket's contents.

While nobody was watching, Petty had levitated from the living room and now squatted in full view of reception. The size of a smallish balloon, the plant sported a rosette of nubby green leaves that covered the rim of the bucket. Pink flowers created a gaudy display on top like an old-fashioned bathing cap. Only a shrewd observer would note the faint tremor of the leaves or the tiny sparks winking among the blooms.

Gravity tugged at my stomach.

"Oh, how pretty," said Mrs. Enderby.

"Primulas in June?" asked her husband.

"It's, uh, a special Himalayan species that flowers all year long. You said you're allergic? Let me remove the flower for you."

I stepped away from the counter to block the little menace from view. When I glared at the plant, the bucket gave the tiniest twitch and shifted on the carpet.

"You're aware we also have a cat?" I spoke over my shoulder.

"Of the common allergens, only bees and, to a lesser degree, mites cause me problems," Enderby said. "However, thanks for your concern."

Don't move, I mouthed, and in my mind willed the primula to obey.

Why would she go walkies today of all days when she rarely did so otherwise?

Hang on, walkies? The lid slipped halfway off my memory box.

I executed a half-turn to face the Enderbys while keeping the floral nuisance in view. "Am I imagining things or have we met somewhere?"

Enderby's gaze dropped to the carpet. Thankfully, the Simpkins sisters had been around to hoover this morning. "Ehem, yes. I'm afraid my colleague tricked me into inspecting your establishment. Back in spring, you remember? Frightfully sorry."

The lid blew off. Jenna's husband, Jeff, a Health and Safety inspector, turned up one memorable Tuesday with his colleague Enderby after planting a dead rat in my kitchen. To save my sorry hide, Petty revealed her supernatural powers. Not only did she deal with the rat but she also knocked out Alan, the crooked police officer responsible for Auntie's death, nearly killing herself doing so. The primula must have recognized Enderby's voice and shown up for a repeat performance.

Not bad for a small houseplant. But downright scary in front of guests.

"No worries," I said. "I feel honored you chose to return." A quick glance at the bucket revealed it was still in the same place, though the leaves quivered more noticeably. I bent over the plant, stroked a nubby leaf, and whispered, "It's okay. He's harmless."

That was only partially correct. Health and Safety staying at the Witch's Retreat meant I needed Alma and Cecily more than ever.

I straightened and beamed at my guests with fake cheerfulness. "Shall we go upstairs?"

Enderby made a beeline for the handrail, where he ran a finger over the top of the blond wood.

"James," Mrs. Enderby hissed. "You're on holiday."

Her husband had the decency to look chagrined.

Behind us, a key scraped in the lock, the front door banged open, and the Simpkins sisters barged in.

For once, they weren't clad in their customary frocks but wore brown slacks and polka-dotted blouses, red dots for Alma and blue ones for Cecily. Damp curls escaped from their perms and were plastered across their sweaty foreheads.

Upon seeing me, both ladies drew deep breaths, and a split second later I was battered by a double verbal tornado. I caught only some of the words they hurled at me, such as "roadblock," "police," and "disaster at the Whacky Bramble." While the storm was raging, the Enderbys looked on with something resembling amusement.

Had Constable Cameron lost his marbles?

I raised first my hands and then my voice. "Calm down, will you? You'll explain it later. Could I ask you, Alma, to please escort our guests to number four? And you, Cecily—"

That was as far as I got. "Tisn't right," Cecily said. "We're not dressed properly."

"Are those your housekeepers?" Enderby's tone was hopeful.

"Yes, we are," Alma said. "Be right with you. First, we need to change." They shot past us and headed toward the utility room under the stairs.

Clunk. The handle of the bucket fell, and Petty's leaves shook and then stilled. Plants can't laugh, but I swear Petty was doing just that.

I gave her a meaningful glance, once more willing her to stay rooted, while I showed the Enderbys to their room. It must have worked, for when I returned downstairs the plant was still waiting at reception. From the kitchen came the clatter of crockery, and I deduced the Simpkins sisters must be preparing a medicinal cup of hot tea.

"Right," I said to my primula. "I truly appreciate you coming to my rescue, but it's not necessary yet. At least, I don't think so.

Let me return you to your windowsill."

I reached for the bucket, but it rose on a comet trail of glittery pink sparks. After a few jiggles, Petty shot along the corridor and vanished through the half-open door to the living room.

Talk about communication breakdown.

—

I pushed through the swing doors. The Simpkins sisters, now attired in near-identical acrylic housedresses of pink and sapphire blue, were reliving the rigors of their trip.

"Okay, that's rooms three and four sorted," I said. "I'm all ears. What exactly is going on at the pub? I understood only half of what you were saying."

Cecily placed her mug on the kitchen counter. "We set out well in time, you see? Would've been over in a jiffy if it hadn't been for the fuzz."

"We waited in that queue for over an hour," Alma said. "The cops never told us nothing. Fortunately, Colonel Elmsworth came by and I could ask him. He was walking that cute dog of his."

Cute? Buster, the Chihuahua, was in charge and he knew it. Colonel Elmsworth was a coven member, something Alma and Cecily weren't aware of and hopefully would never find out.

Alma carried on. "He said our new pubkeeper found a body in his basement, and the cops think something's fishy about that death."

"Fishy?"

"Yes." Ghoulish fascination glittered in Cecily's bird-like eyes. "Never had bodies in this village before."

"Yes we have," Alma said. "People die all the time."

"It's not the same." Cecily finished her tea and stepped to the sink to rinse out the mug. "Not to the point traffic goes chocolate block."

"Choc-a-block," Alma and I chorused.

"Yes, that's what I said, didn't I?" Cecily placed the cup on the shelf.

A loud rumbling and blubbering erupted from somewhere outside the Witch's Retreat.

Alma tilted her head. "What's that?"

I hoped whatever it was would go away. I had enough disasters on my hands to keep me busy. The source of the blubber must have heard me since it died off in a gurgle. "No idea. Must be another guest. We're still missing a few."

Alma reached for the list of new arrivals. It was pinned to the industrial-sized fridge with a magnet in the shape of a witch's hat.

"Says here young Randy Johnston is in room number one, the couple from London in number five, the musicians in number six, and that Aaron chappie in number seven."

Cecily winked. "As to the musicians, I spoke to them. They'll arrive around eight, and they're going to pay cash. Since they'll be staying until the solstice, we need to make sure they do it up front."

Alma gave her sister a sharp look and tutted.

Over a week in an upmarket bed and breakfast? Some musicians. It was high time for me to wrestle reservations back from the sisters' eager hands without offending them. Not today, though.

Instead, I asked, "Aaron's the name of Greg's friend, correct?"

This time, I was the recipient of Alma's stink eye. "Yes. Your friend, the new pubkeeper, he who's the reason for that queue, invites his mates from the States when he doesn't have enough space for all of them. Forced you to move out of your room."

Cecily glared at her sister. "People should help each other. I think it was kind of Myrtle to free up number seven."

"Sorry," Alma said in a small voice.

I was about to make soothing noises when the entrance door slammed open. A quick peek over the swing doors revealed that my cousin had arrived.

"Myrtle, you must do something. It's Greg. It's, like, a total disaster."

Daisy stormed along the corridor, threw herself at my chest, and burst into a fit of hysterical sobbing.

5

THE HEAT IS ON

Daisy's wails grew in volume and intensity, shrilling panic into my ear. Her entire body shook like an exotic plant in a hurricane, and neither comforting squeezes nor crooning baby noises made any difference to her anguish. The Simpkins sisters stayed in the kitchen, mumbling something about tea, though I doubted the British panacea would do the trick this time.

Somebody cleared his throat and said, "Perhaps I can help?"

I lifted my head. At the reception desk waited a blushing beanstalk of a man in his late thirties, wearing stiff jeans and a heavy leather jacket. His gloved hand gripped something that might be a motorcycle helmet. If it hadn't been for the Stars and Stripes covering the top, the pot-shaped headgear could have belonged to a German storm trooper.

The man stepped up and bent over my cousin.

"Ms. Coldron, hey, please calm down. Things will sort themselves out. They always do. Greg will be fine. He's helping the police. It's gotta be a crazy misunderstanding."

Whether it took a male voice or she had cried herself out I didn't know, but the bawling quieted and the tremors subsided. My cousin lifted her head. "They'll lock him up, and I'll never see him again." Her voice was choked with tears, but she was talking.

My arms full of upset cousin, I addressed the biker. "Thanks for your help. I'm Myrtle, by the way. You must be Greg's friend, Aaron."

He nodded and blushed to the roots of his mousy brown crewcut. "It was a pleasure, ma'am."

At thirty, I was a bit too young to classify as a ma'am, but some things are better left alone. "Eh, any idea what's happening at the pub? I assume this is to do with the poor guy in the basement?"

Aaron scratched his bristly head with his free hand. He nodded. "From what I understood, the doctor is talking poison. The dude must have lifted something off the shelves, peas or something, and the cops suspect that might have caused his death. They were checking the food. Pub's been shut down until further notice. Greg—"

Daisy burst into a fresh bout of sobbing.

"Daisy, please. How am I supposed to help your man if I don't even know what exactly is wrong?"

The hiccups stopped. She lifted her head, her big brown Spaniel eyes swimming with tears. "You'll sort them out?" Choked with emotion, her voice was hoarse. She must care for Greg more than she let on. And she relied on me far too much.

"I'll try my best." I patted my hips, but the shift dress sported only one pocket and that sheltered my phone. Aaron removed a packet of paper tissues from his jacket and handed it across.

"Thanks." With delicate fingers, Daisy dabbed at her eyes and then straightened.

I put an arm around her shoulder. "Okay, so where exactly is Greg?"

"Still at the pub with the cops," Aaron said.

"Surely they can't arrest him?"

Daisy's body stiffened under my arm, and I gave her a reassuring squeeze. How I wished I possessed Jenna's soothing powers. Right now, Daisy needed a double dose.

"Not to the best of my knowledge. I was taking my rented Harley for a spin while I was waiting for the check-in at your place. When I returned, the pub was blocked off. I had my luggage stored there, so I called Greg, who then gave me a quick update and asked me to look after his girlfriend. At least the sergeant in charge strikes me as a reasonable and competent woman."

Sarah was just that. "She'll get on top of this mystery. Even if the peas are off or whatever, it doesn't mean Greg is responsible."

Daisy sniffed. "Can you call her, Myr?"

"If Sarah doesn't ring me, I'll contact her later. She won't take kindly to me barging in while she's busy. If push comes to shove, I'll help Greg find a lawyer."

Aaron nodded slowly. "That's good. We've known each other since college. Greg wouldn't hurt an earwig. Anyway, he said it's better if Ms. Coldron stayed in her room at your inn for a while."

Daisy bounced us a defiant, albeit watery, smile. "I'll be fine. It was the shock of seeing my poor darling surrounded by all those coppers. Come on, Aaron, the least I can do for you is sign you in."

Alma chose that moment to pop her head over the kitchen's swing doors. "Would you all like a cuppa, then?"

Sudden warmth spread from my heart. No doubt Alma and Cecily had sucked in every single word of our exchange, and in five minutes flat the rumor mill would go off like a firecracker. But the two ladies truly cared and would defend Daisy and me with their last mop.

"I'll take one, thank you. Aaron? We could bring it up to your room?"

"Sure, thanks."

He struck me as being more of a beer or whiskey man, but like Greg he also was incredibly polite.

"Not for me, thanks," Daisy said, with a brave attempt at a smile. "Let's go." She grabbed the key and headed for the stairs, her tight behind straining under her tunic.

Aaron gave me a friendly nod. "Okay, if there ever is anything I can do for you, let me know. Greg told me how you came to his rescue when none of us was around." With that, he followed Daisy, clomping up the steps in his heavy boots.

I couldn't resist a peek through the open entrance at the Harley. The bike was covered in chrome pipes, which reminded me of the spaceship from *Alien,* hopefully minus the monster. The next moment my view was blocked by a flashy white SUV that popped and cracked over the gravel until it came to a stop. Two rotund figures in designer clothes climbed out.

They struck me as the demanding sort of people who would ask lots of questions. My head swimming with Greg's and Daisy's troubles, I was in no shape to receive them.

"Ladies, incoming guest alert. My money's on the Londoners. I need to work out how to help our pubkeeper. Can you deal with them?"

They could and they did, while I fetched my steaming mug and fled into the garden where green grass tickled my feet and flowers, a lot more seasonal than Petty, enjoyed their short lease on life. Mine had tumbled into chaos. Dot was inexorably dragging me into coven matters. And Chris was back. A man lay dead, and while Sarah's cohorts were only doing their jobs, their investigation was spilling toward my home. I needed to come up with a strategy on how to juggle things. Otherwise, I would soon get steamrolled.

—

First on my to-do list was caring for the local flora and fauna. Alma and Cecily loved looking after Tiddles, but by dropping strong and repeated hints about the primula's imagined value and fragility, I kept control over plant care.

The watering can in one hand, I closed the door to the living room behind me and shouted, "Dinner time."

No reaction came from the cat curled up in the cherry-red armchair, but since the Simpkins sisters no doubt fed her, that didn't surprise me in the slightest. Nor did I expect a response from the Coldron grimoire, also known as the recipe book, since it had never done more than finding its way into my hand when I stood too close to the shelves. On the windowsill, however, the primula sparkled and shifted. The handle of her bucket hit the windowpane with a *chink*.

"Cool it, Petty. I'm coming."

When I poured water mixed with fertilizer over the nubby leaves, the plant tilted her bucket and a lemony scent hit my nostrils. Petty was happy.

"Right, that was a full load. Should keep you going for a while."

Petty straightened and wriggled her blossoms, a gesture I took for assent. How she even heard me, or others like Enderby, remained a mystery. But she did. The primula had to be telepathic, or how else would she have come to my rescue back in the spring when I screamed for her in my head? The plant was a genuine miracle and a loyal and protective sprite—the essence of everything good about witchcraft. I loved her dearly.

Petty whirled around to face the golden rays of the evening sun, glittery drops splaying from her leaves. I left her to digest, and not wanting to disturb Tiddles, plonked myself on the beige settee with a sigh.

Thirsty despite the tea, I picked up the bottle of sparkling mineral water from the coffee table where I had left it yesterday and drank. The liquid was flat now, since for the life of me I could never remember to screw lids on properly. When a soft scratching drifted from the windowsill, my eyes were drawn back to my magical flower.

Born from grief, Dot had said. Born because I didn't know who I was and what I could do, more likely. That would have to change.

"Petty, we're in one heck of a muddle, and it's not only the coven anymore. You haven't met Greg, but he's such a meticulous and cautious person. He would never store poison together with his provisions, never." I placed the empty bottle on the table. "Rats, I wish I hadn't called in Sarah. Now I've got two of my friends on a collision course and Daisy in the dumps, with me acting the piggy in the middle."

Sarah would be involved no matter what you did. When not intent on self-sabotage, my inner voice offered excellent advice.

The flower jiggled her blossoms. Sparks swirled around the bucket as it lifted and hovered across to the armchair, where it gave Tiddles a gentle nudge.

"Mrrp?" The cat yawned, stretched, and curled up again in a ball. Still, she had made space for my floral companion, who now landed on the upholstery.

"Well, there's no point in moping. Things are what they are. Maybe I should give Sarah a quick ring? See what's going on?"

I weighed my phone in my hand. Then I entered the passcode and found a message waiting.

This is more complicated than I thought. Don't call. Once I have the prelims from the postmortem on Monday, I should know more. Our evening is off, I'm afraid. Sarah.

Ambushed by relief and guilt all at once—relief, because I wasn't looking forward to the conversation, and guilt, because I wasn't helping with Greg's troubles—I placed the phone on the table.

"Okay, then I won't contact her. At least not right now."

The primula popped a pink spark.

"One thing is clearer than ever, though. Dot must take on the coven. Sure, I'll help her. Learning more about my skylles also is fine. But I have this nasty feeling Jen and Dot want more."

No way. Not while managing a business, looking after Daisy,

juggling the conflicting needs of my assorted friends, and trying to get to grips with a mercurial sentient plant.

Petty turned her blossoms my way as if she could read my mind, which she probably could.

"Cripes, Petty, life has become so weird. Nor will it get any better in a hurry. What if somebody tries out their magical formulas before we have the database and gets something wrong? What if I do something wrong? Imagine the coven getting outed. The hullabaloo this will cause."

I wrestled with the vision, but it refused to budge.

Petty tilted her plastic bucket, teetering on the edge of the seat. A crumb of topsoil spilled and dropped onto the hardwood floor.

I sighed. "Petty, please, you must stay here. In this room. I'm serious, if we're discovered, all hell will break loose."

The bucket slapped back onto the seat, and the plant stilled.

"Yeah, sure. Sorry, but the stunt with Enderby was too close for my comfort. I promise I'll call you the next time somebody wants to shoot me or flings rats in my general direction. Otherwise, take it easy on the rescue missions."

Petty's leaves drooped.

Myrtle, you're such a cow. The poor thing only wanted to help.

I reached over the sofa's armrest and rubbed the sturdy leaves the same way I fondled Tiddles' paw when she suffered from one of her farting fits. Thankfully, after changing her diet, those were few and far between.

"Sorry. I love you, really."

The leaves, straight once more, tickled my fingers, and I sat back with a sigh. I craved a chocolate ice cream, but I had emptied the last pot yesterday. In all fairness, it was Petty who deserved the treat.

"Let's go outside, shall we? You can enjoy some direct sunlight and fresh air."

The bucket bounced up and down, reminding me of a dog

when it heard the word "leash." With a deep sigh, the cat rose once more, dropped from the armchair, and padded to the other end of the sofa where she turned her back on us.

"Don't fret, old grumpypants. We're off."

I didn't dare leave the house via the conservatory since the Simpkins sisters were inside. While the ladies had swallowed my explanations about the Himalayan species that flowered all year round, they would look askance at me taking Petty for a walk.

Bucket pressed to my bust, I eyed the corridor. From farther down thumped music from the seventies, accompanied by the voices of Alma and Cecily arguing over the state of cleanliness achievable for the French windows.

I dashed into the kitchen. Mercifully, the connecting door to the breakfast patio remained shut, allowing me to slip into the backyard. My van, parked beside the annex that bisected the back wall of the Witch's Retreat, provided excellent cover, so I risked a peek at the windows of rooms four and five upstairs. The curtains were drawn, and I headed for the super-sized day bed Daisy and I had placed at the far end of the annex, where I would be out of sight from every part of the house but the attic. Fortunately, these days everything was quiet under the roof.

There was a slight glitch to my getaway—the bed was occupied. Two feet with painted toenails stretched on the cover.

—

"Hello, Daisy." I placed Petty's bucket in a spot of sunlight next to the divan before sitting at its foot end. "Are you feeling better?"

My cousin regarded me over the rims of her oversized sunglasses, radiating a scent more suited to *Arabian Nights* than Wiltshire summer evenings. The skin around her eyes, however, was puffy. "Sort of, thanks. I guess I'll have to be patient. I mean, he hasn't done anything." Her voice trembled but held.

"Of course not. It would be bad enough if he was delivered

a tainted batch of something, but the cops will work that out in no time."

She sat up. "Aaron said the same. He read about someone who poisoned the food in the supermarket and wanted money. He's super sweet, isn't he? Eh, hang on. Is that Petty? Why are you airing the flower in plain daylight?"

"She tried to help me, and I reckoned I owed her."

"The primula tried to help you? How?"

"Petty recognized one of the guests, thought he was after me, and popped up in the corridor."

The corners of Daisy's mouth twitched. "That must've been a hoot. Wish I'd been there."

"Not an experience I recommend. Do you remember the guy I told you about? The one from Health and Safety who turned up when I hexed Alan's gun?"

Daisy nodded.

"He and his wife are in number four. Petty heard his voice and hovered to the rescue."

Daisy snorted, rolled over, and peeped at the primula, who rustled her leaves in what had to be the magical flower version of a greeting.

"Hi there, little one." With a sigh, Daisy rolled back and lifted a bottle from the side table. The bright yellow liquid she slurped reminded me how thirsty I still was. And how overdressed in my linen shift. Compared to my getup, my cousin's turquoise bikini was a true minimalist masterpiece. So minimalist it was straining at the seams.

"Drink?" Daisy waggled hers. The straw was smeared with lipstick.

"Uh, would you have a fresh bottle?"

"Oops, sorry." She bent over and retrieved another bottle from a cooler and passed it to me. When I sipped, artificial oranges assaulted my taste buds and morphed into manna from heaven.

"Thanks, I needed that."

"I so wish I had my own magical flower." Daisy took the now-empty bottle from me and fished two more drinks from her cooler. This time the liquid glittered in a violent shade of ruby. "Dot only ever explained the basics about magic, and with her having ticker problems all the time, things didn't happen."

Hello? The whole village knew Jenna's grandmother had been seriously ill, even to the point that Jenna and Marty thought she might not make it. But for Daisy the world revolved mostly around herself until, more recently, Greg joined the show.

"You heard what Dot said. I had no clue what I was doing when I, uh, created Petty. Plus, it worked only once. I could do with some training myself."

Daisy sipped at her lemonade and I emptied mine. Did I taste cherry? Berries? It was hard to tell. I placed the empty bottle on the ground and rose to wriggle out of my dress. Daisy gave me a cat whistle.

"Har, har." Back on the day bed, I folded my legs and faced my grinning cousin.

"Racy underwear," she said.

Well, yes. Everybody has a right to a secret vice. Expensive silk undies had always been my thing, ever since my mother bought me my first training bra. As much as I appreciated Sarah's support in fashion matters, no intervention was needed from Sarah on that front, thank you very much. I imagined interventions from Chris, and the tips of my ears flamed.

"Um, thanks. I found a great shop in the outlet center if you're interested."

"Nah. Not now, anyway. I'm, like, washed-out, and it's too hot."

My cousin had a point. The shadows were getting longer, but the air still swam with a heavy heat that pressed on my chest like a load of wet sand. All those hazy clouds above us formed a cover that blocked the fresh air from coming to the rescue. Even the insects capitulated. Only a handful of intrepid bees buzzed along the delphiniums, lavender, and tiger lilies slouching in the herbaceous borders. I took a mental note to water them later when something tickled my arm, prompting a twitch. A ladybug opened its wings and whirred toward the expanse of lush lawn beyond the laurel.

"Things will be better tomorrow."

Smack. Daisy's lips slid off the empty bottle. She blew across the top, coaxing a sad, reedy salute. "Tomorrow I'll still suck at magic."

A sigh threatened to rise, but I shoved it back down. "Be honest. What bothers you more? Greg's troubles or your wonky skylles?"

My cousin's expression changed to vexed. "Both. Don't you see it? I'm, like, super upset about Greg, and does this help with my skylles? Does it heck."

A memory of last spring blipped in my mind. Daisy and I dining at the pub. Tea lights flickering in sync with my cousin's rant.

"I think your skylles showed after Auntie died."

Daisy tossed her head. "Hah, I'm surprised you noticed. Anyway, nothing since then. While she was still fit, Dot showed me a couple of times how she did things. So-called easy stuff like pushing feathers around. I'm a Coldron, she said. I've got to be good at hexing. But I've lost what little I had."

Her lower lip trembled, and she turned away from me.

If Dot had been around, I'd have given her an earful. Where Aunt Eve must have tried to protect her vulnerable daughter, Dot egged her on. I reached for Daisy's hand and gave it a gentle squeeze. "You're putting yourself under too much pressure. Anyway, now Dot's back, she'll train the whole coven. Once we have the database, of course. To do this, she'll need both our help."

"She wants you, not me. No matter what I did for her, she kept talking about you, even when she knew I'd do anything to become a proper witch." Daisy swung her long legs over the edge of the divan. "Gotta see if I can get hold of Greg. See how he's doing."

Daisy's mood swings were the stuff of legends. "Good idea. Keep me posted, will you?" My legs tingled, reminding me I had been sitting in one position for too long. I unfolded them and massaged my calves.

My cousin grabbed her cooler. "Sure. Ping me as soon as you hear anything from Sarah. See ya." She sauntered off.

An invisible vise tightened its grip around my head, and I sank into the covers with a groan.

Why me?

Like a specter refusing to be banned, the cloying scent of my cousin's perfume wafted from the pillows.

With a sigh, I rose. I wouldn't get any rest before Greg was in the clear and progress was made on the hexing front.

6

PARTY TIME

Sunday's temperature had reached an all-time high, and at half-past six in the evening, the Ragworts' porch channeled a pizza oven. Instead of baking smells, the place reeked of fresh paint, wet cement, and dust. The old front door, dented and scratched, was propped open with a brick, so I shouted, "Yoo-hoo, the house."

Since I was late for the coven meeting, I didn't expect a response, and I followed the dusty footprints on the pieces of cardboard protecting the floor tiles. They led into a living room decorated in a combo of sage green walls and cream ceilings. From the open door to the terrace floated laughter and a babble of voices, accompanied by a pungent odor that could only be firelighter. I hadn't planned to be tardy, but after mind-boggling hours of sorting my business bills, Greg had come to the B&B feeling in strong need of moral support. The pub was still shut, Daisy once more suffered from hysterics, Sarah had gone incommunicado, and the autopsy wasn't happening before to-morrow morning. Not a good day overall, and the evening was unlikely to improve.

Chris should be back from his trip.

The thought gave me the courage to enter the garden, where I found the unkempt lawn dotted with molehills and people. A bunch of men, Marty included, clustered at the fence where two large Webers sent smoke signals into cloud-free skies.

No Chris, though.

A group of women, Daisy and Jenna among them, were seated on picnic blankets under the birches. Jenna hollered and waved. When I returned the greeting, the babble quieted only to spring up again, louder than before. While scanning the garden for a certain man in black, my gaze stopped at a third group preoccupied with setting up trestle tables, benches, and camping chairs near the overgrown brick wall separating *Maison* Ragwort from the house next door.

Quite the turnout, with all thirty-seven of us plus the kids gathered to pay our honors to Dot. I had expected to find the woman in a deck chair holding court. She proved me wrong by bustling from one end of the buffet to another, squeezing yet more goodies onto a table already creaking under a load of homemade salads, dips, sweets, and loaves in all shapes and sizes.

I stepped up. "Hello, Dot, here's some more bread for you."

"Oh, no."

"Oh, yes."

She laughed. "Put it on the tables. It'll be gone in no time."

That wouldn't surprise me. The baguettes came from a wonderful new bakery in Swindon. Crisp on the outside and fluffy within, the long, thin flutes of bread had become my latest culinary addiction. I was placing a stone crock of Auntie's garlic herb butter next to the bread when a spindly fawn dog with bulging dark eyes and Yoda ears shot across the lawn and halted in front of me, snarling and yapping.

"Buster, stop." Colonel Elmsworth dropped the camping chair he had been carrying. Straight onto his big toe.

"Ouch, curse it." He hopped around on one Birkenstocked foot, reminding me of a gray-haired and mustachioed daddy longlegs on dope. Buster, visibly unimpressed, kept growling.

"Seriously, James, that dog of yours needs discipline," said Emma Bingham. Like her best pal and my neighbor, the gimlet-eyed Gloria Mornings, Mrs. Bingham loved to gossip. Like most of the witch folk, Mrs. Bingham and Mrs. Mornings were recent arrivals to Avebury and cold-shouldered by the longtime residents. Thwarted in their efforts to feed the local rumor mill, the two ladies sniffed after their fellow witches.

Needless to say, they drove me nuts.

"Auntie Myrtle, Auntie Myrtle. Have you brought chocolate?" Robbie and Johnnie sprinted across from the blanket, and the Chihuahua backed away a few steps.

Oops. I hadn't remembered the kids. Not for one moment. Even for an adopted aunt that was pathetic. Lucky for me, their mother intervened.

"You've had cake, you've had chicken wings, and there'll be sausages later." Jenna rolled her eyes. "They're like food processors. I have no idea where they put it."

She pointed at Buster. "Look here, what a sweet doggie."

Doggie jumped and snapped at the air below her digit.

"That's it," Colonel Elmsworth said. "You're going inside, sunshine."

Someone moved at the edge of my vision. A quick glance revealed a smiling Rosie. "Come on, Myrtle, you need to catch up on the alcohol."

She might be gaunt, with fine white hair cut too short for her narrow face, but a spark glinted in her eyes that hadn't been there before. When we first met, she had recently survived the onslaught of big C. As Rosie's cheeks filled out, her determination returned. Bullying a bunch of renovation contractors must have been better than medicine—it gave her something else to worry about than the inner life of stupid cells.

She handed me a glass of Pimm's. Done the proper way, the drink boasted slices of cucumber and lemon floating in a tea-colored liquid that tasted deceptively fruity and light.

"Great stuff. Thanks, Rosie."

She nodded, a frown forming on her forehead. "Is it true Dot called in Mr. Lentulus? Damian's a tick miffed."

Rosie knew of my feelings for Chris, which must have been the reason her gaze dipped and darted away from me.

I couldn't stand people who used others as an excuse for their prejudices. "Miffed about what exactly?"

"Well, you know, it's not so easy, is it?" She found a scraggly piece of lawn to admire. "You're lucky, you have a proper grimoire, but for most of us some precious scraps are all that's left of our magic. Damian, and quite a few others, are adamant that if we share what some of our ancestors died to protect, then only other coven members should see it. Sure, the young man was helpful in spring, but . . . Damian has a point, doesn't he? I mean, Lentulus does come from a family who used to hunt witches back then, so . . ."

A leaden weariness pressed on my shoulders. If level-headed people like Rosie felt this way, Dot's grandiose plan of having Chris help us with the database was jinxed from the start. Where the heck had the woman got to? I could do with some support.

"We want to explore our skylles, correct? This means storing our knowledge in one place, a bit like a super grimoire to serve us all. That sort of program can't be bought off the shelf, and frankly I don't see who else we can trust with the development."

Rosie nodded, but her gaze kept scurrying all over the garden.

"Quite honestly, I didn't like the plan when your aunt first introduced it. Damian and I are not the only ones." This time, Rosie looked up, concern clouding her pale eyes. "It's too risky to have it all in one place."

"Not knowing what we are doing is worse. Don't tell me

people haven't been experimenting. I know they have. That's bound to go pear-shaped sometime soon."

At first, she remained silent. "Fair enough, I see your point. However, if Mr. Lentulus is such a computer whiz, he can copy the texts without batting an eyelid. I mean, I believed him when he said he wasn't conspiring with his uncle. Still . . . don't take it personally, please." The last bit she added rather hastily.

I sipped my Pimm's to buy myself some time. And to stop myself from saying something I might later regret.

"Rosie, we need this program, and we can't bring in an outsider. Chris hates his uncle with a passion, and he hates what his ancestors did."

"Really?"

"Yes, and he's determined to make things right. That's why he wants to help us create our super grimoire. He told me himself the last time we met. And no, I'm not blind because I happen to like him or something."

Against my will, my voice had risen in volume, and quite a few heads turned my way. And not only heads. Mrs. Bingham and Mrs. Mornings were the first to shift across, and soon I was encircled.

I really could've done with some support from Dot. Or Jenna. Or both. A quick look over my shoulder revealed only Daisy, but she had her back to me.

Rats.

Rosie flapped her hands in a soothing motion, distress wrinkling her forehead. "Oh dear, now I put my foot in it."

"No, you didn't." Damian's violet owl eyes were magnified by his thick lenses. "I gave Eve a piece of my mind about her pet project. There's no need to use the latest technology when a good old Excel sheet can do the trick. Think of the hackers hanging around in the clouds or whatever it is they do."

"That's why we need Chris," Marty said in his level voice. "He's one of them. An Excel sheet doesn't cut ice."

Once more, I glanced over my shoulder and finally spotted

the female Wytchetts. Seemingly oblivious to my predicament, they were overseeing a game of apple bobbing for the toddlers that involved a lot of squealing and splashing.

I waved. No response. With a suppressed groan, I tuned back in on the argument.

Damian pinched the bridge of his nose. "Sorry, but no. We need some sort of repository, yes. However, there's no point in fancy hi-tech solutions. And we certainly don't need Lentulus."

"I disagree." Marty's comment kicked off a spat between the coven members gathered around us, so I took a fortifying sip of my Pimm's to keep my mouth occupied. I wouldn't engage. No way.

A whistle pierced the din. "Hey, listen." Linda, the landlady of the Crystal Dawn, shoved her long dark hair behind her pierced ears. She wore a black sleeveless T-shirt over black combat pants. I risked a peek at her feet. Yup, the flip-flops were black, too. If Morticia Addams had ever worn trousers, this was how she would have looked.

"Folks, we need to fix this chaos before we can go to the next level. It's simply too dangerous. If everybody had proper grimoires, like the Coldrons and the Wytchetts, it would be different. In my case, I can't even decipher the crabby handwriting on my parchments. Worse, they're falling apart."

"Hear, hear." Mel, the owner of Avebury's New Age shop, wore her surplus kilos with pride and sheathed herself in fluttery clothes that flattered her ample curves. "Aren't you the lucky one. I don't even have papers—only some cryptic oral instructions that make no sense whatsoever. I would like to change that and soonish."

"Eve made sense of things. She still died," Rosie said.

"Perhaps she didn't think she had enough power to do harm. Who knows," Mel said.

Surreptitious glances stole my way. I nibbled on a slice of boozy cucumber.

"Well, then, how about some discussion groups where we

compare notes?" Linda asked. "No need to involve externals. But the status quo doesn't work."

"No way," said Mrs. Bingham. "There's been enough yacking already. When are we actually going to do something?"

"Quite right, my dear." Mrs. Mornings' pointy chin quivered with indignation. "We missed the equinox. Will we now miss the solstice? Dot and Eve claimed our powers would increase now we're together. I mean, it's fine for people like Jenna. She's had magic all her life. Or think of Myrtle, turning that gun into a cactus. What about me, though? I haven't experienced any supernatural boost. None." She made it sound like a personal slight.

More furtive looks snuck my way.

I waggled my empty glass. Despite its sad state, my mood had lightened and turned sort of floaty. I was less bothered by being regarded as the über-witch whose aunt died in a magical accident or the magical booby trap my fellow coven members treated with kid gloves. Perhaps they worried the air around me might explode into a shower of petals at any time, like it had back in April. And never since.

Would that apple bobbing never end?

"Let me fill that up for you," Rosie said from behind and tipped the remaining contents of her pitcher into my glass.

"Think this through for a second," Mel said. She had a full glass of Rosie's concoction and saluted me before sipping. "Dot is right. We need help. Isn't Mr. Lentulus also a historian? Should be useful. Hey, I'm willing to contribute to our database if he develops it. If Eve trusted the man, I'm prepared to give him a chance."

"Well spoken" and "You can't be serious" were the more intelligible comments in the commotion that broke out.

I swung around, but the apple bobbing was still in full swing.

The floaty sensation evaporated. "Dot? Jenna?"

Dot turned my way, and I jerked my head at the fracas. She nodded and held up two fingers. About time.

"We should have had our magical database ages ago," Colonel Elmsworth said. "Then we would know whether evacuating for the solstice is necessary. It'll look odd if we all hare off at the same time, no matter what cover stories we come up with." His voice was loud enough to carry in a thunderstorm.

The babble died down.

He grinned at me and I smiled back. I liked the man, even without a dose of Pimm's sloshing around inside.

"It's completely unnecessary, since being together at the stone circle hasn't boosted our powers, no matter what Eve promised us," Mrs. Bingham said. "And since the coming solstice hasn't changed anything either, why run?"

The way she kept worrying her bone, the woman was worse than Buster. I could swear she tried her magical instructions every day in case something might have changed.

"Quite right," Mrs. Mornings said. "Did you get visited by your magic recently, Myrtle?"

Too many eyes swiveled my way, and a telltale warmth crept into my cheeks. Teaching hordes of teenagers should have helped with the annoying phenomenon, but occasionally it got the better of me.

"No. That doesn't mean it won't happen. The solstice is still eight days away. We're setting up a contingency plan, that's all. Honestly, if you don't believe in the coven, why are you here?"

Silence dropped on the assembly, pierced only by the splashes and screams from the older children who must have muscled in on the apple bobbing.

The scent of old-fashioned perfume hit my nose as Dot stepped up on my one side, Jenna and Daisy on the other.

"That's your problem in a nutshell, isn't it?" Dot's voice was tired. "You want to do magic to help save the planet, but you don't want to share your personal legacies. You're frustrated about the lack of progress, but you reject the solution without offering an alternative. Despite hoping the solstice will give you a boost, you're not even willing to address the risks involved simply because it's inconvenient."

When Dot wavered, Daisy dashed across and propped her up.

"Thanks, my dear." To the coven, she said, "I understand you had these discussions back in winter, when Eve was alive. She came up with the database idea. She even made a down payment, but we're still standing here, talking. You need to make your minds up."

Other than a few murmurs and mumblings, there was no response. Dot sat in the camping chair Marty had brought over.

"The evacuation is only a backup," Colonel Elmsworth said. "Assuming nothing, eh . . . untoward happens during the next week, we might as well stay here. We can then go ahead with the training, using—what did Myrtle call the database? Super grimoire? If necessary, we activate the plan for the winter solstice. Assuming we've made progress by then."

That got him shouts of protest. Apparently, winter solstice wasn't acceptable, because of it being too far in the future.

All this talk of grimoires made the recipe book take shape in my mind. Bound in graying calf leather, its stiff pages blotched and stained, the Coldrons' legacy consisted of proper recipes, entered by my aunt and my grandmother, and a hundred or so empty pages in the middle. At the back of the tome, the juicy part started, written by my Great-Aunt Petunia, my primula's namesake. In 1804, she recorded "our lore, lest it be lost." Invocations, herbal potions, and personal comments were interspersed with observations and instructions, all written in a curly script rather hard on the eyes.

I took a deep breath. "I agree with the Colonel and Dot when it comes to the emergency plan. Better safe than sorry. Don't, and I mean it, don't, try to apply your skylles in any form. Should you notice any paranormal effects, you must report them so we can trigger the evacuation. As to handing over our heirlooms . . . fair enough, I would never part with the recipe book either. Someone can scan the pages instead. That way, you can read what's in the Coldron grimoire, like I can. Not Auntie's recipes, though."

The laughter was feeble, but it was there.

"We'll contribute the laundry list," Jenna said. "Sweet Earth, folks, we can only do this together. All it takes is a team of supervisors when the documents are scanned or copied. Afterward, it should be easy to enlarge and interpret the texts, which means we might actually be able to understand them, you know?"

Cheers and catcalls burst from the crowd. The mood was shifting. Not by much, as there were still dissenters. I could hear them grumble. And the others could still swing back. But we were getting somewhere.

Dot looked up from her chair and winked. "There's no alternative to having a database. And no, Damian, I might be older than you, but don't give me Excel sheets. I want something safe, state of the art, and future-proof. We'll have to find a means of regulating access, of course. But that's the only way each of you can keep your personal legacies while contributing to and benefiting from a greater whole."

That was a bit bombastic, but the applause proved her right.

Dot levered herself up from her chair. "I know you have reservations about Mr. Lentulus. Initially, I shared them. Still, Eve trusted the young man and, quite honestly, I liked what I saw when I met with him."

So did I. "During her last moments, my aunt asked Chris to look after me and help me find my magic. He never broke his promise. He even had a go at that idiot Alan when he kidnapped Robbie, risking his own life. Why would he do that if he wasn't on our side?"

"To trick us?" Damian said, but his voice lacked conviction.

I pointed my finger at him. "That's ox manure, and you know it."

A breeze found its way into the garden, carrying along an evening freshness. Laughter sprung up. People shifted and moved as if a curse had broken.

At the end of the evening, fueled by Pimm's, grilled sausages, smoked tofu, and homemade food, we settled on an agreement, which the Colonel outlined in Robbie's painting book.

The Avebury witches would contract Chris Lentulus to program a database with the aim of safely storing the information contained in said witches' respective heirlooms. The content of the aforementioned heirlooms was to be entered manually into the to-be-developed database whenever possible. However, it was not to be done by the aforementioned IT specialist. Wherever scanning was required, said specialist would be supervised.

Dot called Chris at his apartment to share the news and invited him over. When she confronted him with the details, an odd expression I couldn't quite interpret surfaced on his face, but then, the man was hard to read at the best of times and not only when one's brain was a trifle fogged, despite stopping after the second Pimm's and switching to apple juice. I was looking forward to a stroll home accompanied by Chris, hopefully crowned by a happy ending. Nothing naughty, mind you. Just . . . happy. For that, I had better be wide awake.

—

During the fifteen minutes it took me and Chris to stroll from the Ragworts' new home to the Witch's Retreat, my mellow mood curdled. Above us, stars twinkled. Distant music blew in from the henge, and the balmy air was filled with the cheerful voices of people sitting on their terraces enjoying life. The peaceful ambience was lost on Chris. Monosyllabic answers were all I received, so eventually I gave up. There was this thing called pride. The last meters to Chris's Beemer, parked next to the front entrance of the B&B, we covered in a loaded silence.

"I suppose this is where we part, and I don't forget a shoe?" I said.

The motion detector over the portico clicked, and a strip of bright light slashed across Chris's face. I jumped. He blinked and raised his hand to shield his eyes. Then he burst into laughter. "You certainly have your own special way of doing things."

"Shh, not so loud. The guests." A spark of hope rekindled in my bosom. Perhaps all wasn't lost. The big question was, should I invite the man inside? Or would that be too special for him?

"Sorry, Myr," Chris said, *sotto voce.* "I guess I'm a bit ticked about the lukewarm reception. You lot don't quite realize how risky your precious project is."

"Risky?" My voice was way too loud, so I turned it down. "For whom?"

The lamp over the portico clicked off, plunging us into darkness. Was the motion sensor on the blink? Or could this be a magical side effect of being upset?

"For you and your friends," Chris said from among the shadows. "There aren't enough specialists around who can develop a software program that's easy to use and almost impossible to hack. You certainly won't find anything in a shop. You wouldn't want to. We hackers love that stuff."

Click. The light turned back on. Chris groaned, squinting. "Stop this, will you?"

"I'm not convinced it's me. I can't hex that well."

"I meant, push the off button."

"Ah, sorry. No idea where it is. As far as the reception is concerned, what did you expect?"

Chris sighed. "Not sure. Too much, I guess. Damn, I'm trying to help you lot."

"Ah. Alas, I fear we're only human."

Chris sniggered, his body a shadow in the gloom since the blasted lamp had turned itself off again. His trademark scent, linen and incense, wafted into my nostrils. That man smelled much too delicious. It probably says a lot about me that an attractive man, a yummy fragrance, and the absence of light sparked a thought that couldn't have been further from romance if it tried.

"Back in spring, you mumbled something about certain annals on the witch folk your family is keeping. Can you get hold of them?"

"Why?"

Click. The light popped back on, and tiny blobs danced across my vision.

"Well, I guess we should get hold of any knowledge hanging around."

"No way," Chris said. "The Ignatius family records are off limits. If I want them searched, dearest Uncle Bob will ask for favors afterward, which is no good to anybody. Instead, I trawled the Internet while I was sitting on my Welsh mountain, on my ownsome lonesome."

"I wish to point out it was your idea."

The light winked back out. Since my mood had lightened, the effect was likely to be caused not by magic but by a motion sensor on a hair trigger.

"Be this as it may, I scoured various . . . unofficial sources for historical evidence on your lot."

"Oh. And?"

"Pretty much zilch," his amused voice said from the shadows. "There are records of wise women and men, sometimes called Earth Wardens, living next to the odd prehistoric sanctuary, with the biggest community of them here in this village. Nothing in Stonehenge, by the way. Accused of dark magic, the stronger ones vanished the same year. Those who didn't leave were in dire trouble. That would mean your lot, the Reds."

"When was that?"

"1601."

"Nothing on where the Whites would have gone, after they left the Reds behind to be hunted and killed? That is one question I'd really like to have answered."

"Sadly, no."

"Did you talk to Dot about it?"

"Can we forget Dot for a moment?" he asked.

My hand had a life of its own, reaching out and caressing Chris's cheek, smooth for once. He took my hand in his and guided it to his lips. A tiny kiss blew on my fingers, and then he released me. Or rather, my hand.

Flash. The velvety darkness splintered into glaring fragments.

Chris groaned. I must have done the same. We moved apart.

"Today is not a good day," he said.

"It's the corpse. The image of that cellar keeps sneaking up on me. Now, why are you laughing? Shh, the guests."

"Sorry." The lovable idiot took his own sweet time until he stopped snorting.

"What?" I asked.

"Myrtle, if I didn't mention I missed you, here's the official confirmation. You're unique and I missed you. Just don't ever give me dark magic, that's where I draw the line. Now, my supernatural Cinderella, hold on to your magical flip-flops and get a bit of shuteye. Tomorrow, I mean later today, the world will be a better place."

That was when I remembered the autopsy.

7

SCAPEGOAT

My bedroom, chilled to subarctic temperatures when I arrived—I should have read the instructions that came with the air conditioner—warmed up during the night. It had taken me a long time to fall asleep, and as a result, I flailed about in confusion when the clock radio started rapping at a disgustingly early hour.

A blurry glance at the display revealed it wasn't early after all. I must have hit the snooze button.

Through the open window of my bedroom drifted clattering and rattling, underscored by the welcome aroma of fresh coffee. Normal services had resumed. Alma and Cecily had risen at dawn to prepare breakfast.

What a lucky landlady I was.

The fog in my brain cleared in a flash of awareness. It was Monday, the day for the autopsy results that would decide Greg's fate. Some people called me a pessimist. To my mind, it betokened realism when one hoped for the best and prepared for the worst. In any case, hanging around in bed was out of the question.

After a rose-scented shower, I felt more human and traipsed across to Auntie's wardrobe to rifle through my clothes. I needed something like the linen dress from yesterday, only more loose-fitting. I had eaten more than planned at the coven meeting. My fingers hit upon a smooth fabric, and I pulled it out. Another shift dress, this time in pale sage and made of washable silk. I held the outfit against myself, liked what I saw in the mirror, and got ready to rock.

Down in the kitchen I was greeted by sizzling. A split second later, the odors of roasting toast and a tangy whiff of smoked fish did a full body tackle on my nostrils.

"Morning, ladies. Good heavens, who's having kippers with another scorcher on its way?" I sat at the table.

Alma's stocky back emerged from the frosty embrace of the fridge. She turned around and shrugged, penciled eyebrows rising toward her brunette poodle perm. "Morning, Myrtle. It's the American in number seven. He wanted the Scottish breakfast."

Something warm and hairy brushed past my ankles. Alma looked down and waggled a finger at Tiddles. "You've been fed, madam."

The door to the conservatory sprang open and Cecily entered, frocked in sapphire blue. "Morning." She pursed her lips. "Good you're here, Myrtle. The musicians in number six are a bit upset. They had a spat with number five about the noise."

"What noise? And who's in five . . . ah, the Londoners. Am I the last to show my face?"

Alma handed me a glass of orange juice. "Don't you worry. Number five has asked for room service, and your cousin is still in bed."

The latter didn't surprise me in the slightest since Daisy had a rough couple of days.

"Since when do we offer room service?"

Alma's bird eyes glittered. "These people are nothing but trouble, so I figured the less we see of them, the better. Told them there'd be a twenty-five percent service fee."

"Hah, clever of you. Now, what about that noise?"

Cecily grabbed a pan and banged it onto the hob. "Looks like the musicians returned during the small hours, something to do with the marmalade, and when they carried their instruments to their room, the mandarin jingled once or twice. They explained and apologized already, but the Londoners were up in arms."

I stared at Alma and received a shrug in return. "Marmalade? Mandarin?"

"Yes, and some tapas. The Blue Lady—sorry, but that's how she looks, blue hair, blue dress, blue everything—said she dropped one right in front of number five, and it rolled around on the floor in the middle of the night. Happens the Londoners are vestment bankers, they're looking for an escape from the stress, and this isn't it."

Tapas rolling around on the floor? I searched for linguistic matches but drew a blank.

Alma huffed and handed Cecily a pack of bacon. "What did they expect? A cloister?"

A scream shrilled from next door, panic lifting the octaves until the voice broke.

I jumped from my seat and barreled through the side entrance into the conservatory, images of warfare between noisy musicians and burned-out bankers crowding my mind.

Instead, I found Pan standing in front of the breakfast buffet gaping at a china bowl. Gerry patted his back, making soothing noises. Most tables were taken, and the guests present were staring. Randy Johnston had his mouth open. Not a pretty sight.

"Nuts," Pan said, a tremor lingering in his voice.

I assumed he wasn't talking about himself and took a gander. Yep. A misguided creative ringed the muesli with hazelnuts.

"Eh, yes, is that a problem?"

"It is, I'm afraid," Gerry said. "Come on, Pan, nothing's happened. You can calm down. Just make sure you keep your EpiPen handy at all times." He guided Pan back to his seat and made him sit before swinging around to face me. "Poor guy's so completely allergic to nuts. A trace of the stuff could be lethal."

"Last night I realized I forgot to mention it when we registered," Pan said breathlessly. "I was ever so worried about what might end up in my food. I even dreamed of the damn things, and when I saw them in the bowl, it was like in my nightmare."

His eyes appealed at me from deep within their sockets, and a lopsided smile made him look like an overgrown, exhausted urchin. "Sorry for causing a fuss. I mean, I know they're harmless if I don't eat them. Still . . ."

My heart went out to him, and I wanted to hug the guy.

Mr. Enderby, seated at the next table with his wife, clucked his sympathy. "You're allergic too? People never understand what it means having to live with a hazard like that threatening your every move."

The crisis over, the four of them swapped tales of life-threatening incidents across their coffees while the other guests busied themselves with their breakfasts. Table legs scraped along the floor, and cutlery clattered against plates. Through the open doors of the conservatory floated birdsong, and a warm breeze sent the gauzy curtains billowing into the room.

My gaze fell on the breakfast buffet, which sported crystal bowls with orange marmalade and raspberry jam.

Marmalade. Jam.

Cecily must have been talking about a jam session. This meant the mandarins were most likely tambourines, and the tapas had to be tablas. I couldn't stop a grin from breaking out. Yes, our friendly musicians had caused quite a racket. Right now, they sat peacefully opposite the French windows. Enough instruments to kit out the modern section of the London Symphony Orchestra were scattered at their feet and around the table. The unsolved trouble in the pub and the part I still had to play in it festering in my mind, I didn't fancy hostilities in the Witch's Retreat. Management intervention was required.

I stepped up. "Good morning, I hope you slept well? From what I hear, there was a spot of bother in the middle of the night?"

"Not again." The woman slapped her napkin onto the table and jumped up, her indigo dreadlocks lashing around like Medusa's snakes. One whipped into her face and caught on the studs piercing her brows and nose. She shoved it aside. A second later, her companion followed her example. Apart from a pointed goatee, the man sported an amazing amount of muscle. His tee was black and covered in skulls. He struck me as being the more harmless of the two.

My mood curdled. Today was shaping up to be worse than its predecessors.

"We apologized twice already. We didn't mean to wake up those morons," said Blue Lady.

"I'm sure you didn't. Since you're booked until the solstice, we better find a solution for your instruments. It can't be fun to lug your gear up and down those steps every time, correct?"

Blue Lady relaxed her stance. "Er, no, you're damn right about that."

"Thank you for being so understanding," I said. "We've got a utility room under the staircase. How about if you store your instruments there? It's dry, and there's plenty of space. I'll give you the key so you can lock up."

When she smiled, the woman became fiercely beautiful. "That's a terrific idea. We didn't want to leave our babies in the car."

"Would that room be safe during the day?" Goatee asked.

"Of course," I said. "Apart from myself, only the housekeepers have access, and you'll have the key. At any other time of year, your possessions could stay in your car, but right now there are lots of visitors in the village. I wouldn't run the risk."

"Great stuff. We'll move whatever we don't need later." Goatee sat, and Blue Lady followed his example.

Phew. Another crisis mastered. I was earning my keep.

He snapped his fingers. "Actually, we'll only need the clarinets."

Blue Lady frowned at her partner. "We do?"

"Yup. Session with the guys from Bucharest."

Her brow cleared as if dragged down by all that metal. "Ah, the flutists. They're magical."

I could only hope those flutists weren't truly magical. Otherwise, things would get even more interesting than they already were. "I'll fetch you the key. Enjoy your session."

"That's kind of you," Blue Lady said and tackled the remains of her full English.

I returned to the kitchen where I found Alma perched on the edge of the table, a copy of *The County Messenger* in her chafed hands. That rag wasn't among the reading matter the Witch's Retreat subscribed to, so it had to be her own.

"Says here there's been a dead body found in the pub's cellar. And the publican is 'helping with the inquiry.' Ooh, does it mean that American landlord of ours has offed someone?"

Cecily, who had filled Tiddles' bowl with leftover omelet—something my geriatric pal loved but also something that would trigger a farting fit—flung her sister an annoyed look.

"He wouldn't. The man's ever so kind."

"Dearie me, you can be nice and still be a murderer," her sister said.

How could I clear the cat's bowl without offending the Simpkins sisters? Tiddles solved the problem by sticking her whiskers into the omelet.

Oh well, the odd egg wouldn't kill the cat, and her sulfurous winds would pass. Greg was more important.

"Does it say anything else? I mean, do they have an idea what the guy actually died of?"

"Doesn't look like it," Alma said. "The coppers don't even

have a clue who the dead chap is. He's got no papers on him."
She stabbed her newspaper. "Hah."

"What?" Cecily and I asked simultaneously.

Tiddles licked her chops. "Mrrp?"

"Says here, it's a suspicious death. Does mean murder, doesn't it?" Alma waved her reading matter in our general direction.

"No, Alma. My aunt's death was suspicious at first, remember?"

"Yes, that's true," Cecily said. "Ms. Coldron trundled from the attic and 'twas nobody's fault in the end." She grabbed a Brillo pad and attacked the nearest pot.

"Tumbled," Alma said, with an uneasy glance at me.

"It's okay," I said. No, it wasn't, not really, but such is life.

The phone on the kitchen table buzzed and broke out into a tinny rendition of "Love Hurts."

I dashed across and checked the caller ID. Chris.

My heart did a cheerful hop. "Hello, Myrtle here?"

"You sound as if you're suffering from an identity crisis." The trademark amusement in his voice had been replaced by stressed vibes, which was out of character for the man. A leaden ball materialized where my stomach had been.

"There are moments when I feel a bit lost. This is one of them. What's wrong?"

"You better find yourself pronto. We've got a problem. Or rather, Greg has. I wanted to see how he was doing and found him in real trouble. If that tosser has his way, Greg will be arrested. Sergeant Sarah has emphasized the lack of evidence, but she's not getting through to that idiot. You can do two things—organize a lawyer and provide some moral support. And . . . what are you saying?"

Somebody shouted in the background.

"Ah, Greg says to keep Daisy out of it, please. She doesn't seem to be coping well."

She never did, but that wasn't exactly news. "Tosser? Idiot?

Don't tell me, DI Diloff is on the case."

Behind my back, something clattered onto the drying board. Whistling sounds followed as if the ladies were sucking in air in preparation for a free dive.

"Thinning hair? Silly little mustache? Awful taste in jackets?" Chris asked.

"That's him. Crap. I'll contact my legal advisor and see if he knows any competent solicitors. Once done, I'll come over. Can you stay with Greg?"

"I have every intention of doing so, no matter what Sergeant Widdlethorpe or DI Diloff might think."

"Ta, on it." I disconnected.

My head swam, flooded with too many thoughts. I swung around to face the ladies.

"Got some calls to do, and then I'll scoot across to the pub. I'll take the phone, so you can reach me in case the Londoners or anybody else acts up again. Oh, the musicians need the key to the utility room."

"We'll sort things out, don't you worry," Alma said. They would, but they would also want the full report as soon as I returned.

If I returned. Diloff and I weren't exactly besties. I might end up behind bars if I wasn't careful.

I grabbed the car keys from the hook stuck to the side of the fridge and was about to sprint outside when I remembered Petty. "Ugh, the plant."

"We can—"

"Thanks, Cecily. She's sensitive, so it's better if I do it."

I raced into the living room to water the primula while giving her a somewhat sketchy update on things. A fusillade of pink sparks shot from the blossoms, which hopefully meant Petty was fine. I stuck a Post-it Note for Daisy on the bucket asking her to look after the primula. As flighty and stressed as my cousin might be, she cared for my floral pal and would keep her safe. A few phone calls later, I had a solicitor on standby.

That sorted, I dashed to my car and broke my personal speed record for driving to the pub.

—

The Whacky Bramble was besieged by two police cars and the sort of windowless white van that belonged to either Eastern European workers or scene-of-crime officers. Only two days ago the beer garden had been teeming with people. Today it was empty, and the entrance was blocked off with police tape. A handful of tourists clustered on the street side of the barrier, and I had no idea whether they craved a drink or were hoping for photo opportunities.

On the bench closest to the entrance, I spotted three people I knew. Greg, slumped at the table, was staring into space. Next to him sat Chris, legs stretched out, arms crossed on his chest, and a scowl on his face. My friend Sarah, whose dark hedgehog hairdo I would have recognized anywhere, was leaning against the wall, talking into her phone. What was she doing out here? Guarding Greg? They had uniforms for that, but none of them were in sight.

"Excuse me?" I hollered across the police barrier to the entrance to the beer garden. Greg and Chris looked up. The tourists next to me shifted and shuffled.

Sarah finished her call. The hungry expression on her lean face segued to predatory. "Mr. Lentulus, did you call Myrtle in?" she asked, loud enough for me and the tourists to hear.

Chris nodded.

Sarah slapped her hand to her forehead and rolled her eyes.

"What's going on here?" The question had been asked by a man in shorts and a tee shirt not long enough to cover his substantial paunch.

"I'm about to find out." I clambered over the barrier and joined the threesome at the hard bench. "Keep your voices down. The vultures are circling. We might want to sit inside, actually."

"That's where my boss is," Sarah said.

"Ah. Care to put me in the picture?"

"I'd rather if you weren't here, but since Mr. Lentulus—"

"Call me Chris," he said in a silky voice.

"Since Mr. Lentulus chose to involve you, I guess you won't give me a moment of peace if I try to send you packing."

"They think I've poisoned the man in the cellar," Greg said in a listless tone. "They don't know yet what with. Looks like that guy died because of something he ate. The way the head honcho is going on, I left contaminated jars on the shelves because I hated burglars." Greg massaged his forehead. "Tell you what, he's got it in for me because I'm Black."

"Please calm down, Mr. Winters. We'll find the answer," Sarah said.

Our gazes crossed over Greg's bent head, shiny like a dark bowling ball. No further explanations were necessary. After being at the receiving end of DI Diloff's attitude and tank-style approach to investigations, I knew Greg's fears were justified.

Even if the entire mess wasn't of Sarah's design, I was plenty pissed off, which injected a certain sharpness into my voice. "How can Greg calm down when he stands accused of murder? Especially when the theory is so outlandish. It sounds as if your boss wants to scare my friend out of sheer spite."

A small tic at the corner of Sarah's left eye was the only sign the shot hit home. "Myrtle, you do your job, and I'll do mine. The symptoms are a bit contradictory, but it appears the deceased indeed died because of something he ingested. We don't know exactly what it might have been, but his stomach contents included crackers, pesto, and peas, whereof we found a jar next to the sleeping bag and further specimens on the shelves. We have to follow up on that."

The more stressed my friend was, the more her language disintegrated into cop-speak.

"The one next to the bag was closed, wasn't it?" I asked.

"Yes, but the deceased might have already consumed the peas from another jar and disposed of it."

"You don't need to use officialese with me. I'm not blaming you," I said.

A wry smile tugged at her lips. "I know, okay? As I said, the evidence is inconclusive, and our DI can't make his mind up whether the deceased lifted lethal food off the shelves or broke into the kitchen and consumed equally lethal leftovers."

"But that's not possible either." Greg slammed his ham-like fist on the table. "The kitchen door hasn't been jimmied. Why would I want to poison my guests? Tell me that. None of this makes any sense whatsoever. That idiot cop is inventing his story as he goes along."

"Not so loud, Mr. Winters," Sarah said in glacial tones. "As yet, we don't know where exactly in the pub the victim has been or what he might have picked up. Or how. We can't take any risks. That's why I had to shut down the place. You've been co-operative, and I appreciate that."

"Why does your boss want to drag him back to the cop shop, then?" Chris asked in the same silky voice as before.

The tic at Sarah's eye twitched faster.

"Told you he's trying to frame me for murder." Greg glared at Sarah. "He thinks he can slam-dunk this case. He admitted as much when he popped up on my doorstep earlier. What makes him so sure it was my food that did the guy in? Those cans, for example, aren't from the pub. We would never use spaghetti rings in our kitchen. I bet you I'm to be another notch on the barrel of that bastard's gun."

Sarah made soothing motions with her hand. "Rest assured, we'll follow all possible leads." A ringtone trilled from the pocket of her pearl-gray linen blazer. "Ah, that's Cameron. He's supposed to be with Diloff. Must have sneaked outside. Excuse me for a moment." She walked off, with the phone pressed to her ear.

"Oh man," Greg moaned. "I'm done for. Where do I find a lawyer?"

"Taken care of already, in case you need help. I still think this is an unfortunate combination of unclear circumstances and a pig-headed copper.”

“It’ll be all right, mate,” Chris said.

Greg growled. “That Diloff guy has his facts upside down. The connecting door to the kitchen wouldn’t exactly qualify for Fort Knox, but as I said before, it’s warped. And nobody’s tampered with it, I’m sure of that. My bet is the dead man never went farther than the storeroom and the cellar. The sergeant sort of believed me. But that boss of hers doesn’t want to listen. Not to forget those blasted peas—which aren’t poisoned.” He banged his fist on the table once more.

“Listening is not Diloff’s forte. Nor is using whatever brain cells he has,” I said.

“Yeah. As if I would ever keep poisoned jars of food on my shelves to surprise burglars. I mean, come on. I’m no Dr. Crippen.”

“Did he really say that?” Even for Diloff, such an accusation was wild.

“Well, he backpedaled when I pointed out should they trace poison in the jars, I wasn’t the one who put it there. Hah, I betcha he’s trying to come up with something, anything, to call me a murderer and drag me to jail.”

“Has the DI any explanation for the body being down in the beer cellar?” I asked.

“That seems to be straightforward. Sergeant Widdlethorpe told me they found traces of vomit on the stairs,” Greg said. “He must have eaten . . . whatever, had tummy problems, lost his orientation, and staggered down the steps. It all happened during closing hours since the pub shut at eleven on Friday, as usual. Everything was locked. Well, as much as we could lock it.”

“You checked the place before leaving, I assume?” I asked.

“Of course. I did my last round just before midnight. It’s my own fault. I should have ordered a replacement for that back door earlier. Oh man.” He buried his head in his arms.

“Hindsight is a wonderful thing,” I said.

Sarah returned. I tried telling myself she wouldn't talk to us if she believed Greg guilty of gross negligence, or worse, murder. I didn't convince myself.

With a glance at the growing gaggle of spectators, she said under her breath, "There's a development. Mr. Winters, you don't happen to own a small black leather case? It's been found shoved under a shelf close to the sleeping bag."

Her expression was blank, but I knew her well enough by now to suspect somebody was in for a good, old-fashioned wrist-slapping. It wasn't super smart of her troops to miss evidence only to discover it when the DI happened to be around to claim the find as his own.

Greg straightened. "What? No. Why would I? It's a storeroom, not a luggage shop."

"Not to worry. We suspected the case might have belonged to the deceased. I guess none of you noticed it yesterday?"

Chris looked at me. I looked at him. We shook our heads simultaneously.

"Your assorted minions didn't find it yesterday either," Chris said.

Sarah's jaw muscles clenched. "Unfortunately, they didn't, but then it had been hidden in a cardboard box. Mr. Winters, you still owe me an answer?"

Greg shrugged. "Huh? I noticed only those two cans, the peas, the water, and the carrier bag the stuff stood on."

"The case appears to be old, but it's of good quality and lined with velvet. There's a concert flute inside." Her gaze did the round as if begging for offers.

A flute?

The hard bench, the hot sun, the voices—everything slid away. I had heard about flutes recently. This morning, in fact. Back at the Witch's Retreat.

The dam broke. Insight flooded my head. Goatee and the Blue Lady were going to meet up with flutists from Bucharest.

8

CONCERTO FOR A CORPSE

I was arguing with myself whether to share my brain wave with Sarah when Chris scissored his long legs over the bench, narrowly missing the geraniums on the windowsill. "Hey, Greg, are your bottled beverages also off limits, or could we have something to drink?"

If the comment was meant to drag Greg from his well of misery, it did the job. He heaved himself from his seat. "Where are my manners? I've got soda. That's gotta be harmless. I mean, not that the rest isn't. Dammit, hold on, I'll get you something." He entered his pub.

That wasn't a clever move, since he might run into Diloff. "Sarah, where's your boss right now?"

"No doubt boring the officers with his superior reasoning. Don't worry, he'll have leather cases on his mind. It's unlikely he'll notice Mr. Winters' presence."

"I loathe saying this, but shouldn't you be involved in whatever is going on back there?"

Her gaze flitted across to Chris, hovered, and then found me again. "Normally, I would be. Now, the old water buffalo—The DI in his eternal wisdom nabbed Constable Cameron and left me behind, after telling me to do my job. Whatever that might mean."

"I wouldn't have thought babysitting suspects should be in your remit," Chris said.

"Normally not, no. Mind you, it's not the first time in the recent past that he's swapped my role with Cameron's. I reckon he's invented this nifty plan where I get so upset I give up and ask for a transfer." Sarah was a pro, but even she couldn't hide the resentment clogging her voice.

My innards knotted with guilt. "It's my fault."

"Because I went over Diloff's head in spring and made the DCI reopen your aunt's case? Probably, but it was the right thing to do, and I would do it again given half a chance."

"You might have to if your boss continues in the same vein," Chris said, not without sympathy. "Sorry, wasn't aware how that tonker treats his officers. Be careful, though. He strikes me as the sort of person who'll carry a grudge to his grave. I wish there was a way to help you."

Sarah's mouth twitched. "Thank you, Mr. Lentulus, but my boss is my problem. I'll deal with him. I'll start by doing what he told me to do. My job."

Something clattered in the pub's backyard. A loud bang followed, and Sarah whisked around, her nose twitching like a terrier's. "What is Diloff up to now?"

Chris sighed and sat on the bench. "Sounds like they're taking the kitchen apart. Let's hope Greg doesn't catch them in the act. Otherwise, you'll have another dead body on your hands. Maybe you should check?"

"No need to. I can guess what might be going on. And in that case, I prefer to leave them well alone."

"Care to share?" I asked.

"Well, I bet you my latest pair of bargain designer pumps they're searching the bins for discarded bottles and stuff." She bit her lip.

"Bottles? Then why is your boss so het up about peas in glass jars? And what about those cans?" Chris asked. "Ah, I get it. You were trying to slip us some insider information."

Sarah groaned. "No, I wasn't. Oh, to heck with it. I mean it when I say bottles. Don't tell anybody."

"As if we ever would," I said.

Chris made a zipping motion across his mouth. Then he said, "Since you've started, how about if you tell us more. We might be able to help you."

Sarah tugged at her ear. "Hmm, to be honest, I could do with a bit of support. It appears Diloff has received the analysis of the contents of the cans with the spaghetti rings, the water, and all the pea jars, and guess what—they're fine. No poison. He won't like that, which is why he hasn't told me. But Cameron did."

"Would that mean Greg is off the hook?" I asked.

"Not yet, since there's another point I didn't mention. The deceased also had alcohol in his stomach. Not much, but it was there. Neither the alcohol nor the food had been digested properly, indicating our dead man must have eaten his last meal shortly before he died. So they're looking for bottles and other rubbish the deceased might have binned."

The thought of diving into those refuse containers, coveralls or not, made my stomach wriggle. Then I remembered something. "The rubbish collectors did their special solstice round on Saturday morning. I doubt those poor officers will be rewarded for their bravery."

"Call of duty and all that," Chris mumbled under his breath. He refocused on Sarah. "Has it ever occurred to your lord and master to establish who that poor dead bloke is and where he hails from? The reason for his death might be unrelated to whatever drinks or food Greg keeps in his pub."

Sarah balled her fist. "No, but it has occurred to me. The

DI doesn't care for 'bums,' to use his own words. People don't count, especially if they're already dead. He doesn't care an iota about giving them back their names. Solving the case in record time while making a splash with the media is paramount."

"Good for the budget," I said.

She formed her thumb and digit into a pistol and made a shooting motion. "You got it."

I hesitated, but Sarah needed help. "Don't laugh, but I had this brain wave—"

Chris placed a hand on his heart and pretended to collapse onto the tabletop.

Sarah ignored his theatrics and focused her laser gaze on me. What had been a possibility seconds ago suddenly appeared ludicrous and far-fetched.

"To be honest, it's more like a hunch. Something to do with the flute your people found."

Sarah's fingers curled in a gimme gesture. "You're good with hunches. Let's hear it."

"I have some guests at the B&B—Chris, shut up, will you?" He hadn't actually said anything, but his mouth had opened, and the last thing I needed was the man's well-oiled tongue on the run. "She and her partner are musicians. They're a bit like a two-person mini-orchestra. This morning, they mentioned a group of flute artists from Bucharest. What if the dead man is one of them?"

Blessed silence. Even Chris said nothing.

For a moment, Sarah regarded the silvery wood of the beer garden table as if it harbored the answer to the secrets of the cosmos. She raised her head. "Do you hear this?" She hooked her thumb at the henge from where floated a cacophony of tablas, string instruments, bagpipes, and castanets.

"No flutes?"

"Not right now," Sarah said. "But I'm sure your mysterious Romanians aren't the only flutists around. There's got to be plenty. How to spot the right ones? If Diloff authorizes a search, that is, which he won't. He doesn't care for hunches."

"Especially if they come from your friend who gave him a hard time in spring."

"Exactly. Not that I would tell him."

Chris snorted. "Even if he caved in, you wouldn't catch the buggers. They'll vanish quicker than you can say 'police raid.'"

"Don't you think I know that?"

The pub's door slammed into the wall as Greg emerged, carrying a cooler in one hand and a baseball cap in the other. "Okay, guys, here's some soda and a hat for you, Myrtle. You need to get your face out of the sun."

"*Mucho obrigado.* It's not that hot."

"It will be soon."

The cap was cobalt blue and bore the insignia of the Charlotte Moles, complete with the mole stitched in blood-red. It was kind of him.

"Can you be certain this is safe?" Sarah pointed at the cans of soda Greg was fishing from the cooler. My traitorous tongue decided this was the right moment to stick to the roof of my mouth.

"Of course it is. Let me demonstrate." Greg popped the first can and emptied his drink in one go. A big belch followed, which he hid behind his hand. "Oh, pardon me. They're from the fridge in the bar. They've never been near the cellar or the storeroom. Or the kitchen. Soda, anyone?" He suppressed another belch.

Chris was the first to move. "Thanks, mate." He took two drinks and waved one at me. Condensation formed tiny pearls on its side, clustering and dribbling down the shiny metal, beckoning to me.

What are you waiting for? I snatched the can from Chris's hand, ripped it open, and drank. My fillings ached as a chilled fluid slipped down my throat, settling as a polar layer in my stomach.

Bliss.

"Oh, all right." Sarah accepted a can. "If I'm to go on a search for elusive musicians, I'd better stock up on water."

Chris slanted a brow, which made him look like an attractive satyr. "Can you walk off without asking your handler?"

Sarah grinned. "Told you already. I'll be doing what Diloff told me to do—my job. That means I must act on additional information, no matter how I heard about it. Should my investigations yield a result, Diloff's got something to brag about." She rose.

I did likewise. "You'll need me."

"Will I?"

"Yes. Much easier if we search for my two musicians rather than the flute players themselves. They can identify them for us. And I'll identify the musicians for you." I gave her a friendly grin.

"Myrtle, while I appreciate your suggestions, this is police business. Strictly off limits. Describe them, and I'll take it from there."

"Uh, unfortunately there's an awful lot of folks running around. I don't have photos, so you might walk past my guests and never notice." That was a bit of a stretch, since Blue Lady and her partner would stand out in any crowd, but she wasn't getting rid of me that easily. "Remember what Chris said earlier? They'll bolt if you turn up on your own. Let me come with you. I can explain things."

Sarah growled under her breath, but her stiff stance slackened. "I hate it when you're right. I might as well stick a blue flashing light on my head. People always spot me for who I am."

I gave her outfit a quick glance. Over her cream blouse she wore a no-nonsense linen pantsuit. All she carried was an overly large caramel-colored handbag. No name tags, aviator sunglasses, or other cliché accessories were evident, and yet her whole getup yelled "cop." I suspected the jaded cynicism seeping from Sarah's pores was to blame. That, and the quiet authority she projected.

"Off you go then, ladies," Chris said. "I'll stay with Greg in case DI Dickhead gets funny notions into his head while you're gone."

The corner of Sarah's mouth hitched upward. "Diloff, if you please."

"Let me give you the solicitor's details." I rummaged in my backpack for my phone and swished for the number. "Tell him about the state of play."

"As long as you don't mention stomach contents, I'm fine." Once more, Sarah's face turned into a blank mask. "Okay, Myrtle, you can help me with the identification of the possible informants, but you are not, and I repeat not, to take any action."

"Yes, officer."

"Myrtle . . ."

"Don't forget your hat. And take some water with you." Chris slapped the cap on my head and winked, making me feel even warmer than I already was. Time to go.

As we left, Greg and Chris retreated into the shaded interior of the pub. Given the circumstances, I hoped they would stick to nonalcoholic drinks. Somehow, I doubted that.

—

Once we approached the barrier, the sweating crowd shifted. Smartphones and cameras came up, and we were broadsided with questions. The media had joined the circus.

Sarah plowed ahead, an elegant icebreaker. "Sorry to disappoint you, folks, but I'm only a lowly sergeant. If you want details, talk to the DI in charge of the investigation. In the meantime, I'd appreciate if you let me do my job."

A handful of the gawkers, including the journalists, seemed inclined to stick with us, but they were no match for Sergeant Widdlethorpe.

"You know I can't stop you from following. But you know what happens if you mess with me."

The tourists took a step back. The journalists laughed. One gave her a thumbs-up and Sarah responded with a friendly nod.

She then skirted the people littering her path, and I followed, dropping friendly smiles like sweets. The maneuver worked. We passed the crowd and moved onto the henge.

"Uh, nicely played. You appear to know those media types."

"In a way. They're locals. If I can, I cooperate, and it usually pays off. They have their uses. With the nationals and the broadcasting companies, it's a different story."

I threw a quick glance over my shoulder. "They're coming after us."

She nodded. "I expected no less. It's okay. They're pros. Apropos, where to go from here?"

"There's a copse where the artists hang out. It's located on the other end of that bank." I pointed down the trail ahead of us. "I'll show you."

Drawn by the distant strains of music, Sarah and I trudged along the trail, a band of ocher soil that led across an expanse of grass dotted with daisies and dandelions. Here and there standing stones rose from the ground, the grass between them trampled to straw by reverent feet. Bags, cans, bottles, and crushed fast food packs littered the place, the offerings of a civilization that threw everything to the winds, including its past.

Sarah stopped and ran the heel of her hand over her forehead. "Phew, this weather is getting a bit much. Hey, look at those stones. Pretty they aren't, but impressive, eh?"

"I come out here quite regularly. There's something new to discover every time."

The one thing I searched for—an inspiration of what the ancient rocks might mean for the witches—I had yet to find.

Sarah moved on and climbed a set of rough steps that led to the path on top of the steep bank surrounding the stone circle. Like before, a gauzy veil had drawn across the skies, adding an almost tropical humidity into the mix. Even the leaves of the trees in the small copse ahead of us drooped in limp-wristed depression. Sarah flung her jacket over her shoulder, and moisture beaded her upper lip. I was drenched. If the next salesperson visiting the Witch's Retreat was peddling swimming pools, I'd buy one.

Sarah's phone rang. She gave me a warning glance and pulled ahead, speaking little, and listening instead. Her call finished, she dropped her phone back into her purse.

"Mh," she said. "That was the pathologist who did the post-mortem. Some more results have come in, which confirmed his theory. Let's keep moving before our media friends catch up with us and want to know who called me."

"Hah, you're not going to get away with that. What results have come in to confirm which theory?"

"You shouldn't be asking such questions, and I shouldn't be answering you. Since we both know what I'm doing is illegal and must be kept confidential, I'm willing to tell you we're talking cardiac glycosides. They seem also to have entered the poor guy's bloodstream impossibly fast."

"Cardiac . . . oh, I see." Foxglove featured in my recipe book. Helpful for heart conditions if taken in the right doses. Lethal, if not.

"Of course you do." She pressed her lips closed and pushed on.

There was no point in prodding for more, so I asked the next question that popped into my mind. "Won't Diloff be peeved the chap rang you instead of him?"

A grin blipped on her face before it was gone again. "They can't stand each other. Use me as a go-between. Has its advantages."

We reached the copse and dove into the shade of the drooping beeches and birches. As if to compensate for the brief relief, the trail went up a steep incline. A peek over my shoulder revealed the two journalists sweating along the trail. They didn't look happy. The music, now close by, broke into a discordant jangle of stray tunes, as if the open-air orchestra had reverted back to practicing mode. Only a lonely drum persisted, strumming out an earthy rhythm.

"Mamma Mia," Sarah said, panting. "I thought the area was supposed to be a plain. Aren't those flat?"

"A bit more respect, please. This sanctuary was built by pre-historic people with elk antlers for shovels. Originally the ditch was a lot deeper. Think fifty-five feet. This is nothing."

"Thanks for the guided tour. Oh, and give my regards to the architects should you ever consider a séance."

Like a graceful ghost lured by her words, flute music floated from behind the warty tree trunks. The tones soared toward the clouds until they returned to Earth. A second flute joined, and together the tones mounted again, playfully skimming the summer skies.

For a moment I lost myself to the melody. But we had come on a mission.

"That could be them." Pulled along by the enchanting notes, I pushed through the dusty greenery. I bent under a large branch and found myself in a clearing populated by a group of men in shabby clothes.

"See those carrier bags?" Sarah whispered behind me. "Says 'Bucharesti' on them, like on the one we discovered in the store-room. That's the first decent lead we have on the poor bloke's identity. Well done, Myrtle."

———

"Magical," Blue Lady had called the Romanians, and magical their music was. Two of them were playing their silvery instruments while the others lounged in the shade, their eyes half closed. Blue Lady and Goatee squatted to one side, their hands on the tablas, bodies as limp as puppets.

Our arrival broke the spell, and the warble died away.

Blue Lady's eyes snapped open. They narrowed. Her glance slid over me, but it was Sarah whose appearance drew a sneer.

"Politie," she hissed. The Romanians stiffened.

She jumped up, dreadlocks bouncing, and took a stand in front of the flutists, a mother hen protecting her brood. "What do you want?"

"More likely my friend can do something for your friends," I said, trying hard to keep my tone nonthreatening. Sarah stepped beside me, her hands hanging at her side, her poise relaxed. Hopefully, the journalists had enough common sense not to interrupt.

One flutist, a skinny elderly man with a thatch of steel gray hair, stood next to Blue Lady. His lips pressed together as if the air that had given voice to his beautiful music had been sucked back inside, leaving behind hollow cheeks covered in stubble.

"We no problem." His hooded eyes regarded Sarah, watchful and angry.

"Please, don't worry. I mean you no harm," Sarah said. "I might be able to help you."

The man spat onto the ground. His fellow musicians, all of them wiry and mean-eyed, jumped up. Hard living had taken its toll, but it would have also hardened their fists.

Crap. Me and my great ideas.

Blue Lady was on the move, heading for us. Her partner followed, a tabla in each of his hands.

Panic crawled over my skin. This could get nasty.

"Myrtle, you better go." Sarah reached into her handbag, but with one can of hairspray she couldn't fend off a mob.

It was too late, anyway. Grim expressions on their faces, the musicians crept nearer, closing the ring around us. Blue Lady and Goatee stood and watched, but their muscles were tense and coiled to spring.

"I asked you a question," Blue Lady said, a predatory purr in her voice.

"Trust me, I'm not here to arrest anybody," Sarah said. "I'm here to help."

"You're a liar. All pigs are." Goatee's voice was a snarl.

They need to relax. Now.

What could I do when words were my only weapon? I raised my hands, palms out. "Listen."

A rose petal tumbled from my fingers. Then another. A clean scent filled my nostrils, like freshly mown grass. The ground under my feet vibrated with life. I had been sweating before—now my core turned to ice. Time stretched on an elastic band.

My magic wanted to help. Here. In public.

A bizarre green sheen drew over the landscape and the grassy scent strengthened. The ring of assailants blurred. If I lost control, my—our—secret was out. I couldn't let that happen, consequences be damned.

Focus. When Alan attacked me, I willed the primula to come to my rescue. Could I will my magic away?

Skylles be gone. Now, blast it.

The greenness coalesced into a splotch and then vanished from the landscape. The vibrations stopped. My nose filled with the rank odor of bodies sweating in the heat. I drew a deep breath and crushed the velvety petals between my fingers.

I must have swayed. An arm wrapped around my shoulder, clad in a blue fabric. Somebody waved a plastic water bottle in front of my face. I shoved the crushed petals into the pockets of my dress and gulped the tepid fluid. When I looked up, the musicians smiled back, sleepy concern in their faces. Sarah stood on my other side, her purse open but her hands empty. She cracked a yawn and shook herself.

"Sit down," Blue Lady said in a level voice. "You got heatstroke or something?"

Or something, yes.

"I'm fine." Oddly enough, there didn't seem to be any side effects from my magical outburst other than dizziness and a faint throbbing in my temples. But even that faded away.

Blue Lady removed her arm and narrowed her eyes. "Uh, I feel sort of weird."

The urge to apologize became overwhelming, but I wrestled it down. "It's much too hot. Listen, we really want to help. Are you perhaps missing a fellow musician?"

Blue Lady tilted her head. The old flutist took a step backward. "How you know?"

The musician regarded Sarah, who had stepped up, her gaze not settling on anybody in particular.

"Lock up?" the old flutist said, defeat in his voice.

"Nobody's been locked up and nobody will be," I said soothingly. It would have been better. "It's just . . . we found someone. In the basement of the pub, you see, and—"

"Who you found?" interrupted the other, younger player. He had to be in his forties, but it was hard to judge given the worry graying his angular face.

"We don't know," Sarah interjected, her voice soft. "This is why we're here. The person we discovered carried a flute with him. In a leather case."

Blue Lady's gaze had been darting between us. Now, she homed in on me. "What does she mean when she says 'found'?"

"Boian. My brother," the second flutist said. He never moved, and instead pressed his instrument to his chest and fixed his liquid dark gaze on me. "Restaurant closes. We come later, we eat and we drink on benches outside. Like normal people. Not sitting on ground always. Nobody there. We clear up afterward." His tone had become apologetic.

"It's fine," Sarah said. "Please continue."

"Boian go to back. He not good. Heart not good. He say door to back not close good and he sleep in cool. He do before. We go to restaurant next morning, but politie there. We not like. We go."

"Watch it. You've admitted to breaking in," Blue Lady hissed.

The old flutist grimaced and directed a torrent of Romanian at his fellow musician, most likely telling him to shut up.

The man shook his head. "Boian where?" he asked, the sadness in his voice struggling with hope.

I couldn't blame them for their initial hostility. Their encounters with the officials couldn't have been pleasant. The news we were bringing was worse.

Sarah faced the dead man's—Boian's—brother. "It doesn't

matter how your brother gained access to that room or what he might have taken. That's not why I'm here. I'm afraid I don't have good news for you, Mr. . . . ?"

Boian's brother paled. "Albu. Cornel Albu."

"Thank you, Mr. Albu. Perhaps you would like to sit down?"

Blue Lady pressed her lips together as if she wanted to catch a sob. Goatee spoke instead. "He's dead, isn't he?"

Sarah ignored them.

"Is this your brother?" She removed a photo from her handbag and showed it to Cornel. He pressed his lips together and nodded, tears running over his face. The old flutist walked across and put his arm around his friend's shoulder.

"I'm so sorry," Sarah said. I knew her. She meant it.

The silence stretched, interrupted by Cornel's stifled crying and a rustle coming from the bushes. The journalists must have caught up with us.

"So, you say you brought your food with you," Sarah said.

"He just told you so," Blue Lady snapped.

Whatever my skylles did, it didn't seem to have any lasting effects on her.

"I need to be sure. Mr. Albu's brother left two cans of spaghetti and some water, but we've examined them already. They're harmless."

I didn't expect Sarah to mention the pilfered peas, and she didn't.

Cornel rubbed first his eyes and then his belly. "He need to eat little bits often. Stomach also not good."

The old man glared from under his gray thatch. "We play. We get money. People give food. We can save money."

"Jeez, what a nightmare," Blue Lady said. "But it's true, they get donated all sorts of things. Bars of chocolate, crackers, sandwiches, tinned food, drinks, the lot."

Sarah's eyes narrowed. "Your brother's heart condition was pretty serious, correct? I would have expected him to be on medication."

Ah, it appeared the pathologist had told her more than she let on.

Cornel sniffed once. "Too hot. Not good for Boian heart. Not bring enough medicina, but not can go see doctor, not here."

"Yes, the heat might have made things worse," Sarah agreed. "However, isn't it odd that despite suffering from symptoms typical for a massive case of glycoside poisoning, the actual amount of cardioactive glycosides in your brother's system was negligible? Nor did we find any medication on his, uh, on-site."

Silence fell. Feet shuffled. Looks glazed over. Even I took a moment to translate Sarah's gibberish into something meaningful.

"Medicine as in digitalis?" Blue Lady asked.

Boian's brother stared first at me and then at her, and I could almost watch the thought taking root in his brain. "Digitalis. Yes. Boian meet kind ladies. Give water, give wine, give medicina for heart. I forget. I apologize."

Sarah pounced. "What 'kind ladies'? Are you telling me your brother accepted pills from strangers?" She struggled to keep the bite out of her voice but didn't quite succeed.

The older man looked crestfallen. "They hear music. Boian stop, not enough breath. They say blue lips not right. They give drink, food. They give plant medicina."

Kind ladies. Herbal medicine. A thought bubbled, and my synapses popped in a second epiphany in under an hour.

The gift shop. The Wiccans.

9

A TOUCH OF MAGIC

Once I'd shared with Sarah my scanty knowledge of the Wiccans and where they might be found, I returned to the pub and gave Greg the good—well, goodish—news about the latest developments. He wasn't in the clear yet, since the poison might have been in whatever alcohol poor Boian had drunk and the pub offered booze in large amounts.

Back at the Witch's Retreat, I found a note from the Simpkins sisters telling me Chris was waiting on the daybed outside. When I joined him, freshly showered and carrying Petty in her bucket, he dropped the book he was reading and gave me a languid wave.

"Ah, you're home."

"Sorry for making you wait."

"Nah, you didn't know I'd be coming. It was only twenty minutes or so."

I placed my floral friend on the ground and swung my legs

onto the mattress, careful not to disturb Tiddles, asleep at the foot of the bed. Caught in a kitty dream, she twitched her paws and made smacking noises. I'd much rather have her inside and protected by the cool walls of the old house, but my feline pal had a mind of her own.

"I should apologize for leaving you and Greg in the lurch," Chris said. "The moment Diloff barged outside, he considered my presence surplus to requirements. He told me so in no uncertain terms."

"No worries. Greg gave me a graphic report."

"Did you find the people you were looking for?"

"Not only that."

I shared this morning's adventure, editing out my little hexing stunt. Chris would only get excited and pepper me with questions when I didn't have any answers myself. Surely, Dot would be able to help. Later. Right now, it was too hot to move.

A breeze whispered through the birches that framed the garden of the Witch's Retreat, sending dappled shadows across the lawn on Chris's side of the sunbed. Somewhere up there the coming evening might be dragging in cooler air, but the heat didn't budge. Even Petty was still, apart from the odd rustle of a leaf and her unique citrus fragrance that filled the air.

I plucked a cherry from the bowl on the side table and popped it into my mouth. No matter how perfect it might look, the fruit tasted sour, as if it had been picked too early. I bent over and spat the cherry pit at the plate next to the primula's bucket, but it landed on the gravel. Petty lazily wriggled her blossoms and then calmed again.

"Why do you keep your plant in that ugly plastic bucket?" Chris asked. He had his arms crossed behind his head and his eyes closed as if dozing. Acutely aware of his presence, I was too hyped up for a snooze. Even if I made sure not to move and not to touch, I sensed a dizzy tingle in my left leg. I could swear my ears were burning.

"At first, I planted her in a proper pot, but she was too weak and had trouble lifting it, so she ended up in the bucket. It gives her roots more space as well. I'm wondering if that was such a good idea."

"Mph. Maybe not." Chris opened one eye and turned his head. "Your hunches today were spot on, though."

I sank back into the cushions. "Don't remind me. I've caused grief for Mr. Albu and dumped the Wiccans right in it."

"I think you should be kinder to yourself. The Wiccans caused trouble for themselves if you ask me. Pass those cherries, will you? I bought them at your local store. Are they any good?"

I handed him the bowl. "Uh, try them. And I can't help feeling guilty about the Wiccan doctor. I'm sure she meant well. She struck me as being a good person, and I liked her."

"There's nothing more you can do for the moment," Chris said.

"True. If I want to find out what's going on, I'll have to check the media. Those articles will be a hoot and a half."

Chris faced me, a pair of cherries dangling from his index finger. "Don't worry. It's not your problem. You helped your friend—both of your friends. Greg's no longer the only suspect and Sarah found the leads, not Diloff. Because of you. Great job, Sherlock."

"Yeah, and he'll hate her for it."

"She's one tough cookie, so she can cope."

Would she have coped without my magic? I doubted that. The enormity of what I'd done washed over me. I had wanted something to happen, and happen it did. Propelled by naked panic, I had protected Sarah and myself from a scary situation. Since nobody had acted up, my intervention must have gone unnoticed. Unlike last time, I suffered few side effects. Why? There must be a lot more to the skylles than what Dot had told me.

The pocket of my shorts buzzed, and the theme from the Midsomer Murders series warbled into the muggy afternoon. Tiddles sat up and twitched her ears. My phone was ringing. The darn thing kept changing tunes all the time.

"Myrtle Coldron here."

"Oh, hello." Linda's voice was reedy, at odds with her force-ful personality. "It's the call chain, I'm afraid."

My stomach sank. The call chain was the coven's way of spreading news. Yes, we could use social media. No, we didn't trust it.

"Oops. What's up?"

"Buster's gone missing. We've already got a search party organized, no need to join, but if you happen to spot the little monster, better tell Elmsworth immediately. He's close to losing it. Who's next after you? I keep forgetting."

"Wytchett Farm. I'll call them now."

Linda thanked me and disconnected. I fumbled with my screen.

"More trouble?" Chris asked.

"Elmsworth has mislaid his Chihuahua, and we're spread-ing the news."

"Don't think you can blame that one on the DI. I reckon, there's quite a few hungry people out there."

Mirth bubbled up my throat. "You're rotten, you know? Let me call Jenna." I released a deep breath. *Might as well tell him.*

"I need to contact her or Dot anyway. Uh, to tell the truth, I had a hexing fit when I was out at the henge."

Where other men might have stampeded there and then, Chris only quirked a brow. Relief rushed in and, with it, a giddi-ness not unlike the one I had experienced after my latest run-in with the paranormal. "It happened when we met the musicians. They didn't simply back down. I must have stopped them with my skylles."

"Surely you have an idea what happened?" He sat up, his black eyes keen.

"Well, the situation was getting out of hand, and I wanted them to relax. I was dead scared. I hate physical violence. Dot says the skylles are powered by emotions and by having a purpose. So, I must have pulled my act together."

"And?"

"And bingo. The musicians lost the urge to rearrange our faces with their fists."

"Just like that?"

"Well, yes. The effect didn't last long, though. I'm more worried why my skylles manifested when they've been dormant for so long. Was the henge giving me a boost? The solstice? The waxing moon? The stress with Greg?"

"How about all these factors together? Well done with controlling your powers, though. Fascinating."

He sounded like Spock. Only the ears were wrong.

"Mh, I'm not so sure about that. It was a bit hit and miss. Anyway, I need to run this past the experts, and the sooner the better." I raised my phone once more and scrolled for Jenna's number.

It took a moment before the ringtone in my ear was replaced by a boyish giggle. "Hello?"

I had a 50 percent chance. "Robbie?"

"No, it's Johnnie."

Typical. "Okay, Johnnie, it's Auntie Myrtle here. Can I talk to your mum?"

A clattering noise reached my ear. The boy must have dumped the phone, but he also had gone in search of his parent, for it was her I heard next. I passed on Linda's message.

"Oh, I hope the Colonel gets reunited with his poor mite," Jenna said in her soft voice. "This weather is rather hard on the animals. Actually, I meant to call you. Would you fancy eating with us later? In an hour or so? Nothing special, only cutlets, corncobs, and a salad. Gran mentioned you seemed rather worried about your skylles, and she'd said she could explain a few things."

"That would be great, since they saved my bacon today."

Silence on the other end of the line. "Sweet Earth, *what?*"

"I was drawn into the police investigation on Greg, and at one point, out on the henge, Sarah and I ran into some very upset people. The next moment, I had petals dropping from my hands, and the world turned fizzy and green. And things smelled funny."

A hiss of indrawn breath. "What happened next?"

"I told the skylles to vamoose. Luckily for everybody, they did, after calming things down."

A heavy silence hung in the air. Then Jenna said, "I'll tell Gran. Time to activate the evacuation plan, I'd say."

"Not until the Colonel has found Buster. Right now, he won't be able to concentrate."

"You're right. Oh, could you bring your recipe book? Gran would love to have another peck at it. It's been a long while since she last read it. And we'll show you our laundry list. You've never seen it, have you?"

Something deep inside of me knotted, and I wanted to brush her off. The recipe book was mine. Okay, mine and Daisy's.

But this attitude was behind the coven's many troubles.

"Will do. I'd love to come for dinner."

"Be prepared for a grilling. I'm not talking about the cutlets, by the way."

"Your gran?"

Jenna burst into laughter. "No, me actually. I'm absolutely dying to find out what's going on with Greg. I keep hearing all sorts of rumors."

Unlike Mrs. Bingham and Mrs. Mornings, the Wytchetts were local and tapped into the village grapevine.

"Oh, by the way, Marty's got a present for your primula."

"A present for Petty?"

The bucket rose and hovered next to my hand holding the phone while sparks whizzed off in all directions. "Shoo," I said. "She heard you."

Chris laughed out loud.

"Who's that? Is Chris with you?" A silvery giggle tinkled in my ear. "Woo-hoo. Ask him if he would like to join us. What? Oh, sweet Earth, Marty tells me the British team is playing rugby in South Africa or something, and they could watch it together after dinner. Don't understand what's so exciting about a bunch of hairy men scrumming about on a pitch. Does Chris even care for that sort of thing?"

I held the phone away from my ear. "Fancy dinner at the farm in an hour, followed by some rugby on telly? Marty wants to know."

Chris checked his watch and grimaced. "Thanks, I'll have to give dinner a miss, but I'll join for the rugby. First, I need to earn the outrageous fee your aunt paid me."

"Hah." More likely the coven got itself an excellent deal.

"Wouldn't like to disappoint Dot. She doesn't strike me as the warm and fuzzy type."

With a wink, he was off, leaving me stranded with a snoring cat, a hyperactive primula, and a jittery hollowness inside. On second thought, the queasiness may have been caused by the cherries.

—

Compared to my boiling backyard, the atmosphere in the Wytchett apple orchard was downright refreshing. Not only had evening finally arrived, which made the temperatures bearable, but the place also lay open to the plain, allowing the drafts that flowed around the gnarled trees to find us. What had been festive white flowers in spring had turned to green. Among the leaves, tiny new fruit had taken hold, safe now from killer frosts. At the other end of the orchard, the chimneys of another house poked over the tops of the false acacias. They filled the place with their sweet scent, and had it not been for the distant growl of the M4, the orchard could have been an enchanted garden.

"Jen's set up dinner on the lawn." Marty pointed at two camping tables covered in white tablecloths sitting next to a wooden Hollywood swing. The ensemble was completed by a set of mismatched folding chairs, which were placed well away from the walled terrace. A wise move, since the place had baked in the sun the whole day and radiated warmth onto my back.

From somewhere atop the closest tree piped a youthful voice. "Yoo-hoo, Auntie Myrtle."

I squinted into the evening light, but the twin's perch was hidden by the glossy foliage. Instead of a proper greeting, I waved at a quivering branch and placed the shopping bag with the Coldron grimoire and the promised chocolate on the nearest chair. Afraid of prying eyes and chocolate stains, I had wrapped the tome with the only paper I could find. Shiny and green, it was covered in gilded inscriptions wishing us a Merry Christmas in ten different languages.

Jenna arrived, carrying a tray loaded with plates and cutlery. "Hiya, have you heard more about Buster?"

"Nope. Let's hope Elmsworth finds his micro-hound."

Dot shuffled out of the house and across the lawn, leaning heavily on a cane. "Can't say I'm a big fan of small dogs. Strange that a grown man should be so besotted with a pet." With a sigh, she sagged onto the swing.

"Speaking of pets, here's something we wanted you to have." Marty presented me with an oversized terra-cotta planter decorated with garlands and snarly lions, Renaissance-style.

"Whoa, thanks a bunch, Marty, but Petty's no weightlifter." I braced myself for impact, but the container was surprisingly light.

"Fiberglass," Marty said. "I saw it in a garden shop the other day and had to buy one for your primula."

Dot compressed her lips into a tight line and thumped her cane onto the ground. "Martyn, you need to be more serious about the skylles. Myrtle's plant is no pet. She's a familiar."

I'd suspected something along these lines, but the recipe book was a tad vague about magical critters. Reality bites, and in my case, literally. An acid cherry burp seared my throat.

I placed the planter on the ground. "Are you sure?"

A brief grimace pulled at Dot's calm face, and then it was gone again. Concern? Envy? Hard to tell.

"Yes. I can show you the paragraph in the laundry list."

"Oopsie, that reminds me. I'm going to get it." Jenna dashed into the house.

"You created her," Dot said. "You might not have known what you were doing, but you did it. Your magic called her into being. That's what she is—pure magic. She'll be there for you. She'll help you grow. And she'll protect you. That's the true purpose of a familiar. Never forget yours is immature, though. She's learning herself." The strange expression blipped on her face again. "We haven't had a familiar for centuries."

I turned away from Dot, reached for the shopper, and unwrapped my grimoire. Then I stopped. "What about the boys?"

When I looked up, she was smiling like an imp, as if Jenna were looking out of her tired eyes. "They're not interested in books unless they feature astronauts, knights, or dinosaurs."

"They've learned from an early age that there are certain things one must never talk about," Marty said.

"If we get this right, they'll be able to grow up being who they are and not hiding and keeping secrets all the time." Dot's voice had grown bitter. "Unlike Jenna. Or myself. Or you. At least, that's the plan."

My hand rested on the warm, smooth leather of the Coldron grimoire. "I thought that was the reason you and my aunt called the coven in the first place. To come out and be useful to society."

"You're right, but with all this to-ing and fro-ing I doubt we'll ever make it." The pained expression was back, and now I could read it—a frustration so deep it hurt.

"You'll have your hands full for sure, Myrtle. These people are incredibly weak. Not even the slightest trace of magic showing after all the time they've been here. How are you supposed to get the rituals going when their skylles are lacking, huh? Tell me that. This so-called coven is a disgrace." She thwacked her cane against the swing, two bright red spots shining on her pale cheeks.

What does she mean by "you"?

"Gran, you mustn't stress," Marty said in his unruffled way. "Remember what the doctor said?"

"Pah." She slumped like a deflated balloon. "Oh well, I've always wanted too much. We're a sad caricature of what once was possible. Most of that lot is no better than the plain vanilla humans desecrating our henge."

Marty frowned. "Gran, give it a rest."

Here was my cue. "My skylles showed today. At the stone circle."

I recalled my paranormal achievements, and by the time I finished Dot was smiling again.

"Excellent. There is hope yet. Perhaps you're only the first, and the others will follow? Even without proper training, you controlled your powers. And you used them in the proper fashion."

"Did I?"

"Yes. Our skylles are defensive in nature, meant to nurture and protect, and that's what you did. You're stronger than any of us, and with your teaching background, you'll make an excellent leader."

Hang on. "Later, perhaps. You're the expert, after all."

Dot smiled, rubbed her hands, and pointed at the gift-wrapped recipe book. "Oh, is that your grimoire? Thanks for bringing it. I remember it being in such good shape."

Happy to change the subject, I removed the paper. "Great-Aunt Petunia recorded her knowledge in 1804. I would have thought the book itself is older, but short of having it examined, there's no proof."

Dot groaned. "They left it that late? Sweet Earth, imagine how much wisdom must've been lost by the time somebody picked up a quill."

Hello? Her set of ancestors had drawn the cushy number and waited out the centuries here at Avebury. Mine must have been on the run. What was she thinking?

"It is what it is."

Dot shifted in her seat. "Mph. Hopefully, the laundry list will give you some inspiration."

"For what?"

"It's obvious I can't take charge of the coven with the way my health is going. Jenna and I will support you, of course."

My pulse whipped my blood into a furious froth. "Sorry, Dot, but I can't. I'm willing to support you, but I'm not cut out for coven leadership."

Wood smoke hit my nostrils and was immediately followed by the acrid stench of firelighter. Marty had fired up the grill as the sun disappeared behind the first solid bank of clouds I had seen in days. Elongated like Plasticine snakes, they crowded the skies above the drystone wall at the end of the apple orchard.

"You're still not comfortable being you, correct?"

"Sorry, but no. Can we stop this, please?"

"Listen—"

"No." It popped out sharper than I meant it to be, but I wouldn't let her bowl me over.

When footsteps sounded from the terrace, I whirled around. Jenna returned, wearing a pair of cotton gloves and carrying a scruffy old tome. Reverently, she placed the book on the tablecloth. The laundry list had lost both panels, and only the frazzled spine held the pages together.

"This is from 1620," Jenna said. "We keep it in a climate-controlled box. It's actually sturdier than it appears to be. Have a look for yourself, but make sure to use my gloves. In the meantime, we'll study yours. If you don't mind, that is."

In a way I did, but that sort of thinking would get us nowhere.

"Go for it. No idea if it will cooperate, though. Each time the Simpkins sisters dust the shelf, I find the book in a different location. Daisy and me it seems to like. It almost jumps into our hands. Oh, and you need to start at the back. After the empty pages."

Jenna and her grandmother were staring at me, Jen's eyes big and round, Dot's expression unreadable.

"Eh, what's up?"

"Sweet Earth," Jenna said. "It sounds almost as if your grimoire's been spelled."

At first, her words made me proud. Worry came next. "Is it a problem?"

Jenna blew a maroon strand away from her face. "No. Not per se. However, for the hex to stick like that, it's got to be pretty nifty. It's like with Petty. Nobody else has a familiar. Nobody can cast spells on this level anymore. Though canned magic is actually easier than the direct variety you and Eve seem to prefer." She nodded to herself.

Dot cackled. There was no other word for it. "Jenna, you're moving too fast. Let me explain. Spells and potions are indirect or 'canned' magic, as my granddaughter insists on calling it. You use an incantation to transfer magical energy to an object and it changes in look or the way it behaves. Alternatively, you transfer your magical energy into a brew to achieve a certain effect. If enough skylles are invested, the spelled objects stay changed, even if the spell weaver is no longer around. Well, that's the theory."

"Which would indicate Aunt Eve spelled the recipe book."

"Or somebody before her," Jenna said. "Don't take it the wrong way, but I don't think your Aunt Eve knew enough about the skylles to make this happen. Cue her idea with the database."

Dot waggled her finger. "Mh, not so fast. The Coldrons were always supposed to be special."

"In what respect?" I asked.

"I'm afraid I don't know," Dot said.

Jenna sought my gaze and rolled her eyes. "There's more, but that's the upshot of it. Oh, indirect magic is also less complicated and risky than direct magic where you project your skylles, well, directly. Like you did today."

"I never thought of roses," I said.

Dot snorted. "They're the essence of your skylles. Magic you can touch. Magic that lingers. It's rare, though. In my youth, I could conjure up violets. Not anymore."

"Sometimes they show up for me," Jenna said coyly.

"Anyway," Dot said. "You'll learn to control the manifestations, together with the side effects, as you improve. Once we have our database and start our training, the others should follow suit. Of course, that's assuming the skylles of those . . . weaklings will ever manifest. And you'll have to fulfill your role."

Oh, now it's my fault?

Jenna rolled her eyes once more. "Gran, stop pushing her. Think of direct magic as freestyle, Myr. It's highly unstable, sucks more of the skylles, and is accompanied by manifestations like your petals. Oh, and it can backfire with bad results if you use it for the wrong purpose. Not that the other variety can't. Only, it tends not to be quite so nasty. Odd that you and your aunt should both go for direct, but you seem to be getting to grips with it. That's good."

"Did I have a choice?"

"I guess not. Don't fret, Myr. It worked."

"Mh, you mentioned backfire. Last time, my hands were covered in thorn pricks and I had the mother of all headaches. This time, I only was tired."

Dot tutted. "Did you listen at all? You used the skylles in a way that served their purpose, so you only suffered some minor side effects, not proper backfire. It's logical."

My jaw hurt, but I didn't dish her the comeback she deserved. Sometimes it's better not to engage. "Uh, I'll need time to get my head around the concept."

Dot huffed and reached for the recipe book. I couldn't stop my muscles from tensing, but nothing happened. She opened the book at the back and looked up.

"Fascinating. I remember the potions and spells from my discussions with your aunt. The laundry list is a bit thin on that front. Instead, it focuses on the direct magic. Also, the style is totally different. Our grimoire is more like a treatise. Yours is more practical. A proper recipe book."

She raised her chin at the laundry list. "Perhaps the inspiration to accept your natural role is in there."

Determined, are you? But so am I.

I donned the gloves Jenna had handed over. When I turned the first page of the Wytchett grimoire, an odd scent hit my nose. A combination of vanilla and dust, it was the unique perfume of old manuscripts. Like the recipe book, the laundry list was covered in curly handwriting, but it was even harder on the eyes than Great-Aunt Petunia's ramblings. But the paper felt the same. Stiff and sturdy, it crackled as I opened the book.

Inspiration was sadly lacking. Line after line of mangled English ran past my unwilling eyes, pontificating on the correct application of one's "skylles," the moral obligations of the practitioner, the backfire if one got things wrong, and similarly hair-raising statements. Sentences like "Iu needeth to be hale of boddy for magicke" were hard to read and difficult to decipher. I forced myself to turn another page, and here it was. The first directive of the witches, except this one read something like, "It's never evylle we serfe."

"Two minutes to dinner, ladies. You'd better pack away your books," Marty called out from among wafts of frying fat.

Saved by the dinner bell. "I'd need a lot more time."

"Not exactly a page-turner, eh?" Jenna carefully closed the cover of the recipe book.

"Grimoires are not meant to be page-turners," Dot said stiffly. "It was good to be able to read this again. Thank you, Myrtle. Seriously, you ought to take better care of your legacy. I find it appalling this precious text should have been used in the kitchen."

With an expression of disgust, Dot swept crumbs off the pristine tablecloth that must have fallen from the tome's gutter. Suitably chastised on my aunt's behalf, I wrapped up my grimoire while Jenna returned the laundry list to its box.

My view on Diloff's shenanigans shared and the last cutlet

gnawed and placed on the side plate, I was reaching for the lemonade when my phone buzzed. The doorbell also chose that moment to shrill away. Marty went to answer the latter, while I responded to the call.

It was Linda. Buster had returned. Her next words made the fine hairs on my arms rise all at once as if magnetized.

10

LETHAL FLORA

"You'd better believe this. Elmsworth has found Buster, and it was divination that did the trick," Linda said, her voice in my ear breathless as if the woman had just run a marathon.

"Eh, what? Hang on, I'm with Dot and Jenna. Let me put you on speaker. Okay, shoot. What's going on?"

"Well, divination is perhaps too grandiose. Call it accidental scrying. Anyway, after running around all day searching for his dog, Elmsworth is in the shower. Seems like the plughole's blocked, and water is pooling at the bottom. He looks closer and spots a blurry reflection in the puddle at his feet. It's his pet, sitting on a motorbike in a garage. Can you imagine? Elmsworth recognizes the bike and knows who it belongs to. Amazing, eh?"

From the depths of the farmhouse rumbled male voices, followed by a door banging shut. Silence fell and then was broken by the twins, who clambered onto the Hollywood swing and started a pillow fight.

Linda continued. "Looks like the guy who owns the garage was in Marlborough for the day and never realized the little blighter was locked in. Doggie is safe now. But there's a problem."

Dot's gaze intensified. "Magical side effects."

"Couldn't hear a word. What did she say?"

"Dot mentioned hexing-related fallout."

"Ah, yup, exactly that. This is so totally out there. It started with a blinding headache immediately after the scrying. The Colonel fumbles through his mirror cabinet in search of paracetamol, staggers around in pain, and grips the cabinet. Next thing he knows, the mirror is cracked and his headache gone. Poof. Vanished."

"Oh, dearie me," Jenna said, hands pressed to her face. "How's he doing? The poor man."

"He's all right. Rather exhausted, though. Says the critter is worth a broken mirror. Uh, the doorbell. Must be the next lot of visitors. Talk to you later." She was gone.

"Out there?" Dot asked. "It's what I would call reassuring. The man successfully deflected the side effects into an object. Glass, especially mirrors, and liquids are great for that."

"Why did he have to suffer in the first place?" I asked. "He was trying to save his dog. Isn't that how the skylles are supposed to be used?"

"Yes, but he used direct magic. And don't forget, these people are inexperienced, not in full control of their skylles, and therefore accident-prone. It doesn't matter. Everything's coming together beautifully." She stared at the apple trees with an oddly serene smile on her lips.

"Gran, are you running a fever?" Jenna reached out and touched her grandmother's perspiring forehead. "I don't like this. You'd better lie down."

Dot swatted the hand away. "Don't treat me like a doddery old fool. It's been a long day. Call the boys. I'll bring them to bed, and then you'll have more time for your friend."

Dot's smile did nothing to hide the whiteness lurking in the wrinkled skin around her mouth. The woman was flying on willpower alone.

"Robbie, Johnnie." Jenna's voice had turned sing-songy. "Time to go to bed. Gran is coming, too. Say goodbye to Auntie Myrtle."

"But Mu-um, we're not tired," hollered the boy I took to be Johnnie, his cute ferret face scrunched up in protest.

"But Mu-um, it's light outside," the other tyke wailed, the gingery mop on top of his head sticky and unkempt. "We can't sleep yet."

Dot hoisted herself from the chair. "Come on, we'll read the next chapter from *Watership Down*. Let's see if our bunny friends truly have found their new home."

To my surprise that clinched it. Amazing that in the age of electronic toys, computers, and robots, a storytelling granny could still kick butt. Well, this one did.

The boys were right about the light, though. We had reached that time of the evening when the blue of the sky deepens, but the day has left so much sunshine behind it seems to cling to the landscape, illuminating shrubs, trees, and buildings from within. Together with the smoke from the barbecue and the scent of unseen flowers, the remains of the day kept me company as I swayed on the swing, mulling over strategies to get Dot off my back while waiting for the others to return.

Jenna emerged first, worrying her lower lip with her teeth. With a sigh, she sat next to me, pulled up her legs, and hugged her knees.

"Has your grandmother calmed down?" I asked. "Oh, and did I hear Chris earlier?"

"Yes, to the last question. He's in the den with Marty. Rugby has started."

Great. That was me—beaten by an egg-shaped leather ball.

"As to Gran, I fear she's not well. Myr, I'm so sorry. She can be super stubborn." Jenna slipped me a furtive glance.

I slapped on an extra-bright smile. "Not your fault. Eh, why is she so keen on me running the show? She has ten times my knowledge, if not more."

"To be honest, that came as a bit of a surprise. She might have overdone it again, like in May. She gets better, feels fit, and bang. It might be the heat. The doctor's run another battery of tests, but we're still waiting for the outcome. If it were something dreadful, he would have rung, wouldn't he?"

Jenna's eyes, huge in her pale face, implored me to say yes, so I did. Given the state of the National Health Service, the results couldn't be in yet, not in such a short time frame. For Jenna's sake, as well as for the coven, I fervently hoped Dot's weakness was caused by the high temperatures and overexertion and not more serious health issues. If we needed proof that clustering wonky magical beings near the stone circle indeed boosted their skylles, here it was. I had been the first, and the Colonel followed suit. What would happen next?

—

By the time the menfolk surfaced from the den, darkness was complete—as complete as it could be this close to the solstice.

"That was a great game," Marty said. The bug trap behind him flashed blue as another moth met its maker. The resident mosquitos were too smart for traps and kept whining by.

"Wasn't it, quite?" Chris said. "Sorry, Myr, I arrived a bit later than planned. The first half had already begun."

"No problem. We used the time to trigger the evacuation." And warned the witches to be on the lookout for rogue magical activity, its symptoms, and the resulting fallout.

Once the light had waned, Jenna turned on the lanterns that dotted the orchard. Their soft glow illuminated the trees, prompting visions of rugged fairies dancing under a canopy pinpricked with stars. Out on the henge, the festivities were in full swing. A hodgepodge of drums, string instruments, and flutes competed with singers and stomping feet.

Chris tilted his head. "Apart from the violins, that gig

sounds suitably prehistoric." He swung around. "Why don't we join them?"

Marty checked his watch. "Hate to be the party pooper, but the milking robot is acting up, and if I don't fix it, my cows won't love me anymore."

Jenna gave me a sly look before she shook her head. "You heard the boys. They'll take a while before they fall asleep. And I need to kiss them goodnight. At least they don't seem to miss their father." She pulled a face. "Nor do I."

Bully that he was, Jeff Burns had been warned to stay away from his future ex-wife and the kids.

"They've got the greatest uncle in the world," I said. Patchwork families came in all shapes and sizes.

If I didn't want to rise late again, I should go to bed myself. But to walk under the stars with Chris? The temptation was impossible to resist.

"Come on, Myr, this is probably our summer. Make the most of it." Jenna pointed at a gate set into the stone wall. "Why don't you take the shortcut? If I'm not up when you get back, use the gate and walk around the house. Much easier than taking the trail through the fields. Do you need a torch?"

"Got one." Chris pulled a Maglite from his pocket.

I hugged the Wytchetts and Chris shook their hands before we passed into the benevolent night.

—

Life is a string of memories, some more vivid than others. Some eventually fade while others shape our future, be it in a good or a bad way. That Monday night will forever be etched in my memory.

Chris and I strolled along the rough track flooded with the rays of an almost full moon. Its perfection was slightly marred by discolorations that looked like a figure, one hand raised in warning. Like the breath of a specter, cold air found my neck. My world was changing, whether I wanted it to or not.

"Out of curiosity, are you okay after this morning's, eh . . . achievement?" Chris asked, echoing my thoughts.

"So far, so good. Oh, I need to tell you about Elmsworth."

When I finished the tale, there was enough light for me to see Chris's mobile brows twitch. "The old boy did that? Respect." He frowned at the skies. "I wonder whether the moon might play a role."

"Dot didn't mention it, but I wouldn't be surprised. If the trend continues, though, we risk exposure. Which means we must get our guerrilla magical skylles under control. I hope Dot is up to it. We need her."

Her, not *me.*

We followed the trail until it reached the river Kennet and the bridge leading to the standing stones. Like the prehistoric monument, the river had become a hotspot. Along its banks a motley collection of tents had sprung up, washing lines strung out between them, clothes limp in the feeble breeze. Some shelters were lit from within, and silhouettes flitted across polyester walls like actors in a shadow play.

People talked, cooked, and laughed while music blared from radios and phones. With the crowd filling the space under the willows, the stream's friendly burble was lost in a soup of noise.

Once we passed the tent hamlet, Chris hooked his thumb over his shoulder. "I'm surprised the cops let the great unwashed stay."

"Marty says there's no point in rousing the wild campers. They'll come back. They'll sleep anywhere."

No sooner had the words left my lips than the image of the bundle that had been Boian rose in my mind. The poor man's eternal sleep had begun in a beer cellar.

I stumbled and Chris grabbed my arm. "Watch out. Path's getting a bit iffy."

His hand slid down the inside of my wrist, drawing instant goose bumps in response. His fingers found mine.

More goose bumps.

My fingers intertwined with his and we walked on, the trail branching off to the bridge and from there winding along to the party at the stones. No words passed between us. As one, we turned the other way, heading for the sleepy village. Chris stopped, and with his free hand caressed my chin, my temples, and my hair. The moon poured its silvery light over us, and I could see every hair in his stubbled face.

"Myrtle," my witch hunter murmured, his eyes closing.

I allowed mine to follow his lead. The next moment, a scream shrilled from the riverbank.

—

For a split second, my heart stopped, I swear it did. My eyes snapped open. The live music broke off. The babble in the tent hamlet died down. Some radios and phones continued until they too fell silent.

Another scream broke the night, louder and sharper this time. A mosquito whined past my ear.

"Blast it all. What's up now?" Chris heeled around.

I was facing the riverbank and had a full view of the scene, illuminated by the campfires. People were running in from all sides, clustering around two figures center stage. Arms flailing and long skirts billowing, they moved in a parody of a dance. It was hard to tell what they might be doing. A fight? A ritual gone wrong?

The screams rose in pitch. The babble of voices swelled. The figures jerked, melted into each other, sprang apart again. A fight, then. The throng of campers grew thicker until they hid the two figures from view.

My fury unsheathed its claws and lashed its tail. Why had those blasted hippies chosen this moment to have a go at each other? Thankfully, they were out of reach. Otherwise, I might have strangled them. Chris's tense stance and scowl showed me he too must be wrestling with the beast inside.

We stared at each other. And then broke out laughing.

"Talk about *interruptus*," he said.

I sensed heat creeping up my ears yet again. "Indeed, Mr. Lentulus. Indeed."

The moment was saved, but the mood had been broken. Chris turned away from me, glaring at the romance killers gathered on the riverbank. "What are those morons up to?"

With the tourists crawling about like upset ants, it was hard to tell. At least the yelling had ceased.

"At first, I thought they might have been Druids or Wiccans because of the robes," I said. "Some sort of ritual, maybe?"

"To me, it sounded as if somebody was in real pain. Why would they celebrate their rites on the campground and not on the henge?"

"Search me, I'm fresh out of inspiration."

Together, we observed the distant scene, revealed once more by a shift in the crowd. A third person in a flowing robe had arrived, carrying some sort of clunky suitcase.

A jolt of recognition zapped through me. "You know what? I think those three in the middle, the ones wearing the long skirts, are Wiccans. Probably even the ones I met in the gift shop."

"How can you tell somebody by their skirt? Sorry, that's female logic."

My fury, already piqued, showed its teeth. "Female logic? Now listen—"

He took a step backward. "Abject apologies, I didn't mean it like that. Watch your eyes. They're flaring like searchlights."

"Seriously?"

"Oh yes. It's gone now."

These—what did Dot call them?—manifestations of my skylles would get me into trouble if I didn't watch it. "Sorry for the magic, but if you don't mean something, don't say it."

"Whoa, tiger." He raised his hands, palms up. From what I could make out, the infernal grin was back on his face. "How can you be sure from over here? Telepathy? That moon must be giving you guys a real boost."

"Very funny. No, I recognize the case the tall woman is carrying. I think she's the doctor who gave Boian his medicine. Perhaps we should have a look? Find out what is going on?"

A flash sparkled among the group. Were they taking photos now?

"Yeah, you and all those others." Chris waved his hand at the gawkers.

The inner beast growled. Who did he take me for? "It's not like that at all. I feel responsible."

"For what?"

"I sicced the cops on the Wiccans."

"You did your civic duty and gave Sarah her leads. Let her do her job. No need to take responsibility for anything."

My gaze flicked back to the riverbank in time to see one of the three long-skirted figures drop to the floor. There she lay, with the two others kneeling next to her, while the crowd looked on.

"Oh, bugger, forget what I said. I fear my questionable first aid skills are called for. Excuse me." With that, Chris sprinted off.

My anger evaporated with a whoosh. In its stead, something bristly entrenched itself in my stomach.

I started after Chris but stumbled over the same root that tripped me earlier. After picking myself up, I headed for the camp, puffing like a frustrated dragon.

A gap in the crowd revealed a young woman on the ground, her puce skirts pushed up and twisted around her knees and her blonde hair sweaty and tangled. As she moaned and thrashed about, a glittery pentagram on a chain whipped across the woman's chest, and the charms wrapped around her skinny arms jingled in unsuitable merriment. The poor girl was clearly a practitioner. To one side sat another Wiccan, clad in green. Her face was a frozen mask of horror, and whimpering noises came from her throat. Opposite her knelt a woman in black, rummaging through a leather pilot case, her full sleeves flapping like the wings of a dark bird.

The Wiccan doctor from the shop.

She grabbed the girl's wrist. "Mother Hecate, that pulse is much too slow. Hannah, hang in there, the paramedics are on their way." She rubbed her arm over her forehead, addressing Chris. "This is simply impossible. From one minute to the other, she . . . I'd say it's glycosides, but they don't act that fast. And they should be out of her system. I mean, with all that vomiting they can't . . . Hannah? Hannah?"

A surge in the crowd hid the scene from my view, for which I was supremely grateful.

Others were not.

"Oi, I can't see anymore." A pimply youth in a pair of saggy Bermuda shorts stood on his toes, phone at the ready.

Bloody ghouls.

"She's done for," said his friend with grim relish. "She looked, like, totally gray in the face. Then she doubled over. Couldn't breathe, she said. Saw halos around the moon or something stupid. Guts on fire. Heart going nuts. As sick as a dog, I tell you."

"Gross." Bermuda shorts pocketed his phone. "I hope it's nothing catching?" He licked his lips as if suddenly uncertain.

"I tell you, I'm outta here," his mate said.

They melted away from the crowd.

I pocketed my phone. The paramedics were coming, and Chris had offered his help. As dodgy as he claimed his skills were, he was trying, which was more than others—including me—had done.

Ahead, the wall of bodies shifted once more, giving me another unwelcome glimpse of the sick woman. Chris and the doctor were kneeling on either side of her. The woman in green was behind them, weeping. The young Wiccan lay quiet now, her legs stretched out and the soles of her feet black with dirt.

The crowd gasped, and the ring of spectators shifted, dragging me with them away from the scene. If Jenna had been here, she might have calmed the patient down. I could only recall what I'd read.

Glycosides. Again. Great-Aunt Petunia had been quite specific about herbal medicine. Foxglove and lily of the valley both yielded strong heart tonics and diuretics that had been used by doctors throughout the centuries. They were tricky to administer, though. Overdoses would cause precisely the symptoms the young Wiccan suffered from—symptoms reminding me of Boian.

Another freak shift in the crowd, and I could see the young woman once more, lying still. Where was that ambulance?

As if in response, the woman's arm, reddish splotches showing here and there, flopped through the air and came to lie on the grass, palm upward. The pale fingers cramped once and opened one final time, like a flower unfolding.

11

SELFIE WITH GRIMOIRE

The bells in the distant church tower pealed away the day and ushered in the next, and still I sat in my stuffy living room accompanied by my magical primula and my geriatric cat. Too tired to open the windows and too wired to sleep, I could only sip Auntie's best Burgundy, spooked by the images of that poor dead woman. Over and over again, I kept seeing those pathetic feet of hers with their grubby soles and her flower-like hand.

Perhaps if Chris were around, the haunting would go away. He had escorted me to the door of my B&B before he walked back to his flat, needing to be alone. The man had my fullest sympathy. He had been so much closer to the horror.

Tears pricked my eyes. "Girls, this is going over my head. First, all this haywire magic, and now another awful death. That poor, poor woman."

Tiddles, snuggled up by my side, yawned once, and dropped back into sleep. Her warm, furry presence radiated comfort.

Petty, her bucket resting at my feet, fired off two sympathetic sparks.

I pulled up my legs and hugged them. "And there's Dot, wanting me to run the show. Blasted woman is like a bulldozer. How am I supposed to lead when half the time I don't know what I'm doing?"

Tiddles grunted in her sleep. Petty shared another spark. She shifted her bucket on the floorboards, tilted, and a full dose of her flowery scent wafted in my general direction. My primula, my familiar, trying her best to comfort one confused, sucky witch.

"I know, I know. Selfish of me to complain. I'm still alive. I can still hope."

Hannah, dead under the uncaring glare of the moon, had run out of the gift that is life. Correction: Somebody had stolen that gift from her. The woman's death couldn't be a coincidence. Not when her symptoms mirrored Boian's end.

"His last minutes must have passed just like hers. Only, he was alone. Nobody around to listen or care. Not even the gawkers. How ghastly is that?"

More tears welled up, and I swiped them away. But I couldn't clear the memories that mired my mind in a noxious sludge.

"How can Hannah be dead?" the Wiccan doctor had asked the paramedics more than once. "It's not possible, but I could swear it's glycosides. Though, why would she have taken medicine? She wasn't ill like the poor musician. Whatever that stuff is, it acted impossibly fast. Ten minutes after the first symptoms, she was gone."

I let go of my legs. Two people in a small village died one after the other, suffering from the same symptoms. There had to be a link. The doctor herself? No way. Not when genuine bafflement rang in her voice and shock dulled the woman's eyes.

Shock or guilt?

I reached for my laptop and scrolled through the information I had called up three times already, modern findings that supported Great-Aunt Petunia's words written almost two hundred years ago. Every part of foxglove or lily of the valley was lethal, but the adult body usually purged itself in time. It was different for kids, but even there it seemed to be a case of hours, not minutes.

"They must both have been given a massive overdose. But if I remember correctly, the pathologist found only a minimal amount. Girls, this doesn't make sense."

Tiddles rose from the settee and stretched, her tail a question mark over her bony rump. The cat sat up and licked a beige paw the same moment Petty launched into the air, flying toward the coffee table and landing on the recipe book with its unseasonable cover. With my brain on the blink, I had so far lacked the strength to unwrap the tome.

"Rats. Guess what I've forgotten to bring? Your new pot."

Petty tilted her bucket and, with its rim, nudged the recipe book, once, twice.

"The recipe book won't help us, little one. I know the passage on the herbal potions and poisons by heart. That's what gave me the idea, see? That and the rash. Both victims had it. Boian and Hannah, I mean."

Names meant the world when talking about the dead. Names were all that remained after the loss of the most precious thing we're given—life.

Rustle. Petty's leaves were flopping about and rubbing against each other, the blossoms shaking. Tiddles gave me an inscrutable look that might have been born of cross-species sympathy. With a contented sigh, she settled again, closer this time, her bony spine pressing into my thigh.

"Sorry, girls, I'm rather maudlin tonight. There must be somebody out there poisoning people. Maybe it's the Wiccan doc. Personally, I don't think so. And don't tell me the cops are on the case so it's no longer my business."

"Mrrp?" Tiddles said, reopening one rheumy green eye.

"Sweetie, these deaths bother me. There's something odd

about them." Impossible had been the word the Wiccan doctor used. Sarah said something similar. "Odd isn't good. Odd means media attention. That's the last thing we need with our skylles acting up."

Tiddles shut her eye and grunted. Petty hovered over the gift-wrapped grimoire, and then she tilted her pot and gave the book a shove. It shifted my way.

"Oh, all right. I'll have another look."

With a sigh, I ripped off the wrapping paper and leafed through the tome. I hit upon warnings about skylles, instructions on how to prepare a restorative gruel, and comments on invisible familiars, but not a single herbal lecture.

"It's here somewhere." My gaze slid across the curly script. There it was.

"Listen to this, Petty. 'They might be helpful, but it is hard to believe how deadly exuberant foxglove and delicate lily of the valley are. An overdose can cause immense discomfort and possibly death.'"

How ironic. Here I was, lecturing a plant on herbal poisons. I shook my head and continued. "Farther down she talks about symptoms. Headache, nausea, vomiting, diarrhea, and irregular heartbeat when the body tries to purge itself of the poison. Plus, what she calls inflammation of the skin. It fits for both Boian and Hannah."

I rubbed my tired eyes. "I'd love to see those toxicology reports."

Wide awake, I rose and ambled through the living room, passing under the archway into the office and back again, the recipe book pressed against my chest. My thoughts drifted back to the riverbank and the shadows lurking between the many lamps. Strangely, it was not the hand my thoughts always tripped over but the grubby pair of bare feet.

The distant church tower bonged one.

"Specters begone," I whispered, knowing it was never that easy.

After placing the book on the table, I threw myself onto the sofa. The cat jerked and raised her head, her tongue hanging out of the side of her mouth like a tiny pink slug.

Sudden mirth bubbled in my nose.

"Thanks for turning my parlor into a bathroom, Tiddles. And for cheering me up." I was scratching the fur between her pointy ears when something rustled softly.

"What are you up to now?" I turned around to face my plant and found her motionless.

Ripple.

My gaze skittered across to the recipe book. My heart skipped a beat. The grimoire was lying open, but page after page flipped by, as if an invisible presence was leafing through the book and taking the time to lick a finger each time before reading on. Funnily enough, the tome seemed to have started with the wasteland of empty pages in the middle.

Mouth drier than a dust bunny—not that the Simpkins sisters would allow those inside the B&B—I kept staring at the old manuscript. It continued to crackle—no, that was now Petty, who had moved next to me, tilting her bucket at a crazy angle as if to watch the show. Sparks ran over her blossoms, and she radiated waves of lemony happiness.

What the heck was going on?

Well, duh, my grimoire was reading itself. And the plant appeared to be unconcerned, if not pleased. A hysterical giggle burst from my lips, and I pushed the heel of my hand against them.

The next moment, my helpful imagination whirred and conjured the image of an invisible presence studying the text. That I liked even less. "Hello? Anybody here?"

No response. The book read on. Petty's leaves shook. The little floral monster was on a roll.

"Petty, what if it doesn't stop? Think of the Simpkins sisters."

My primula shot off a pink spark. Then the bucket rose and bumped against my laptop. This time, I grasped her meaning in a flash.

With wobbly fingers, I hit the Internet and searched popular fiction for a freezing spell. Since I was dealing with a book, it might work. A lame idea, but what else was I supposed to do? I had no other options other than ring Dot or Jenna, which was impossible in the small hours.

Gosh, there was so much rubbish out there. Mangled Latin seemed to be my best bet. Even Harry Dresden used it, though his spells tended to be on the explosive side of the spectrum. When I looked up, the book reached the last of the empty pages. A page quivered once, and then the tome proceeded to reread from the end of the empty section.

"Okay." I cleared a throat as scratchy as Weetabix. "Listen— uh, grimoire?"

The book read on. The cat, on the other hand, arched her back and hopped onto the table.

"Oh, cripes, no, Tiddles. Stay away. Shoo. Oi, you, grimoire, stop it. Now. Uh—Immobulus? Immobulus."

The book read on. The cat, oblivious to my orders, sniffed at the fluttering pages. I always knew that Harry Potter stuff was complete hogwash. To be fair, I had based my reasoning on the firm belief that witches didn't exist. After the recent revelations, my views on that point had shifted. Talking of witches, what about wands? Fictional wizards used them all the time. Perhaps I needed one. I looked around the room and spotted a pen lying on the sideboard.

"Petty, do you think I can use a pen instead of a wand?"

The plant sparked and shook her leaves. She was laughing at me.

"Not helpful, you know?"

"Merow." Tiddles was even less helpful and kept batting at the old manuscript with her front paws.

"Watch it." I jumped up, but the recipe book was faster. The next page slid from under my cat's claws and turned over, giving Tiddles a good thwack on her nose. She sneezed.

The book read on.

"You know what, I don't think we're talking ghostly presence here. Somebody must have triggered the wretched thing into flipping through the empty pages, and that somebody is most likely me."

Dot's comment about emotions rang in my mind, louder than the bell had sounded in the church tower. Not only did I suffer from rogue magic, but also I witnessed a woman die a horrid death. Not to forget, we had been looking for answers in the grimoires earlier that evening, so here was our purpose. Add in Petty, who made me touch the book, and *kazoom*. At least that was my best, and only, explanation. Far from requiring eye of newt and toe of frog, my magic ran on grief, compassion, and a pesky floral familiar egging me on.

Oddly enough, there wasn't a single rose petal in sight.

The book kept leafing through the empty pages with dogged determination, once more going front to back.

"What are you looking for? If you're looking for something."

Could the recipe book be waiting for my input? What would happen if I touched it? Tiddles had done so and didn't get far even if she hadn't gotten hurt. If I was right and the grimoire's nightly reading session was kicked off by yours truly, perhaps the outcome would be different.

"I'm supposed to be in charge here, right?"

Petty rustled her leaves and sparked, which I took to mean assent.

My heart sprinting in my chest, I bent over the recipe book. Another page slipped by, free of text like the others, virgin apart from brownish discolorations at the bottom and tiny splotches that looked like fly poo. Once it flipped over, I let my finger swoop in and land on the paper.

The page, silky and warm under my finger, curled up at the edges and then it flattened. And from my finger, like ripples in an inky pool, spread an image.

Scribbles appeared, first in pale gray and then in sepia

tones. They flowed to the edges until they covered the page my digit was resting on. The tinge of the markings changed, turning washed-out blue and staying that way.

At first, I couldn't work out what it was I was seeing. Blurry lines and circles seemed superimposed on each other, embedded within a jelly-like substance. Slowly, the image cleared, morphing into a crude engineering sketch displaying two small circles within a bigger one. Scraggly asterisks with lines doodled between them sat atop. Inside and outside the circle marched stick people. Some wore hats and some long skirts. Above it all sat a ball, most likely the sun, with uneven lines pointing in all directions. The whole masterpiece reminded me strongly of the wonky drawings Robbie and Johnnie churned out by the ton. In the bottom right corner, the unknown artist had doodled something that might be a plant with broad pointy leaves and little bells. It was placed next to an undecipherable word.

I withdrew my index finger. The image faded, so I quickly stabbed the page again. The bluish color returned. That bode ill. It appeared I was bound to the recipe book if I wanted to keep what I discovered. A quick glance showed me the smartphone was at the other end of the table.

"Crap. Petty, it fades if I lift my finger. I need my phone."

My familiar bumped her bucket against the table, causing my smartphone to slide across.

"Thanks, dear."

With my right index finger fixing the picture, I groped for the phone with my left. Then I pushed on the camera icon with my thumb. To my monumental relief, I got the app to open and pointed the phone at the page.

And just in time. Despite having my finger firmly pressed against the parchment, the strange image was fading.

I pushed the button. The camera flashed and clicked away. By the time I was finished, the sketch was a faint memory on the page. A few heartbeats later, it was gone. The book, cooperative at last, remained immobile, which allowed me to flex fingers as stiff as twigs.

"Okay, let's see what we have here."

Petty hovered behind me as I swished my way through the photos I had taken. I halfway expected the image not to be visible, but I got lucky. While the last shots were useless, the first seemed halfway okay, even if blurry, especially when I tried to zoom in.

"Mh. If you ask me, the scene shows a group of people at the stone circle. It's probably daytime, otherwise we wouldn't need the sun. Oh, hang on. Maybe this is meant to depict the solstice since that sun is right at the top? Given their outfits, I dare say we're talking seventeenth century. I can't make any sense of that scribble in the corner. A name or a place? That leafy thing is probably a plant. A shame the photo is out of focus. There are some more elements I can't work out. Perhaps I should try and get a better picture."

Apart from a woozy sensation in my brain and fatigue probably caused by the recent stress, I didn't suffer any side effects, which was reassuring.

"Let's have another go, shall we? Okay, if I remember correctly, I was pacing the room."

The recipe book once more clutched to my bosom and a bookmark in the page I had made visible, I stalked from the living room into the den, swung around, and returned. Tiddles, waiting by the door, tilted her head and gave me a concerned "Mrow?"

"I'm fine. It's an experiment."

Dr. Frankenstein's famous last words?

Reverently, I returned the book to the table and sat in the armchair, waiting. The Coldron grimoire remained still. Circling my flat palm over the blotchy page drew no reaction either.

I slumped in my seat, overcome by a sudden weariness that spread from my brain to my limbs. Mental shutters rattled down, one after the other. Whatever emotions and sensations might have triggered the magic, they must have burned themselves out. The next moment, a yawn of monumental proportions pushed its way up from deep inside. No way would I perform more miracles today.

"Petty, thanks a bunch for your help, but I'm going to bed. And you stay here." While I slotted the recipe book on the shelf, its leather smooth under my fingers, Petty hovered to the windowsill and landed with a soft plop. Perhaps we finally understood each other.

As I headed for the exit, Tiddles' solid little body slipped past my ankles. She preceded me up the stairs and into my room, where she scrambled onto my bed. I followed her example—and ended up wide awake.

Why that picture? Was it a random choice, or had the grimoire's magic guided my fumbling finger? For what purpose? The solstice was obviously affecting the coven, but we had expected that and were preparing for evacuation. We also knew the Whites, our more competent magical cousins, disappeared via the circle, leaving the feebler Reds, my ancestors, at the mercy of the witch hunters. This information wasn't new. The exercise might have been nothing but a paranormal training session. Lesson one—empty pages aren't always empty. Would it take a corpse each time to make them visible? In that case, I had better give up on the whole magical shebang and run. I tossed and turned in my bed, and it must have taken hours until my synapses declared a cease-fire.

—

When I resurfaced from a black void, rays of sunshine were tickling my nose. I lay sprawled across the duvet in yesterday's clothes, my head pounding away and a funky taste in my mouth. I ran my tongue over my teeth, which seemed to be covered in mildew, they felt that furry.

I dragged myself upright with a groan and lurched into the bathroom. Grabbing the peppermint mouthwash Daisy had presented me with, home-produced by the Women's Institute as one of their many projects to support the community, I gargled long enough to chafe the inside of my cheeks. Then I ripped off my smelly clothes and stepped into the shower. As strong jets massaged my skin and a vanilla scent wrapped around me, my consciousness slowly emerged from the fog. Unfortunately, the shower did nothing for the pounding in my head, nor could it stop the memories from knocking.

A dead Wiccan. A self-reading book. The empty pages not empty after all—

Oh blast, the photos.

With the water still running, I shot from the stall and rummaged through the pile of discarded clothes on the floor until I found my phone. With trembling and wet fingers, I tapped the camera icon, slipped, and opened the navigation app instead.

"Turn around, if possible," it said.

Various unspeakable swear words later, I hit upon the photos. They were still there, as fuzzy as ever, but they hadn't vanished during the hours I lay lost in slumberland. If I wanted to make sense of my discovery, I would need help.

First things first. Witching and murders were getting in the way of my business.

The shower turned off, I dry swallowed two headache pills and threw on a flowery muumuu and a sleeveless white blouse. A matching scarf tamed the flyaway hair that had half-dried already.

I needn't have worried. This time I arrived before the guests. Not before the Simpkins sisters, though, who had set up the buffet and bustled about in the kitchen.

The moment I pushed through the swing doors, Cecily opened the fridge and Alma switched on the kettle. "Have you heard about the death?" she said.

"You mean the Wiccan?"

"Yes. One of the wild campers, they say. Poison, they say. Exactly like for the other one. Don't bother with the *Messenger* or the radio—they're still on the first corpse. The Druids staying at the Crystal Dawn told my friend Elsie about it last night." Alma's friend Elsie cleaned at Linda's B&B. Their rumor mill was much more efficient than the coven's call chain.

Cecily nodded eagerly. "Said the police had the killer but didn't do anything. Bingo, he killed again."

She poured three glasses of orange juice. "So, 'twasn't the pubkeeper who did it after all. I think that police friend of yours is in a lot of trouble. She was the one who let the killer go, apparently."

Oh, poor Sarah. "It's not like that . . ." I bit my tongue, but it was too late.

"Would you know more?" Alma's eyes glinted with anticipation. "Actually, what happened when you went to the pub? You didn't happen to be at the river, did you?"

Urgh. Payday.

I gave them a sanitized version of my recent exploits, trying to dampen down my qualms about the Wiccans. They must have seeped through, no matter how hard I tried.

"Hah," Alma said. "Heard that, too. They're not allowed to leave, but what good is that to anybody now?"

Cecily nodded. "Huh. Guilty as hell if you ask me. But the Druids claim it's all hearsay and unfair cushions."

"Percy Cution, Cec," Alma said. "You want eggs this morning, Myrtle, or just bird food?" A smile crinkled the fine lines around her eyes.

"Muesli and fruits will do, thanks, Alma," I said. "The young woman who died belonged to the group that was taken in for questioning. Why would they kill one of their own?"

Alma's and Cecily's expressions told me what they thought of that comment.

"No matter what, we're in trouble. The village, I mean," Alma said in a tone as excited as it was lugubrious.

"Why?"

"Some guests are already leaving. Mind my words, soon we'll all be out of work."

As usual, she was exaggerating wildly—we were booked solid—but the unease clogging my throat thickened. Perhaps I should act on my early morning heebie-jeebies and run. But then, acting the chicken had never been my style.

12

MOVING ON

Fragrant steam rose from my cup of coffee and wafted to the windowsill where Petty sunbathed, calm and content after absorbing her fluid breakfast. Not turning my back on this muddle meant I would have to stick my nose into a few things. The only question was whether to start with the mysterious magical image or my qualms about the killings.

Sarah would be the harder nut to crack, so I'd better tackle her first.

I called her number, dread pooling at the bottom of my stomach. She wouldn't thank me for my efforts. With a bit of luck, she might have slept well and picked up some doughnuts on the way to work.

"Sergeant Widdlethorpe, Swindon CID," a harassed voice said. Luck and I don't go well together.

"It's me, Myrtle. Before you tell me to go away, I was at the river yesterday evening."

"That's the last thing I need."

"I could have done without the experience, believe me. Those symptoms—"

"Myrtle, hold it right there. I've got enough ox manure on my plate without you sticking an oar in."

That was a super-confused metaphor, which also seemed a tick unfair. Sarah must have come to the same conclusion. "Look, I appreciate your leads, but it's my job to nail the perp."

"You'd better do that pronto. The gossips are having a field day."

Sarah groaned. "And the media won't be far behind. Them I need even less. Not when the evidence is not exactly straight-forward."

That was cop-speak for "I don't have a clue what's going on here."

"Sarah, I was there. I heard what the Wiccan doctor said. She was totally baffled by the symptoms and the speed at which they developed."

Sarah was quiet. Then she drew a deep breath. "I can rely on you not to blab? Well, some of it you know already."

"Who do you take me for?"

"Sorry, I had two hours of sleep last night, if that much. The coffee is crap, this case a nightmare, and the DI is worse. Right, our sawbones tells me Mr. Cornel stood no chance. The poison, however he might have ingested it, swamped his body, despite copious vomiting and . . . eh, let's not go there. Funny thing is, there wasn't even enough to kill a child or a pet. Doc says the man's death is, let me quote him, 'quite impossible.'"

The vaguest of notions surfaced briefly in my consciousness but sunk again too quickly for me to grasp it.

"He had a dicky ticker."

"Indeed. Until yesterday evening, I was thinking tragic ac-cident for the reason you mentioned. Not anymore. I quizzed the Wicca practitioner about Ms. Turner's symptoms—eh, that's the victim's name—once more this morning, and she confirmed what you just said."

"Mh. Okay, if I learn anything, I'll let you know."

"Please do. Even if you think it's not related, it might help me. Well, after Ms. Turner's postmortem we should have a better idea. And I need those lab tests." She yawned. "Sorry. Ah, there's one more thing I can tell you. Mr. Winters is in the clear. He's free to open shop." With that, she cut the connection.

The pub could open, but would there be any customers?

I drained my coffee and flipped through my contacts for the next number. The phone rang. And rang.

"Hellooo?" piped a youthful voice.

As usual, there was a 50 percent chance. "Johnnie?"

"No, it's Robbie."

Foiled again. "Robbie, is your mum around?"

"She's with Gran. Upstairs. The doctor is here. I don't like doctors. Will Gran be all right?"

My stomach cramped. "If the doctor is with her, then she'll be fine," I said with cheer I didn't feel. "Can I talk to your Uncle Marty, then?"

"No, there's a problem with the robot." That Robbie didn't make mooing or other animal noises told me how upset he was.

"Okay, please tell your mum and uncle I called. And don't worry. Your gran isn't young anymore. Visits from the doctors are normal. I'm sure it's just the weather." I struggled to keep the chipper tone in my voice.

It seemed to work. "Okay, Auntie Myrtle. I'll tell Johnnie. He was crying. I wasn't."

He hadn't been far off it. "That's great, Robbie. There's nothing wrong with tears if one is upset. Believe me, your gran is in good hands." The twins were at an age where the word of an adult still counted. That would soon change. Hopefully, I wouldn't be the one responsible.

With Jenna fighting her personal battle, who else might help me interpret a wacky magical image? A joyful flutter in my chest was the response. Chris. By now he should be awake. My finger hovered over the number. The next instant, it swooped.

"Hello, you have reached Lentulus IT Solutions. I'm unable to answer your call. Please leave a message after the beep."

Beep.

"Uh. It's Myrtle. Are you okay? Perhaps you can ring me back. Oh, and I found something odd in the recipe book. Looks like a magical doodle. Will explain, but not on the phone."

A more patient person would have waited for people to call back. Patience not being my biggest virtue, I ran down a mental list of suitable friends and settled on the Ragworts. Damian was a retired librarian, so Internet searches were in his blood.

This time I connected, and I arranged to meet them in an hour. That allowed me enough time to visit the commercial cleaners beforehand. Feeling efficient, I hopped into the van, its back filled with the Witch's Retreat's dirty laundry. Through the open roof drifted birdsong, and I caught glimpses of swallows spiraling into the cloudless skies. Then a preppy voice blared from the radio. When he mentioned "Avebury," I pricked up my ears.

" . . . the second suspicious death last night. When asked about potential links between the two incidents, Detective Inspector Diloff from Wiltshire Police pointed out investigations are ongoing, and there was no cause for concern. Citizens are advised to keep their comestibles refrigerated since the heat wave is expected to continue."

Pull the other one, you moron. It's got bells on.

The presenter switched to a church fête in Upper Little Piddlesborough, so I changed stations.

My errand completed, I drove back and parked close to the Ragworts' new home. I walked up and found it blocked by a monster of a removal van. A gold and cream brocade sofa wobbled along, one sweaty muscle man at each end. I followed the bumping and swearing into the living room from where the same preppy voice on the radio enthused over the latest hit they were about to play.

"A bit more to the left," said Rosie, standing by the garden entrance and waving her arms like an overexcited octopus. "No, that's too far. Back a bit. Back a bit more. No, that's too much. The other way. Stop, that's it."

The muscle men dumped the sofa and stomped into the corridor. From the radio in the corner drifted the unwelcome strains of an overconfident singer and a rookie with a synthesizer riffing on the theme from *Titanic*. They both failed miserably.

"It's coming together ever so nicely, isn't it?" Rosie said. Her face was flushed, damp white strands of hair stuck to her forehead, but she sounded as happy as pie. "Uh, tell me, I'm curious. What was it exactly you discovered in your recipe book?"

Heavy footsteps, grunts, and swearing from the entrance announced the return of the movers.

"Can we go somewhere more private? Like the terrace, for example?"

"Sure. Let's see if Damian has sorted out the watering system. He got het up about these blokes mauling our furniture, so I asked him to make himself useful."

Outside, we found Damian standing on the trampled lawn and flattened molehills, threading a hose into an oscillating sprinkler he held in his hand. With the other hand he turned on the tap.

"Myrtle's here," Rosie trilled.

Damian shot around and dropped the sprinkler. The hose detached itself from the sprinkler, whipped up, and a jet of water exploded from its front end and drenched him in two seconds flat.

"Oh, dear." Rosie turned off the tap. "I didn't mean to surprise you."

Damian pulled a handkerchief from the pocket of his soggy shorts. "Never mind, dear, it's actually quite refreshing. Hello, Myrtle. So, you found a ghostly image in your grimoire?"

"Shhh." Rosie raised a finger to her lips. She kept her gaze glued on the living room where the movers appeared to have dumped a small elephant.

The taller and beefier of the two blokes stuck his face out the back door, toweling his neck with a rag. "Where does the bed go, then?"

"Upstairs, luv, first door to the right," Rosie said.

The mover mumbled something under his breath and withdrew.

"Let's stand under the trees for a while," Rosie suggested. "They won't hear us, but I can hear them."

"I wish I couldn't," Damian said, dripping.

Once we had put some distance between us and the movers, I gave the Ragworts the condensed version of my exploits with the recipe book and handed my phone to Rosie.

An airplane crossed the deep blue skies, a tractor rattled over the fields behind the garden, and still the Ragworts were staring at the photos.

"What's this, then, when it's at home?" Damian wiped his brow with the hankie.

"I was hoping you'd be able to tell me. My money is on our ancestors' exodus via the stone circle."

"May I?" Damian pocketed his hankie and reached for the phone. "Yes, you're right. I would say that's the big circle, the one still standing, together with the two lost ones. Proportions are about right. In a pinch, I'd say these squiggles and lines are star constellations. Not sure. That scraggly object is a sun, obviously."

"Yes, that occurred to me as well," I said. "Looks like a drawing made by one of Jenna's twins. Since it's high up in the sky, I'm pretty sure we're talking solstice."

He adjusted his glasses. "Agreed. Mh, can't read the word at the bottom, and the funny doodle next to it could be anything."

"A plant?"

"Perhaps. Look at this." Damian pointed at rows of zigzagging lines I had previously disregarded. "This reminds me of something."

He snapped his fingers, his eyes widening. "Our Neolithic plaques have the same chevrons running across."

Looking again, I saw it. The two famous plaques of the witches featured the same spiky wave pattern that crowded one corner of the image. "Could also be running water. The Kennet, for example."

"Mh, perhaps the chevron pattern is by default meant to depict water. How about if you ask Chris? Chap's supposed to be an expert in the matter, isn't he?" Damian's voice was cautiously neutral.

"The more opinions, the merrier, but I'd value yours."

"Oh, I'll try," Damian said. "However, my computer is not set up yet. I'll do it when I'm back at the B&B. Can you email me your photo?"

"If this is a magical image, I doubt you'll find instructions on the Internet, luv," Rosie said gently.

Her husband rolled his eyes. Since his thick lenses magnified everything, the overall effect was distinctly disconcerting.

Apparently engrossed by the image, Rosie didn't react. "What's that third circle? I mean, the little ball the people are heading for?"

"A full moon?" said Damian. "Eh, tell me, why did you pick this particular image?"

"I didn't. I hit the page at random. At least, I think so. The grimoire kept oscillating through the empty section. On the other hand, the departure of the Whites is something that truly irks me. Could it be the grimoire wanted to drop me a friendly hint?"

Damian took off his glasses and polished them. For a moment nobody said anything—nobody in the garden, that is. Inside the house, the movers were swearing their way up the stairs.

"I would have your book examined." Damian put his spectacles back on. "Figure out how old it really is. I wonder what other secrets it might be hiding."

The upstairs window slammed open and a bald head appeared. "Those wardrobes of yours also go up here?"

"Yes, luv, it's in the plan I gave you," Rosie said.

"Blast," said the head and disappeared.

Rosie's hands fluttered to her mouth like startled sparrows. "Well, I've also got news. Nothing spectacular. Nothing like yours." She looked coyly at Damian, whose face softened.

"This morning, I . . . see, I was excited the move was finally happening," Rosie said. "And when I reached for the roll in the picnic basket, it lifted. Not by much, mind you. It fell back the next instant and never moved again. Then it turned all black and smokey. Can you imagine, Myrtle? I've levitated a breakfast roll."

The summery garden seemed to sway for a nanosecond and then it settled. I had always taken for granted that Rosie and Damian were witches, but I assumed their powers were so feeble they would never show. I also had pegged Colonel Elmsworth for a magical loser. Now both he and Rosie had—what was one supposed to call it? Performed?

The coven was coming into its own. The recipe book had yielded a secret. Not something useful right at this moment, but there were many empty pages in the Coldron grimoire where in the laundry list I found none. Could that be the reason for Dot wanting me to assume leadership?

"Are you all right?" Rosie asked.

"I'm fine. So happy for you."

"It didn't fly high, mind you. And there was very little smoke. The movers didn't notice a thing."

"Isn't she amazing?" Damian asked.

"So she is. Did you suffer from a headache afterward?"

A tiny furrow appeared between Rosie's brows. "Should I?"

"It can happen. I bet the charring was some sort of side effect."

"Oh, dear." She smiled again.

Inside the bedroom, something crashed. Damian and Rosie stared at the upper window.

"Uh," he said.

I could take a hint, even if it wasn't expressed in so many words. I'd better go home, wait for Jenna and Chris to ring back, and do my accounts. Or I could do something else entirely, like help Sarah solve her case.

"I'd better get out of your hair. I might have a word with the Wicca practitioners, actually."

A wry smile tugged at Damian's lips. "Sleuthing again, eh? Shouldn't you leave the job to your friendly copper?"

"Unfortunately, her boss is an idiot. The Wiccans might be more open with a sympathetic local like me." I batted my lashes. I had put mascara on them, so they were no longer invisible.

Damian snorted. "With one of them dead, I would imagine they'll cooperate with the police."

"If the same man is in charge who caused that kerfuffle in spring, then no, they won't," Rosie said.

"I want these deaths to stop," I said. "They're awful and cruel, and they place the village in the limelight. With the way the coven is going, this isn't a good thing."

"True. In this case, your best bet is the Magic Mushroom Café," Damian said. "That's where the pagans meet. I had a friendly chat there with a group of shamans the other day."

"Thanks, I'll try there." It was that or visiting the tent hamlet on the riverbank. Not to forget, the café offered the distinct advantage of Chris's flat being close by. I would have a sneak peek to see if his Beemer was parked there, on the off chance he might be around.

Back in my car, I was reaching for the ignition button when my phone broke into a discordant jingle.

"Myrtle? It's Jenna. Robbie passed on your message."

"Jen, how are you? What about your grandmother?"

"Exhausted, but better. The doc gave her something, and she's sleeping now. Uh, could you come over? I could do with a bit of company. By the way, you forgot your pot last night."

How I wished my skylles allowed me to send supportive

vibes via the phone. "I know, silly of me. Of course I'll come. Hey, should I bring Petty along? She can try the pot for size." In doing so, she might cheer poor Jenna up.

Jenna gave a squeal of delight. "Oh, would you? You're a genuine friend, Myr."

"Give me fifteen minutes."

When I arrived, I found the front door of Wytchett Farm closed. When nobody responded to either the knocker or the doorbell, I traipsed my way along the old farmhouse to the patio at the back, Petty's bucket in my arms. One never knew who might be looking, so having her float was out of the question.

The kitchen door stood open. "Jen?"

All remained quiet, so I entered the house. To the left of the iron Aga stove, an opening gaped, light seeping onto the oven's turquoise doors. I risked a peek down a steep staircase built of brick, where worn steps lead into the cellar.

Mustiness found its way into my nose, followed by Petty's citrusy slipstream when she zipped past the entrance and down the stairs.

"Hey, Petty, not so fast."

"Myrtle?" Jenna's voice echoed oddly. "Oopsie, your familiar's here. Hang on, I'll take her back up."

"I'm coming."

"No, no, wait. Sweet Earth, where's the primula gone?"

"Jen?"

Supercharged stillness sizzled in my ear.

"Jenna?" What was going on down there? I gripped the chilly handrail and headed down the steps.

13

DOWN AND OUT

The mildewy gloom of the farm's cellar was broken here and there by light bulbs dangling from the ceiling. Like a frozen rag, the sudden drop in temperature slapped into my face, sending shivers up my arms and down my spine.

The spooky ambience raised the stakes. Mottled and cracked after what must have been centuries, the arched brickwork shouldered the farmhouse above. To my amateur eyes, the cellar appeared to be a lot older than the building itself, which hailed from the seventeen hundreds. This cellar had been around for a while, had seen too much, and hid its secrets in dim nooks and crannies, cobwebbed and echoing for good measure. How large was this place, really? It seemed to reach far beyond the confines of the Wytchetts' home.

Slowly, I rotated a full turn to work out where Petty and Jenna might have gone. The shelf facing the nearest archway was one possible hiding place. Filled with preserves and jams, it also housed boxes full of apples from last year's crop, all of them now wrinkled and wasted. Through the space above the dusty glasses that crowded the shelves, I spotted gardening implements leaning against the far wall. The rusted scythe fitted right in with the *Hammer House of Horror* look and feel. Petty and Jenna, however, were still missing in action.

"Jenna?" My voice rolled into the cellar, drawing eerie echoes but no response.

Whoosh. Clink.

A pale face peeked from behind a column, accompanied by the familiar bucket crowned with an unruly mass of pink flowers. Behind the two, a ragged curtain was swaying.

"Sorry, Myr, I would have come up, but I thought I'd lost your primula. Turns out, she was playing hide and seek among the columns. Eh, in case you're wondering, I went down here to find some special soil I was pretty sure we stowed somewhere. If I only knew where."

My friend stepped away from the pillar, the bucket floating next to her at hip height.

"Come on, I'll buy something in the garden center." Anything to get me out of this place.

"No, no, for your familiar you should always do your best. Was it about her you rang earlier?"

"Not quite. I discovered an image in the recipe book. In the empty pages. I'll tell you more when we're back upstairs."

Jenna's lusterless gaze lit up. "Really? Sweet Earth, how utterly amazeboggling. Come on, I must know more."

I sighed. Told her all about finding the image and Rosie's achievements.

Her woes apparently forgotten, at least for the moment, Jenna clapped her hands. Petty in her scruffy bucket bounced around until she landed on an old apple crate.

"Ooh, that's incredible. Where are those photos?"

"Please, let's go upstairs. They're all blurry and the lighting here is totally impossible."

Impossible. Like an echo in the shadowy vastness of the cellar, the word rang through my mind, where it swelled until it filled my head.

Impossible, the Wiccan doctor had said. Suspected glycosides that acted too fast for her young friend's body to purge itself.

"Impossible" had been the term used by the pathologist. A tiny portion of cardiac glycosides had overwhelmed Boian, an aging, sick musician.

Impossible. Absurd, unimaginable, unrealistic. In other words, magic.

Magic was killing these people.

A soft hand touched my shoulder as a concerned voice hushed into my ear. Petty lifted off the nearest apple crate and floated in front of my face, leaves whispering and blooms wriggling.

"Myr, what's up? You're white like a ghost."

"It's magic."

Jenna straightened. "Your image? Of course it is. You've done it again. That's why I want to see it. Pretty please with sprinkles on top?"

Frantic thoughts crashed like breakers in my head. My stomach churning and my throat tighter than a steel hawser, I searched for the photos and handed her the phone.

That done, I paced the floor. Movement usually helped with stress. Not this time. If anything, the mental turmoil spiked. I was wrong, I had to be.

Calm down, Myrtle, you've got no proof. You're acting on hunches.

Sarah claimed I was good with hunches.

"Wonderful." Jenna's titter grated on my nerves. "Completely and absolutely amazeboggling. This must show the exodus of the Whites when they left our ancestors behind."

I willed words past my lips. "Yes, Damian and Rosie agreed."

"So far we only knew by hearsay. Here we have the proof.

Oh, Myr, well done, you. Look at the image. So detailed. Oh, and I love those cute lilies at the bottom."

"Eh, what lilies?"

She waggled the phone in front of my face. "At the right bottom edge. Next to that scrawl I can't read."

She must have phenomenal eyesight.

Jenna swished through the pictures on my phone. "Mh, zooming doesn't help a lot, but they've got to be lilies of the valley. Can't you see the pointy leaves and the tiny bells? And I bet those asterisks around them are sparks. Oooh, maybe it's a familiar, like Petty? Huh, a magical lily. How cool is that?"

The roaring in my head stopped, and only a terrible stillness remained.

Magic. Magical lily of the valley glycosides doing the impossible, and a magical book pointing the way?

No, I wasn't acting on hunches. I was right, I sensed it in every fiber of my paranormal being. The coven sheltered a killer.

Perhaps it had been an accident? Haywire skylles manifesting in mysterious ways? Magical fallout harming the innocent?

Desperation surged and swallowed me whole. From deep inside, a primal scream rose and exploded from my mouth.

"No, no, I've had enough of this! I don't want magic. I don't want to be a witch. I just want to be me."

In a blur of pink sparks, the miracle flower floated across, her soothing lemony scent reaching for me, leaves rustling with concern. A veil of tears and with it a wall of hurt rose between me and Petty. Petty—the embodiment of everything wrong with my world.

"No, you're magic. I don't want you. Go away."

"Myrtle, *no*." Jenna's face was masked by horror.

The primula stopped dead, wriggled once as if to acknowledge my words, before she zipped into the murky depths of the cellar.

In the wake of her sudden disappearance, a wave of sadness washed over me. It carried along the whimper of a puppy left to die in icy winter woods and the hopeless grief of a teenager whose parents died a fiery death. *My* parents. *My* grief. From deep inside, the long-forgotten but all too familiar pain rose, gripping my heart and twisting it with greedy fingers. Gasping for breath, I leaned into a dank pillar when suddenly the sadness burned out, leaving behind nothing but the taste of ashes and loss.

"What have you done?" Jenna whispered.

What had I done? Oh, I knew. By rejecting my magical plant, I had condemned her to death. She had come back twice. There would be no third time lucky.

My Petty.

"Oh no, first Dot, now this . . ." With a sob, Jenna swung away from me and raced up the cellar stairs.

I needed to know. To see Petty one last time. I stumbled off, blindly dodging pillar after pillar, fleeing the feeble glow thrown by the bulbs into a half-light that seemed to take on a presence, squeezing my chest with the weight of centuries gone by.

This place was enormous.

My shoes slapped on packed earth. No footsteps followed. I was alone, looking for sparks in the dark. The ashy taste on my tongue faded away, and I sensed only emptiness.

Ahead of me, a wall loomed, the end of an endless place.

The air was filled with the stink of moldering potatoes, together with something else. Something sickly sweet, like rotten citrus fruit.

"Petty?"

An unseen creature scratched over the floor and scuttled away from me.

I moved closer to the back wall, fumbling my way through the gloom. Why was there no electricity in this part of the blasted cellar?

I need light.

No sooner had I finished the thought than a fizzing warmth sped through my blood. It peaked on the scent of roses, and the next moment the cellar exploded into a blinding glare that stabbed into my head. My hands flew to my eyes, and violet flashes danced across the inside of my eyelids while fire rushed to my cheeks, followed by a velvety patter of something that feathered over my fingers and my arms.

Slowly, my vision adjusted to the brightness. The heat cooled down, even if my head still throbbed. Eons later, my pulse slowed until nothing but a faint niggle was left in my temples.

I dropped my hands, covered in the fading pinpricks of tiny thorns and stinging as if I had grasped a bunch of nettles. I looked at the floor. The ground was dotted with red rose petals.

The glare surrounded me, but there was no shadow at my feet.

I had hexed myself into some sort of torch.

In the bright light, I could make out something small and white next to the nearest pillar. I stepped closer, and the glow fell on Petty's bucket.

The primula's leaves and flowers, shriveled and bleached into the paleness of bones, lay spread across the cracked surface of the topsoil. Dark liquid stained the broken sides of the bucket. The ground underneath was moist. Petty must have expelled her water and withered away.

Because of me. Because I hated my magic. Because she thought I hated her. Yes, I had shouted at her to go away.

But I didn't mean it.

"Oh, Petty." Pain so savage I could hardly breathe stabbed my ribs. In the fading magical illumination, I fumbled for a leaf, nubby and vigorous when I last touched her. Brittle as autumn foliage now, it broke apart in my hand.

I need you. Please.

I was too late. She was gone.

I knelt on the hard ground and cradled the broken bucket. "Why is the bloody magic still here when you aren't?"

I don't know how long I stayed in that awful place as my witch light dimmed into the gloom sheltering my dead familiar.

It must have been a long, long time.

—

When I rose, one thought burned in my mind. Revenge. Whoever was killing those people carried Petty's death on their conscience.

You said the words.

"I didn't mean them." The whisper got swallowed into the dusk. Everything was pointless now.

No, not everything. I would find whoever was behind this. Then I would leave Avebury.

It shouldn't be too difficult. There weren't too many people with sufficient magic to do harm. Among the Wytchetts, Marty had no skylles, the boys were too young, and Dot wasn't "hale of body to do magic."

That left only Jenna.

My thoughts scuttled aside. There were others. There had to be.

Rosie and the Colonel had shown their skylles. Daisy once made candle flames dance. What about Mel or Linda? Mrs. Bingham? Mrs. Mornings? None of them could be responsible for such monstrous crimes, surely.

Nor could Jenna. She was a healer, for fright's sake.

Healers know about medicine.

My thoughts whizzed and whirled. Not to forget, with Dot down for the count, Jenna and I were the strongest of the lot. An iron band tightened around my chest, making it impossible to breathe.

Impossible. Oh yes, it all started with a word. As a result, my adorable, lively, clever magical primula left me forever.

"Oh, Petty, I never wanted you dead. Not you. Never you."

A monstrous wave of pain rolled out of the gloom, forcing me back down to the uncaring chill of the ground. Blindly, I reached out and found the bucket. My tears dropped on the blackened blooms, the rotting stalks barely visible in the somber darkness.

Zing. A spark flared. A second followed, hovering like a kindly eye. Together, they illuminated the scene.

Where my tears had fallen, the colors were brightening, spreading into the body of the plant. The shriveled stems filled out and the blooms returned. They flexed their petals, which turned a washed-out pink, barely visible in the halo that flickered around the primula. From underneath the bucket came a slurping sound, and the moist scent of fresh earth hit my nostrils.

Another pale spark shot from the center of one bloom and landed on my hand like the caress of a cat's paw. I bent closer, greedily inhaled the familiar lemony fragrance and listened to Petty's soothing whisper. I lowered my face to silky blooms that tickled the tears from my cheeks. The flowers still hung limp, but it didn't matter.

Petty was back. And never again must I lose her.

Remorse squeezed my heart. How many lives did a small spring plant possess? Nine like a cat? Less? More? I better not find out. Even a zombie primula would have its limits. Petty needed water, and I needed her. I knew that now. She was pure magic—my magic.

I couldn't change my nature. But if somebody had been careless enough to cause accidents, or—worse—been twisting the skylles to kill, that witch mustn't get away. No matter who they were.

Jenna's sweet, heart-shaped face blipped in my mind.

Intentional malice would be out of character. But then, I'd only known her for a couple of months. If it was her, there'd be a purpose behind the poisonings. She always had been in control of her powers.

Whatever was going on, I would have to find the truth, and do so quickly, before the cops got too close and exposed the coven.

With a heavy heart, a pounding head, and dirty knees, I rose from the floor. Petty's fractured bucket lifted with me, this time without the glitter. I had never been green-fingered, but my treatment of my familiar was the pits.

Zing. A pinkish flash zapped from pale pink blooms. Moral support from my mistreated floral companion.

"You're wonderful." I ran my hand through the floppy blossoms. There was so much about that miracle plant I didn't understand. Perhaps I never would.

Back at the stairs, I found my phone lying on the edge of the apple crate and Jenna nowhere in sight. I strode to the curtain, ripped it aside, and faced a longish painter's table snuggled against a wall daubed in a white saltpeter fluff. On the table-top, five massive glass jugs with fat bellies and narrow necks sat lined up in a row. Jars with preserves and a green gunk that was likely pesto stood at the edge.

What was wrong with this picture? Nothing, as far as I could see, so I heaved Petty's bucket back into the kitchen.

"Let me give you more water before we leave."

The bucket leaked, leaving brownish soil stains in the sink. A plastic bag I found on a chair would serve as a makeshift fix, but I needed the fiberglass pot.

Looking around, I found it on the terrace, brimming with soil.

Huh? Why would Jenna fill the pot when she must have thought the plant gone? A second, nastier thought nudged the first aside. What if she filled the pot before we arrived? If that was the case, what had my friend been doing in the cellar? She couldn't have been looking for soil. Why would she lie to me?

—

It took Petty and me over a day to recover from the horror in the cellar. I even sent Chris away when he called. Thursday at lunchtime, however, my plant restored to her former robustness and my demons back in their boxes, I headed for the café to search for the Wiccans—and answers.

14

COP CHASE

All the tables in the Magic Mushroom Café were taken, but here and there a chair, metal and the same fire-engine red as the tables, remained unoccupied. The air-conditioned interior of the café echoed with the chatter of many voices, its patrons displaying a colorful blend of piercings, Goth makeup, and white robes. Chairs scraped over slate gray tiles, the vintage farming implements strung up on the wall—sickles, seed planters, and even a yoke—clashing in style. Pan and Gerry, both in spanking new hiking gear but sans locust wings, were sitting at the rear. No doubt they would offer me a seat. But I was after the Wiccans.

Both my mother and Aunt Eve had scolded me for "shooting from the hip," and they had been right. Before doing anything rash I might later regret—such as confronting Jenna—I needed facts. Sarah had told me what she could. More than that, actually. The Wiccans were my only other lead.

For once, I got lucky. Quiet where others were chatting, the sleeves of her black dress pushed up her brawny arms, the Wiccan doctor sat in a corner alone at a table for two. With a vacant expression, she nursed a cup of tea, an untouched slice of carrot cake waiting on a plate at her elbow.

What nosy parker would intrude on her grief? Only someone desperate to find the truth before the police did.

I stepped up to the service counter. For once, I didn't suffer from hunger pangs, but I needed an excuse to join the Wiccan. The mozzarella, tomato, and pesto sandwich looked appetizing enough, and it might come in handy later.

"Would you like that toasted?" the girl behind the glass display asked me with a grin that made the freckles on her nose dance.

"Yes, please. And an iced tea."

My snack paid for, I weaved my way around the tables, the tray a protective shield in front of my chest.

"Is this seat taken?"

The Wiccan looked up and gave me a ghost of a smile. She waved at the empty chair. I thanked her and sat on a metal surface hard enough to serve as penance. When I sipped my tea, my innards twisted into knots. This wouldn't be easy.

The woman lowered her head once more. Her grizzled afro, almost buzzing with energy, belied her listless pose. A tear coursed down a tawny cheek.

I handed her a tissue.

"Thank you. Sorry, but a dear friend of mine just died." She dabbed at her face.

Sometimes honesty is all we have. "I was there when it happened. My . . . friend supported you with the first aid. You did what you could."

"I'm a physician. I should've been able to save her. Hannah was as healthy as a horse."

I laced my voice with calmness. "You'll think I'm crowding you, and you're right. Still, I find your friend's death deeply disturbing. What disturbs me even more—apart from the bull-dozer approach taken by certain police officials—is that you were talking about glycosides."

Her head came up. Alertness returned to her eyes. "Who are you?"

"Not the police, for one thing. DI Diloff is giving you a hard time, correct?"

She raised her chin and then dropped it.

"I'm Myrtle. I run the Witch's Retreat B&B here in the village. We met in Knick-Knack's . . . the gift shop a few days ago. Not sure if you remember. I'm also a friend of the pubkeep-er. He called me after he found the dead musician. You shared your food with them, didn't you?"

For a moment it was touch and go. Then the tension flowed out of her muscles. "Oh, yes. That poor man. They played their beautiful, beautiful music, but he ran out of air. His lips were blue. You didn't need a medical background to spot the guy's heart trouble."

"The cops seem to think you gave him some medicine."

"Mother Hecate, no. I advised them to see a specialist, but they were too scared. They're probably illegals. He told me he suffered from insomnia because of the weather, but I tell you that must've been the least of his problems. Anyway, I'm guilty of slipping him a mild sedative made of hops and valerian. After ensuring he would be okay with it, of course. I prepare the pills myself. They're tried and trusted, and I took some the other night."

"Did you tell the cops?"

"Hah, yes. They confiscated the lot, looking for their murder weapon. We're not supposed to leave the area while they're running tests. Let them—they won't find anything amiss with my sedatives. I would never, ever, put anybody on heart medi-cation without a proper checkup. That's insane." She balled her hands into fists.

"Ah, but the investigating officer doesn't listen, correct?"

I took a bite of my sandwich. Not because I was hungry, but because she looked like she needed the comfort of food and wouldn't eat without me.

It worked. The Wiccan cut off a piece of carrot cake with her fork, chewed, and swallowed. "You know that moron?"

"Oh, yes. He's prone to quick fixes."

"He won't fix me. I've never used lily of the valley for my heart patients, so there's no way they can pin this on me."

A bucket of ice water poured down my back wouldn't have chilled me more. My hunch triggered by the magical image had been spot on.

"Lily of the valley? Not digitalis?"

"No, the DI kept harping on about the lily, but I don't think his sergeant was pleased about that. She mentioned only cardiac glycosides in general. Both foxglove and lily of the valley are highly poisonous, and they have similar uses. Personally, I prefer foxglove, but I ran out of stock."

She wagged her head. "Ah, I remember. I considered ordering digitalis in the gift shop, didn't I? That gorgeous saleswoman told me she couldn't get it for me. Are you two related? You look quite a bit alike."

That was probably meant as a compliment. "Well-spotted— we're cousins. Uh, since you seem to know your herbs, am I right that the symptoms of an overdose are similar both for the lily and for foxglove?"

"They are. Trouble is, I've no idea when and how Hannah would've taken either. We were together all the time, saying a prayer for the departed flutist." She pulled a face. "Or, we tried. The henge was crawling with tourists. These idiots despoil a sacred place. We come to worship and what do we get? Noise pollution and people who stumble all over the place and take selfies with the stones. It's a disgrace."

"Mh, maybe you should meet our Dot. She's harboring the same gripe. Never mind. Did Hannah leave the group at any point?"

"No. We arrived together, and we stayed together. We had dinner, and she fell sick soon after. Complained about queasiness and was hyperventilating. I didn't like that one bit, but I thought it might be food poisoning. We have no fridge or anything. When she went downhill in a hurry, I called the ambulance. I wanted her to walk around to work off some adrenaline. Lorna, she's another member of my coven, came with us. Hannah freaked, saw halos around things, and screamed Lorna was attacking her. Then her stomach troubles worsened."

She drained her cup in one go. Her fingers, broad and capable, crumbled the rest of the carrot cake.

My mouth dry, I took a sip of my iced tea. The ice cubes floating in the drink had melted and diluted the brew.

My gaze slipped from the glass to her plate. "Tell me, did you all eat the same food?"

"Yes, that's the funny part, and none of which we prepared ourselves. We've got stoves, but only to heat things up. I live in Marlborough. Theoretically, I could go home, but the days before the solstice are sacred to us. It's all about being together and away from our daily lives. So, we camp here and shop in the grocery. Oh, and we bought some spreads and wines from the gift shop and some sandwiches here at the café."

All of it local, which wasn't good. "Each time?"

"Once our original provisions ran out, yes. It's exactly what we did the day we met the musicians. Those guys were half-starving, so we did the decent thing and shared."

"Including the cans."

"Spaghetti rings were Hannah's favorite, and the last thing she ever ate. But Lorna and Aimée ate them, too. They even cooked the contents of three cans in one pot. We all drank wine. Mother Hecate, this has got to be a bad dream." She clawed at her hair.

I reached across the table and squeezed her clammy hand. If I were Jenna, I might send comforting thoughts. Being who I was, I could only share my touch.

It must have helped though, since her features softened. I debated whether to hold my questioning right there and to stop causing her pain. But I was on the track of something monstrously important, and every fiber in my body quivered with the need to learn more.

"I heard the contents of the cans were okay, at least the ones Boian had with him. The dead flutist, I mean. Can you recollect what you bought and where and when? It might help you with the cops."

She looked up. "The sergeant tried to ask the same question, but her moronic boss stopped her. I swear to you, he's got medicine on his mind."

"He operates that way, unfortunately. Now, if it's not medicine, perhaps there's a problem with the food. And if that's true, you're off the hook."

That was assuming the Wiccan had told me the truth. But her grief and shock struck me as genuine. For a fleeting instant I hated the woman seated next to me. If she wasn't guilty, my fears about magic, about Jenna, might be justified. But that was hardly the Wiccan's fault.

"Well, after shopping on Friday, we shared with the musicians. That much I remember. We then bought some more of those lovely dips and nibbles on . . . Saturday, I think it was. On Monday, we ran out of stuff because we had given so much away. We visited the grocery, the gift shop, and the café. They do great sandwiches here."

I looked at my plate. A lonely tomato slice remained, and I hadn't tasted a thing.

My companion tapped her teeth. "You know what? This is odd. We shop, we share the stuff, and a musician dies. We do more shopping and Hannah dies."

The Wiccan and I traded gazes.

"Once the provisions we brought with us ran out, we only ever shopped in the village," she said slowly. "You're right. It's got to be something we bought here. But as I told you, we shared everything during our last dinner. Why Hannah and not anybody else?"

"I've got no clue whatsoever, but you'd better talk to your legal person. He or she can drip feed this idea to the police." With a bit of luck, it would take them long enough for me to work out what was going on and then come up with a solution that didn't feature magic. No idea how to pull off such a stunt, but I had to. I'd need luck on my side, though.

The door slammed open, and I glanced over my shoulder.

Rats. It appeared luck was indeed on my side, but it wasn't of the kind I needed.

Sarah and her beastly boss, DI Diloff, entered the café.

Human instincts are amazing. Nothing about Sarah or Diloff announced their profession. His crumpled white shirt and stained tie might have belonged to a third-class accountant. Sarah wore another of her lightweight suits, this one in muted blues. It was elegant enough to be worn in a boardroom by an expensive consultant. But still the chatter in the café died down. The clatter of crockery stilled and many pairs of eyes sought the exit, most likely working out how to get out before the questioning began.

A whisper sprang up and spread through the café. "It's the pigs."

The two officers stepped closer to the counter, and I twisted in my seat to keep them in sight. Diloff's bulging eyes glittered, his nose on the twitch as he scanned the room. Once his gaze hooked on my companion, a pleased smirk tugged at the corners of his babyish mouth, framed by a sharply clipped graying beard.

"Hello, everybody," he boomed. "Relax, we're not here for you. Well, not this time. We're here for her." He pointed across the room at my companion.

Sarah seemed intrigued by the straw wreath decorated with poppies and cornflowers that decorated the wall behind the serving counter. She stood to Diloff's left, as far away from his stocky body as was possible without running into the cash counter.

The eyes of the Wiccan blazed, and she rose in her seat. I seized her hand and whispered, "Don't let him rile you. He's waiting for that."

She sat again, her nails digging into the soft flesh of her palms.

I had spoken under my breath, but since the café had fallen quiet, my remark was heard.

Crap.

Sarah's head swiveled my way. I blipped a smile. She didn't return it.

"My, my, what have we got here? Ms. Coldron to the rescue." Diloff's voice pierced the clouds of resentment filling the room. The girl at the counter restacked the napkins she had been straightening.

The two Goths at the first table rose, their chairs scraping over the concrete floor like nails over a blackboard. With an insolent shuffle, they pushed through the entrance, their expression of disdain wasted on Diloff.

The door creaked shut behind them.

"You've interviewed, as you choose to call it, all of us," the Wiccan said into the calm that sizzled through the café. "You've searched our tents and our cars. Especially mine. Since we've got nothing to hide, we let you do your duty. Stop harassing us. Stop harassing me."

A murmur sprang up, and angry glances were fired at the police officers and bounced off them as if they were shielded.

Diloff's eyes narrowed and a sneer distorted his face. "Sergeant Widdlethorpe, do the honors."

"We have reason to believe you are in the habit of dispensing the type of toxin instrumental in the two deaths we are investigating." Sarah's voice was so wooden, she might have been reading from a textbook. She could do better than that, and she usually did. "We need to search your practice. I would ask you to accompany us."

"How dare you? Why?"

"Somebody had better open the door, lady. Unless you would prefer us to break it down." Diloff's smirk widened. "Before you ask, yes, we have a warrant." He curled his index finger in a come-hither gesture.

This time I couldn't stop my companion from jumping up. "Are you arresting me? I'll call my lawyer."

Diloff opened his mouth, but Sarah was faster. "No, we aren't. I suggest we discuss this outside." She swung around and opened the door.

"What about my friends? They'll worry when I don't return."

"You can ring those ladies from our nice, air-conditioned police vehicle. There's plenty of time," Diloff said. "Do we need to repeat the invitation? I wouldn't advise it."

Anger flared up in the café like a bushfire. People jumped from their seats, chairs fell over, whistling and shouting broke out. I rose with the others, digging in my backpack for a business card. I pressed it into the Wiccan's hand.

"Here, take this. If there's anything you need, call me."

"Thank you. They'll regret that." Her eyes blazing, she stormed for the door and barged outside.

For a moment, Sarah's gaze and mine met across the room. She gave her head a quick shake and then snapped her professional mask back in place and followed the Wiccan.

Diloff's gaze homed in on me. "Ms. Coldron, I'm telling you once and only once—keep your nose out of police business. If I get even an inkling you might be involved, I'll have your place turned upside down. Bet your guests won't like that."

Fueled by the Petty disaster, my worries over Jenna, and the coven's fate, my heart accelerated to a flat-out gallop, shooting adrenaline into my bloodstream. Not that I needed another incentive, but I would move the world to find the truth ahead of DI Dickhead, if it was the last thing I did. First, however, that ponce deserved a downer.

The eyes of the crowd were on me when I spoke. "Mr. Diloff

. . . oops, Detective Inspector, rest assured, I have no intention of interfering with your investigations. I'm sure there's plenty of people around willing to help you." I winked at him and sat, letting my arm dangle over the backrest of the chair with fake insouciance.

The café erupted with cheering and catcalls. Several rather large men headed for the inspector, their expressions a lot less than amicable.

Diloff, in an untypical display of intelligence, backed through the door. Outside, a motor fired up.

Somewhat out of breath, I bounced off my chair and shot after him. I weaved my way around the tables, accompanied by applause and shouted advice on how to deal with the force. Sadly, the suggestions were rather violent and mostly impractical.

As I popped from the exit, the police car rolled toward the corner of the café before it disappeared down the small access road to the car park.

The Wiccan had drawn the fire, but for how long?

15

A DASH OF PESTO

"Myrtle?" The male voice sounded familiar. I swung around and there was Chris, appearing from behind the trolley stacked with used trays, a concerned expression on his face.

"What are you doing?" I asked.

"Hiding. I called from the balcony when you crossed the car park, but you didn't hear me. Gave me the impression you were on a mission and better left alone for the moment. When Diloff and Sarah joined the party, I decided I might be useful as a backup. I figured you'd sort out Diloff in no time. Had blood seeped out from under the door, I could always have galloped to the rescue."

The door sprang open and guests trickled out, recalling their run-in with the cops and bouncing me friendly smiles and nods.

"Sorry for brushing you off yesterday."

"No worries. Are you okay?" He reached out, and I held on

to his hand.

"I am now. Thanks a million for your patience."

"All part of the service. Though, you can't tease me with magical doodles and then go into hiding." Chris winked.

I owed him the truth. The whole sordid story about the murders and the magic. How in the world was I supposed to share a revelation like that with the man I would love to get to know a bit—a lot—better?

Frantic butterflies beat their wings in my throat. I had no idea how he would take the news. But he needed to hear it.

I swallowed hard. Poor butterflies.

"That image is only one problem."

"Let me guess. You won't leave things well alone."

"Would you? And there's more. You don't even have the full picture yet."

He tilted his head. "What I saw Monday night was bad enough. Until your friend Sarah runs the show, I'm not confident the cops will ever find the truth. Should you wish to, eh, assist her, you can count on me. Ah, had a word with Greg earlier, and he's plenty pissed off. He sends his regards and asks if you need lamb chops. Apparently, he's got tons and nobody to eat them."

"Isn't the pub open?"

"Yes, but there isn't much going on. Word has spread and quite a few of the tourists are leaving."

"That's exactly what Alma feared would happen. Okay, where can we talk?"

"You're herewith invited to my humble abode." Chris pressed his palms together in front of his chest and bowed from the waist.

His antics triggered a giggle, and for a precious moment life was almost normal.

—

Chris's studio was functional, cool, and free of the clutter I had discovered the one time I "cleaned" in his room when he was staying at the Witch's Retreat. No boxer shorts on the hairy coconut runner that led to a closed door at the end of the corridor. The kitchenette behind the high counter and barstools sported aluminum cupboards, their space-age look fit only for catalogs. They stain if you so much as breathe on them. Yet not a single thumbprint showed on their immaculate surface. What I could see of the living area also appeared pristine. The furnishings were a bit wild for my taste. Black shelves and two settees in a red-and-black houndstooth pattern faced a coffee table lacquered a virulent shade of candy apple. Maybe Chris had cleared the space in the hope I would show up? Now that would be a true sign of affection. A lonely butterfly fluttered in my throat, still hopeful.

Chris opened the mini fridge. "How about something to drink? You've got the choice between beer, lemonade—well, Irn Bru, or a Coke."

"Coffee, perhaps?"

"Sorry, no time to buy coffee pods and the mobile bakery didn't sell them, which is why I bought some cake things instead." He hooked his thumb at brown paper bags lying on the microwave.

He was guilty as charged—the man had come prepared. A second butterfly joined its buddy. "Would you have water?"

He pointed at the tap and smirked.

"That'll do, thanks."

Chris banged cupboards open and took out mismatched plates and glasses that must have been peanut butter jars in a previous life. He then opened the freezer compartment and removed a tray with posh metal ice cubes. They clinked into the glass, which he filled at the tap before handing it over. Chris had style, but I knew that already.

I drank, balancing my glass with utmost care lest the cubes slid out and down my décolleté or something similarly embarrassing. I also have style, even if mine is on a different planet from Chris's.

"Ahh, that's better." He rolled the can over his forehead. "Right, let's sit down, and you can tell me what you've been up to when I wasn't watching." Chris popped another Irn Bru, which he lifted to his mouth but didn't drink from. Instead, his inky eyes observed me from over the rim of the can. Deep and dark, they seemed to suck me right in.

"Did you know your nose twitches when you're annoyed or upset?"

"No. And I'm not annoyed." Upset, yes. He nailed that one.

"Let's sit outside. There's a nice breeze." He grabbed the brown paper bags, and I followed him, my glass in one hand.

Chris pushed open the sliding glass door that opened on a narrow balcony built from the same dark wood as the stairs. It was shaded by beech trees that rustled in the wind. Two rickety deck chairs were the only furniture, so I lowered myself onto the faded green canvas and handed Chris his can.

"Ta. Fancy a doughnut?" He dangled the bag in front of me. "They're filled with cream. I figured you'd like them."

I wasn't hungry, but I welcomed any opportunity to push off the inevitable for a little while longer. When I bit into the fluffy dough, a fat white dollop landed on my shorts.

"Cripes." I grabbed a napkin from the paper bag, dunked it into my water, and rubbed away. The tissue disintegrated.

Chris's lips twitched. "So, what did you find in your grimoire? Can I see it? And what else has been going on that made you go into hiding for two days?"

I freaked over my magic and killed my familiar.

"Let's start with the picture. Remember what you told me about the people living close to stone circles? I'm pretty sure this image tried to tell us where some of them might have gone."

"Didn't you notice the picture before?"

"Not really, since it was invisible."

"Myrtle—"

"I'll explain in a minute. First, look at this." I thumbed for the photos and handed my phone to Chris.

That done, I leaned back in my deck chair and watched as the sunlight twinkled through the soothing green canopy of leaves. Cocooned in the afternoon warmth, I should have relaxed. Instead, my shoulder muscles hardened into rocky lumps and the butterflies beat up a storm.

How should I voice my suspicions about the magic and the murders? Wouldn't he run? Perhaps I was doing him an injustice.

Chris's voice cut across the turmoil. "Okay, I need to print this out and take a closer look. If you ask me, your theory is spot on. This looks to depict the exodus of the Whites. Unfortunately, I don't think we're any wiser about their ultimate destination. How old is your recipe book?" He glanced at me, dark curls falling over his elegant brows.

He wouldn't have looked better if I had dreamed him up. A whole swarm of ever-hopeful butterflies migrated to my stomach. I shouldn't have eaten that doughnut.

"Ah, Damian also wondered about that. No idea. My great-etcetera-aunt penned her notes to posterity over two hundred years ago. Interestingly enough, she started at the back of the book, as if she knew the empty pages weren't truly empty."

My phone in his hand, Chris stared into the greenery as if enlightenment were to be found among the leaves. In the car park, people were talking while engines idled their exhaust fumes into the country air.

"Right. Let's start at the beginning. How did you make that image visible?"

"Well, I wasn't planning to. Things just happened. And it's gone again. Luckily, Petty helped me take a photo before it faded."

Chris raised his head and observed me for a moment before he sank back into his chair with a groan.

The butterflies belly flopped. "Hello? The recipe book doesn't come with a Q&A on hexing."

"Such a shame. How is Damian involved?"

"Internet searches."

Chris nodded. "I'll do the same. I'll focus on those scribbles I believe to be two sets of star constellations. They might help us with dating the image."

"Damian also thought of star patterns. You two had better coordinate your efforts."

"I'll try. Are you okay with me emailing myself a copy?" He waggled my phone.

"Sure."

Chris's nimble fingers danced over the screen. "Done." He bent forward, to the deck chair's creaked protest, and handed back my phone. "Now, let's hear whatever else is bothering you."

I gave him a boiled-down version of my conversations with Sarah and the Wiccan but held back my suspicions about the magic. One step at a time.

"The poison must originate from lily of the valley, and somehow it ended up in the food. Nothing else makes sense. I bet you Sarah had the same idea, hence the questions she asked before she got steamrolled by Diloff."

The last words left my mouth when my brain connected thoughts it had previously stored in separate compartments. I struggled to stand up, and the chair collapsed under me.

Chris, ever the valiant knight, burst out laughing. "Myr, you're funny. You really are."

"Blast it, help me."

He levered himself from his chair to pull me from the wreckage, sniggering. Too agitated to sit, I paced the few steps it took to stalk the balcony, turned around, and faced him again.

"The Wiccan doc told me her coven bought the canned spaghetti rings at the grocery."

"Yeah, and? You might want to verify her statements."

"Eh, the ones Boian had been given were harmless, Sarah said so, and I could bet the same applies to the contents of the three cans consumed by the Wiccans. Otherwise, they'd all be dead. Don't you see? It means the poison must've been in the stuff they picked up at Knick-Knack's or in the café's sandwiches."

Another mental compartment sprung open and spat out the drawing on the magical image with its leaves and bells that Jenna had suspected to be a lily of the valley. Then the vision changed, morphing into broad, flowerless fronds of wild garlic growing on the barren soil of early spring. The pesto jars on the table in Jenna's cellar could have been standing on the balustrade, so clearly could I see them in my mind.

Panic flared, hot and urgent. I had eaten a pesto sandwich earlier. Then the panic ebbed away. I was still alive.

"The pesto." I faced Chris.

"What about it?"

"Lily of the valley can get mistaken for wild garlic. It's silly, honestly. They don't even grow at the same time."

"You're not trying to tell me the pesto in this place is poisoned? People would be dying like flies."

"Not all of it, for sure. However, unless my memory's gone on the blink, Boian's stomach contents included the stuff."

Chris pulled at his earlobe. "Mh, I vaguely remember words to that effect. In any case, he must have eaten a bizarre mixture of things."

"Let's run with the pesto theory for the moment. If I'm right, we might be dealing with something worse than murder."

"What do you mean 'worse'?" He slapped his forehead with his palm. "Now I get it. Mutant garlic. Taking over the village. All is lost. Run."

That wasn't even remotely funny. "Not mutants. Magic."

Chris stilled, and his brows quirked into a V. "You'd better explain."

Here it comes.

I couldn't look him in the eyes anymore. "What if somebody's hexed the pesto?"

"Uh, what? You must be joking. Who would do such a thing? And why?"

"Unless it's all a horrid accident, Jenna is the only logical candidate who comes to mind. Search me as to the why—I have no clue." My voice had taken on an odd squeak.

He stood and leaned on the balustrade. "The complete story, if you'd be so kind."

There it was, the silkiness in his tone I didn't like. Still, what could I do? I mustered my courage and relived Tuesday's panic, horrors, and suspicions while Chris listened without butting in a single word until I was finished.

"Blast it, Myrtle, you need to be more careful. You're lucky you didn't lose your plant. The poor little thing."

"I know that, all right?"

"Good. As to the rest of your harebrained story, you keep telling me your posse doesn't command enough magic to butter their toasts, and now you want me to believe paranormal fallout can kill? How would a random effect manifest in a specific location? The other theory is even worse. I mean, come on, why would Jenna hex the pesto?"

"Told you, I don't know. Given the bizarre symptoms, magic is the only explanation I have. I fear you're right about it being deliberate, though. It's more in line with what Dot says about the skylles. Not every jar either, by any means. Just a few of them, and most likely they get slipped into the local outlets in intervals. That's the only way it can work. Chris, I hate the whole idea. But I can't discard it."

"Mh, perhaps not. But Jenna? Just because you saw pesto jars in her cellar and you ate a sandwich with the stuff? That's wild."

"She's the strongest of the lot. Apart from myself, of course. Dot's too ill. The laundry list was quite clear on the physical fitness required for hexing."

The V formed by Chris's brows grew more pronounced. "What if it's someone you don't have on the radar?"

"Then I don't know what to do." My words came out as a wail. "I don't know," I repeated, forcing myself to sound calm and reasonable. "I'm sorry. This is a complete and utter shambles. But there's a chance I'm right, and in that case, I fully understand if you don't want to have anything more to do with us."

"Myrtle."

I swung away from him, tears blurring my vision. Chris grabbed my arm and pulled me hard against his chest.

"Myrtle, stop it." His voice a soft hush in my ear. "Who do you take me for? I won't run just because you're haring off on another tangent."

"What if it's no tangent?"

"In that case, you aren't responsible for anything. Instead, you're trying to work out what's going on. And you will, you know?"

His arms pressed tighter, and I was acutely aware of his body close to mine.

"Will I?" I suppressed a sniffle.

"Oh yes, and I'll help you, you adorable idiot. I can't say I like the scenario, but there might be a perfectly rational explanation. You got ambushed by magic, and you nearly offed your primula. It's all a bit much," he said in a soothing tone.

"Mh," I responded, somewhat distracted, the butterflies revived. He still wanted me, and it was all that counted.

"I won't kiss you."

What? I turned my head and searched his concerned eyes.

"The last time I tried, somebody died. And even if I think you're no better than Diloff, conjuring up theories and suspects, I suspect you might be on to something, even if I'm not sure what exactly it is. That thought is a bit—disturbing."

Reluctantly, I broke contact. "You mean I'm right about the food being tainted? Or the hexing? Or both?"

Chris's slender fingers drummed on the railing. "The food scenario strikes me as being quite realistic, especially since Sarah must have come to the same conclusion. The hexing I'm not sure about since somebody in the know could have souped up the poison. Like your friendly Wiccan. I think you ought to establish if the good doctor was talking the truth. Otherwise, I agree that you can't risk having the coven exposed. Jenna I find an unlikely suspect. Okay, I understand she's more competent than the rest, but still."

My head spun. "If not her, who else? We're missing something."

"Mh, you might want to find out who produces that blasted pesto. On the off chance there's a connection. What about your cousin?"

"Daisy? What about her? For one thing, she's no cook. Plus, her skylles seem to be missing in action. Nor is she a bad person. A tick flighty is all."

"Your aunt was pretty clued up, wasn't she? So are you. Why not your cousin? Still waters can run deep, you know? She's definitely selling the pesto. I was in the shop this morning to get myself some marmalade, and I'm sure I saw it on the shelves."

Daisy? She craved to be a real witch. However, my cousin's bellyaching about her missing skylles rang true. But there was more.

"The gift shop delicacies are prepared by the local WI. My cousin's a member. So are Jenna, Mel, and Linda."

"Witches Institute?"

"Efforts to lighten the mood are appreciated. Institute, yes. Witches, no. At least to the best of my knowledge most of those women aren't witches. They wanted me to join, but a lot of effort is involved. They support the community. You know, church fairs, charity events, excursions for the elderly—the works."

"Between running a B&B, protecting your fellow witches from themselves, and acting the sleuth, I agree you won't have time for that."

"Nope. Okay, fair enough. I'll talk to my cousin and see how she reacts. At the very least she'll be able to confirm if the Wiccan was speaking the truth, and she can put me in touch with the other WI members. Might be useful."

"Do that. You'll also need to wheedle more information out of

Sarah. If these victims suffered from the same symptoms, they must indeed come from the same source, pesto or no pesto. The police lab must be able to work that out. How come these pagans ate the same stuff and only one of them died? What is the connection between a dead musician and a dead Wiccan? Those are the questions you need to ask yourself. And once Sarah gets rid of that bigoted rhino, she'll do the same."

The conversation was bizarre. Here we were, standing close to each other discussing sleuthing strategies and murderous magic. On the plus side, Chris was still with me, and he had joined my crusade. One thing, however, still wasn't right.

"I'll talk to Daisy and take it from there. But not now."

"Why not? She's definitely in the shop."

I stepped closer to him, a smile tickling the corners of my mouth. "Right now, I would like to continue where we left off the other day."

His eyes crinkled as he smiled back and closed his arms around my waist. "Can you promise there won't be more dead bodies?"

"I've forgotten my crystal ball. Even if I hadn't, I'd probably drop it, and glass shards are bad news. Can we pretend everything's okay? Just for a moment? Is it?" I nuzzled his cheek and breathed in his spicy scent.

"It is."

It was.

16

TAINTED GOODS

High on cloud nine, I would have floated down the stairs to Chris's apartment if only I had sussed out the bit with the self-levitation. The murders, the image, the coven, the heat—they all had withdrawn to the recess of my consciousness, giving way to a heady bliss as if my bloodstream were fizzling with magic. Chris was with me and, better still, we were drifting closer. In a wild moment after our kiss, I had promised to make good use of Greg's proffered lamb chops and cook us dinner tomorrow. As much as we wanted to see each other beforehand, he was leaving again for a brief assignment. Such is life.

As daydreams go, mine was short-lived. Once my espadrilles thudded onto the pavement, I returned to solid ground on more than one count. It was time to park my cloud with its pals piling up in the east and zoom back in on the tasks at hand.

Like last time, the discordant jangling of cowbells announced my arrival at Knick-Knack's. Unlike last time, my cousin did not waylay me in the aisles, but waited at the counter, yawning.

"Oh, sorry, Myr, this place has gone, like, totally dead." Daisy pulled her auburn braid through her fingers, the beginnings of a frown wrinkling the porcelain perfection of her face. "You look a bit out of sorts. What's wrong?"

Apart from two corpses, potentially lethal magic, and the coven at risk of exposure? Not much, really.

Before I could respond, Daisy dropped her braid and leaned over the counter, her eyes brighter than the ceiling lights. "Have you heard? You must have—it's all over the news. There's a killer on the loose. Poison, they say. People dying all over the place, they say."

"They? With slogans like that, it's no wonder the tourists are on the run. That's why it's so quiet in here. To be fair, the pagans are still around."

"Ah. I didn't think of that."

I swallowed a sarcastic comment, as it wouldn't be appreciated and most likely would stop Daisy from answering the questions burning in my mind. First, I needed her to verify the Wiccan's statement. Following up on my suspicions concerning the magic and her potential involvement would be a lot trickier.

"Do you remember the Wiccans? They shopped here when I visited last Friday. The coven leader tried to order digitalis. Tall, black dress, and a grizzled afro."

A blank gaze was the only response.

"Actually, they showed up more than once. When I was with you on Saturday, it must've been their second visit. You were amazing, the way you made them buy every single silk scarf. You're ever so good at selling stuff."

If the deepening wrinkles on Daisy's forehead were anything to go by, she was cranking up her brain processes.

Her response, when it finally came, was a non sequitur. "I guess it's an okay job. Told you, I like it better than the bar. This place is full of beautiful things."

I took a deep breath. "Eh, you do recall them? The Wiccans, I mean?"

"Of course."

Progress at last. "They bought some WI delicacies. Can you remember which ones?"

Did I say Daisy's brain worked in mysterious ways? She raised her head and twitched her perky nose like a hound on the scent. "Ooh, you mean they bought something to poison people with? Have they got arrested, then?"

"Not to the best of my knowledge. I have the nasty suspicion the products were already compromised before these ladies even put their hands on them."

A furtive peek at my cousin revealed nothing more incriminating than a puzzled frown. "You're telling me one of the WI is selling poisoned goodies? Or let somebody tamper with them? No way."

Never forget Daisy is a lot more intelligent than she lets on.

"Way. The products from the grocery must've been okay, which tends to indicate the café or this shop as the source. Of course, that's assuming I'm on the right track. I don't have the same intel as the cops."

Daisy clacked her lacquered nails on the counter. "Why do you even bother? I mean, Greg's safe, so why are you doing Sarah's job for her?"

A good question, which called for a doctored version of the truth. "Uh, her boss will arrest anything not up in the trees on the count of three. There's no point in giving her more hints because he'll muscle in. First, he went after Greg. Now the Wiccan is under fire as we speak. No idea what that moron is up to next. Daisy, somebody's got to stop him. It might as well be me."

My cousin played with the tip of her braid. "All right, then. They paid with plastic. Both times. I found it funny. Those traditional costumes and then credit cards. Made them stand out from the crowd."

"I get your point. But it doesn't tell me what exactly they bought."

"They only play at being witches. They're not real." Daisy hid a giggle behind her hand. "If only they knew who served them. Dot vented a bit once they were gone."

Oh, cripes. It never occurred to me to talk to Dot, preoccupied as I was with the Petty disaster. She might be hard to handle, but she was also the only person who could run a reality check on my theory about the murderous magic. I took a mental note to get hold of Jen's gran.

"What do you mean by 'vented'?"

"Dot believes people shouldn't pretend they're witch folk when they're not. They're normal human beings with a lot of imagination but no skylles."

Magical weaklings, all of us. Our ancestors were found wanting and left behind, and the coven was struggling with our guerrilla magical powers, but there was nothing like despising somebody else if one needed to feel superior.

"Sounds as if she's suffering from a Muggle complex."

"Muddle?" Daisy wiggled her nose, and we were now seriously off-topic.

"Forget about Dot. Let's come back to the Wiccans. Would you have a list of their purchases somewhere?"

"Nothing detailed, but give me a mo." Daisy bent under the counter to retrieve a slim ledger. She licked her fingers as she flipped through and speared an entry with her fingernail. "Here they are. I enter every transaction. For the inventory, see?"

"Clever." And useful.

"Bear with me. It's funny, but when I see the total and the date, I can remember what most people bought. It's like a film rolling in here." She tapped her temple.

I thought of *Titanic*.

"Right, all coming back to me now. On Friday, that group of Wiccans bought mainly dips, nibbles, marmalades, and wines. We offer elderberry and rosehip, and they took both. The biggest sale was on Saturday, when they purchased the scarves, some herbs, and dips and stuff. They returned on Monday, and they shopped for more of the same."

"It would really help me to know what exactly they bought."

She scrutinized her ledger. "Says here 'delicatessen miscellaneous,' but as I told you, I remember these things. They didn't seem to like the lemon curd—they bought it only once. Otherwise, they must have gone through a lot of Jen's apple chutney, the nut sauce, and the wine. Hm, what else? Ah, yes. On each occasion they purchased a jar of pesto together with the garlic crackers, and almond biscuits." Daisy closed the little ledger and gave me a caustic look. "I don't get it. Sorry, but this is, like, loopy?"

It was, but it confirmed what the doctor had told me. Boian had died Friday night after accepting the fatal gift and Hannah on Monday night after the third shopping spree. Each time, the Wiccans seemed to have gone for the same products—pesto included.

"Mh," I said. "The Wiccan who died had spaghetti rings for dinner. However, her friends ate from the same pot, so it can't have been that. Plus, the cans and the water the dead musician had with him were harmless. No, it's got to be something else."

I took the plunge and explained my theory about the lily poison ending up in the pesto. "Not sure if the young woman ate it. The musician definitely did."

When I sneaked another glance at Daisy, she appeared surprised.

"Sorry, I don't buy it. No way would the ladies make such a nasty mistake." She hooked a thumb at the shelves behind us. "Our goodies are ever so popular. The café even uses our dips and sauces. Surely if something were wrong, we'd have noticed by now."

"Not every jar would be poisoned, obviously. Listen, I'd better talk to the WI. I need to understand how this all works."

Daisy rubbed her nose in thought. "Health and Safety is

forever sniffing through the WI's kitchens and ensuring the lids are sealed properly. Makes me glad I'm just the hired help." She laughed, but it sounded bitter.

"Care to explain?"

Her expression segued to sullen. "Oh, it's nothing. I fetch things and bring them here. Stock the shelves. I do it for most of them. Gives me a reason for driving my new car."

What was my cousin's problem? I had no time to fumble my way through the maze that was Daisy's mind. And we were getting off-topic again. That happened a lot when I was around her.

Daisy must have reached the same conclusion. She gave me another dose of the furtive look. "Come on, give. I know you. There's something else."

Here was my cue. Caught by surprise, she wouldn't be able to mask her feelings, so I made sure to keep her gaze. "Spot on. A few of the coven members joined the WI, correct?"

Daisy jerked. "You mean tainted as in hexed? Oh, no, no, that's impossible." She giggled, but it fizzled out. "You're kidding me. We can't." Her face had paled, and she took a step backward. "Oh, no. This would be beyond awful."

"I kid you not. See, the poison seems to be super strong, and it acts fiendishly quickly. The first victim was ill—had a dicky ticker. But the medical examiner appears to be quite baffled about the symptoms. The second victim was a healthy young woman who shouldn't have died."

"That alone doesn't mean things are hexed." My cousin fingered her braid again, and her gaze was anywhere but on me. She reminded me of my pupils when they hadn't done their homework and were searching for an excuse.

"Daise, you look a trifle pale around the gills."

"You have a pretty wild imagination. Next, you'll suspect me."

Well, she wasn't out of the running. "Whatever's going on with these delicacies, I need facts, and for that I need to talk to the WI members. Our fellow witches I'll tackle in a separate meeting afterward. Will you help me?"

Jenna would hopefully join the meeting, which would give me the perfect opportunity to quiz her in a neutral environment. Unlike my cousin, my friend was easy to read.

Daisy tapped her lips, and then she sighed. "All right, I guess we better tell them. I'll see whether I can get them to arrange a meeting. Rest assured, they won't be happy."

"They'll be even less happy if more people die and law enforcement storms their kitchens."

"Eek, no. Give me a mo." My cousin disappeared in the office behind the counter to make her phone call.

I stepped across to the shelf with the dips, marmalades, and homemade wines in all shapes and sizes. Labels, some of them handwritten, advertised blackberry jam, rosehip preserves, quince jellies, and more of the same.

My gaze slid over the spreads and from there on to the sauces. Then it stopped, returning to the spreads. My heart skipped a beat. I grabbed the jar to the right and read *Linda's homemade pesto*. As in Linda, the landlady of the Crystal Dawn and fellow coven member? I rotated the glass to check the ingredients. Pine kernels, olive oil, and wild garlic.

Wild garlic. A nerve in my temple twinged.

One after the other, I removed small jars from the shelf. Nut sauce, Jenna's apple chutney, cherry preserves, and lemon curd, together with two selections of country wines, one made of elderberry and the other of rosehip, as Daisy said. The bottles with the elderberry wine looked medicinal, but their alcohol content wasn't. They struck a chord that twanged through my memory and resonated with my favorite film, *Arsenic and Old Lace*. Unless both the police and I were mistaken, arsenic wasn't the problem.

"Sorted," Daisy hollered from the counter. "Sunday at two in the old stable's gallery. I told them you'd be coming. Do you know your way around?"

"Sunday? They can't make it earlier?"

"Nope. They're all running businesses or households. Plus, I ought to be there to introduce and support you, and given our opening hours, I can't make it to the regular meeting."

"Ah, when is that?"

"Tomorrow at six, same place. But please, Myr, you're better off waiting a bit, trust me."

"Mh, I see." The twinge became a throb. The WI wasn't taking me seriously, that much was clear. Should I alert Sarah? But that would push her too close to the coven. On the other hand, I didn't want to be responsible for more deaths.

I urgently needed to get hold of Dot.

—

Once again, I was out of luck. The Wytchetts didn't answer their phones, and when I drove to the farm, all the doors were closed. Dot wasn't at her cottage either, but with being unwell, she likely wouldn't be. When I tried once more on Friday morning, she still wasn't there. The coven's rumor mill insisted she was at the doctor again, and Jenna was ferrying her around while the kids stayed with a friend.

Something sharp knifed into my belly. Jenna could have asked me for help. In the past, she would have done so.

Sarah had gone incommunicado. I received no response to any of my messages, which meant no updates on useful things like lab reports and general investigative progress. When my conscience screamed too loudly, I left Sarah a warning about the pesto. Without the magic, of course.

The Coldron grimoire had fallen into the sulks and jealously guarded its secrets. No matter how hard I tried, the empty pages remained empty. Magic was so fickle.

What I needed was a large dose of something powerful to combat the constant ache twinging away in my head. I massaged my temples and checked my watch. The figures glaring from my wrist made me jump up from the office chair.

"Cripes."

After fretting away another day, I had run out of time. A six o'clock meeting gave me just over ninety minutes to pick up the lamb chops, drive back home—it was still too hot and humid for cycling—prep the food for tonight's dinner with Chris, once more check on the Wytchetts, and get tarted up for the WI. If I wanted to gate-crash their meeting, I'd better look my best. Perhaps I could even snatch ten minutes of shut-eye to ease that bloody headache. I couldn't pop tablets all the time.

My plan unraveled as soon as I entered the pub. Greg was his usual generous self, and when he heard about the impromptu dinner for two, he supplied me not only with lamb chops but also fresh peas, already shelled, dill, and enough cream to send Tiddles into kitty heaven.

"Do you need potatoes to go with that?"

"No, thanks, we've got plenty. Alma and Cecily have become expert hash brown makers. You must come for breakfast one day and give us your verdict."

"Sure. Speaking of potatoes, you should have seen my store-room when the police were done with it."

He embarked on a rant, which meant most of my precious margin was gone when I left the pub.

It shrank further once I got back into the Witch's Retreat, where Alma lay in wait behind the counter, eager to share news of the latest disaster.

"Told you the Londoners would be trouble. They wanted to leave without paying for today, but I put my foot down."

"That's brave of you."

"They'll give us a bad review."

"They would have anyway, don't you worry."

"Hah, they're going on the blacklist."

The blacklist meant upmarket B&Bs across the UK would be full when the Londoners wanted to book. Not all of them. But enough.

"You do that. Thanks for drawing the fire."

"'Twas a pleasure. Good riddance to bad rubbish."

The hassle, even if once removed, did nothing for either my head or my stress levels. Despite driving around in an air-conditioned car, my cheeks were burning. After depositing Greg's generous gift in the fridge, I opened the tap and let the water run over my wrists.

Apropos of water, I grabbed the can and tanked up on fluids for Petty and then pushed sideways through the swing doors.

"Alma?" There was no response. Instead, footsteps stomped down the stairs and a motor roared its anger into the super-heated air outside. Gravel exploded in all directions as the SUV carrying the Londoners accelerated out of the driveway.

Five minutes of rest would be enough. Five minutes to sit down and catch my breath. It was my own fault, really. I shouldn't have left things so late.

Once inside the living room, my gaze fell on the windowsill. It was empty. No plant.

I swung around, can in hand. No primula on the coffee table either.

Nor did she sit on the floor. Or in the corner. Or anywhere. With mounting dread, I placed the can on the sofa and searched the room.

Petty was gone.

17

CUCINA ALLA MAMMA

White noise filled the parlor like a sneaky whisper. Through the window behind the half-pulled blinds filtered sunlight, which cut a swath across the floorboards and highlighted the abandoned watering can.

Petty couldn't have gone. Not again. Not twice in one week.

Strangely enough, the room was saturated with the citrus scent she released when thrilled, so she must have left recently. Was it possible she overheard the uproar caused by the Londoners and wanted to sort them out? That would be in character. My heart going full sprint, I opened the door and peeked into the corridor.

"Petty?" I didn't dare raise my voice. Not with the Simpkins sisters pottering about.

My mind, ever so helpful, spat out a nasty vision. What if Petty had snuck out the front door and was now trapped in the SUV on her way to London? With the truckload of baggage those people carried, one small primula in a fiberglass pot would get lost—

Rustle.

From the floor behind me floated a sleepy hushing of leaves. I whirled around. The air shimmered, bubbled, and took on the shape of a fake terracotta pot with greenery draped over its rim, crowned by a heap of pink blossoms. The blossoms stretched to their full height, and so did the leaves, like a human being after a nap. The pot sparked, lifted, and hovered across until it floated at a level with my face.

My legs noodled with relief. A split second later, the truth hit home, and I staggered backward until I hit the sofa. As I slumped onto the velvety upholstering, my jaw snapped shut, a narrow miss for my tongue. My mouth must have gaped open.

"What the—you're invisible?" Well, duh, right now she wasn't. But she had been, without apparent effort. The pot hovered across to the settee and landed beside me. "Well done, girl," I said, not knowing whether to laugh or cry.

Petty raised her leaves to hide her blossoms as if she were flirting. The lemony scent strengthened.

I swallowed twice, trying to contain the bubbles of hysteria popping up in my throat. Had the little monster vanished before and I never noticed? Unlikely, since my primula was such a helpful creature. She would never let me stress over sneaking her outside when she could become invisible. No, her trick had to be more recent. Perhaps even related to her temporary demise.

Didn't the recipe book have something on invisibility? I could swear it did. If only Great-Aunt Petunia's notes were a bit more organized. The sheer notion of having to scan the curly handwriting in a hurry didn't help with my aching head.

"Uh, grimoire? Are you listening? Could you come over here? I'm feeling a bit wonky."

The recipe book ignored my plea. Petty, however, waved her leaves about with wild abandon and popped sparks.

Fun was had by all, apart from yours truly.

I snatched the grimoire from the shelf and found the relevant part almost immediately, scribbled into a margin. "Few familiars have the gyft of invisibility. Only the strong ones do. Grandmother's was the last of its kind."

What kind would it have belonged to? Another flower?

Leaves and blossoms swished behind me. I raised the book and pointed it at the pot. "See that?"

With a pale pink pop, the plant shifted aside. The leaves drooped. Fair enough, Petty couldn't read. I couldn't become invisible. I reckoned between us we'd do swimmingly.

With Petty hovering after me, I slotted the recipe book into its place on the shelf. "It's getting late, and I still need to come up with a decent recipe. I'll be cooking for Chris tonight."

The plant fired off pink and red mini-fireworks followed by a scent that reminded me of roses. She'd never done that before either.

"Hah. It's got to happen first. You can try the vanishing stunt with him. See what he says."

Petty winked out. There was no other way to describe it. One moment she was there and the next she wasn't. The shimmery show from earlier must have resulted from her being asleep. My primula commanded a cloaking device that would put the Klingons to shame. Had beaming herself away become part of her brand-new bag of tricks and she was no longer with me? I stretched out my hand and touched dry soil while amused rustling reached my ears.

"Jolly good. You need watering, though. Better if you reappear."

The plant winked back into existence and landed on the coffee table. I reached for the can and returned to witness Tiddles twist around in the pot, a dreamy expression in her pale green eyes, her hind legs kicking at the soil.

Oh, bugger. "Tiddles, no. Go find your litterbox."

The pot gyrated wildly and sent the cat flying. Tiddles landed on the wooden floor, her claws scraping for purchase.

"Mrrow." With a flick of her tail, my furry friend stalked from the den.

Take a deep breath, Myrtle. Relax.

No time for that.

I had forty minutes to Google a dummy-proof recipe, prep dinner, and change before barging in on the WI. Fifty, if I allowed the ladies enough time to get seated. However, I mustn't leave it too late either. Once they had started on their agenda, they'd be unlikely to lend me their ears. My fingers flew over the screen of my smartphone. I chose jacket potatoes—no need to wash or peel anything—and marinated lamb. That, however, meant I would have to dress the cutlets before I left. The pureed peas I had in mind as a dip could be done later. It needed a few sprigs of mint, but the herb had taken over the garden and there was enough to season a flock of sheep.

With Petty digesting on the sill, visible this time, I dashed into the kitchen and banged through the cupboards in search of balsamic vinegar, dried thyme, cinnamon, and a few cloves of garlic.

The cutlets and condiments I slapped into a plastic bowl, the potatoes I nuked in the microwave and wrapped in foil, and the peas landed in another dish where I could puree them and mix in the cream once I was back.

Finito, prep done.

I tore upstairs and found the first-floor landing barred by Alma and Cecily.

"There you are. We're done cleaning," Cecily explained. "Mrs. Shuttlecock called, and she needs a room tonight, so we did number five. Mrs. Saddler also called to confirm she's coming."

Three cheers for the salespeople.

As to Alma and Cecily, they were no longer on duty. Anybody else would have gone home. Not them. Not ever. I gushed my thanks, hopping from foot to foot and feeling guilty for it.

"Mr. Johnston checked out. He wants you to know that he will be back, no matter what happens. Oh, any news about the killer?" Alma asked. "Would it be that Wiccan? She got arrested again, didn't she?"

To heck with small villages. There was no chance of cleaning your teeth unobserved. One wrong word and I would be stuck for absolute ages.

"Uh, no. But she gave me an idea. I need to follow up on that, but I'm late. I'll tell you as soon as I know what's going on." The prospect of getting first dibs at the gossip did the trick. Alma and Cecily cleared the steps.

Shower finished, I threw on a white blouse and a blue batik skirt, grabbed a pair of red slingbacks with low heels—an outfit that classified as professional without being too formal—and raced down the stairs, late already.

The traffic deities were off duty, and it took me fifteen minutes to drive to the car park, which meant the meeting would be well under way by the time I arrived. It couldn't be helped. I was here, so I might as well try.

The slings of my shoes kept slipping, so I shuffled into the gallery where I found myself surrounded by oversized canvasses featuring designs as cubic as they were garish. They were vaguely inspired by Mondrian but not quite getting there. I made for the two doors on the opposite wall and tried the first—locked—and then the second. The knob turned, and I pushed the door open.

The WI's meeting room was square and reeked faintly of mildew. An air-conditioning unit under the ceiling was going full blast, but it only stirred the tepid atmosphere. The furnishings were nondescript. Gray meeting tables, arranged in a U-formation, were matched with clunky black chairs and a stained gray carpet. Whitish walls that had seen no fresh paint in millennia were peppered with pins, some of which had little scraps of paper sticking to them. Greasy windows looked out on the beech hedge that ran around the grounds of Avebury Manor.

The leaves sucked up the light, which gave the assembly a some-what sinister look and feel despite the old-fashioned neon lamps buzzing overhead.

The women seated around the table looked up, their gazes drilling into me, and I sensed a telltale blush spreading over my cheeks.

The mascara was supposed to be waterproof, but what if it had run in the shower and I was giving them panda eyes? "Hello, everybody. I'm frightfully sorry to bother you like this, but what I have to tell you can't wait until Sunday."

My introduction met with a stony silence. The chill of ostracism crept down my spine, and the urge to withdraw in shame grew. Instead of caving in to the impulse, I let my gaze travel over the group until it found a smile in a sea of frowns.

"I know her," Mel said. "If Myrtle says something is urgent, then it is. We must hear her out."

A murmur sprung up, but it didn't sound overly hostile, only annoyed.

Phew.

"Well, then. Let's hear it." Linda pointed at the empty chair at the flat end of the U. The whole setup screamed job interview. A furtive glance into the round gave me a grand total of sixteen women, only two of them coven members, since Daisy and Jenna weren't around.

A shame about Jenna, really.

"Sorry for the rotten timing," I said. "I was planning to arrive earlier, but two of my guests left in a hurry. They didn't want to pay—"

"Yes, yes, same here." A tired-looking woman banged on the table, bowling over three of the mineral waters lined up on its surface. I recognized her from my trips to the commercial laundry. She owned a B&B in the neighboring village of Calston. "Two of mine buggered off this morning, and the rest are totally spooked."

Linda nodded. "People are upset. Though nobody's deserted

me yet. Looks like I've calmed them down." A smirk spread over her sharp features. I was wrong when I compared her to Morticia Addams. She wasn't half as nice. Still, her words stung. I took a mental note to touch base with my guests tomorrow.

"Is it even safe to eat anything around here?" Mel asked. She wore one of her filmy tents, her heavy blonde locks pinned back with Hello Kitty barrettes.

"I'm no longer sure." I rubbed my sweaty hands on my skirt. "To be frank, I suspect somebody has tampered with your goodies. That's why I'm here, actually."

"Daisy mentioned it," Linda said, her reedy voice even. "Care to explain?"

"I will in a moment. Did you hear from Dot or Jenna? I'm worried. I can't get hold of them."

I'd also left messages about the primula being okay. Why was Jenna avoiding me? Empath that she was, would Jenna sense my suspicions?

"I've closed the shop for the afternoon," Mel said. "Wasn't worth it. I drove to the farm, oh, about two hours ago or so. Jenna told me the medication seemed to be helping Dot, but that her grandmother now needs to catch up on sleep. Poor girl's got her hands full."

How rotten of me to suspect she might have other motives.

The room fell silent. All stares directed at me. I hated exams, especially when sitting on the wrong side of the table.

"About your theory," a petite Asian woman prompted. Her I knew as well. She hailed from Upper Little Piddlesborough, where she ran a small hotel. Had our trouble spread that far?

Bit by painful bit, I laid it out before them. The shopping sprees of the Wiccans. The two deaths that followed. "Looks like the police have ruled out the pub as a source for the poison. Once they ran out of provisions, the Wiccans shopped locally, and the dead musician's last meal must have come from them. The spaghetti rings were okay. That leaves the café and the goodies you sell from the gift shop."

"Is that all you have?" Linda's voice dripped disdain.

"Give it a rest," Mel said. "Though I'm not sure how this is supposed to have worked. Health and Safety sniff around my place all the time. You know, I sometimes wonder whether all this bother is worth the money we make."

Her words were followed by nodding and "hear, hear" and "well spoken, Mel."

As the tension seeped from the room, my courage grew. "Do you prepare all those products in your own homes?"

"Yes," the B&B owner from Calston said. "Some of us, like Linda and myself, have commercial kitchens. Makes things a lot easier. You should think of joining us, Myrtle. Your place is great."

Linda thrust out her chin. "I'm not in the habit of poisoning my customers."

"I'm not saying you poison them," I said. "However, it appears we're talking toxins derived from lily of the valley. Does this ring a bell?"

Linda's dark eyes narrowed. "Are you insinuating I mixed up my plants? You've got to be stupid to mistake *Convallaria majalis* for *Allium ursinum*."

"I never insinuated anything. It could be a genuine oversight." Or something more sinister.

"Quite a few people get poisoned every year," the woman from Piddlesborough said. "The idea isn't outrageous."

Linda shook her head and sent her dark hair flying. "No way. I pluck my wild garlic when it comes out in spring and process it straight away. I was late this year because of the rain, but come mid-April it was marinating in olive oil. The lilies hadn't popped out by then." Eyes blazing, she continued. "I know my herbs. I don't make stupid mistakes. And I won't let anybody near my creations." With the last word, she stabbed the table and meant me. "You've. Got. No. Proof."

"Fine, so I don't. Did you give some to Jenna by any chance?"

"Yes, why? She liked it and I let her have a few jars. Wouldn't ever poison her, you know."

I massaged my aching head. "All I want is to make sure we're not selling contaminated food to our guests."

"Which I'm not," Linda said, deep red spots showing on her cheeks.

"Let's talk this through," Mel said. "Could somebody have tampered with the jars without you noticing?"

The woman from Piddlesborough shook her head. "How? The lids are sealed."

Mutters of assent skittered up and down the table, and accusing looks turned my way. If this were a proper job interview, I would've blown it.

Mel pursed her lips. "There was this case where somebody blackmailed a supermarket. The guy used a strong needle and pierced the lids. Another time, they did open the jars, and then they closed them again once they had done whatever they wanted to. With the corks it's even easier."

A clever suggestion? Or something else entirely? These days, suspects lurked in every corner. The throb in my temples graduated to a full-blown drumbeat. The table, however, calmed.

"Mh," said the woman from Calston. "Okay, let's say it's possible. Why only the pesto? The poison could've been in anything. The jams, the sauces . . ."

"Given the type of toxin, I suspected the pesto. But yes, you're right," I said.

Linda threw herself back in her chair with a sigh, her cheeks flushed. "This is nothing but wild speculation, and I'll tell you why. For argument's sake, let's assume somebody messed with my product. The Wiccans buy and open it. Was the dead woman the only person to eat the dip?"

Her line of reasoning was all too obvious. "I don't know whether she had any, but they must have shared everything. However, the flutist definitely ate pesto."

"Why aren't there more deaths, then?" Linda crowed. "You can get four helpings out of each jar. More, if you make sandwiches. The café goes through a lot of the stuff. One jar is way too much for one person. It's like garlic overkill." She grimaced. "Sorry."

"Let me play devil's advocate," the woman from Calston said. "Okay, so the poor woman alone ate from the poisoned jar, whatever it might have been. What next?"

Linda shot her a venomous look.

Thoughts whirled around in my head like a swarm of upset midges. The midges turned into wasps and stung. I rubbed my temples where an idea was forming, but it was taking its own sweet time.

Linda stabbed the table again. "I want to see this sorted out. I refuse to take the blame for something I haven't done."

Chris's comment about connections zapped through me like an electric shock. "Listen, if a group of people or even only two have dinner together and one dies, then either that person was the only one to touch the tainted food or the poison must be in something that comes in single portions."

"You're right," Linda said, obviously not liking it. "Can't be the dips, sauces, or marmalades, then." That she liked a lot more.

"What about the wines?" Mel asked, a determined tone in her voice.

Silence fell. Only the air-conditioning unit hissed, stirring the heavy ambience.

Mel leaned forward. "Jenna's elderberry wine. The rosehip comes in liter bottles, but hers are quarter-liters. It's not too much for one person."

I flexed aching fingers I must have balled into fists and rotated my stiffening shoulders. My worries had zigzagged from Jenna to Daisy, and from there to Linda and back again. Next, I would turn myself into a suspect.

"Come on. There must be something else with single por-tions. If that's what happened," the woman from Calston said.

"Not really." Mel's voice was purged of emotion. "We did away with those a while ago. Not sustainable, remember?"

"It can't be the wine," I said. "I checked up on the lily poison. It has a bitter taste. Surely people would notice."

Mel shook her head. "Wrong. Those wines are sweet. Far too sweet, if you ask me. Elderberry, for example, is quite potent. It would mask the bitterness. Quite frankly, if you're at an outdoor party, you won't pay much attention to the taste. You'd guzzle whatever gets plonked in front of you."

Didn't Boian have alcohol in his stomach?

The meeting exploded with shouts, booing, and accusations. And fear. As wacky as my theory might sound, the ladies now suspected Jenna—I saw it in their faces. It was all my fault. I'd opened the can of worms. They were now crawling around, with no way of putting them back in.

"Listen, hey," Mel said. "Let's assume somebody had a go at Jen's wine. Since it's got a cork, tampering is even easier. The poor girl needs to know pronto. Before the police show up. And we need to act. The risk is simply too high."

"Act?" a WI member asked, sounding bewildered.

"She's right. We have to pull our products," another said. "All of them. To be on the safe side."

Shouts of outrage. More hissing and booing.

I managed to catch first Linda's and then Mel's attention and tilted my head at the exit. Linda shot me an acid glare, but she rose from her seat nevertheless.

The WI members seemed happy to see me gone. Unlikely I would receive another invitation to join the club.

"Where can we talk?" I asked Mel once we had shut the door behind us.

"The manor," she said. "It's just round the corner and we're after opening hours. The gardens should be empty."

"If it's closed, how do we get in?"

She smiled. "I'm a volunteer. I have keys and can unlock things. After you, ladies."

18

A COMING STORM

Blight-free and manicured boxwood hedges framed the benches Mel had chosen for our impromptu gathering. While our backs might be protected, the rest of our bodies were not. A gray mass billowed into the heavens despite the sun's brave attempt to fight back, with the occasional ray breaking through in blinding flashes of brightness. Unlike Saturday's haze, these clouds meant business. I could smell it in the electric freshness of the breeze that tossed hair and plastered skirts against legs. Over the shrubs on our left peeked the thatched roof of the stable gallery where another type of storm raged, audible since a WI member must have ripped open a window. Would these people ever do anything apart from arguing?

"Tell me why I'm sitting here with you when I could be at home trying to figure out algebra with my daughter?" Linda asked.

"Because algebra sucks," Mel said.

A brief smile flitted over Linda's austere features. "There's that."

"You've got something horrid up your sleeve, don't you, Myr?" Mel asked. The wind grabbed her gauzy scarf and blew the ends into my face.

I flipped them aside. "I wish I didn't. Looks like I've wreaked enough havoc for one evening."

"Okay, I accept you had to warn us. Still, I don't make that sort of mistake."

"Linda, please." Mel wrung her hands, soft and pale with dimples along the knuckles.

Linda reminded me of Buster. She showed as many teeth, and she would never stop yacking.

"My other theory you'll like even less. I don't like it myself. Unfortunately, I'm not the cops, so it's not like I'm rolling in facts. Still, there's enough evidence to make me rather nervous."

"Is there?" Linda asked.

"Yes. See, I'm worried these murders might be caused by magic."

For a moment, the other two women must have been too gob-smacked to speak. The wind picked up once more, and Linda's black hair lashed about like angry snakes.

"Are you seriously suggesting one of us would or, more importantly, could do such a thing?" she asked.

"Frankly, I've got no clue what's going on here. Fact is, a mini dose of the poison seems to be a lot, and I mean a heck of a lot, stronger than it should be. It also acted incredibly fast, especially with the young pagan. Two medical experts consider the effect to be quite . . . improbable." I couldn't make myself use that other word. Perhaps I would never use it again.

Linda frowned. "It takes a massive dose for the stuff to be lethal. Yes, those plants are dangerous. Yes, their toxins can kill you—more so if your heart is weak. However, an adult can't just nibble a few leaves and snuff it. Even if we're talking a severe case of poisoning, the body reacts. With vomiting and diarrhea, which is how most people survive."

"Most people, correct," I said. "Not these two."

Linda grabbed her hair with both her hands and twisted it into a coil. "And you're thinking magic because . . . ?"

"Told you already. Because of the severity of the symptoms and the speed at which they manifested. Because at least one person died despite having ingested only a tiny amount of the poison. Because the symptoms and effects baffle the pros."

"Doesn't wow me," said Linda. "Are you sure the poison acted the same in both cases? What about your cop friend? Did she share the autopsy results with you? What we need are facts and not all these airy-fairy theories."

Well, Sarah had in fact informed me, but only as far as Boian was concerned. "I don't have the full picture yet. I've been trying to reach my friend at Swindon CID to find out more about the second victim, but she's busy."

Linda shrugged. "There you go. I agree, there's a remote possibility something could be wrong with our products, so we'd better not take any risks. It's really a job for the cops, but I don't want to be responsible for dead tourists. But magic? Come on."

Mel jumped up from the bench, a sudden flare of golden sunlight shining through the layers of her garment. Much more than a tent, the colorful veils highlighted the soft curves of her body. She seemed to find something fascinating to observe among the foamy green wall of boxwood leaves. When she swirled around, she reminded me of Salome.

"I'm not sure. This morning, when I listened to the news, I wondered if we're somehow responsible for this horror. Witches are evil, aren't they?" Mel's hands dropped to her sides like dead butterflies.

"Evil, my backside," said Linda, her face flushed. "Don't even go there. The entire theory has holes in it the size of a barn. Yes, over the last days a few of us improved our skylles. But magical murders to my mind require significant powers. Not to forget these deaths are random. Do you see any connection between the victims? I don't."

Sweat trickled down my spine. Chris had been as skeptical as Linda, but he had acted a lot nicer about it. "Agreed, I've read enough murder mysteries to know motives are important. Here, I don't see any. Linda, I'd love to be proven wrong. I don't want a coven member to be responsible. But I can't rule out the possibility that I could be right. Otherwise, we might be exposed before we're ready."

"Ugh, no," said Mel, flapping her hands.

Linda pursed her lips. "Is there nothing in your recipe book?"

"Information on the medicinal use of foxglove and lily of the valley, yes. Nothing on hexing them to kill people."

I should have studied the laundry list more closely, but hindsight was a wonderful thing.

The wind flapped Mel's scarf about and threatened to blow open my skirt. Linda wore pants, so she was fine.

"Can we ignore this?" I asked. "Are you sure we can discard my theory?"

"No," Linda said slowly.

"You're on to something, I can feel it." Mel lay a hand on her ample bosom. "It's as I feared. An evil witch. When is our next coven meeting?"

"Tomorrow," Linda said. "We wanted to discuss evacuation arrangements, remember?"

"Can't wait that long. Let's start the call chain," Mel said.

"To do what?" Linda asked. "Tell them what's going on and see if somebody acts suspiciously? On the contrary, we might alert that person and they'll hide the evidence. Jeez, now you've got me aboard the paranoia train."

"There's no way around it," I said. "Perhaps that'll nip more murders in the bud. Maybe one of the others has seen or heard something that might help us. We can't just sit on our hands."

"Even if you were right, and if we found the person responsible, what are we going to do?" Linda was pacing the gravel, reminding me of a hungry Tiddles.

"We'll consult Dot." I reached into my backpack for the phone.

"No. Call Jenna instead. She needs to know about the wine," Mel said. "If Dot's in such bad shape, we'd better not bother her."

Linda nodded eagerly. "Good point. Let's talk to Jenna."

She might know about the wine already.

"I've tried before. She doesn't answer the phone."

I tapped the screen to call her number. Of course, this time I reached Jenna on the first attempt.

"Hello, Myrtle," she said. Her voice, usually so melodious, sounded listless.

"The wine," Linda hissed.

"Sorry for not responding to your messages, Myr, but life got a bit hectic."

"No problem. Look, Jenna—"

"Tell her about the wine," Linda hissed.

"I guess we should talk, but I'm not feeling up to it right now. Give me until tomorrow, okay? Try not to fret so much. It'll all work out. Gotta dash, Marty and I are taking the kids out for a burger. They were ever so sweet with Gran."

"She needs to know about the wine."

I turned my back on Linda. "Jenna, sorry, but is Dot around?"

"Yes, don't worry, Gran's better. She was sleeping when I last looked. The weather's changing, and that's never good for her. She's staying with us for a few days. I didn't want to leave her alone in her cottage. Do me one favor and please, please don't bother her. That'll only upset the apple cart again. See, I fear— No, can't do this over the phone. Thanks for caring. You're the best. We'll talk tomorrow."

She disconnected, and I stared at my phone.

"Why didn't you tell her about the wine?" Linda asked.

"Never stood a chance. And she doesn't want me to contact her grandmother."

How ill was Dot really? Could this be a ruse to cut us off from the one person who could tell us what was going on?

"Mh, can't be helped," Mel said. "Someone has to warn Jen before the scat enters the ventilation system. Which it will."

"I'll see what I can do for her. Not now, though—she and Marty are taking the kids for a burger."

That would give me the perfect opportunity to talk to Dot, no matter what Jenna or Mel might think or want.

"Good. I'll kick off the call chain," Mel said. "What message shall we give out?"

"Let's be upfront," I said. "We'll tell the others we suspect a magical cause for these deaths. We're asking them to search whatever documents they own for instructions on poisonings. I doubt it, but it might prevent . . . uh, the person responsible from doing any more damage, simply because they know we've noticed."

Linda barked a laugh. "Yeah, or it kicks them into a killing spree."

"Do you always have to snipe at everything Myrtle says?" Mel arched her brow. "You're welcome to share your theories or contribute solutions. Otherwise, I suggest you keep quiet."

"I'm not sniping in the slightest. Just pointing out facts. Oh, okay, go ahead. Really, I don't know what else we can do."

She hadn't finished speaking when another thought ambushed me, forcing a groan to my lips.

Linda rolled her eyes. "Now what? Don't tell me, you've had more hunches."

"Not a hunch, but a problem. You see, some visitors might have bought goodies before they left."

For a moment, nobody said a word. The angry voices from the barn distorted, sounding unreal as if a glass bowl had been placed over us. Every breath turned into a struggle, and the pain drilled from my temples into my eye sockets.

"Oh bugger," Linda said, running both her hands through her hair. "For a change, that makes sense. That's assuming something's wrong with our products."

"I guess this is where I call the cops." I toyed with my phone as if I still had an option.

"About the magic?" Mel's voice was shrill.

"No, of course not. But they need to know the rest."

"I doubt magic can be traced in a lab," Linda said, her tone remarkably sympathetic. "It shouldn't be a big deal."

"Mh, if the police find the person responsible, assuming there is one, you never know how they'll react to interrogations."

Far above our heads, a rumble sounded from the menacing skies.

"We tell them in the call chain to keep their traps shut. Uh, we better take cover somewhere," Linda said. "I don't like the look of those clouds."

I didn't like the look of anything right now, but who cared about me? I tapped on Sarah's number, pressed the phone to my ear, and listened to a ring followed by another.

"Sergeant Widdlethorpe, Swindon CID."

"Sarah, thank the heavens."

The heavens rumbled in response.

"Myrtle, sorry for not responding earlier. First, let me apologize for the scene in the café. My boss is an absolute . . . well, you know. Of course, we found nothing in that woman's practice. No self-respecting physician would hand out pills like M&M's. It was only ever about Diloff's prejudices. He wanted her to be guilty because she's a pagan."

I changed the phone from one sweaty hand to another. "You're right about the problem not being related to medicine. Seems like I might have found the source."

"Of what?" Sarah's voice went calm. That was never a good sign.

"Eh, the poisonings."

"So have we."

Fear spidered down my spine.

"But let me hear your theory. Oh, I hope you don't mind Cameron listening in?" Sarah said.

"Afternoon," an unsuitably cheerful male voice hollered

from the background.

"I'm with the WI." I pushed the speaker button and shifted the phone to my other hand since it was less sweaty. "We believe the poison might be in their products. More specifically, the wine."

"Wine? Mh, both victims indeed had drunk alcohol, and the second victim more than the first. Like him, she's also consumed a variety of comestibles, which makes it hard for the lab to establish the exact poisoning agent."

"See, that's why I worried about the pesto sandwiches. Apparently Diloff mentioned lily of the valley poison when he was grilling the Wiccan, and she told me."

"She shouldn't have done that," Sarah snapped.

I said nothing. In the background, Cameron's level voice rumbled recriminations.

"I know, I know. Sorry, that was uncalled for."

"It's okay. Anyway, she did, and it made me think of the pesto. The lily can get mistaken for wild garlic. And there are lots of dips and sauces on sale at the souvenir shop, including pesto, prepared by the local WI. They get spread on the café's sandwiches, and the Wiccans bought some. That's how I made the connection, which I told you about."

Linda growled. I placed a finger on my lips and glared at her.

"Fair enough," Sarah said. "I got your message, thanks, and I passed it on to the lab. They tell me while glycoside poisoning is the cause of death for both victims, they found no trace of lily leaves. That much they could work out."

Linda punched the air. "Hah."

"Once we found nothing at the physician's practice and the reports on the stomach contents came in, it was obvious the food must be the connection. I liked your pesto theory. Still do, but it doesn't work."

A burst of babble from a cop radio cut her short. A screeching of brakes followed.

"Where are you?"

"In a car on the way to the village. As soon as we got the results, I roped in the DCI."

"Oh, great. That means Diloff is out of it, right?"

"Sidelined, but still in charge, sorry. Now, what makes you think it's the wine?"

"It's got to be in something that comes in single portions. Otherwise, more people would have died."

"Ah, clever," Sarah said. "Should have thought of that myself. You might be on to something, you know? This morning, I interviewed Mr. Albu once more—once I got hold of him—who confirmed that he and his brother not only took all the spaghetti rings, which were harmless, but also pesto, crackers, and a small bottle of country wine for their dinner. Boian took a sip after the meal—only one, mind you—but found the wine much too sweet, which stopped his brother from drinking anything. The victim then developed symptoms, but they thought it was his heart trouble. He retired to the storeroom and his lonely death. After disposing of the bottle, of course, as these are conscientious people. Don't ask me why he then consumed the peas, but he did. They weren't even digested."

"You never found bottles in the pub's wheelie bins, did you?"

"No. A shame, since that might have prevented the second death. Nor did we find anything lying around at the camp."

"Why not?"

"Hah, once its denizens realized we were on our way, they dutifully collected their rubbish. We've confiscated the bags, of course, but it'll take a while to sieve through their contents. Anyway, we've issued a warning about the food and drinks. Sorry, Myr, I fear your village is in for a rough ride."

"We'll pull the goodies from the shelves."

"Good. But keep them handy. We'll analyze the lot. In any case, I'll start with the wine now. Can you describe what we're looking for? That will help us with the rubbish."

"Small glass bottles. Translucent. Roundish. What a pharmacy might use. Complete with cork stopper and an octagonal label. The wine is a deep dark red like Burgundy."

"Great, thanks. One more question."

I dreaded her words. I knew what she would ask. The boxwood hedges seemed to creep closer, and the vise around my temples tightened the squeeze.

"Any idea who produced the wine?"

Bingo. "It's not that person's fault. Somebody must have tampered with the bottles."

"That's entirely possible, Myrtle. The name."

Mel raised her arms like a veiled semaphore while Linda looked mutinous. What were they thinking? Yes, Sarah was a friend, but the coven had to remain a secret. We needed time to come up with a smoke screen. It was all about choices.

"The producer of the wine won't go anywhere in a hurry. As long as your idiot boss is involved, I can't rat on that person. Sorry, but I just can't."

Static followed, interrupted by more cop babble. When Sarah spoke, her voice could have flash frozen Niagara. "I see. You're protecting a friend. But fair warning—if I find out you're obstructing justice, Myrtle, you'll be the one in trouble."

The connection broke.

From the wall of clouds climbing toward the stratosphere emitted another rumble, sounding like the freight train that had just rolled over me.

"Whoa, that's one scary lady," Mel said. "Who is she?"

"My friend in the police force." At least, she had been until the phone call.

"And now?" Mel asked.

"Now I'll call the Wytchetts to warn them. Sarah won't take long to work out who produced the wine."

There was no response to my repeated rings of Marty's and Jenna's mobile numbers. For the first time since I met them, I cursed our mutual dislike of social media.

"I'll drive across and leave a note, since they're likely still out with the boys. There are two more things you can do, Linda,"

I said. A fat raindrop landed on my nose. A second one hit the bench. "Ensure the ladies stop arguing and remove their products. Once you've done that, I suggest you tell the café to stop selling the WI goodies. I'm not sure the ladies will think of that. The cops will take over once they arrive, but one never knows."

"On it." She dipped her chin once and marched off.

The wind, warm like a hair dryer, tore at the birch trees behind the hedge, their branches whipping up and down.

"Uh, it's starting." Mel pulled the scarf over her head as if that would make a difference. "Let's get back to our cars. I'll kick off the chain from mine."

We hurried out of the manor garden, pursued by fat raindrops that dotted the tarmac. Mel sketched a hurried goodbye and flung herself into her silver Honda.

Once inside my van, I turned on the radio.

"Police have issued a strong caution against consuming food or drinks bought at Avebury stores and restaurants. Should you have purchased such items, please report to Swindon CID immediately. The number to call is on our website. Now, on a lighter note, here are the results of the guinea pig race in Bloxham village . . ."

Any other time I would have been impressed with Sarah's efficiency.

A ray of light fell into my eyes as the sun reappeared in full glory. The raindrops on the windshield had dried already, leaving behind circular splotches on the dusty glass. I turned the key in the ignition, and the motor of my minivan roared to life. Did we block the storm or only buy ourselves a breather? If the latter were the case, how long would the peace last?

19

HISTORY LESSONS

Pointless fretting wouldn't get me anywhere in a hurry. I rummaged in my purse for another headache pill, which I dry swallowed. Spurred on by my worry demons, I didn't wait for the chemicals to kick in but started the motor and drove to Wytchett Farm. Once I arrived, Daisy's wheels were the first thing I spotted, followed by my cousin herself as she banged shut the trunk of her Cabrio.

She leaned against the electric-blue back fender, a glum expression on her lovely face. "What are you doing here?"

That was typical. Daisy did something that made me like her, and immediately afterward she kicked me in the shins. "I might ask you the same question. Shouldn't you be at the shop?"

"Since when do you control my movements?"

I had neither the time nor the nerves for her histrionics. "I'm not doing anything of the sort. The cops issued a warning about the WI's products—"

Daisy gave a little shriek. Her hands flew to her face.

"Good grief, not the bit with the hexing, if that's what you think. No, the problem is that people might have bought souvenirs before leaving."

She dropped her hands. "Oh."

"Anyway, I really need to leave Jenna a note. Sorry for the rush, but I'm late for an appointment." My date with Chris, to be precise, but that was none of Daisy's business.

A frown broke the porcelain perfection of my cousin's forehead. "What's wrong?"

"I'll tell you another time. Is Dot around by any chance?"

"I spoke to her. That's why I closed the shop early. Nothing going on anyway."

"She's awake? Oh, good." I started for the entrance, but Daisy waved me off.

"No, don't. She was asleep before I'd even left her room. Actually, there's something—"

"Daisy, not now. Told you, I'm running late."

She tossed her braid. "Oh, but for Dot you would've found the time, right? Forgive me for breathing." She stormed to her car, slammed the door shut, and raced away, missing my van by inches.

I pinched the bridge of my nose, but that did nothing for either the invisible band squeezing my head or the stiffness in my shoulders.

I entered the kitchen via the back entrance and scribbled a note for Jenna, explaining recent developments, without mentioning the role I feared she might have played, and asking her to call me as soon as she returned. After calling Dot's name a few times and not getting a response, I took myself home, with Chris due in less than forty minutes.

Blast. Should I beg off?

Resentment surged. I'd warned Sarah about the wine, which wasn't in my personal interest but might save lives, ensured that the coven was up to date, and alerted Jenna to incoming coppers. With Dot and Jenna both making themselves scarce, I couldn't do more. I had a right to a break. Make hay while the sun shines, or words to that effect. Not to forget, Chris promised he would help me.

It still meant beating the rural record for dinner preparations. Not that the food was my biggest problem—getting dressed was. This was my first proper date with the man, and I wanted to look the part.

That was easier said than done. After I had rummaged through my wardrobe twice, the ticking of an imagined clock overloud in my ear, something blue slid off the hanger and dropped to the floor. I bent over and retrieved a faux-jeans dress made of a silky viscose I had seen in a shop last month and bought on impulse. I tried it on and preened in front of the mirror.

Goes nicely with the strawberry hair. The dress also displayed my curves without being too provocative.

Shoes were less of an issue. I'd slip on the slingbacks once I'd navigated the stairs. The straps were unreliable, and the last thing I needed was a tumble down the steps. First, I fluffed up my mane, discovered I was out of spray, and searched my backpack for the can of extra-strong I carried for defense ever since the trouble in April. With a floral familiar acting the bodyguard, at least inside my house there was no need for chemical warfare.

Slingbacks dangling from my hand, I raced into a kitchen reeking of garlic. I donned a frilly apron, the type of garment I wouldn't otherwise touch with a barge pole, but grease and classy outfits don't go together. It took ages to mash the peas into a dip since the little beasts fought me all the way. The top of the Tabasco bottle was caked with sauce and wouldn't yield a drop, and then the bottle disgorged its contents in a fiery rush. I spooned the gunk from the bowl and then dashed into the garden to cut the mint.

In between, I laid the table—in the kitchen, since we were short of a dining room. There was the conservatory, but as the only diners, Chris and I would rattle in the large room. Outside, the wind picked up again, so the kitchen it would have to be. My grandmother's silver candleholders looked stylish enough on the polished wood of the table, and they matched my best place mats. I slapped the potatoes into the oven but kept the lamb cutlets for Chris, who would know how to treat them right. Left to my own devices, I would only fry them to death.

They are already dead.

The bell gonged into that happy thought.

When I opened the door, I was greeted first by a red amaryllis and, behind it, a smiling Chris.

"For me?" I asked, a cheerful warmth spreading inside. Christmassy, yes, but I liked amaryllis. How had he known? And how had he found one out of season?

"For you. Don't eat it all at once." The grin on his face spread across his smooth-shaven cheeks as he handed me the flower. The teensiest tease of a kiss followed. He looked great and he smelled fantastic, and without that silly comment, I would have given him five out of five.

I retaliated in kind. "Thanks, that won't be necessary. Dinner isn't burned yet. Come on in, and I'll make it happen."

Chris trailed after me into the smelly kitchen where I rummaged around for a vase.

"Do you think you could take care of the meat?" I asked over my shoulder.

"With pleasure. If you're looking for a vase, your aunt kept them here," Chris said, opening a cupboard and striking gold at first try. I took out champagne flutes and fetched the bottle from the fridge.

The swing doors flapped open and closed again. Likely Petty wanted to sneak up on Chris. I swung around to watch the show.

Chris had placed the vase with his gift on the table. He reached for the bowl with the cutlets sitting on the draining board the same moment Petty materialized beside him.

To give him his due, he didn't scream. Instead, he dropped

the bowl. Fortunately, it was made of plastic. Even more fortunately, the cutlets landed in the sink and not on the terracotta floor tiles where Tiddles was circling like a furry mini-shark.

The primula bobbed through the kitchen airspace, pot swaying like a gong, soil scattering over the tiles.

"It's her latest trick. Neat, eh?"

Chris stared at the plant. Petty floated closer, rustled her leaves, and fired a broadside of pink sparks at him.

"Bloody hell. Is that normal?"

"Normal? She can hover, she can spark, she can move her leaves. Somewhere she's hiding a brain, but don't ask me where. Why not go invisible? I checked in the recipe book. If a familiar is capable of such a trick, she's quite the powerhouse. Or he." Not that Petty could ever be male—she acted far too girlie for that.

He tilted his head. "Familiar? Is that what she is?"

Of course, he hadn't known. "Looks like it. Sworn to protect me, it appears. Well, it's what Dot says."

His grin returned. "Trust you to create a pretty bouncer."

Give that man a medal for open-mindedness.

Instead, I handed him a glass of champers. Our fingertips touched and something like an electric shock, only nicer, zinged from my fingertips straight to my navel. Cheeks on fire, I turned on the hob. "One thing Petty can't do is help me with the cooking."

Chris, who had swung away from me and was stroking Petty's leaves, bent down to fetch a pan. "What was it I nearly dropped? Ah, spicy garlic with chunks of lamb. Great stuff."

"Har, har."

With Chris in charge, the cutlets turned out crispy brown outside and pink and succulent in the middle, and we dug in.

"This isn't bad, you know?" Chris held out his plate. "Could I have another spud, please?"

I passed him a baked potato, still wrapped in aluminum foil. Something, perhaps the tasty food, acted as a conversation killer, and we swapped nothing but banalities until we had scraped our plates clean and emptied the bottle. Only when a soft alcoholic haze blurred the edges of my consciousness did I dare share the latest developments.

"Ho, you're moving too fast for my mushy brain. Okay, it's not dips now, but wine?" Chris pulled his eyebrows into his trademark V. "At least you did the right thing and called in the coppers. Sarah can take care of this mess."

"Oh, she will. That's bad news, assuming I'm right and there is a magical link."

The fingers of his right hand drummed the tabletop, and the V turned more pronounced. "I'm still not keen on your theory."

"Linda isn't sold on the idea either. Anyway, we've started the call chain to tell people what's going on. I wish I could get hold of Dot, but she seems to be down for the count."

Chris shifted in his chair. "That's a shame. I suspect she'd be able to stop you from stressing unnecessarily. Yes, your witchy friends have been pulling some amazing stunts in the last few days, but even you or your friend Jenna would find it difficult to place a killer spell on the drink, am I right or am I right?"

He eyed the empty bottle of champagne.

"For the record, I didn't even try. But 'last few days' nails it on the head. The poison must have entered the wine fairly recently."

"What makes you so sure?"

"Duh, isn't it obvious? Otherwise, people would have died a lot earlier."

"I guess, anything is possible, but . . . do you have even the faintest clue how long that wine's been on the market? You and Jenna need to have a conversation. It won't be pleasant, but it's necessary. Until you do, stop driving yourself nuts. Actually, I can offer you something to stop you mulling over imagined magical murderers." Chris winked.

I had a vision of another kiss. Instead, he pushed his plate aside before digging into the pockets of his khaki chinos from where he retrieved first his car key, and then his wallet, and finally a sheet of paper, which he unfolded.

A copy of my mystery image. Amid the latest hassle, I had all but forgotten its existence.

"When I first saw these doodles, they reminded me of an Ignatius family secret." Chris tapped the procession of stick people crawling across the stone circles like ants until they ran into some sort of mothball. Then he tapped the squiggles Damian had claimed were star constellations.

"What would that be?"

"Well, since it's a secret, nobody talks about it."

"Chris."

He sniggered. Through the open kitchen window drifted the sounds and smells of another balmy summer evening. Once more, the skies had cleared of the clouds and the wind had died down. It would do that. Had I opted for an alfresco dinner, we would have been blown away.

"I told you before, my lot was plenty pissed off that the Whites escaped the pyres. They still chalked up the event as a success."

"Meaning?"

"Meaning, the Ignatius tribe prides itself on driving your lot away from Earth and straight into hell."

"Seen from my side of the fence, they might well have blown your lot a magical raspberry and vanished of their own accord to somewhere a lot more pleasant than an overheated underworld."

"Very likely. Anyway, wherever your magical cousins disappeared to, the magical artifacts of the witch folk must have served as door openers. At least, according to Uncle Bob's research they did, which is why he wants them." Chris pointed at the chevrons rippling at the top of the drawing. "What do they remind you of?"

"Waves? A bit spiky, though."

"Ripples or wavelets, yes. Only, I'm pretty sure we're not talking solid medium, like water, but impulses from a remote control. A bit like age-old signals trapped on paper.”

“Mh, sounds intriguing. I wonder whether they still work.”

Chris quirked a brow.

“Don’t worry, I’m not going to try. But my aunt was right to protect the plaques the way she did.”

“There’s more, so bear with me for a moment. I need to share some backstory. Did you never ask yourself why your ancestors would place so much value on two Neolithic plaques when there are tons of them around?”

“Not really, no. Certainly not in the recent past.”

“Shame. The ancients chose the building sites for their temples for a reason. They’re hotspots of power. It would explain why so many of the wise women and men lived next to the old sanctuaries.”

“Not exactly breaking news.”

“Patience, my dear. If the old monuments can channel supernatural energies, it stands to reason somebody with para-normal powers was around back when they were built. Those people left the access keys behind. Maybe they hid them. Maybe all these plaques were keys once. Maybe the chevron pattern became popular because it signified power. No idea.”

“But the Whites found the right plaques.”

“Yes, and they used them to escape the madness that erupted at the dawn of the age of reason.” Chris broke eye contact and stared out of the window.

“You’re feeling responsible again. Don’t.” I longed to touch his hand. Instead, I tapped the little ball drawn on the edge of the paper, the ball Damian had considered a full moon. “The million-pound question remains the same. Where did they go? These figures seem to be headed for this mothball. What is it? Another planet? A wormhole?”

“Think lateral. Think myth and white gods. Viracocha for the Incas or Quetzalcoatl for the Aztecs. There are similar myths among the Carib people.” His gaze searched mine and held it. “Don’t look so skeptical. It’s one theory among many. Whatever they did, it happened either at or around the solstice."

"Because of your family rumors."

"That, and the fact those doodles represent star constellations that only appear in summer. As wonky as it might look, the drawing is actually quite precise. This here," he said, indicating the squiggle on the left, "depicts the summer sky over Britain as seen back when the henge was built."

"Seriously?"

"Trust me, Damian and I checked. Stars change positions slowly, but they do change. While the nightly firmament might have looked similar back then, it wouldn't have looked the same." He tapped the paper again. "The second constellation here on the right is almost like ours, but there are subtle shifts. Our research confirms these are the skies over the same place as they appeared over four hundred years ago." His eyes sparkled.

Cor blimey, the man was good. Let him loose with a computer and he dished up some mind-boggling revelations. "To sum it up, the super witches used the powers of an ancient monument to disappear during the summer solstice. Where they ended up, we don't know, but they left their access keys behind. These access keys were originally created back in the Neolithic period, like the monument itself."

"Something along those lines, yes."

"What do you make of this?" I pointed at the doodle Jenna had taken for a plant—the doodle that had triggered me into a full meltdown.

"Ah, yes. I'd say it's a crude drawing of a lily plant. Next to it is a name. Took me a while to figure it out."

"So?"

He grinned. "I'd wager the artist signed her drawing. The name is Coldron. Together with the lily drawing, that gives you—"

"Lily Coldron? Oh, wow. Never heard of her, though."

"Shame, I was hoping you would. Anyway, that's all for the moment."

"You've done an amazing job."

"Make sure to thank Damian for his cross-referencing. The man is a pro, and he'll take over now, since I need to get on with the programming."

"Will do. Now, what does this mean for us?"

"It certainly means the coven is right to be a bit cautious around the monument at this time of the year. The evacuation plan is a reasonable measure, and in case anybody has an issue with it, you can show them your image."

"With the cops sniffing around, I'm not sure we'll be able to leave." I rose, fetched the plates, and opened the dishwasher.

"Myrtle, your mob didn't make the cut, was left behind, and disbanded. Now you're all back together and you're drawing sparks from each other, or whatever it is you're doing. Perhaps the solstice indeed eggs you on. Still, I think you guys have your limits. That's why I don't think your murders are caused by magic. Should evacuation not be on the cards, simply ensure that you all stay at home. Don't invite anybody uninitiated, in case your skylles go a bit haywire. With some luck, you should be fine."

His gaze fell on Petty, and a smile twitched in the corners of his mouth. "On a good day, you can challenge the laws of nature. That other mob must have twisted them. I've said it once before, and I'll repeat it. I've got no sympathy for my ancestors for what they did. But there is one thing I'd count in their favor. They must've been dead scared of the Whites."

I placed the plates in the dishwasher and fetched the cutlery. "If they were that formidable, how could the witch hunters catch them?"

"Perhaps there was a way to block their magic, and my lot sussed it out. It doesn't change that the Whites must've been damn powerful and scary. I wouldn't want to meet a real witch. Ever."

What? "Hey, I am a real witch."

Chris winced. "Sorry. You're a miracle. But your lost magical cousins must've been a force of nature."

I closed the dishwasher and turned my back on him. In a way, he was right. I was flying blind by the seat of my silky knickers. We all were. And without brooms. On the plus side, I had managed to solve the riddle of the empty pages, and with a lot of help from Chris and Damian, had thrown some light onto the mystery of the disappearing witch folk.

I still was a failure. Left behind when what Chris called the real witches went away and took their magic with them.

Chris stepped up. "If I think about it, perhaps I would like to."

"Would like what?"

"Meet a White. With some safety measures in place. Yes, it might be scary. But it would also be fascinating. I mean, how do you live with powers like that?"

"Dangerously?" My voice trembled, and I hated myself for it.

"Sorry, now I've hurt you."

I sought his deep, dark gaze. "You didn't mean to. It's just . . . oh, forget it."

He grabbed my hand, and I let him. "I shouldn't have said that. It was thoughtless of me. You feel inferior. You shouldn't. Myrtle, you're absolutely amazing simply because you're you. I bet no White ever had a magical primula."

His words sent a warm glow of contentedness spreading from my midriff. Chris understood me. More than that, he cared for me, no matter who or what I was. None of the men in my previous romantic entanglements had truly bothered. Back then, I'd been nothing scarier than a grammar school teacher.

As the glow surged through my body, the recent troubles dropped out of sight. Not forgotten by far, but not important for a little while. I had found a friend. Perhaps, with a bit of luck, I had even found my soul mate.

20

A LOVER'S SPAT

As much as I fancied Chris and he seemed to fancy me, we did not take the plunge between the sheets that evening. The reason is best explained in culinary terms—we both preferred a slow simmer over a flash in the pan.

After we had said a lengthy goodbye to each other, I went to bed. At first, I slept like a baby. Then the dreams interfered. My cat, my primula, the recipe book, cobwebbed rows of wine bottles—they were all mixed in with the pesto, and corpses littered the streets. When somebody screamed, I woke up in a cold sweat, but it was only the clock radio. Tired and edgy after my wild night, I hated leaving my bed and wanted to relive my evening with Chris. But no, the guests needed TLC, and I had to get hold of Jenna before the cops did.

I rang her number, but the call went to voicemail.

"Jenna, we need to talk. It's hyper-urgent."

A quick check from the window revealed the heat wave was

still going strong, though the telltale cauliflower clouds had already seeded the sky with turmoil.

None of those thoughts did anything for my mood, so I treated myself to a verbena and peppermint shower.

When I padded out of the foggy bathroom, the radio was chattering away about dead bodies, suspects, and general mayhem, bringing back the breathless anguish of my dream.

Get a grip on yourself.

I placed my washing in a plastic hamper and shrugged into a rayon dress in cheerful traffic-cone orange. Once I had put on my face, I snapped on the golden ear clips, the last present from Mum on my fourteenth birthday, and slipped into fawn-colored suede moccasins—one instant landlady at your service.

Secure in the knowledge I looked okay, no matter how gnarly my mood, I descended to the utility room to run a load. To reach the machine, I had to pick my way between tambourines, tablas, ukuleles, and other assorted instruments, which told me the musicians were still around. That gave me hope for the others. After drawing a deep breath, I headed for the conservatory.

A quick head count from the entrance boosted my budding optimism. Apart from the Londoners, nobody had run.

Instruments on my mind, I beelined for the Blue Lady and her partner, who must have guts as robust as my cat's. Steaming lumps of fried black pudding with eggs over easy were piled on their plates, while helpings of bacon lurked on the side.

"Good morning. I wanted to thank you for continuing your stay with us. I gather you heard the police warning about the poisoned food in the village?"

Blue Lady wiped her mouth with a napkin. "Yes. We never bought anything in the shops. No need to worry. This is typical police bullshit." She stared at her plate, shook her head, and speared a sizable chunk of bacon.

Her partner gave her a grim little smile. "Not everybody can afford a place like this, dear. If I were living rough, I would also run."

"Pah." Blue Lady raised her chin at the empty table for number five. "The poshies have bolted, haven't they?"

"Yes," I said. "I must admit, I'm not unhappy about it."

"Me neither." She bounced me a conspiratorial grin before tackling her breakfast with renewed vigor.

The two sales ladies were swapping pitch strategies, so I left them alone and approached the Enderbys.

Big mistake.

I hadn't yet reached their table when Mr. Enderby launched into a tirade. "Ms. Coldron, good to see you. You heard about the tainted products? That's the result of allowing amateurs to sell homemade foodstuff. Never advisable. As I have said on many occasions—"

"Too many occasions." Anne Enderby sighed.

I slapped a cheerful smile onto my face. "Dear me, yes, so worrying, isn't it? However, I can assure you we don't use compromised products in our kitchen." Not a lie, not quite. Our bacon hailed from the same place as the wine, but it wasn't produced in the village. Marty got it from a pig farmer over in Devon.

Anne spread orange marmalade on a slice of toast. "Here, dear. Try this. It's ever so nice."

"Honestly, my dear, sometimes I wonder. Citrus fruits aren't good for my stomach when it's acidic already. Don't even think of it. I might take some cherry jam instead."

Amazing how his wife coped, but her eyes never lost their twinkle.

"Have you made any plans for the day?" I asked.

"We thought of visiting the locks at Caen Hill. We've run out of sights here in the village," she said.

Her husband pulled a list from the breast pocket of his polo shirt. "We've seen the henge, the manor, the alley of standing stones, Kennet Long Barrow, the museum, the gallery, the church, and the dovecote. And we've done the four recommended rambles. That should cover it."

The sheer thought of running around in this weather,

ticking off touristic highlights, made me break out in a sweat. "The locks are quite the drive. How about a visit to the Swindon Sports Pool?"

Enderby dropped the toast his wife had passed him onto the tablecloth, sticky side down. "No way. Ms. Coldron, I appreciate your suggestion, but pools are extremely unsanitary places. Chlorine always gives me a migraine, and you won't see me dead in swimming trunks."

I took a moment to work out that he must have cracked a joke.

Mrs. Enderby patted her husband's hand. "Yes, dear. It's a shame about this health of yours."

Those two seemed fine enough, so I swung away from them and was about to have a word with Aaron when my gaze fell on Pan.

Something was wrong.

For one thing, he was alone. When I had counted heads, I had spotted Pan's back and had assumed Gerry to be with him. But the other chair at the table was unoccupied. I stepped closer. Pan's face was waxen, and a sheen of perspiration covered his forehead. The same moment I reached the table for number three, he winced and pressed his hands to his stomach, making mine lurch in response.

I bent over him. "Pan, what's the matter?"

He looked up and tried a brave smile but failed miserably. Fresh tears glittered in his eyes. "It's nothing. I've been up the entire night with stupid cramps. Gerry isn't around, I'm afraid."

With a bang of the door and a lusty "Morning, all," Cecily burst into the conservatory, carrying a tray with Aaron's breakfast. I caught her eye, pointed at Pan, and mimicked emptying a cup. After a brief nod, she served Aaron and returned to the kitchen.

I sat in Gerry's chair. "We'll get you more tea. That'll help with the cramps." It wouldn't fix whatever had gone wrong in their marriage, but tea was the one thing I could do for him.

"We had a row yesterday," he said, his sunken eyes begging me to understand. "Gerry arranged this lovely picnic, but I couldn't eat anything. These poor dead people. I can't stop thinking about them. It has totally ruined our trip. I didn't want to leave, I mean we came for the celebrations, but everything's so awful." The last word was a sob.

My heart went out to him. To cope with this madness, one needed the hide of an armadillo, which Pan didn't have.

"Do you know where Gerry is?"

Pan ran his tongue over his lips. "No idea. I'm afraid I stormed off. Left him in the clearing. It's not far, somewhere near that farm. Upwind—the place stinks to high heaven." He tried another brief, tragic smile, failed as miserably as before, and sagged in his chair.

What was Cecily doing with the tea? This was taking way too long. "I know it sounds strange, but you need to eat something. How about some antacids?"

Pan sighed again. "I had some, thanks. I tried eating. Got myself some yogurt. Toast on its own is too dry." He dipped his spoon into a small bowl. The spoon reached the mouth, wavered. He swallowed.

Pan forced a grin. "You're correct about the fluids. I should have used the kettle in our room." Once more, he dipped into the bowl, his hand trembling until the spoon dropped onto the tablecloth, splattering its load of creamy Bircher muesli.

My sluggish brain was trying to make sense of what I had seen when Pan reached for his throat. "Ugh, it's getting worse." He half-rose and then fell back on his chair.

My brain shifted gears. Muesli. Muesli contained nuts. Pan was allergic to nuts. My stomach responded to the pull of gravity. A hot wave of panic surged through my body.

My gaze snapped to the buffet and to the big red warning sign next to the muesli bowl.

Oh, rats.

Allergies. How did one cope with an allergic reaction? I had no idea—

Enderby. He suffered from allergies, and he had an EpiPen. He had shown it to me when he checked in.

In the short time it had taken me to reach a decision, Pan's breathing became labored. His face reddened. When I rushed to his side, my chair fell over, interrupting the breakfast chatter. Cutlery clattered onto plates. Teacups got lowered and eyes fixed on me.

"Mr. Enderby, I need your help. Now, please."

Pan's breathing turned squeaky, and once more he struggled up from his chair. His face red, he clawed at his throat.

"Air. Need . . . air."

Chairs scraped over the tiles. Someone spoke, but I didn't understand a word. This was going way too fast. We needed a doctor, an ambulance.

They'll never make it in time.

Enderby stepped up. "If you ask me, the young man suffers from anaphylactic shock. That can be life-threatening. In fact, I—"

"Mr. Enderby, Pan is madly allergic to nuts. He's just eaten some. We need your EpiPen."

A sharp intake of breath somewhere in the room.

Pan slumped in his chair, sliding sideways. I caught him as he was slipping off his seat.

"For heaven's sake, James, don't stand there. Do something." Anne's voice, her body close to mine. "Let's get the poor man onto the floor, Ms. Coldron, before he hurts himself."

Enderby rummaged in his leather purse and retrieved the EpiPen. It still reminded me of a Magic Marker. He looked up. "Keep his upper body upright, otherwise he'll have even more breathing problems."

Once Anne and I had lowered Pan to the floor and propped him up with seat cushions. All I found was a frantic flutter under the tips of my fingers.

Enderby knelt next to me, pulled a stopper or something

from the top of the pen, shook it once, and jabbed it against Pan's chino-clad thigh.

"Uh, shouldn't you have removed his trousers? Or injected him somewhere else?" I asked.

"No need to. This is how it's done. Trust me, I have verified and tested the procedure many times." Enderby's voice sounded as calm and unfazed as if he were carrying out a routine inspection. "He'll require medical assistance. I don't like those blue lips."

Somebody spoke from behind me. "Ma'am, what can I do to help?"

Aaron.

"Could you call the emergency services for me?"

"Nine-one-one, gotcha."

Mrs. Shuttlecock shifted into my field of vision, a smartphone in her hand. "Won't work, luv. It's triple nine in this country. Let me do it."

"No need, I've already called them," the Blue Lady said from behind. "They'll come as quickly as possible."

By that time it might be too late. Why on earth would Pan eat nuts? The last time, he had freaked at the sight of them.

What if Pan dies?

The pulse under my hands raced so fast, I kept losing it. The wheezing and the terrible squeaky rasps increased in volume until they filled my head, the breakfast room, the world. I was caught in a rerun of the horror on the riverbank. Like the other day, there was nothing more we could do. Mr. Enderby acted his part. Now, we would have to wait.

He mustn't die.

My vision wavered. The voices were swallowed into a fizzy greenish light until only a hushing of leaves was left. A faint scent of roses reached my nose. Something velvety tickled the inside of my fists.

Rose petals. The essence of my magic.

You'll learn to control the manifestations together with the side effects as you improve, Dot's voice whispered in my mind.

Purpose, it was all about purpose, about wanting or needing something.

Pan mustn't die, and I don't want any petals.

Mr. Enderby blipped back into view, grim-faced as he knelt next to Pan. I was dimly aware of the other guests, who were drifting in and out of sight. Seconds stretched on an elastic band, pulling and reaching the breaking point.

A lump of moist petals filled my fists. Two or three of them tumbled past my vision.

He mustn't die. My vision fizzed and wobbled. Fire lanced into my head. Then it was gone. And Pan was still alive.

The wheeze eased off. Slowly, he sagged into the pillows. I slipped the crushed petals into my pockets. When I checked his pulse, it was slowing.

Mr. Enderby nodded once more and faced me, concern in his brown eyes. "I wasn't sure whether the epinephrine would do the trick. He was in a pretty bad shape."

Something inside of me uncoiled, leaving me limp and dizzy. Without Enderby's EpiPen we hadn't stood a chance, but my skylles must have made the difference between life and death. "Thank you so much."

Pan moaned. His eyes snapped wide open. He pushed me aside and scrambled to his feet.

"Careful, luv," Mrs. Shuttlecock said. "You're not fit to walk around."

His hand in front of his mouth, Pan stumbled into the garden.

"Oh, dear," said Anne. "That man needs to get to a hospital."

"Emergency is aware," Blue Lady hollered from across the room. "Called them again."

I bounced her a breathless "thank you" before joining Pan on the lawn.

"So sorry." He panted.

I sensed a presence next to me. Cecily, bearing not tea but a wet dishrag. Wordlessly, she plastered it across Pan's forehead and sucked her teeth. "What have you done to yourself?"

Pan slumped, pressing the towel to his forehead. "I don't know," he moaned. "Everything's so weird. I want my Gerry."

"Do you have your phone on you? I can call him." Behind me, many feet shuffled on the terrace as the other guests followed us outside.

Pan sat there, staring at the tiger lilies.

I felt like calling him to order, which was rather uncaring. Perhaps the latest hexing gig was to blame for my impatience. What had possessed the man to eat muesli when he knew nuts could kill him? And when we had put up a warning sign five times the size of the original one? It made no sense. He was highly strung, and perhaps the quarrel with Gerry, the murders, his upset stomach, and a sleepless night had broken glass in his brain cabinet.

"Pan?"

"Sorry." He fumbled for his phone, unlocked it after three attempts, and handed it across. It was a more modern model than mine, but I found the contact list eventually. I pushed the button with Gerry's number and waited. The call went to his voicemail.

"Gerry? Can you please call back? Pan is seriously ill. He needs you." I thumbed away the call. "He's not answering his phone."

There could be many explanations for Gerry's lack of response, wounded pride being one of them. The man could have spent the night anywhere.

Pan said nothing and kept ogling the lilies with a vacant expression on his face.

A siren wailed its way up Long Street.

"I hope it's them," I said.

"They're not usually that fast," Mrs. Saddler said.

"The girl at the switchboard told me an ambulance was already in Avebury," the Blue Lady said. "When I told them Pan was dying, they moved their backsides quicker than usual."

She was a competent person, but her whole demeanor made me concerned for anybody who dared to cough during her concerts. Most likely she would whack them over the head with a trombone.

That wasn't nice of me either, and since my headache had improved, there was no excuse for my surliness.

We didn't have to wait long for the doorbell to gong and two sturdy paramedics to show up. They took one look at Pan and declared that while he might not be at death's door, he needed immediate medical attention.

Strapped on the stretcher, he called for me in a weak voice. "Myrtle? Could you try Gerry again? He needs to know. Do you need his number?"

"It's on the reservation. Don't you worry."

My phone buzzed, and for a brief, happy moment I thought it would be Pan's husband.

Instead, it was Jenna. In tears. "Myrtle, can you come, please? Gran's taken a turn for the worse. She had problems last night and again this morning. We called an ambulance, but it never arrived. Marty is taking her to Swindon. I've got the kids here and . . ." Her voice dissolved into sobs.

"On my way."

—

The front door to Wytchett Farm stood wide open. Marty must have been in one heck of a rush when he took his grandmother to Swindon hospital.

"Jenna?"

My call echoed into the dim hallway that smelled of burned milk, burned toast, burned everything. When I received no answer, I hurried into the garden. No Robbie and Johnnie were there to greet me in high-pitched excitement. No Jenna. Only rows and rows of apple trees dreaming under the sun. Not for much longer, though—the clouds were building cauliflower castles in the heavens while little airplanes zipped across, headed for turbulence.

"Jenna?"

The chirp of a thrush was the only response. Inside the farmhouse, I faced the steep oak staircase, where a thick red cord led the way upstairs. From the space under the stairs peeped an old spinning wheel, together with two Bobby cars, one red and one blue. The clutter was comfortable. The house was a real home, its solid walls sheltering the patchwork family living within. But something had disturbed the peace. Perhaps it was all in my mind. Maybe my misgivings were owed to the faint medicinal odor that wafted from the upper floor.

With dread squeezing my throat, I climbed the treads, step by creaky step, until I arrived in the upper corridor. Whitewashed uneven walls and white doors greeted me—the place would have looked bland had it not been for the butterfly flurry of childlike drawings and the woven Navajo rugs covering the floor, threadbare but beautiful.

From the other end of the corridor drifted sobs.

"Jenna?"

I found her in a small bedroom, its oak floorboards covered in a wildly patterned carpet at odds with the antique bedstead that occupied the wall to my left. On the bed sat Jenna, pressing an embroidered pillow to her chest, tears wetting her face. The room was the origin of the odd smell. Fusty and metallic, it crept into my nostrils and made me sneeze. Jenna looked up, saw me, and broke down crying.

For a moment I hesitated. But only for a moment. "It'll be all right," I said, not believing one word.

Jenna didn't either and continued her sobbing

"Come on, tell me what happened."

Jenna pulled away from me, fumbled in her pockets for a disintegrating tissue, and blew her nose. "Gran was fine until some point early this morning. I heard a thump and dashed across the hall. She was lying on the carpet in her nightie, lips blue. She said she was dizzy and not to mind. You know how she is. I shared my skylles and wished her well. It helped a bit, but I was fretting myself into a knot."

"I bet you were."

"We rang the hospital. They told us to bring Gran across, but Marty thought the drive would be too much for her. I insisted on an ambulance, but there's been another accident on the motorway, they were out of paramedics—these cuts, you know—and she was breathing okay, so she wasn't at the top of their list. They said they would try. Gran got better, and then worse, and then we rang emergency again. Nobody came." Jenna's hands pulled at the sodden tissue, so I rummaged around in my backpack and pushed a fresh one into her hand.

"Thanks." She sniffed.

Tissues weren't good enough compensation for having hijacked Dot's ambulance.

"About what happened the other day . . . in the cellar, I mean. I'm sorry, I shouldn't have run away and left you alone. It was just the shock."

I clenched my fists. "Yes. It was wrong of me, but I didn't mean it that way. I didn't know."

"No, how could you? Something must have really rocked your boat, and I made it worse. When I returned to help, you'd gone."

Odd. I had spent ages in Jenna's horrid cellar. "Petty's back and it's all that counts."

"Yes. Oh, I found your note. Myrtle, this is horrible. Why would anybody want to poison my wine? It's for people to enjoy. Now, they're dying." She burst into another bout of sobbing.

That didn't sound like a confession, and Jenna had never hidden her emotions. The pale face and the sorrow clogging her voice were genuine. Had to be. My mood soared and then plunged.

If not her, who else? Daisy? The poison must have been in the wine, since nothing else made sense. But why? And how? Or was Jen guilty and I was being naive? What the heck was going on here?

21

ANGEL WINGS

The bedroom door creaked open, and in traipsed one subdued little urchin. His brother waited on the doorstep, gripping something in his grubby fingers, something translucent and glittery that teased my memory, telling me I should recognize it.

"Mum?"

Jenna sat upright and wiped the heel of her hand across her eyes. "Yes, sweetheart?"

"Mum, we have a present for you."

Jenna's smile was a ghost of its former self, but it did the job. The kid's face lit up like a sparkler, and his brother rushed into the room, the shiny object in his hands. I'd seen it somewhere before. But where?

"Johnnie, how lovely. What is it?" Jenna said. Johnnie skipped across, a grin splitting his face, and placed his gift in her lap. The gadget was the size of a baseball bat, round on one end but splintered at the other where it must have broken off from whatever it had been attached to. Made of shiny plastic, the object reflected the light in a rainbow sheen, with strands of silvery metal running through the material like veins. It reminded me of a giant locust wing.

Finally, my sluggish synapses deigned to spark. Wrong insect. Not locusts—dragonflies.

Pan's dragonfly wing.

"What's up?"

I must have stiffened.

"Isn't it lovely? Look, Myrtle."

"Amazing. Well done, you two. Do you remember where you found this?" There was no reason dread should squeeze my chest. No reason whatsoever. Pan had mentioned a farm, and this was the closest to the Witch's Retreat. He told me he stormed off. He could have lost his wing around the corner.

"Outside. Under some trees," Johnnie said. His mother had identified him for me, and they remained in the same positions. He also sported fewer freckles across his button of a nose than his brother.

"It's not far." Yup, Robbie definitely displayed more freckles. On any other day, I would've been proud of myself.

"You only found this one, right?"

"Are there more, Auntie Myrtle?" Robbie's eyes lit up. "They're pretty. We can give the other to Gran."

Jenna's eyes were on me, begging me not to blab. She needn't have worried. I was preoccupied with the geography. If Pan lost his wing where the boys could find it, the picnic place couldn't be far. Upwind of the farm, my stricken guest had said. I argued with myself that it didn't matter—Gerry would be long gone. He would have found somewhere to spend the night and was now playing hard to get. Where would he have stayed? Not with Linda, whose bed and breakfast was still full, or so she had claimed. Not at the pub either, with its rooms occupied by Greg's friends. Pan and Gerry's car had never moved, I would swear to that.

What had Pan done?

The invisible weight on my chest amped up the squeeze. It was unlikely that somebody would have taken Gerry in. On the other hand, he might have slept rough. Last night had been warm. He would have had food. Perhaps he was still out there, sulking, hoping for Pan to grovel.

"Can you show me where you found this? There's another one, yes. I'm sure your gran would love to have it."

"Let's search for it," Jenna said. "I need to move or I'll go stir-crazy. Run ahead, you two. We'll follow in a minute."

"Treasure hunt, treasure hunt." The boys shot out of the door and sprinted down the corridor in a two-child stampede that reverberated through the old building. Jenna gave me a watery grin. "That's them sorted. What is this thing?" She placed the wing on the bed. "Is there something I should know?"

"It belongs to a guest. It's part of his midsummer night getup. He's not well and needs his partner. Only, the man has gone AWOL. The way I see it, they picnicked in the woods close to the farm, argued, and Pan must've broken off one of his wings when he left in a huff. Gerry, that's the other fellow, is not responding to calls, most likely nursing a good grump. I wonder whether he's doing so somewhere around here."

"Right, let's see if we can find him." Jenna stuffed the tissue into the pocket of her shapeless cotton dress. It was too mumsy for her, but then, fashion must have been the last thing on her mind this morning.

We were descending the stairs when Jenna spoke again. "You're sure that man is okay?"

"Gerry? He's lovely. He'll probably blame himself for the row and what happened to Pan. The guy was so upset this morning, he ate muesli."

"That's a problem because . . . ?"

"He's allergic. He almost died and got taken to the hospital."

"Ah." She gave me a caustic look.

A telltale flush crept into my cheeks. We had nicked Dot's

ambulance and Jenna knew it.

"Mum? Auntie Myrtle? Where are you?"

"We're coming," Jenna trilled.

Saved not by the bell but by a small boy.

Out on the terrace, we ran into a wall of humid, hot air. No breeze stirred the oppressive atmosphere, and sweat steamed from my pores, soaking me in an instant. An excellent excuse to change the subject. If in doubt, discuss the weather.

"Phew, it's hot."

Jenna fanned her flushed face with her hand. "Yes, it's getting unbearable. I can't imagine that guest of yours braving the great outdoors when he's rented a nice, cool bedroom."

Fear fluttered at the base of my throat. Jenna had given voice to my qualms. Even if Pan and Gerry had the mother of all rows, it would be nuts to stay out in this heat to prove a point. Perhaps he had returned. However, if that was the case, why didn't the man respond to my calls?

Because Pan, in a fit of madness, had killed him? No way— that was wrong thinking. There were plenty of reasons, all of them perfectly valid.

Such as? I pushed the niggles aside and scanned the grayish clouds bubbling up in the east.

"It'll be worse when the weather breaks."

Jenna nodded. "Sometime this evening. Marty is certain. Better find your guest first."

"Are you sure you want to come?"

"Told you, I need to move. So do the boys. And they know where to go."

We followed the twins through the gate and into pastures overrun by weeds and wilting wildflowers. I expected the children to take the trail that led to the river, but they kept to the brick wall, passing the garden of the next house. Once we reached the final plot in Tadpole Lane, the wall turned crumbly and was covered in ivy. All the time, the boys were leaping ahead like cheerful spaniels.

"How is Dot?" I asked, to say something. "Did Marty call?"

"Yes, the nurses were trying to find a bed for Gran."

"That's good news, I suppose."

"One should hope so."

In the abandoned garden to our right, disheveled beeches and birches were running the show. The house appeared desolate, its windows turning blind eyes on the weather.

Robbie and Johnnie stopped at the corner of the wall where it doglegged to the right, only to be swallowed by greenery that had broken through the bricks and reclaimed the land. The victory was old, for the shrubs stood tall and the shady ground below was covered in a tangled mess of nettles and grasses. A squirrel chittered its protest at our presence before it shot up a false acacia, showering us with blossoms.

The kids squealed and brushed the petals from their hair. Robbie pointed at a bushel of wilting ferns. "Here. We found Mum's present here."

Pan had spoken of a clearing. If Pan lost his wing after a long flight, I stood no chance of ever finding Gerry.

This is pointless. No way is he still out there. Unless Pan had . . .

"Is there a picnic place somewhere in the vicinity?"

Jenna pursed her lips. "Mh, there's a small clearing near the far end of the wall. Marty chased a horde of wild campers away from there last week. Blasted litterbugs. No idea why they chose this place over the river. There's no running water here. Though for a picnic it might do."

I had to check. I owed it to Gerry. And my conscience. But I would do so without Jenna and the kids.

"Great. I'll find it on my own, don't you worry. You'd better turn back."

A sticky hand stole into mine. A second later, another one followed on the other side. "We know that place, Auntie Myrtle. You think the other treasure is there?"

"If it is, I'll bring it to you. Deal?"

"Come on. Let's see what we can find," Jenna said, regaining her confidence at the wrong moment.

"Jen—"

She powered ahead and the twins dragged me on. Soon, a latticework of twigs barred our way at face height, while clusters of dusty nettles waited to nip our ankles. The boys tore loose, passed underneath the branches, and dashed off, yelling.

Sunlight filtered through the leaves, and Jenna and I emerged in the open. Ahead of us lay fields crisscrossed by double tractor tracks. To our right extended a rough crescent of grass, while on the far side the old garden wall left only an overgrown trail for access. Where the wall had disintegrated, vermilion bricks spilled to the ground in a picturesque tumble. The twins scuttled up the heap and entered the garden.

"You two come out of there at once," Jenna shouted. "Excuse me, Myrtle." She dashed off.

I scanned the surroundings and liked what I saw. The place had a morbid charm, as if an actual ruin played the romantic folly. I could imagine Chris and I enjoying dinner under the stars. Protected by the half-circle of trees on one side and the broken wall on the other, this place would be sheltered from prying eyes, especially at night.

My gaze hitched on something in the far corner. As I shaded my eyes, an object checkered in red and white swam into view.

A picnic blanket.

—

A swift glance confirmed Jenna was busy with coaxing her offspring from the unkempt garden, so I stepped closer to the picnic spot. The plaid had been spread on the grass, a basket on one side, a champagne cooler, the tops of bottles peeking over its rim, on the other. Plates and glasses had been arranged in the middle, and a baguette, still wrapped in paper, waited for a romantic dinner that never happened.

"Gerry? Are you here?"

There was no reaction other than a buzzing of bees, bird-song, and distant noises, most likely from the riverbank.

"Gerry, it's Myrtle, the owner of the B&B. I need your help. Pan is seriously ill."

Such a peaceful scene. At the same time, it wasn't. Something felt off. I told myself it was only the lack of reply. Gerry had no beef with me, and he was a polite person. He would have shown himself. Ergo, Gerry was no longer around.

Laughter rang out behind me. One of the kids. It was followed by the voice of his mother, scolding him. Other than that, the place was eerily quiet.

Apart from the buzzing in the air, that is. Bees? I wasn't allergic, but I didn't fancy upsetting a hive either. Surely Pan would have mentioned irate insects? Yet, the man had been in quite a state. Did bees sleep at night? Surely they did. Gerry and Pan would never have noticed.

My gaze was drawn in by those little bottles, so innocent in their cooler, the ice long since melted.

Bottles? Deep in my abdomen, a nerve cramped. Surely Gerry wouldn't have . . .

I rushed to the checkered plaid. Something glinted in the shade thrown by the cooler, something that wasn't visible from where I had been standing a moment before. Two used wine glasses. A reddish residue stuck to the bottom of one glass, while the other one remained almost full. In the grass beside the picnic blanket lay two empty bottles. Not the ones for sale in the supermarket or at a liquor merchant. They were small, round, and reminiscent of old medicine flasks.

Jenna's country wine.

Shock punched me in the stomach, and I took a step backward. Gerry never heard the warning. Instead, he bought the wine and poured those drinks. Perhaps he had bought them before the warning was broadcasted, as I feared somebody would. Then the two men drank.

I looked at the glass still filled with wine.

Wrong. One of them did.

Pan. His must have been the poisoned bottle, but since so much of the wine was left, he would have only taken a sip. Unlike Boian, he didn't suffer from a heart condition. That had saved his life.

And still the poison had been potent enough to cause stomach problems and hallucinations. Why else would the man eat muesli when it could kill him?

What about Gerry? The niggles returned and swarmed my brain.

Both bottles were empty. The contents of one remained in the glass, but the other had been drained. Drunk? Poured away, perhaps? Unless I had the wrong end of the stick, and it had been Gerry who sipped and Pan who emptied his glass and suffered the consequences. No matter what, since not every wine bottle was lethal, Gerry might be perfectly fine. That was a good thought. I sucked hope from that thought.

"Gerry?"

The buzzing increased in volume. It didn't sound like bees at all.

Once more I looked at the full glass. How could I miss them before? Fat bluebottles and flesh flies in iridescent green circled the glass. A bluebottle landed and crawled along the rim. As I stared, the fly lost its balance and fell into the wine.

My heart skipped a beat.

The insect hadn't been the first to drop in. A blackened crust of them floated on the liquid. The newcomer quivered once and then calmed. Two flesh flies circling the rim plopped onto the plaid, where they landed on their backs, their little legs clawing the air. I had stumbled over evidence that something was wrong, and I mean seriously wrong, with that wine.

Sarah would need to know, and now. I reached into my pocket and then hesitated. First, I had to get Jenna and the kids out of the way.

Perhaps she knows? An icy hand squeezed my throat.

The buzzing increased in anger. Impossible. Not enough of the flies remained alive to make such a noise.

The buzzing seemed to come from somewhere along the wall Jenna was scrambling over in pursuit of her boys. They flitted through the wild garden behind the wall, cheerful, playful, innocent. For the moment, they were out of harm's way.

Buzz.

That noise was sawing on my nerves. I should ring Sarah and get the heck out of here. Instead, I stood rooted to the spot and listened to something that was more ominous by the second.

Buzz.

What I heard sounded like a chorus composed of lots of busy little wings. It set my teeth on edge and caused the hairs on my arms to rise. The sound originated from the thicket of butterfly bushes caressing the ruined wall. Soon, they would bring out their beautiful flowers. Buddleia was aptly named lilac of summer.

Buzz.

Some flowers had to be out early because I spotted something violet hidden behind a shimmering veil.

My heart skipped a beat.

Not a veil at all. Something was moving. Flies. A whole swarm of them, buzzing, shimmying, soaring.

If the veil wasn't a veil, the flower couldn't be a flower.

My legs turned to jelly, and my head swam. My vision rose and dropped and rose again, like the macabre dance of the flies weaving in and out of the butterfly bushes.

Drawn by the flower that wasn't a flower but had been a person.

Gerry.

Nausea rose at the back of my throat. I could have sworn there was a funky smell in the air that didn't register before.

Stop it right there.

This was all too much. And there was no way out.

With shaky fingers, I dug for the smartphone in my pocket.

Somehow my fingers hit upon the right number on the first try. A quick glance at the garden revealed Jenna and her kids were out of sight. I couldn't hear them over that buzzing, which now seemed to come from inside my head.

"Sergeant Widdlethorpe, Swindon CID."

Relief streamed through me, and my fingers slackened and lost their grip on the phone. I caught the thing before it slipped out of my hands.

"Sarah? Myrtle here."

"What's wrong now?" Sharp like the lash from a whip, her voice smacked my ear.

"How do you know—"

"Your pitch. When there's trouble afoot, it's a lot higher than normal."

"Yes."

"Yes, what? We know who's made the wine, if that's what you wanted to tell me."

"No, that's not why I'm calling."

She carried on relentlessly. "Based on our evidence and your tip, the DCI pulled in plenty of favors and two labs worked through the night. We found about twenty poisoned bottles of elderberry wine among the lot we confiscated. I suspect there are more out there, since people are still calling us. We're now screening the rest of the foodstuff, but that seems to be okay. I was about to head for Wytchett Farm to make sure your friend is there."

My insides melted into mush. It was too late. "Bring your team. I found more poisoned wine. And a corpse. At least I think so. I'm not getting any closer, I can tell you that now."

"Closer? Where are you? Hang on, did you say corpse?"

"Can't be anything else." I swallowed, but my throat was dry. "All these flies," I whispered.

She was quiet for a moment. When she spoke again, her voice had changed. Warm and gentle, it hugged my ear. "We're coming. Don't worry, we'll be there. Where are you?"

Relief rushed through me. The police would deal with the flies. I wouldn't have to inspect those bushes and whatever I suspected lay behind, hidden by the moving, buzzing swarm.

"Behind Wytchett Farm. The abandoned property. I'll wait for you at the top of Tadpole Lane."

"You do that. See you in half an hour. Stay away from . . . you know what I mean. And take care." She disconnected.

How I hated those flies.

22

LIGHT REFRESHMENTS

Thirty minutes was all I had until the cops arrived, which gave me barely enough time to scramble after Jenna, break as gently as possible the news about the wineglass and its grisly contents, announce the imminent arrival of the troops, and urge her to return to the farm.

Never once did I mention the butterfly bush and what lay beyond.

I simply couldn't.

After Jen and the kids left, I followed the trail to the end of the cul-de-sac that was Tadpole Lane and waited in the shade of a copper beech for the cops to arrive. It took nail-biting ages until an unmarked vehicle rolled up, tracked by a squad car. A white van in much better shape than Marty's brought up the rear. My heartbeat accelerated, and the buzzing was back in my ears as my thoughts dipped and dove, too fast to catch.

The car doors opened and Sarah climbed out. By now, my

heartbeat clocked a hundred miles an hour. The man emerging on the other side wasn't Diloff. Of plump middle age, he featured the sort of face one tends to skim over in a crowd. His outfit of a lightweight gray suit, a cream shirt, and no tie was business-like and nondescript. The doors of the squad car banged open. Cameron and two constables, a man and a woman, spilled from the vehicle. They were soon joined by the passengers from the van, two unhappy-looking women in the type of white coveralls I had learned to associate with the scene of crime officers. Nothing beat walking around snugly wrapped in plastic on a hot summer's day.

The new copper must have spotted me in the shade because he sauntered across. Despite his mild and nonthreatening posture, the man radiated competence. It was his eyes, I decided. Lighter than his suit, they were razor sharp.

"DCI Peter Christie. You must be Ms. Coldron." He gave me a curt nod but didn't extend his hand. Not many people shook hands these days.

"Let me show you what I discovered," I said, eager to get the horror over and done with. "It's not far."

"Good," Christie responded. "Sarah assured me you wouldn't have entered the crime scene."

"Not for the life of me. If there is one. I spotted some poisoned wine, which I believe a guest of mine must have drunk. He's alive, by the way. He's the reason I was looking for this place, actually. His partner is missing. From what I can see, I think I might have found him."

I was babbling—I always did when stressed. The alternative was screaming.

Christie gave me another measured nod. "You're doing fine. Show us the way, then."

I headed for the clearing, the DCI on one side of me and Sarah on the other, with the rest of the coppers trailing behind. When we reached the picnic area, I stopped short of the blanket.

"See this?" I pointed at the insect death trap one wineglass had become. "My best guess is Pan—my guest—sipped from the wine. He had severe stomach trouble this morning, plus he was totally spaced out. He even ate muesli, when he's allergic to nuts."

"Where is that man?" Sarah said, anxiety creeping into her expression.

"Swindon Central. He should be okay. Another guest had an EpiPen."

And I used my skylles.

"Yes, but we need the medics to run a few tests." She whipped out her phone. "What's the bloke's family name?"

I told her what she wanted to know. Sarah must have the hospital on speed dial. She pressed the phone to her ear, chewing her lower lip.

All the while, the DCI said nothing. He seemed to take my friend for granted and let her get on with things. The guy rose another notch in my respect. He knew about delegation, something DI Diloff wouldn't ever understand, even if he memorized all of *Management for Dummies*. However, Christie's competence wasn't good news for the coven.

Still, those thoughts were good, since they stopped me from worrying about the eerie non-flower at the edge of the clearing. The lilac splotch always remained at the corner of my vision. The lilac—and the cloud of flies busily buzzing around. I could hear their hum over the soft voices of the officers and the radio chatter.

Without hurry, Christie scanned the trees, the pasture, and the butterfly bushes at the back. "I guess those flies drew your attention?"

"Yes."

He nodded to a scene of crime officer. "Over to you," he said.

I took a few steps backward.

Unhurried, the woman in the white coverall headed for the broken wall, pushed the bushes aside with one hand, bent forward, and stopped. The SOCO's arrival drove the insects into a frenzy, their buzz rising to an angry drone as they whizzed around the intruder.

Dread sat on my stomach, heavy and chill. How silly. If Gerry was there, I would no longer be alone with him. If he wasn't there, I might end up with egg on my face, but I had only done what any sensible citizen would do in such a situation. But I didn't believe that would be my biggest problem. Not the way those flies were carrying on.

The SOCO let go of the bushes, swatted at the insects, and returned to us as placidly as before. She nodded once. "Dead less than a day, I would say."

"Mh, that's for Doc to figure out." Christie turned to the second SOCO. "I want the van here." Cameron he ordered to flush out the doctor, who apparently should have turned up by now. The uniforms were last. Their job was to secure the scene and scan the perimeter for further clues.

When the DCI was finished, I felt sick at heart.

"I need to ask you a few questions, Ms. Coldron. Not here, though. This isn't a good place for you to be."

That was decent of him. Poor Gerry. Poor Pan. On their honeymoon, of all things. I fought the rising tears and faced Sarah, who had finished her phone calls.

"Myrtle, are you okay? You're as gray as yesterday's porridge." She squeezed my shoulder, her sharp eyes filled with concern. "Good news. Your guest is on the mend, so we won't have to worry about him. The medics pumped out his stomach to be on the safe side. I reached them in time. They'll do lab checks of the contents now."

"Who will tell him about Gerry?"

Sarah winced. "That'll be me. I'll take a liaison officer with me. Later."

DCI Christie, who had waited patiently for us to finish, gave me a little nod. "After you. I reckon you know the way to Wytchett Farm? You can accompany me there."

My stomach churned, and a fresh load of acid seared my

throat. My troubles were far from over. Jenna's had just begun.

"Right. Okay. The easy way is down Tadpole Lane. Or would you prefer the shortcut I took through the woods?"

The male officer fastened one end of a blue-and-white police barrier to a birch and marched across the lawn, unrolling the plastic band as he went. The DCI held up the barrier. "After you. Let's not make our lives more difficult than they already are. We'll take the road and you can tell me once more how you found the victim."

—

Suffering from mental chilblains, even with the thermometer showing thirty degrees in the shade, is possible. I am the living proof. Not because Christie made me recall every single step I took to the clearing and my moves afterward—that I could cope with, since the DCI had been kind enough to reassure me I was a witness, not a suspect. However, worries about Jenna kept interfering with my thoughts. In my memory, her face was superimposed on the scene.

Labs could trace anything these days. Why not magic?

We rounded the last corner and the farmhouse lay ahead, asleep in the stifling calm. I could swear the row of windows in the mansard roof observed our approach from above, like mistrustful eyes.

Christie had taken off his jacket and now carried it over his shoulder, his only concession to the weather. From above sounded a deep rumble. I craned my neck and watched the sun disappear behind a rather ominous mass.

Christie followed my gaze. "Looks like we might be in for a good soak. Let's hope this holds off for a while."

"Because of the crime scene."

"Indeed. Ah, we're expected." My escort raised his chin at the front door, wide open as it was when I arrived earlier this morning.

That didn't stop me from banging the knocker.

"Myrtle, is that you? We're on the terrace," Marty hollered in response.

"Yes, and I've brought the police with me." Not the most brilliant of warnings, but the only thing I could do for my friends.

Christie slipped me a sidelong glance, but he didn't comment.

When we arrived on the terrace, Marty was alone. He was scrutinizing the drama unfolding above our heads. "Need to get the cattle and chickens in this afternoon. The weather is about to break." He sucked his teeth and nodded to himself. With his rugged face and cheerful apple cheeks, he looked the local yokel, but I doubted my not-so-tame copper would let himself be hoodwinked.

"That would be a massive relief," he said. "Sorry, I should have introduced myself. Name's Christie. I'm the DCI at Swindon CID."

"Martyn Wytchett. I guess you know that already." Marty's face gave nothing away, but his rigid stance spoke volumes.

Since Christie hadn't dismissed me yet, I was determined to stay on as long as possible.

"Of course. I need to talk to Mrs. Jenna Burns. Would she be around?"

Jenna chose that moment to show up, bearing a tray with homemade lemonade. The glasses jingled slightly as she placed them on the table. "I prefer to be called by my maiden name, if you please. Take a seat. Is Sergeant Sarah not with you?" she asked, her voice purged of all emotion.

Christie waited with his response until we were sitting around the garden table. "She's busy. I hope you can accept me in her stead. I've taken over from DI Diloff, as things were getting . . . urgent." His smile intended to charm, but his eyes were busy scanning the environs. Eventually, his gaze found the lemonade.

Jenna poured. Her brother shot the police officer a quick glance, grabbed a glass, downed the contents in one go, and held the glass out for more. "Great stuff. Just what the doctor ordered."

I thought of coroners, and my hand hovered over the drink. Whose side was I on?

To heck with it.

I took the glass and followed Marty's example. The concoction was fantastic, like everything Jenna made. Crisp, sour, and sweet at the same time, the cool fluid ran down my throat. Surely I had imagined the bitter aftertaste?

Christie didn't touch his drink. "You're the winemaker of the Women's Institute?"

Jenna tilted her head, anxiety clouding her eyes. "There are two of us. Have you found out what rotter is poisoning our products?" Her lower lip quivered, and she was kneading her hands in her lap.

Christie turned his glass around and around on the table. "I hate to say this, but the products seem to be fine apart from one."

At least he had allowed both me and Marty to stay while he spoke with Jenna. She would be no match for the bloke—he would tie her into a knot in five seconds flat. Yes, he struck me as being both competent and fair. But he was police. They now had three deaths on their hands, which screamed serial killer. Diloff had effed things up. The media were baying for blood. The police needed to solve the case and fast.

"What product would that be?" Marty asked.

"The elderberry wine," Christie said.

Jenna tossed a swift glance in my direction. With a sharp hiss of indrawn breath, she said, "No."

"I'm afraid so," Christie said. "The first victim received one of your bottles as a gift. We didn't find it, but his friends confirmed the Wicca practitioners donated wine and food to their group. The head flutist gave us a detailed description of the bottles. Looks like they were fine apart from one."

Bolder now that Christie hadn't thrown me out, I said, "Only some bottles are affected."

Christie's voice never changed in pitch. "Yes. Ms. Turner

also drank the one compromised bottle of wine in the batch her friends bought. That one we seem to have found, by the way. We've analyzed the bottles that have been turned in, and about twenty contain the toxin. I feared there would be more around. Sometimes I hate to be right."

"No." A tear coursed down Jenna's cheek.

Marty stood and placed his hands on his sister's shoulders. His eyes were sharp. The Joe Farmer pretense was stripped away. "Jen has done nothing wrong."

"We compared the bottles," Christie said. "There's no visible difference between the tainted and the untainted ones. As to the ones with the poison, you can, of course, insert needles into corks. It's been done. Our experts carried out only preliminary tests, but they're reasonably sure this didn't happen here."

"How does winemaking work?" I asked. "I mean, in terms of fermenting, storing, and bottling? There must be other people involved."

Christie ran his hand through his thinning hair. "You took the words right out of my mouth, Ms. Coldron." A grin blipped on his face only to vanish again. "Sarah said you would."

"The boys and I collected the berries where we used to live." Jenna's voice trembled and steadied again. "Robbie and Johnnie have nothing to do with this."

I reached across the table and squeezed her hand.

"We're not suspecting your sons, Ms. Wytchett," Christie said. "Please carry on."

"Oh, sorry. It's only the second season we're doing this. It's all new for me."

"Sure. What about the first batch?"

"All sold last year. Right, so the wine matures in the carboys. Our cellar is old, and it keeps the temperature perfectly. Once the wine is ready, we transfer it into barrels, which Marty then drives to a bottling plant. They also do the corking and label- ing."

The table down in the cellar with the big glass jars must

have been Jen's winemaking facility, which she had pulled the curtain on. Why?

Christie reached into his jacket and removed a paper notepad. "Name of that outfit, please?"

"Oh, no way. It can't be Screwed Limited. They're ever so kind to take on my humble brew and at such a reasonable price. It makes my life so much easier."

"Unfortunately, we'll have to verify things with them," Christie said.

Her face as white as a sheet, Jenna dictated the address to Christie.

High time you did something to throw that copper off the scent. Dutifully, I prodded my brain, but it refused to cooperate. At least Sarah's boss wasn't accusing Jenna of mass murder. Not yet. He wasn't far off, though. I knew it, and Marty did, too. I could see it in his gaze, searching mine, imploring me to help.

An idea popped up like a submerged rubber duck. There had to be a reason not every bottle contained the poison. "Jenna, how many bottles in total did you put up for sale and when?"

Jenna fixed her panicked gaze on me. "Uh, all of it. About a week ago. It sold quickly, surprising me no end."

"Let's stick with the production for a moment. How many of these containers do you have?" Christie asked.

Rats.

"Five. They take ten liters each, and we ended up with around a hundred forty bottles."

"Why?" Christie asked. "I would have expected more like two hundred."

"Well, you always lose a bit, plus my filter broke and there was quite some spillage. I was so proud of my wine. It got bottled and I wanted it to mature. Makes it smoother and richer. For that, it has to age for a while." She sniffed.

Marty handed her a tissue, looking grimmer than ever.

"If you started out with close to one hundred forty bottles, then we seem to have most of them at the labs," Christie said.

"That's a great relief, though we're still missing a few. To make sure I've all the facts correct—other than yourself, who else is involved in making the wine?"

"My brother, for the mash. But he would never do something so rotten."

"Why would anybody?" Christie asked, still with his deceptive calm. "Twenty-one tainted bottles, and assuming nobody tampered with the corks, my money would be on one poisoned carboy. Does that make sense?"

His sharp gaze raked over Jenna's elfin frame, but it was Marty who responded. "Unfortunately, it does. This doesn't mean that Jenna is responsible. Or me."

"All right, let me rephrase that," Christie said. "Who apart from you and your sister has access to the cellar?"

"Everybody and their dog," Marty said through gritted teeth. "Doors in this place are always open."

Christie pushed back his chair. "Right, Ms. Wytchett, I would like you to show me your winemaking facility. Our specialists will thoroughly go over it later. You don't have to allow it, but I can get a warrant. However, I would most appreciate it if I could have a look now. Time is of the essence, and I'm afraid you're our only lead."

How kind of him not to say suspect. Jenna nodded, defeat in her anxious eyes. Marty rose, and I followed his example.

Christie shook his head. "I think Ms. Wytchett can perfectly show me on her own. After you."

Jenna shuffled toward the door, shadowed by the DCI. Marty and I were left behind on the terrace, together with one untouched lemonade.

23

TROUBLE BREWING

Marty slammed his fists on the garden table. The shock wave sent Christie's glass into a spin, and it toppled and spilled its contents onto the wood, from where the liquid dripped down the cracks.

"Damn him," Marty spat. A flush spread from his cheeks and on to his throat, and there was a dangerous gleam in his eyes. I had never seen Jenna's mellow brother explode like that and was glad to have the table between him and me.

"I feel like a traitor," I said. "When I visited the WI yesterday, we agreed something had to be wrong with the wine since it's the only product that comes in single portions. I had to rat on you and tell Sarah."

Marty heaved a deep breath. His hands, broad and strong, rested on the tabletop. "Not your fault. The cops would have sussed it out eventually. Somebody is trying to frame Jen. And it's working. I can see the inspector has her in his crosshairs."

"Somebody's also killing people willy-nilly." My subconscious, sluggish and useless when Christie was around, whirred along and spat out an idea. "Could Jen's ex be involved? He's with Health and Safety, and he's missing a few keys on his piano. He might have tampered with the bottles."

Marty straightened. "Jeff? No way. He got fired for trying to set you up. Anyway, with the injunction, he's left the area. He's been gone for quite a while. I'd say it can't be him."

My brain whirred more, remembering something Chris had said. "No, wait. Jenna said she matured her wine for what—half a year?"

"Oh, longer. The bottling took place in early May. And as she said, it came out fairly recently. Gran and I had a hard time convincing her it was good enough."

"Hubby might have messed with her carboy while he was still around in spring. That would explain why the murders are so random. They're not murders. It's all about revenge."

Marty rubbed his nose. "Hm. Not a bad theory, but our Jeff's a trifle trigger-tempered. Poisoning doesn't quite fit his profile. Nor would he have the patience to wait for the results."

Blast. He was right. Not to forget that Jeff also didn't have any skylles.

"Mind you, better to tell that copper about Jeff," Marty said, "before he finds evidence to suit his theories."

"Christie doesn't strike me as that type of person. Still, it would be nice if we had a few more suspects for him."

Marty fell quiet. The entire garden was unnaturally silent.

"Where are Robbie and Johnnie?"

Marty raised his chin at the chimneys poking above the trees at the end of the orchard. "With Elsie. Jen didn't want them around."

Did she fear an arrest?

"In a way, I wish she'd never started the wine business," Marty said. "She was ever so stressed about it. As to the cellar, well, like I told that copper, the farmhands, the neighbors, your cousin, you . . . everybody is in and out of there all the time. If somebody wanted to sneak down there, they could easily do so."

"If we're lucky, the same somebody left fingerprints."

Marty blew an auburn strand of hair from his face. "That would be way too convenient. And if your suspicions about a magical influence are correct, Jeff can't be involved. Though, quite honestly, I don't understand how a fellow coven member could do such a thing."

"Who told you?"

"Linda. She took your place in the call chain."

"Ah. Sorry, too much going on. I forgot."

Marty shoved his hands into his pockets and observed the threatening skies. "Oh, crap. I should help with bringing in the animals. It's going to be a bad one." He swung around to face me. "Be honest with me. Do you suspect Jen?"

"At some point, I wasn't sure."

His smile was bitter. "You still aren't."

Something hot stabbed my innards. "What would you do in my place? The poison acts unnaturally fast. Nor does it normally kill adults—not with the tiny amounts the police lab found. Something rather unusual is going on, and magic is the only explanation I have."

Marty's jaw muscles bunched. "Jen's innocent. She's a healer, not a killer. Told you, somebody is framing her."

"But who? And why? Tell me, what's the purpose of this?"

Marty sank into the nearest chair and clawed at his scalp. "It's madness."

A rumble came from above. When I looked up, I found the clouds in possession of the sky, with only a blue fringe hanging on for dear life. I couldn't tell whether it was coming or going. Twigs shivered in the first stirrings of a breeze that brought a welcome freshness into the garden.

I reached for the pitcher that had survived Marty's outburst and poured the rest of the lemonade.

"What is taking them so long?" Marty scrolled through the

messages on his phone and sighed.

"Give them another five minutes, and then I'll go down and act the general nuisance. You sort out your beasts."

"No way. I won't abandon my sister." He emptied his glass, and I followed his lead. More gusts, stronger this time, stirred the hot air of the terrace.

"Let's assume you're right about the magic," Marty said. "It's got to be accidental. None of us would do something like that."

"How can it be accidental? What I've experienced of magic recently has always been linked to a purpose, as your gran explained. Emotions fire up the skylles and . . . things happen." Things like Pan's survival. I had helped keep him alive with my magic. How cool was that?

"Then I've no clue. Since her relapse, Gran's been too ill to hex, Jen's too soft, you too decent, the rest of us useless, and frankly I can't see anybody slinging such a nifty spell. Not even after the coven's recent paranormal upgrades. At least, I don't think so. I'm not your top specialist for these things."

That Marty had included me in his list I didn't like one bit.

Before I could string together a suitable response, a door slammed at the other end of the house. For a moment, nothing happened, and then footsteps hurried along the corridor. Jenna reappeared on the terrace.

Marty jumped up and smothered his sister in a bear hug.

"Has that copper buggered off, then?" he asked into her hair.

"For the moment," was the muffled response. Jenna pushed herself off his chest and faced me. "He'll return with a bunch of techies to search our cellar. In the meantime, we're not to go down there and aren't allowed to touch anything. I asked him outright whether he thought I'm guilty. He said they'll find out the truth."

What should have been reassuring sounded decidedly ominous.

"Jen, Myrtle thinks someone might have spelled the wine, since a little poison seems to have super nasty effects," Marty said.

Confusion clouded Jenna's pale face. "Huh? Rubbish."

"The first victim was old, not very healthy, and a sip must've been enough. My guest survived, but it messed with his system. His partner, however, died . . ." The words had not left my mouth when realization whacked me over the head. The Wytchetts didn't know about Gerry.

Two pairs of eyes fixed on me, expressions of surprise and dismay flitting over faces that looked so different—hers elfin, pale and delicate, his ruddy and strong-boned. But it was Jenna who nodded when Marty kept staring at me.

"I feared as much when you shooed us away like you did. That's why I sent Robbie and Johnnie to play at the neighbors'. You found your missing guest, then?"

"The police did. I couldn't bring myself to check, and not because I was worried about fingerprints and stuff. The last thing I wanted was you or the kids stumbling over it—him."

Jenna shuddered. "What an absolute nightmare."

Wait, fingerprints. A crazy notion careered into my head and screeched to a halt.

"Tell me, does magic show? For example, if somebody has spelled an object, could the application of the skylles be traced like DNA or prints?"

"Not by the police, no way," Jenna said. "But yes, magic leaves traces behind, though they fade over time. It wasn't me, by the way."

I sought her gaze and held it. "I believe you. As to this supposed magical fingerprint, how would it work?"

"Well, the skylles are basically some form of energy. We can generate it inside—please don't ask me how—and we can then transfer it to things or people directly or can create objects that carry the energy. Like your recipe book. That power is triggered by emotions. Again, no idea how exactly it works. But by transferring energy, you leave a record behind. Unfortunately, I have no idea how one spots magical energy. Not sure Gran could either." She wrinkled her nose. "What about you?"

"What do you mean?" I asked.

"Because now that Gran's ill, you're the most skilled witch of us all. In any case, you're the only one with a familiar." Her eyes narrowed. "Actually, that might work. Petty's pure magic, so she should be able to spot it. Not sure she can tell us who, but why not try?"

Marty rubbed his nose. "You want to use the primula as a supernatural truffle hound? Would she know what to do?"

The more I thought about it, the better the idea sounded. "Petty never ceases to amaze me. Her latest trick is invisibility. If you ask me, that takes a lot of magical energy. She might spot traces of magic since she's using it. In any case, she's our last hope."

"Yes," Jenna said slowly. "Yes, she is."

—

Between leaving a message for Chris to join me at Wytchett Farm as soon as possible, driving to the Witch's Retreat, fetching an exuberant Petty, and rejoining my friends with my invisible plant, I spent no more than fifteen minutes.

"Do you think you can do without me for a while, at least until the coppers return?" Marty thumbed away a message and pocketed his phone. "Things are getting a bit desperate on the farming front. Call in case the DCI acts antsy. You might need a solicitor, you know?"

"I know one," I said. "Got his address for Greg."

"Off you go, bro." Jenna smiled over-brightly and stroked Petty's leaves. "We'll cope."

"I've called Chris. Let's hope he checks his voicemail."

What the man saw in me was beyond me. A wonky witch with murder problems. How could that be attractive?

"Oh, jolly good," Marty said, his brow clearing. "I hate to leave you in the lurch, but the man carries a good head on his shoulders. And he isn't a suspect. Better if I'm not easily accessible, in case that DCI chap wants to interrogate me. I'm sure he'll do it at some point."

Framed by a mini-vortex of glittery sparks, Petty twirled away from Jenna, winked in and out, and settled once more, a floral ballerina.

"When did she start her vanishing act?" Jenna asked, the admiration in her voice laced with a dash of jealousy.

"Not long ago. After, uh, that day in the cellar. You're the only people after Chris to watch the show."

"I want my own Petty," Jenna said wistfully.

"As long as this condition doesn't spread to my livestock," Marty said. "Righto, I'm off. Should you need me, give me a holler. First, let me draw up the drawbridge for you. No need to make it easy for them." Jenna's brother stomped off and, a few instants later, the front door slammed shut, followed by the sound of a key turning in the lock.

"Oh, cripes, that's typical. Big bro has forgotten there's more than one way into the house."

"Let's go inside, and then you can close the back door."

Jenna did, shutting us in with the olfactory remnants of yesterday's curry that mingled with the tantalizing aromas of a glossy, dark goodie cooling next to the oven.

"I always bake a chocolate cake when I'm stressed," she said.

"We're a team made in heaven. When I'm stressed, I eat lots of chocolate."

"Sold. Yours is the first slice. Shall we go?" Jenna asked.

The doorbell rang.

Jenna's head snapped around. "Sweet Earth. The police." Her face gone white as milk, my friend grabbed the cellar door for support.

For a second I wished I had something or someone to hold on to myself. "Blast it, that was way too fast for my taste. Fine, I'll deal with them. Go down to the cellar with Petty and let her sniff for magic. Hurry, I don't think I can stop them for long."

Jenna sucked in a deep breath. "I'll try my best. The keys for the front door are on the coat rack next to the entrance. Petty, are you coming?" Without further ado, Jenna raced down the steps. Petty fired off a salvo of pink sparks and rushed after her.

I rushed the other way, through a cramped corridor blocked by a solid oak door at its other end. Drawbridge, Marty had called it. The banging that echoed into the hallway made me wonder whether the police might have brought a battering ram.

To make matters worse, the doorbell shrilled into the din, refusing to stop.

"Hello, the law?" I called out.

The banging and ringing continued. *Duh.* The door was too massive for the coppers to hear me, so I pounded on the panel from the inside. That stopped them.

Then the handle rattled madly.

I banged on the door again, and the handle stilled. Communications were established, but we would never get far that way. As long as the iterations wasted time, everything was hunky-dory.

On the right side of the entrance, a small stained glass window promised easy access to our unwelcome visitors. If I opened it, negotiations could begin, which would hopefully enable Petty and Jenna time to finish their job in the cellar. The window was out of reach, so I grabbed the antique milking stool placed under the coat rack and stepped on it.

I threw open the window and shouted, "That door is locked, and I don't have a key." That was technically correct—I wasn't carrying one.

"Whoa, cool it with the decibels," said Chris from below.

Chris? Ah, right. Good of him to come, and fast, too.

Other than the barn on the other side, I couldn't see much. "Are the police with you?" I asked.

"No, should they be? I was on my way to the B&B when I got your message. No cops in sight, though I haven't checked the back entrance. More polite to try the front first."

"Okay, hang on a sec. I might be able to unlock the door after all." I hopped off the stool and let him in.

When I smiled at Chris, he smiled back. We then stepped closer, and for a moment neither of us bothered with smiling. Or talking. Then an alarm went off in my head—now wasn't the time to romance my witch hunter.

"Bother." I broke contact.

He grinned. "Do I kiss that badly?"

"You're doing fine, but I have a small problem."

Chris laughed out loud. "You said as much. What's wrong this time? I can smell chocolate cake. Don't tell me it's hexed or poisoned or something."

A frantic peek over his shoulder revealed no minions of officialdom, but that could change any moment. I grabbed his hand, yanked him inside, and locked the door behind us.

"Not the cake. Jenna is down in the cellar with Petty, seeing if she notices any traces of magic on the carboys."

Chris's expressive eyebrows formed another V on his forehead, but he was kind enough to keep his questions to himself, and I didn't give him a chance to change his mind. Down the worn stone slabs we went until we passed under the archway.

No Jenna. No Petty. The cellar was empty.

24

ON THE DARK SIDE

Our footfalls bounced off the archways until the sound was lost in the depths of the gloomy cellar. A light bulb flickered and buzzed, reminding me of those flies in the clearing. The air was chilly down here where sunlight couldn't penetrate the never-ending winter. Shivering, I wrapped my arms around my body.

"Brrr," said Chris. "Do they shoot horror flicks in this place?"

"I hope not. Jenna?" My voice rolled into the open space, drawing echoes but no reply. "It's okay. That wasn't the police. Chris has arrived."

Something moved in my peripheral vision, and then Jenna emerged from behind the thick folds of the curtain that had been pulled aside, giving a full view of the painter's table.

"Sweet Earth, you two made such an unholy racket, I thought the coppers were storming the farm. I really don't want to be caught, not after Christie warned me the cellar was off limits."

"Good morning," Chris said. "Now that we're reunited, I'd appreciate if you could put me in the picture. I'm not sure I understood things correctly. Are you telling me somebody truly magicked your wine?"

Jenna didn't answer. Instead, she waved for us to come closer—and entangled her hand in dusty cobwebs.

Disgust on her face, she flicked them off. "I ought to clean down here more often. Never mind, Petty and I have something to show you. You might want to come closer."

Want wasn't the operative word, but I did as bid, and Chris followed.

Jenna pointed at the second carboy to the left. "Petty didn't hesitate one moment. She shot across and landed right in front of it. Her blossoms turned blue and the leaves drooped. Even I sussed out what she wanted to tell me without knowing her that well. She did a repeat performance with those four bottles under the table that I'd kept for myself. I touched them to find out if I'd notice anything."

"And?" Chris asked.

With a tremolo in her voice, she said, "Difficult to describe. Let's say, I'd rather put my hand through a web full of spiders."

"Did you try the carboy?" I asked.

"Yes. Didn't work. I cleaned them all, so there won't be much tainted magic left to trace. Petty is so amazeboggling, she found it anyway. Could you show them, sweetie?"

Petty shot forward like an obedient bloodhound, coming to an abrupt halt in front of the second carboy. As Jenna said, for a moment her flowers turned blue and her leaves sagged. Then the primula went back to normal.

I tossed Chris a quick glance. His lips were flatlined, and there was a glint in his eye. Something bristly formed in my stomach. The man had never fully bought my theory, and this evidence had to be a rude awakening.

"That's . . . impressive," Chris said.

Jenna shivered and rubbed her arms. "Evil, that's what it is."

"I meant the primula."

"I'm talking about dark magic," Jenna hissed. "Magic that defies the true purpose of the witches."

My brain was reeling under the latest load of bad news, so I latched on to the bit that bothered me most. "Forbidden magic?"

"Yes. Magic used to kill or to harm. Destroying lives. That's as dark as it can get."

Chris's glance flipped from the carboy to the primula and then to Jenna. "So, Myrtle was spot on after all, and we're indeed dealing with a murderous coven member?" His voice glaciered even the chill air.

"Yes." Jenna's face had gone as rigid as Chris's. "I tell you, somebody's crossed the line."

Who's afraid of the wicked witch?

I was. How I hated being right. One of our motley crew of magical misfits had gone to the dark side and killed. Had done what the witch hunters killed the real witches for. Chris's witch-hunting ancestors, to be precise. This was the moment when I would find out how open-minded and flexible he really was.

You haven't gone to the dark side. He can't tar you with the same brush. He said he wouldn't.

The bristly thing in my stomach shifted and grew. He was another person I didn't know all that well.

His gaze flicked from Jenna to me and back again. Came to a rest on the primula, softly shushing her leaves. A spark burped from a blossom and winked out again.

I balled my fists and forced myself to speak. "It's never evil we serve. That's the first directive of the witches."

"It appears somebody didn't pay attention," Chris said, his voice flat, lifeless.

The cold of the cellar seeped into my core.

"One needs to be a warped rotter to use the skylles that way," Jenna said. "Perversely enough, dark magic is much easier than the other kind."

"Easier?" Chris asked.

Jenna fondled the blossoms of the primula, who had parked her fiberglass pot on the table next to the last carboy, one of the four safe ones. "For dark magic, you don't have to pay as much as you do for the other type. Well, when it comes to really big spells, that is."

"I must admit, sometimes I wish I had access to the Ignatius archives," Chris said. "I know for a fact my witch-hunting ancestors, back in the sixteen hundreds, diligently recorded their intel. And I bet dear Uncle Bob, given his obsession with magic, has studied every snippet he could find. Not that I'm going to ask him."

Jenna shook her head. "I doubt your lot ever knew the details. Dark magic feeds on negative emotions like greed, hate, fear. Initially, we humans care only about ourselves. Egotism is our first nature. Love, compassion, empathy—those emotions come later in life and demand more from us. That's why doing positive deeds costs more in magical terms. Plus, if you don't have empathy, you can't be hurt. The less compunction, the easier it gets."

Chris huffed. "Let's be grateful my lot never showed any skylles."

"My aunt died because she twisted her magic when she flipped and wanted to kill."

"She was provoked," Chris said. "She got things wrong and paid for it with her life. For me, that's different from using magic to murder people willy-nilly." The light bulb over his head painted bizarre shadows onto his dear face.

"That's exactly the point," I said. "There's no motive whatsoever. It's like somebody flexed their magical muscles just because they could."

Dread bubbled up deep inside me, and the same list of suspects marched past my inner eye.

"If it's not Jen—"

"Told you, it wasn't me," Jenna spat. "How can you even

think . . ." Her voice broke, and she swung away from us.

"If it's not you, and it's not me—which it isn't—and it's not Dot, then somebody must be shielding their skylles."

Like a specter haunting the shadows, the answer crept up on me. I should have seen it before. But I had been blind.

"Myrtle?" Chris and Jenna spoke as one.

Petty tilted her pot in an unspoken question.

"Given how open Rosie and Colonel Elmsworth were in sharing the news about their magical achievements, only one person comes to mind." How odd my voice should remain stable. "Daisy."

Chris's intense gaze seemed to scan my soul. Slowly, he nodded. "I don't really know Dot, but I do know hexing takes the stuffing out of you, of which she doesn't seem to have a lot left. Somehow, Daisy always topped my list. I'm stumped when it comes to motive, though. Also, she strikes me as being a bit of an airhead, not a killer."

"Because she wanted to? Needed to? Because she's jealous of Myrtle?" Jenna addressed the wall and the rectangular window high above our heads. It was dirty and blocked by a rusty wire mesh. "Gran was never happy with your cousin's progress. She thought as a Coldron, Daisy should do better. Perhaps she did."

"Is the intel on the dark magic to be found in the laundry list? It certainly isn't in the recipe book. Could be Daisy talked Dot into letting her read your grimoire. Once she knew she'd be safe on the dark side, she pounced."

Jenna's eyes were sad. "She can be quite spiteful."

Visions of my teenage years danced across my inner eye. Daisy in a tutu. Daisy painting, colors on her nose, acting in a play. Daisy scowling, the two of us fighting like street cats.

She was the only sister I'd ever had.

Jenna rubbed the back of her neck. "Actually, dark magic doesn't feature in the laundry list. This is oral lore." She snapped her mouth shut. Then she slapped her forehead. "I'm stupid. How could I forget? No, it can't be Daisy."

"Now you've lost me," Chris said.

Jenna raised her face at the feeble ray of light seeping through the grimy window. "In one generation, there can only be one truly strong witch. Doesn't mean the others are complete duds, by no means. But to do this? I doubt it."

Jen swung around, eyes wide. "You're the strong witch in your generation."

What? "Are you now accusing me?"

Jen blinked. She slumped. "I . . . no, not really. I don't know anymore what to think."

Chris's eyes narrowed. "Would it be possible Myr did something without knowing it?"

His words slammed into my gut, taking my breath away.

"No," I whispered.

I cleared my throat. "No. Dot told me. The whole reason I fear magic is that I might do something crazy without ever wanting it. But Dot said it was impossible."

Impossible. We had come back full circle to that day in the cellar, a day still bloody and raw in my mind. Only this time I wouldn't condemn my primula. I would do something else instead.

"Petty, can you please come here?"

The primula rose, gently swaying in front of my head. "You've traced tainted magic to the carboy and the bottles. Can you trace tainted magic on a witch?"

The pot bobbed up and down and tilted toward me. Sparks zinged from the leaves. No saggy blooms going blue. Nothing but her unique lemony scent. She shot back to Jenna and repeated the performance. As if to ram a message home, she then hovered in front of the second carboy, drooped her leaves, her blossoms blue, and came to a standstill on the floor.

"Wow," said Chris. He ran his hand through his hair until it stood all on end. "I mean, wow." His posture slackened. The frown vanished from his forehead. "Okay, works for me. Now you need to try this with your cousin."

It might have been the tsunami of relief that rolled through me, washing away the blockage in my brain, but an oversight so monstrous it should never have happened surfaced in my mind.

"The question is, did somebody hex a whole carboy or slip in a magicked component? Since the wine contains lily glycosides from lily of the valley, the latter is far more likely, correct?"

Jenna nodded. Chris quirked a brow.

"Right. When did your grandmother's health improve? I know she's ill now, but didn't she get better at any point before?"

"Uh, yes. In early May. Why?" Jenna's voice had gone squeaky.

"You bottled your wine at the same time. She must've been home in between hospital visits. Back then, she wouldn't have been as unfit as she is now."

A huff escaped from between Chris's lips.

Horror dawned in Jenna's eyes. "Oh no, no, that's what I feared. She's been on a slippery slope for a long time. Going doo-lally, not her normal self. All this hating and her prejudices . . ."

Nobody in the cellar said a word. Even Petty stilled.

I cleared my throat. "Aye, there's the rub, isn't it? Here we have our motive. She considered the henge to be sacred to our coven. She despised the tourists with a passion. Maybe she didn't want to kill them. Maybe the poison turned out too strong. But I could bet she wanted to sow chaos, if not murder, and wanted to drive them away."

Tears trickled down Jenna's face. "She wouldn't. Not Gran." But her voice lacked conviction. "She wouldn't kill on purpose. Never, ever. Believe me."

How I wanted to.

I faced Chris. "I've got to drive to the hospital. Can you stay with Jenna? The cops are due any minute, and Marty has his hands full."

"Of course."

I stepped across and put my arm around Jenna's shoulder. "Jen, please, help me. Where would she keep the poison, assuming there's some left? You'll need to tell the coppers about your gran, otherwise you'll get arrested, you realize that? But we can't have them find anything that would expose the coven. It's bad enough as it is."

Soft sobs were my answer. Chris's gaze and mine locked over Jen's bowed head.

"You go," he said. "I'll call Elmsworth. He'll have to rustle up a few people to toss Dot's cottage."

"Key's under the mat," Jenna whispered.

"Everything will be all right," I said, disbelieving myself.

Upstairs, the knocker thundered into the empty house. It was soon followed by the shrilling of the doorbell.

Jenna gritted her teeth and looked up. "The police. What shall I tell them?"

"The truth. Minus the magic," I said.

"How am I supposed to know which carboy is tainted?"

"You don't," Chris said. "Let them run their tests and see what they find. You don't know the bottles are poisoned either. Only your testimonial about your grandmother's mental health counts." He fiddled with his phone. "Typical. There's no connection down here. Excuse me, need to ring Elmsworth. I'll handle the cops, but you better get out of here. I won't be able to stop them for long." He shot upstairs.

"Jen, tell the DCI about Dot. It's his job to catch the murderer."

My job was to confront a murderous witch before the cops showed up. My job was to save the coven from exposure.

We returned to the kitchen in time to hear the front door opening. Voices followed.

"Run," Jenna hissed. "Here's the key to the back door."

Petty winked out.

"Ms. Wytchett?"

Blast it, the DCI.

"Showtime." Jenna threw her arms around me. "Thank you for being such a great friend. And for lending me your Chris."

A great friend who accused her beloved grandmother, the woman who had raised her, of murder. Jenna might hate me yet.

Petty's scent in my nose, I slipped into the corridor. As I fumbled the key into the lock, I half-expected the DCI to holler after me, but my familiar and I made it to my van and back to the Witch's Retreat unmolested. Petty back in her parlor, I hit the road, a torrent of thoughts gushing through my head as I prepared myself for an interview with a killer.

Once at the hospital, I climbed an excessive number of stairs since the visitor lifts were broken and trotted along endless corridors until I ended up in front of a door painted an institutional pale green.

Room 4666, cardiology ward, the tired young nurse had said, and she'd warned me the patient might be asleep. Asleep was okay—for sleepers could be woken up. Only a magical zombie primula could ever return from the dead.

25

PURGATORY

I gave the door a perfunctory rap. When nobody responded, I slipped into a storage room on steroids, crammed full of hospital beds. The curtains were drawn, the air stagnant and stuffy. To judge by the number of sockets and fluorescent lights mounted on one wall, an architect with hamsters on his mind had designed the space for three patients.

Three beds were indeed lined up on one side, while the fourth was squeezed into the narrow corridor in front. To create a modicum of privacy, half-screens were slotted between the row of beds where brown blankets and white sheets covered rigid shapes with even whiter faces. From vents high in the ceiling blew cold air, which did nothing to freshen the miasma of sickness and medicine that gripped the place in its stranglehold.

The names on the beds against the wall were unfamiliar. Not so the invader. "Dorothy Violet Wytchett" had become a surplus patient, shoved in here as an afterthought. She hadn't been given even the flimsy pretense of a screen, since there was no space for it.

I wormed my way past the other beds until I stood next to her pillow. Should another patient wake up, my body would serve as a shield. Given the gurgled breathing from the other beds and the hiss of oxygen through clear tubes, it was doubtful we would be disturbed. Anxiety fluttered in my chest. What if Dot was too drugged to talk? However, this place was no intensive care unit, and the nurse hadn't objected to the visit of a stranger. Perhaps things weren't as dire as they looked.

I vowed to stay away from hospitals in future and whispered, "Dot?"

Smooth in its slackness, her face was almost young again. Only the white hair and the loose, splotched skin around her neck remained to tell a different tale. That—and the sunken eyes that hinted at the skull underneath the tired flesh.

Angry, worried, and nauseated all at once, I tugged at her pillow. I would end this horror here and now.

"Dot."

From the beds behind me came a cough and muttered words. I froze, but the other patient stilled once more, the hiss from the oxygen and a faint electrical hum the only sounds in the room. Sterile air, wrathfully blasting from the vent, found my neck and bare arms. In my mad rush to the hospital, I hadn't thought to bring a jacket.

"Dot," I said for the third time.

I bent over the bed, tugged at the shabby blanket that covered Jenna's grandmother to her shoulders, and swallowed a yelp when a skinny, freckled hand shot out from underneath and closed around my wrist with surprising strength. Dot's eyes snapped open and rotated toward me.

"You came," she said, in a voice more toneless than a whisper.

My heartbeat took a moment to sink back down from the stratosphere. "Did you expect me?"

"When Daisy told me about the call chain, I realized you'd

soon work things out. You're as determined as Eve was." She said it without rancor.

I threw a nervous glance at the other occupants of the room, but none of them stirred.

With a soft intake of air, Dot spoke again. "You should accept your heritage. You're stronger than—that other lot. Even Jenna is no match for you. You could rule."

I nearly asked, "The roost?" but stopped myself. Things had progressed beyond flippancy and way beyond anything I had ever wanted.

What *did* I want? To explore my skylles under my own steam and help the others find theirs while staying hidden was the answer. Not more. Not less. But Dot had changed all that and had forced my hand. There would have been a few things I could have told her. Instead, I said, "Why, Dot? It makes no sense."

The ghost of a smile appeared on Dot's papery lips. "You still don't get it, do you?" She groaned. "Pass me some water, please. There's a cup with a straw on that thingy."

"That thingy" was a little tray affixed to the side of the bed. I placed the straw between her lips, and Dot slurped the liquid from the cup. I knew she couldn't help it, but the sound scraped on my nerves, so I balled my free hand into a fist, nails digging into my palms until they twinged worse than my head. Once she had finished, I put the cup aside.

For a moment, her eerie young-old face was calm, but just as I was wondering if she might have fallen asleep with open eyes, Dot spoke again.

"All these people. Crawling over the stones. Soiling them with their presence. Druids. Wiccans. Tourists. Hah. They don't possess any skylles whatsoever. They shouldn't be here. The stone circle is sacred. It's ours, not theirs."

Bingo, smack on target with the motive.

The old eyes went sharp, holding my gaze. "I did what I could. To make them feel unwelcome. But they kept coming back. More every year. It's a disgrace. This mediocre rabble should stay in their filthy cities where they belong."

"The Neolithic people built their temples for themselves. Our ancestors simply found a new use for them."

Dot huffed once, her eyes roaming the ceiling and her fists clenching and unclenching the scruffy blanket. "Somebody with skylles built the henge, and those vermin have no right to be there. They needed a wake-up call. That's why I hexed the poison. It was so hard to do. Then it took absolute ages until Jenna was happy with her brew. Next, she lost confidence and held on to her bottles. I had a hard time convincing her. The wine was put up for sale on the shelves only last week."

Spittle flew from her mouth as she hissed the words.

"How did you do it?"

That penetrating look again. "If you don't know, girl, you're not worth your salt."

Despite the anger knotting my innards, I kept my unruly tongue under control. "Then let me guess. In spring, you collected lilies of the valley and boiled the leaves or did whatever it took to get the poisonous fluid. You then spelled it to make the poison much stronger than it should be. I assume there are some clever instructions hidden in your laundry list, which Jen doesn't know about and I missed when I skimmed through, right?"

Dot sniggered. "No, that sort of knowledge can only be passed on by word of mouth. Carry on, this is most entertaining."

She was at death's door, so wringing her scrawny neck would only hasten the process and get me into trouble. I drew a deep breath and kept talking.

"You sneaked into the cellar and removed the plugs on the carboys. That's easily done. Jenna would have to check on her brew at regular intervals, so they weren't fully sealed. Most likely, you did it right before the wine was ready for corking. You had to be sure Jenna wouldn't taste it again. I can't see you poisoning your offspring."

"You're right and you're wrong," Dot said. "Hexes can't actually hurt a blood relative. Unless you excel at magic, that is. I don't—certainly not now. My revenge cost me all I had left. Nor did I want to cause trouble for Jenna. You see, I never hexed more than a drop of the stuff. Nobody should have noticed."

She wasn't half as smart as she considered herself to be. Or too arrogant for her own good. Even tiny amounts could be traced these days. The police labs proved it.

As did I, with the help of my familiar and my friends.

"Be that as it may, the Wiccans bought the wine, and now a musician and a young woman are dead."

I wouldn't give her the satisfaction of knowing about Gerry.

"Musician? He was a tramp," Dot hissed, her face pulled into a mask of hatred.

Poor Jenna. This wasn't the deed of a woman on the brink of senility. And not a mistake. Madness was the only excuse.

By the time I had gained control again, both my palms throbbed where my nails were digging into them.

"The hex you used is dark magic, correct?"

Dot's laugh segued into a brittle cough. "It's a family tradition. All oral lore, of course. My problem was I had to fill in some gaps. That's where things turned pear-shaped."

Dot raised her head from the pillow, her feverish gaze drilling into my eyes. "I broke the first directive, so what? Never serve evil. Define 'evil.' Can you do that? I couldn't. They had it wrong back then."

"Oh, sure, of course they did." Unfortunately, sarcasm was wasted on the old bat.

"See, we Wytchetts steered clear of direct magic. Didn't attack anybody like your aunt did. Never morphed anything like you did. It's easier that way. I'm not convinced the laundry list was originally ours, since it contains these idiotic lectures on how to be righteous. Anyway, Jenna is into this empathy thing, yes, but she can do the potions and spells. Unfortunately, the girl is too kind for her own good. That makes it much harder for her. I'm not a good person, Myrtle. I don't need to be. I know I'm right."

In a warped way, it made sense.

"By dripping hexed poison into the wine, and only one carboy at that, I left it to happenstance who would die. I reckoned it should be safe enough, since I targeted nobody directly. Not like Eve at all. It's clear we pay a lot less for dark magic, but I was convinced that way I wouldn't have to pay at all. Things were hunky-dory—until I fell ill. One night, it felt like my heart was stampeding in my chest until I had no breath left in my body. Then it slowed down and stopped."

Dot stared at a spot on the ceiling. "Then it started again. That was when I knew. I knew the wine had found its first victim."

She smiled a parody of a smile. "Do you now know, girl, what had happened?"

"I can guess. Like foxglove, lily of the valley can be a heart remedy in proper doses. You twisted the stuff until it became lethal. Somehow, your dark magic rebounded on you, but only when the first person died."

She huffed. "I'm not a monster, Myrtle. I care about our traditions. Marty, Jenna, and the boys mean the world to me. I suspect that's what hit me in the end. Foiled by love."

Break out the violins. "Did you suffer from heart problems before?"

Dot grimaced. "My arrythmia was acting up, but the operation fixed things, until the magical backfire made the condition worse than ever. Still, I got things right. Eve died because she tried to kill someone with direct magic. I rid the henge of three invaders and am still around."

She knew about Gerry. The awful cow was proud of her achievements. Sour acid rose in my throat.

Dot's features softened. She looked so much like Jenna, it wrenched my heart. "I did this for our magical heritage. How unfair the magic should rebound on me. It was worse the second time. Yesterday, it happened again. My heartbeat was all over the place. There's another corpse out there, you know?"

I did. But I wouldn't tell her.

Another dry cough. This time blood flecked the corners of her lips. "Is there more water? Please?"

I should have let the old hulk shrivel and die, but I didn't have it in me. I went to the basin in the corner, filled up the cup, and placed the straw in a mouth bristling with a corona of wrinkles. Dot sucked the liquid greedily and then sank back onto the pillows.

"Whether you like it or not, it's yours now. Whatever is left." She cackled. "You have a familiar. You're the first real witch we've seen in centuries. The others are, in a way, worse than those tourists. The so-called coven is an abomination. Magical weaklings, the lot of them. Unworthy."

The others? Unworthy? Images flashed in my head.

A smiling Rosie, barely recuperated from an onslaught of the big C, levitating breakfast rolls. Damian, her fussy-pants husband, enthusiastically diving into our past. My friend Jenna with her magical touch and her cute boys. The Colonel, devoted to a yapping little mammal—caring so deeply he conjured up long-buried skylles to save his pet. Linda, as annoying as she might be, meant no harm. Fluttery Mel and her kind heart. And all the others. The old bat considered them unworthy?

"How dare you? For the record, I don't care two hoots about leadership."

Dot's lips twisted with a snarl. "No, I noticed. You'd still like to bow out, if I'd let you. You want me to do all the work." A bony finger stabbed the air. "For what happens now, you'll only have yourself to blame."

I backed away, stumbling into the next bed. "What are you on about? You're bonkers, you know?"

She tutted. With a groan, she heaved herself upright, her eyes shining with an eerie light. "So frightfully rude, just like Eve, aren't you? Unlike you, she wanted to lead. You didn't—you made that clear during our dinner—and I'll tell you here and now, that's why I did it."

I should have strangled her when it first occurred to me and not give her the chance to drip poison into my ears. "Wrong. You doctored the wine long before that evening in the orchard."

Dot fell back onto the pillows and closed her eyes. "You never listen. I'm not talking about poisoning the wine. I'm talking about the coven. Those so-called witches don't deserve to bear that name. Well, most of them shouldn't, anyway. We'll find out—oh, yes, we will. I've changed the curse. Only true practitioners will survive. I doubt there will be many left. Saves you from having to lead them. Too bad I won't be around anymore." She blinked once, her eyes bloodshot. "You better watch your back. That young man—he's a good one, as I told you. But he comes from a bad family. Bad for us, I mean. You can never shake off your roots. Never."

Now she was giving me the oracle of doom routine? That was too much.

"Leave Chris alone. He's got more morals in his little finger than you have in your whole body." The words escaped with a hiss.

Her eyes were closing, and with the faintest twitch of her lips, Dot turned away from me. That was the moment her words registered.

"What do you mean by 'curse'? What have you done now?"

When she didn't respond, I shook her limp body. "Tell me."

"Show some consideration and stop making such a racket," a petulant voice behind me rasped. "Where do you think you are?"

"Sorry," I mumbled in impotent fury. Dot must have found a way of putting herself under. She wasn't dead. Her wispy hair fluttered as she breathed. But the beast was beyond my reach.

I squeezed past the bed, ignored the reproachful looks of the patient who had woken up, and dashed for the hospital entrance. My thoughts were crashing and rumbling in my head, but it wasn't the only noise. Finally, the storm had arrived. Rain bucketed down from the pitch-black mass of the sky. Flashes zipped across the heavens, immediately followed by thunder that rattled my teeth. My heart thumped in my chest so loudly, the booms became one with the storm.

Whatever happened now was my fault.

Hold it right there. She wants you to feel guilty, so don't. Work out what she's planned and then stop it from happening.

The coven meeting. She wanted to hit the coven meeting.

I fished for my phone, but my fumbling fingers found crumpled tissues, a lipstick, my wallet, a crumbly toffee, the car key—anything but the phone. In my hurry, I must have left it at the Witch's Retreat. What should I—or could I—do now?

I paced the entrance hall, dodging the people flooding in, driven by the storm.

A gust rattled the windowpanes, and the crowd surged toward the back of the entrance hall to safety. Caught in the melee, I couldn't escape, but the jumbling and jostling shook loose a nasty thought.

What if she had kept some poisoned wine and warped it to attack the coven? If that was the case, how would she make things work?

A second later, the answer kicked me in the solar plexus.

Daisy.

26

MELTDOWN

My cheek resting against the smooth, cold concrete wall of the hospital lobby, I wrestled with my feverish thoughts. I needed to think like Dot. Impossible, really, but vital for the coven's survival.

The coven. Daisy. A lump of ice materialized in my stomach. Thunder rolled and people screamed.

Solid and three-dimensional as if she were standing next to me, my cousin's image rose in my mind. She had been at the farm yesterday evening talking to Dot. Worse, she had closed the trunk of her car. What might she have been transporting?

White lightning flashed thrice in rapid succession. I needed to get back to Avebury. Now.

The clock on the wall revealed I had fifty minutes until the coven meeting started. Once enough people turned up, they would have a go at the drinks as they always did. Given the circumstances, my fellow witches wouldn't touch the wine, surely.

Another thought plopped up in my mind.

What if it wasn't in the wine? Not everybody drank alcohol. What if Dot kept the original poison and gave it to Daisy? She'd do anything to become a real witch. She'd follow Dot's instructions—whatever they might be—to the letter. Had she been an accomplice from the start?

Sweat broke from my pores.

As I measured the distance from the lobby to the car park, lightning zapped a church tower and was chased by a deafening boom. I jumped back from the window, a flimsy barrier between me and the elements. Rain sheeted onto the ground. The storm was closing in.

I mustn't waste another second.

My heartbeat exploded and my surroundings took on a greenish tinge. The buzz of a billion flies droned in my head as I dashed outside and flung myself into the maw of the tempest.

I was soaked in an instant, but the rain was warm and brought along the scent of moist soil. Zigzagging between the cars, I jumped over puddles. The frantic hissing of water on the tarmac was the least of my worries.

Zap.

Another bolt of lightning forked down, its light so bright I yelped and covered my eyes. I had nothing to cover my ears, however, when thunder struck, shaking the ground below me.

Oh no, no, no. This was the wrong time to be out in the open in a car park filled with lumps of metal, and me sticking out above them. I bent over, trying to keep level with the roofs of the vehicles.

Zap. Wrrrooommm.

That bolt had hit even closer. No place to hide and nowhere to shelter, I was on my own with the elements. Terror lashed me on. I dashed through puddles, my heart racketing fast, little black dots zipping through my vision. My car. Where was my blasted car? Why had everything turned a bilious green? Not a splotch of red anywhere—ah, there, on my left. Gone. Now on my right. And gone again.

I squinted into the raindrops. More red flutters, but no minivan. I ran on, water pounding my back, a terrible buzz in my head. And a rose fragrance in my nose.

Oh, crap. My skylles were out.

Another splotch of red. This time it was my minivan. I beeped it open and broke an Olympic sprint record across the tarmac.

Zap, zap. Wroombble. Lightning struck the top of the hospital in a flash of searing white.

With a shriek, I slammed into the van. My elbow hit the side window and pain shot up my arm. The greenness shrank into a speck as I ripped the door open, vaulted into the driver's seat, and slammed the door shut behind me.

Finally safe, I slumped over my steering wheel, trying to catch my breath.

Rainwater flooded my windshield. A faint scent of fresh leaves and roses wafted through the van. Then it was gone. Like bloody tears, ruby red petals settled on the dashboard.

I grabbed a handful of the floral confetti. It felt real enough. Some of it was wet. Did my magic protect me from the storm? Had I been surrounded by a red flurry as I dashed from the cover of the hospital?

More importantly, why did my skylles disappear so abruptly? I never asked them to.

Beside me, something snicked. I twisted in my seat. Cracks feathered over the side window. With a soft hiss, the glass turned opaque, reminding me of rock salt. More snapping noises sounded from the other side of the van and its back.

Crunch.

That had come from the windshield. As I stared in slack-jawed disbelief, the security glass riddled with cracks like a worn skating rink until my view was completely clouded.

This. Was. Not. Possible.

Strangely enough, I felt fitter than I had in quite a while. No headaches squeezed my temples. No pressure tortured my head.

Recently, my magic must have been sitting under my skin, ready to jump at the slightest provocation.

That thought dragged in Dot's words, spoken at Wytchett Farm. *Elmsworth successfully deflected the magical side effects into an object. Glass, especially mirrors, are great for that.*

Glass did more than that. Glass absorbed the skylles themselves.

Like an afterthought, the rearview mirror shattered, and the instrument panel went blank.

Outside, lightning ripped through the sky, the broken windows glittering like a sunburst on snow. Thunder rumbled over the van.

I rested my forehead on the steering wheel. With all of the glass in the van wrecked, it would go nowhere today.

My gaze found the cracked dashboard clock.

I had forty-three minutes.

No phone, no car, and I needed to get to the coven meeting in a hurry. What were my options? There were buses, yes, but I had no idea how often they ran. Plus, they would take far too long, if they even operated in this weather.

Blast it all, I was supposed to be a witch. I needed to pull my act together and gain control of my erratic magic.

Dread clawed at my stomach. What if my skylles had now clocked out for the day?

"I've had it up to here with this rubbish." I banged my fist onto the dashboard. The remaining petals slipped aside. Some floated to the floorboard.

"Hello, skylles? I'm in deep doodoo."

Then I remembered. At the henge and during the Pan emergency, I never used my voice.

Chris, can you hear me? Jenna, Marty, Colonel, hello? Rosie, Damian? I'm stranded at the hospital. I need to get to Avebury. Don't eat or drink anything at the coven meeting. Help me, please.

Something sharp knifed into my temples.

Huh? Did that work?

I couldn't take the risk. I couldn't sit here like a lost whatnot and wait. Taxi? I opened the door and scanned the hospital building. A mile-long sodden queue snaked under the covered stand. Not a single taxi in sight, of course.

Borrow somebody's phone? Some kind soul would surely help me out, but that was no good either. Even the few numbers I knew had vanished into the panic that was clouding my brain.

The only option was hitchhiking. Here and there, figures were dashing through the thinning downpour. Thinning only for the moment, however, as another black wall was headed straight for the hospital. More was yet to come.

I grabbed the umbrella I kept on the backseat, locked the van, and scanned the drizzle. Farther along the aisle, a woman was opening her vehicle, and I splashed toward her as she was getting in.

"Excuse me?"

She stuck her head back out. "Yes?"

"Sorry, my car has broken down, and I have to get to Avebury. It's a matter of life and death. Are you going south by any chance and could drop me off in the village?"

"Life and death, hah. Won't work with me, sweetheart. I've got leather seats and you're soaked. Call the AA." The window whirred up, and she drove off, splashing muddy water over my feet. Lost for words, I stood there and stared after the disappearing taillights, and I did nothing when another vehicle rolled down the next aisle and drove off.

Fury churned inside me, scorching my throat, and it took a few measured breaths to allow me to swallow some of it. Spontaneous magical combustion was the last thing I needed.

I searched the car park once more. No drivers. Instead, I spotted a mangled bicycle locked to a lamppost opposite the hospital entrance.

If I were a proper witch, I could hex the bike to make it fly. I wasn't, so I couldn't.

Less than forty minutes and counting.

Hang on. The lamppost reminded me of something. If I only knew what it was . . . ah, yes. The pole with the bus timetable at the Whacky Bramble Pub where I always tethered the auntiemobile. The pub's phone number would be on the Internet. Somebody could find it for me. I could call Greg and ask him to pass a message to Damian. Greg was no witch, but he was a good friend.

Now I had a plan, and life looked marginally better. The quicker I got inside, the better—the bloody thunderstorm was getting closer. I could hear it rumbling.

"Ms. Coldron?" a concerned voice said next to me. I whipped around and beheld Aaron, dressed in a leather jacket and helmet and sitting astride his gleaming alien spaceship that was still blubbering away merrily.

"Oh, hello. What are you doing here?"

A confused look crept onto his kind horse face. "Uh, not sure, ma'am. I was returning from the biker shop in the outlet, got to the outskirts of Swindon, and was forced to sit out the storm. Suddenly I had this urge to reach the hospital. I just knew if I drove here, I could help someone." Confusion changed into a smile. "Somehow, I figured it might be you. Odd, huh? Anyway, here I am."

Here he was indeed. Human kindness astride a motorbike, beaming goodwill at me with over-white teeth. My frantic summons must have been too feeble to go all the way to Avebury, but it latched onto the one person who was close enough, the one person who could—and would—help me.

"Uh, are you going back to Avebury by any chance?"

He nodded eagerly. "Would you fancy a ride? This is a great hog, I can tell you."

Fancy the ride I did not, but it was better than nothing. "That's ever so sweet of you. I'll take you up on the offer. What about the weather, though?"

We both scanned the skies. Still menacing, still black, but the worst of the front seemed to be drifting north. We might yet make it.

"We'll be fine," Aaron said.

"Oh, would you have the pub's number? See, my van has broken down. I need Greg to pass on a message for me. Everything's going wrong."

Aaron rolled the bike aside, turned off the engine, and kicked out the stand. He searched the pockets of his leather jacket, stopped, and smacked his forehead with his palm. "Ah, he won't be in. He closed the pub. No guests, see? We planned a spin into Wales today, but I couldn't face it after what happened at breakfast. Let me call him."

I waited for an eternity while invisible ants were having a party on my arms.

"Nope, ain't gonna work. They're probably stranded due to the weather." Aaron stowed away the phone before he looked at me. "I'd be honored to take you to Avebury. You deliver your message in person. Then I'll drive us back here."

His kindness made my eyes water. There was hope for this world if it had people like Aaron in it.

But it meant riding that gleaming monster. Motorcycles and I don't gel. They go fast when I want to go slow.

What was the alternative? My struggles must have already bitten a fair chunk out of my remaining time. But they had brought me Aaron. I must have manipulated him, but he didn't seem to be hurt in any form. To the opposite, he was positively hopping with helpfulness.

Think of it as a paranormal distress call.

Aaron shrugged out of his jacket and handed it over. "Do me a favor and put that on. You're soaked to the skin. I don't want you to catch a cold." He reached for my umbrella and stowed it away in a leather bag slung onto the back of the Harley.

He then thrust something at me. "You must wear this, too."

I stared at the storm trooper helmet. "Uh . . ."

"Please, it's safer that way. I hope the coppers don't catch us. We should both be wearing helmets, but I don't have a spare."

The helmet was rather too large for me. Despite fixing the strap as firmly as possible, the thing sat low on my forehead, forcing me to raise my chin if I wanted to see more than tarmac and bits of Harley.

Now I faced the dreaded moment. How did one mount a motorbike in a shift dress? A soggy shift dress at that. At least it was traffic-cone orange, which befit the occasion.

"Right, ma'am, I need you to come over here and climb on from the left. She's sitting on the stand quite safely, see?" He pointed at the gleaming silver tongue that kept the monster in balance.

"Okay, all you do is step on the footrest and then swing onto the seat behind me. You'll find it's very comfy."

A perch the size of a diaper on the back of a motorbike wasn't my idea of comfy, but I took a deep breath, placed one moccasined foot on the protruding metal part, lifted the hem of my dress, and swung my legs over the saddle. A car horn hooted, and somebody gave me a thumbs-up through the window.

Tosser.

In the meantime, the clock was ticking.

"You'll need to hold on to me," Aaron explained, so I did. "If we go around corners, try to lean into the curve with me. I promise I won't go fast and it won't tilt much. Okay?"

No.

What I said was, "I'll do my best, but I've never ridden a bike. But thank you so much for bearing with me."

"It's a pleasure, ma'am," he said, full of cheer. The engine engaged with a brain-shuddering rumble and Aaron kicked the stand away.

Accompanied by fluttery farts from its motor, the bike started moving and rolled onto the street with a plop that shoved the helmet over my eyes. I didn't dare remove my steel grip on Aaron's skinny body, but after raising my chin skyward and tossing back my head, I got the darn thing back where it belonged.

I wished I hadn't. We were on the wrong side of the road. "Left, Aaron. Stick to the left."

"Dang, that gets me every time." The bike swerved across and straightened. With a growl from the engine that vibrated through my entire body, we gathered speed.

I could only hope my magic, having done its job, wouldn't backfire and put a spanner in the wheels.

27

MIDSUMMER NIGHTMARE

One thing was certain—I would never make a decent biker's bride. Crouched on the hot seat behind Aaron, the parody of a helmet obscuring my vision while unseen cars roared past on both sides, I had a hard time not worrying about fiery accidents, crumpled metal, and broken necks. However, things improved once we left Swindon and the traffic thinned.

Some drivers must have been closet bikers. At the lights they buzzed down their windows and shouted technical questions at Aaron. The whole experience was worsened by the permanent vibrations and the nerve-racking noise the contraption made every time it was kicked into speed. I would forever be in Aaron's debt for lending me his jacket and the wretched helmet, which gave some protection against the wind and the disturbing sights.

Neither helped with the clock ticking away in my mind.

The embarrassment at clinging to a male torso other than

Chris's I had dumped immediately. Aaron was a great windbreaker, and I needed something to hold on to, lest I toppled onto the road. Of course, my sodden dress rode up my legs, which was most likely one reason the other traffic kept coming too close.

With practiced ease, Aaron tilted the chrome monster into yet another hedge-framed curve, this one familiar.

Almost there.

I should have known better than to think optimistic thoughts. The bike straightened, slowed down, and rolled onto the shoulder. A rubbish collection van clattered past, trailed by a long queue of cars.

"We're almost out of gas," Aaron yelled over his shoulder. "Can't risk her running dry."

Once he had secured the Harley, he helped me off my perch and caught me when my stiff legs refused their service. Together, we stared at the chrome spaceship.

"Uh," Aaron said. "I'm super sorry. I was so focused on getting to the hospital—I had this weird urge, ya know? I didn't pay much attention to the gas."

He looked so sheepish that I couldn't possibly be mad at him. Plus, he'd showed up when I needed help.

Magic came at a price.

Rats.

I checked my watch and my stomach clenched. Less than ten minutes left.

"Look, I'll be forever in your debt," I said, jittery with impatience and hating myself for my rudeness in deserting the man I had summoned to my rescue.

"I know you're in a hurry. Trouble is, this is a rental. If she runs totally dry—"

"Aaron, please, I understand. Are you okay if I abandon you here and we sort things out later?" I shrugged out of the jacket and handed his helmet across.

Aaron grinned and whipped out his phone. "Nothing to sort

out. My pleasure. You run. I'll organize myself someone with a jerrican."

Out of time and clean out of words, I gripped his shoulder and then sprinted away. The stranded Harley was close to Long Street, but I might as well have found myself on the moon. I would never make it, not with my legs stiff and achy after the ride.

You might already be too late.

That thought was even worse, so I ignored it and speed-shuffled past the rubbish collection van that hunkered beside the road in a cloud of exhaust fumes, stink, and midges. A slender man in an orange vest hopped off and rolled two bins across the street. Another man followed, headed for the rest.

I had seen both before. My brain rifled through my memories and found a match.

Boian's brother, Cornel Albu. And his pal, Iosif.

Would they help me? "Uh, sorry, but I need to get to the cul-de-sac in Nightingale Lane. Like, now. Or my friends might get poisoned."

Cornel stared over the lid of the dustbin. Then a shy smile lightened his face. "You lady who found Boian."

"Uh, yes. Sorry about that. Listen—"

A bald head stuck out of the driver's cabin. "Are you buggers getting a move on back there? Bloody temp helpers." The man slurred his words around a lolly bulging his cheek.

Cornel rolled his eyes. "We need money for bury Boian." He pointed first at his vest and then the bin.

Guilt pooled in the pit of my stomach. By their standards I was as rich as Croesus, and not once had I thought of helping them. "I'll find the cash. Wait a moment."

A thousand ants swarming my guts, I dashed up to the cabin and faced its glowering occupant. "How much if you take me to Field's View? Now?"

The man's laugh sounded surprisingly good-natured. "Lady, I'm no taxi service. It's bad enough that everybody's called in sick and I'm forced to work with temps. The regular chaps are scared stiff of the local grim reaper."

"The killer is in hospital," I said. "She's left some stuff behind, and if you don't take me along, more people will die."

I checked my watch. Four minutes.

Cornel and Iosif abandoned their bins. The eyes of the driver almost popped from their sockets.

"You found killer?" Iosif asked, the sad expression on his face shifting to grim.

"Shit, lady, now you're scaring me," the lollipop man said.

"Sorry. And yes, I found her, and she's after my friends. Will you take me?"

"Hop on in. I won't charge you."

—

The van roaring off behind me, I banged open the door of the Ragworts' home and slammed into a living room filled with people.

"Don't eat or drink anything! It's poisoned!" I shouted.

Conversation stilled. People stopped doing whatever they were doing. Mouths gaped. Eyes widened.

"Buffet's not open yet," Mel said. "We're still missing a few. What are you on about?"

I ignored her. "Where's Daisy?"

Damian's steady regard never wavered. "In the kitchen. Putting the finishing touches on things." He pointed at the freshly painted door beside him. "What's wrong?"

I shook my head and barged into the kitchen—and straight into my cousin's back.

"Oof." Daisy staggered. Something small dropped from her hand to the floor and rolled under the table.

My cousin swung around, glowering. "Oh, it's you. Where have you been?"

"Where's the poison?" My gaze found the object—a perfume dispenser—on the floor. I didn't dare bend down and pick it up.

Not when the knife on the cheeseboard glinted with sharpness. Daisy only had to snatch it and stick it into my back.

She wouldn't, surely.

Silence roared in my ears.

I stepped up and blocked the cheeseboard with my body. Then I grabbed my cousin by the shoulders and shook her. "Daisy, tell me. What have you done?"

Her lip trembled. Fat tears formed on her thick lashes. One coursed down her cheek, leaving a glittery trail.

Anger rolled through me, rumbling like the thunder from earlier. This time, there was no green, no magic. Only a fury too hot to contain. "You knew what Dot was up to. You helped her with the murders."

Daisy's head jerked up. She stared at me as if I had too many legs. "What? No, no, never. Myr, I swear I didn't. Dot hasn't . . . I mean, she wouldn't . . ." Daisy's gaze focused on a faraway place only she could see. Her face spasmed with horror. "Oh my gosh. The boost."

"What boost?"

Daisy stared at the dispenser on the floor. "See, something about Dot was super odd, the way she was going on and on about the tourists. She'd, like, said things before, but never with such hatred and anger, which is why I wanted to talk to you first. But you never have time, you know? So, I went to the farm, to confront her. She got shirty, and said I should do as I was told, and that I wasn't good for anything else. Then you had a go at me as well when we met at the farm." Daisy tossed her head, her auburn braid squirming over her shoulders.

A part of me wanted to shake the woman until her teeth rattled. The other part called for patience, of which I didn't have a lot left.

The door behind my back opened. "Can I help?" Rosie asked.

"No," I said. This wasn't the time for niceties.

The door snicked shut.

"Daisy, I was under time pressure." *Yes, you wanted to have dinner with your lover.* "Anyway, what did Dot say?"

"We would find out who in the coven was a genuine witch. I didn't want to annoy her even more by asking silly questions, so I took the cool pack with the dispenser and stored it in my fridge as she told me to do. She told me once it was out of there, it wouldn't last long, so I had to be, like, fast about it? She also made me swear not to tell you about the boost. It was meant to be a surprise."

Some surprise. "And?"

She pouted like a little girl. "You're still talking in that tone."

"What tone? Daisy—"

"You don't trust me. Don't believe in me. You treat me as if I was five. Just like Mum. And Dot."

Mea culpa. "Daisy. I'm truly sorry and I'll make it up to you later, but what's the business with that bottle? What were you supposed to do with it?"

"Spray it over the food and drink. It would make everybody stronger, she said." Her gaze slipped aside. "Dot played me, didn't she? She knew how I hated being such a failure." Another tear trickled down her cheek.

A wave of tiredness rolled over me. I sank into the nearest chair and buried my head in my hands. "Oh, Daisy."

"When she talked about proper witches, there was a funny look in her eyes that I didn't like at all. I really needed your help, but you weren't here." Quietly sobbing, she swung away from me. "Oh my gosh, what have I done? I'm beyond stupid." Her voice rose to a wail.

I rose, drew my cousin against my body, and closed my arms around her trembling warmth. "You're not stupid, but you keep acting the ditz, and you do it disastrously well. It certainly fooled Dot."

Daisy lifted her head and sought my gaze, her eyes moist and huge in the pale oval of her face. "They would all have died. I would've killed them."

Perhaps not quite all of them. But the outcome would have

been . . . bad.

I guided Daisy's head to my shoulder and rocked her gently, as if she were a baby. Slowly, the trembling went away. "You didn't. Nothing happened. It'll be all right."

I would make sure of that.

On the other side of the door, the babble cranked up the volume. I could have cried with tiredness. But there was still so much to do.

A knock sounded on the door.

Silently, it crept open, and Rosie slipped into the kitchen. "Sorry, Myr, but this won't do. Jenna, Marty, the Colonel, and a few others still haven't arrived. They're not responding to calls either. Please, what's going on?"

Daisy wriggled out of my grasp and ripped a sheet from the roll of kitchen paper. She blew her nose.

I forced a smile on my face. "Too much of the wrong thing. But this will change. We'll need training, and I'll organize it myself. I think I now have a vague notion how we can control our skylles. The rest we'll sort out once we have the database."

"Good." Damian joined his wife. "Time you took charge. What about Dot?"

"Dot is . . . out of it."

From one second to the next, the kitchen walls seemed to warp oddly, and I could swear the tiles were undulating. I wanted to tell my fellow witches that I would be there for them. And for Daisy. Especially for Daisy. But I couldn't. My skylles saved Pan, saved me, and saved the coven. Now they demanded payment.

The kitchen shrank into a tunnel and then a pinpoint. A sharp hiss pierced my ears until it ebbed away, and everything was calm and dark.

28

A GENTLEMAN CALLS

Chris and I spent the solstice in my private parlor. The storm had gone. The rain lingered in a soft but persistent drizzle from the skies, washing away the horrors and cleansing the countryside. Not that it deterred the pagans. Through the half-open window drifted distant strains of music and the thumping of tablas, and from somewhere floated the sweet song of a flute. In their wake trailed the wet scent of damp soil, nature revived after the scorcher.

Drummed on by Colonel Elmsworth, the coven was on the march. They, too, should be safe.

Sarah told me, in confidence of course, that the police had matched Dot's DNA to both the winemaking table and the distilling apparatus Dot had hidden in her garage. The lily leaves she had buried in her compost provided additional evidence. Only the faintest trace of the poison was found on the apparatus—not enough to run major tests, but enough to know it was there. Dot was now in a single hospital room with a police guard at the entrance. Since the doctor didn't expect her to emerge from the coma, Jenna's and Marty's statements about Dot's mental health and my recollection of Dot's confession shored up the case.

My statement had required quite a few edits.

The minivan was at the garage. I blamed my transport's sorry state on vandalism—which it was, in a way. The money for the repair, however, would come out of my own pocket. It wasn't the insurance's fault if my skylles went ballistic.

Jenna and I had a great talk, which cleared the atmosphere. She said she had acted funny in the cellar because she was embarrassed about her wine and didn't want me to see the production line, so to speak. When I shared my concerns over the soil, she had a fit of the giggles.

"You'd give Miss Marple a run for her money. After filling up the pot, I remembered we kept this super stuff somewhere. Well, I thought we did. Still haven't found it."

Anyway, Jenna was out of the crosshairs, the deaths had stopped, and the magical misfits remained a secret. The database—our super grimoire—was under way, and once the coven returned to Avebury, the training would start.

All that was for later. Right now, priority one was lounging on the sofa with my head on Chris's chest, content to watch channels flip by as he searched for football. Everything else was far too strenuous. I had dragged a protesting Tiddles from the armchair and pressed her warm, furry body to my cheek until she deigned to relax and started purring. Now she curled up in my lap, fast asleep. Empty pizza boxes yawned on the coffee table, their cheesy aroma mingling with the fresh air from outside. From behind, the occasional spark sailed over my shoulder. In other circumstances, I wouldn't have drunk bubbly with pizza, but right now I couldn't face red wine. Petty had tilted her pot, eager for a sip. I needed to watch my plant, lest she turn into an alcoholic.

Into that peaceful scene of domestic bliss, the doorbell gonged.

Chris dropped the remote control. "Are you expecting more guests?"

"Not really." I had called Greg and instructed him to ply Aaron and his friends with the best his cellars offered. No way would I allow my guest to pay his bill. It was the least I could do. Perhaps Aaron biked over on his blessed hog and wanted to express his gratitude once more? If not him, this might be Cornel, equally grateful for something he was owed. He and his fellow musicians now had enough money to return to Romania without having to sleep rough, while Boian in his coffin would travel by air. Oh, and I'd invited them to stay in the Witch's Retreat the next time they played at the village. Cornel and Iosif insisted I was a good woman.

That remained to be seen.

Mr. Enderby and I might have saved Pan's life, but he had lost his love. No happily ever after for the poor man, and that hurt.

I placed the cat on the sofa and scrambled to my feet. "Let me go and see."

The air had cooled down, so I was wearing gray leggings and a light sea-green jersey jumper. Not something I would typically want to greet guests in, but I couldn't care less.

I left the living room door ajar, walked along the corridor, and opened the entrance door. I was confronted by a meticulously groomed gentleman, dressed like a golf pro minus the clubs. He was neither too tall nor too small and in no way remarkable. But his presence filled the porch.

I plastered a professional smile on my face. "Good evening. If you're looking for a room, I'm afraid we're not taking any guests right now."

His eyes crinkled in an amusement that seemed familiar. White, even teeth appeared in the well-shaven face.

The better to eat you.

When he spoke, his voice sounded both educated and amused. "Don't worry, Ms. Coldron. I don't need a room. All I wanted was to meet you in person."

Why did these simple words spoken in a civilized fashion spook me so much?

His eyes slid over me as if I were an ambulant dust bunny.

"I assume given the recent developments that you're in charge here?"

"At the B&B, you mean?" I asked, my voice higher than usual.

"No."

Somewhere deep inside me, a spark of anger took hold. Who was this man? What was he doing here? Where had I seen him before? Because I was sure I had.

"I'm talking about your . . . eh, coven? Is this still the correct term? You might have changed things over the last centuries."

Suddenly, I recognized him. Chris's uncle. Bob Ignatius. Multimillionaire, political mover and shaker—and descendant of the witch hunters.

The man responsible for the deaths of my parents and my aunt was standing on the doorstep of the Witch's Retreat.

"Look, Ms. Coldron, I don't want to prolong this unnecessarily. Your clan departed this world a while back, which, from my family's perspective, is a good thing. For whatever reason, they left a few of you behind. Against all odds, you flourished. I'm happy for you."

His head inclined to one side, he regarded me like an evil sparrow. Where was Chris? Probably glued to the television because some silly football team was scoring even sillier goals. As the thought sailed through my head, I sensed a draft of displaced air. Then I heard angry rustling and swishing before something brushed past me.

"Let me guess. You now want to deliver a final ultimatum and warn me off using magic, right?"

Ignatius snorted. "Tsk, tsk. I'm not convinced your team has a lot of magic left to use. In any case, I don't have the time to play games. I'm a businessman, Ms. Coldron. And I've got a business proposal for you. First of all, I'm interested in those plaques of yours. The other Ms. Coldron misunderstood my intentions. I was offering her a deal."

Fury lanced into my abdomen and sent acid heat up my gorge. Of course, my aunt had misunderstood things, despite being a shrewd businessperson herself.

Blink.

For a fraction of a second, Petty winked into vision. She hovered in the air above Ignatius's head, the pot swinging like a bell. If she socked him one, he'd be out in a wink.

He must have taken my silence as encouragement to continue. "So many misunderstandings. The incident concerning your parents was the same."

Blink.

I shook my head ever so slightly. There was no point in Petty getting involved, but it was a relief to know she was there. Hang on. What did Ignatius say?

My unwanted visitor must have caught the small move and thought it was meant for him. "But that's not why I'm here." He raised his soft hands toward me with a pleading gesture that did nothing to drown the roaring in my ears or the fire running through my veins.

The jerk on my doorstep was talking about misunderstandings when he meant the near-extinction of my family.

With a strange detachment, I noted that fury could indeed make people see red. Except, in my case, it was green. Everything—the door, the porch, the man—fizzed in a bright emerald haze. There was a pounding in my head. I smelled roses. This time, I understood what was happening. This time, I was ready.

Ignatius's voice continued, cultured and calm. "Now, I have a second point I want to discuss with you. Your magical skills might be not on a par with those of the Whites, but you do have them. I wonder whether you would consider employing them occasionally? On my behalf?" He tilted his head and said something else, but his face and words were lost in a deepening frothy, green glare.

A smidgen of the wrath raging through me must have shown, for he took a step backward. "Ah, I understand. I knew you wouldn't agree immediately. Do consider my offer, Ms. Coldron. I'll make it worth your while."

"You want me to use magic to improve your return on investment? Is that what you're saying?"

Blink.

Ignatius took another step, stumbled on the doorstep, and caught himself at the last moment. "Think about it," he said, now rather hastily. "I'll contact you."

He turned to leave.

My nose filled with the perfume of a thousand roses. Heat flared through my veins and the green haze roared toward his retreating back, the urge to mangle and hurt impossible to control.

No, you mustn't. My inner voice sounded like Aunt Eve. Some of the greenness fizzled away.

I want him out of my sight.

Petty winked in and out. A bramble hedge burst from the gravel, entangling Ignatius with its scratchy creepers.

He yelped and beat at branches that grew in mass and wrapped themselves around him, ripping, pricking. Red rose petals zipped across the tangled mess.

"Myrtle, what on earth . . . ?"

Chris.

Burning shot down my arms and into my hands, the pricks of many little thorns wrapping themselves around my throat, creepers covering my legs, feet, and torso. A monster migraine swept through my head.

Magical backfire, the penalty for using the skylles to attack.

I whirled around, spotted the water container under the drainpipe, and aimed the green fizz toward it. Amid more whooshing, steam rose from the barrel. Next, the lid flew off and landed on the ground with a *whump*. The magical hedge vanished. Only the petals and the torment raging through my body remained.

I opened my mouth to scream. And found the pain was gone.

Ignatius stood in front of an expensive dark limousine, his eyes wide with fright. But he was unharmed. Not a mark showed on his body.

Chris pushed past me into the yard. "Go," he spat at his uncle. "Don't come back. You don't know what you're dealing with."

Ignatius's expression shifted, and he smiled again. "To the contrary, I think I do. Amazing, really. Tell your—friend the offer still stands. Now more than ever."

He nodded and entered the passenger side of the car, which then slid away in silence.

Chris turned toward me.

I ignored him and stumbled onto the porch. "Petty?"

Blink.

This time she stayed visible, pirouetting in the air above the yard and shooting off multicolored fireworks as if supercharged. Well, she probably was, and I'd been responsible. Petty must have acted as a catalyst. Or something to that effect. There was so much we still didn't know. My legs refused to function, and I sagged onto the stoop and buried my face in my hands.

"Myrtle? Sorry I came so late. I was wondering where you had got to."

"It's fine," I mumbled.

"No, it isn't. I should've been there when that wanker . . . What did you do to him?"

"Magic. He pissed me off royally, and I wanted him out of my sight. My skylles are rather literal, and I seem to have a natural affinity for prickly plants."

A hand found my neck, and a finger stroked the soft skin along my chin. "Doesn't surprise me. I better avoid pissing you off, then."

I looked into his eyes, a grateful warmth ballooning in my chest. He still hadn't run. Not even after watching the live show of my latest tricks. I allowed my muscles to unclench and let Chris's pull me upright.

"Hold me," I mumbled. "Don't you ever leave me."

His face nuzzled my freshly washed hair. "Told you before, I won't. I know who and what you are. I find you and your cute botanical friend fascinating, not scary. Just don't ever lose control and head toward the dark side. That's where I draw the line. Get that in your head, will you?"

In the past, men like him had explored the jungles, found passages through ice floes, and flown to the moon. Helping one budding witch wrestle with her paranormal powers would be right down his street.

"I'll try my best."

I would. He was worth it. And so was my magic.

Acknowledgments

A big, fat thank you is owed to my husband, Keith. Not only does he support my wild writing sprees (and fits of passion where I threaten to burn my manuscripts) but also he had his reading preferences severely impacted by my editing journey. These days he even spots bloopers in his favorite novels. And many thanks for your patience, your staunch support, and for believing in me when I do not. I love you.

A very special round of applause goes to Sharon Salonen, for her sage editorial advice and amazing insight. You make my writing sparkle! And since this is the acknowledgment section, I'm surely allowed a few exclamation marks and parentheses... Hah! A special thank you also to Susie Brooks, Chief Editor of Literary Wanderlust, for your kindness, your patience, and your professionalism. Ladies, you rock.

Much praise is owed to my fellow authors in The Scribblers' Society Critique Club, the Ladies on Life author circle, and the wonderful writers and readers of Wattpad who help me chase the bloopers. You all rock as well.

And last but certainly not least, another round of applause to my parents, for igniting my lifetime love of books. Well, it cost them and me a pretty penny over all those years, but it was worth it.

About the Author

Lina Hansen has been a freelance travel journalist, teacher, belly dancer, postal clerk, and science communication specialist stranded in the space sector. Numbed by factoid technical texts, she set out to write the stories she loves to read—cozy and romantic mysteries with a dollop of humor and a magical twist. After living and working in the UK, Lina, her husband, and their feline companions now share a home in the foothills of Castle Frankenstein. Lina is a double Watty Award Winner, Featured Author, and a Wattpad Star.

Down the Hatch is the second of the Magical Misfits series of mysteries. More information and Lina's blog can be found at www.linahansenauthor.com or connect via Twitter @lhansenauthor or Facebook @linahansenauthor.